THE
ULTIMATE

SPIDER-MAN: THE VENOM FACTOR
by Diane Duane

THE ULTIMATE SPIDER-MAN
Stan Lee, Editor

IRON MAN: THE ARMOR TRAP
by Greg Cox

SPIDER-MAN: CARNAGE IN NEW YORK
by David Michelinie & Dean Wesley Smith

THE INCREDIBLE HULK: WHAT SAVAGE BEAST
by Peter David

SPIDER-MAN: THE LIZARD SANCTION
by Diane Duane

THE ULTIMATE SILVER SURFER
Stan Lee, Editor

Coming soon:

FANTASTIC FOUR: TO FREE ATLANTIS
by Nancy A. Collins

DAREDEVIL: PREDATOR'S SMILE
by Christopher Golden

THE ULTIMATE SILVER SURFER

STAN LEE, EDITOR

BYRON PREISS MULTIMEDIA COMPANY, INC.
New York

BOULEVARD BOOKS
New York

Special thanks to Lou Aronica, Ginjer Buchanan, Julia Molino, Stacy Gittelman, the gang at Marvel Creative Services, and especially Ken Grobe and Keith R.A. DeCandido.

THE ULTIMATE SILVER SURFER

A Boulevard Book
A Byron Preiss Multimedia Company, Inc. Book

PRINTING HISTORY
Boulevard edition / November 1995

ISBN: 1-57297-029-4

BOULEVARD
Boulevard Books are published by The Berkley Publishing Group,
200 Madison Avenue, New York, New York 10016.
BOULEVARD and its logo
are trademarks belonging to Berkley Publishing Corporation.

PRINTED IN THE UNITED STATES OF AMERICA

10   9   8   7   6   5   4   3   2   1

This one has to be for Jack "King" Kirby

CONTENTS

CONTENTS

CONTENTS

THE ULTIMATE

INTRODUCTION

STAN LEE

Illustration by Dave Gibbons

Blame it on Jack Kirby! It's his fault. He's the one who first drew the Silver Surfer.

Since you probably weren't there at the time, let me tell you how it happened—before I forget.

There we were, Jack and I, merrily tooling along, producing one *Fantastic Four* comic book after another. Talk about fun! It was one of the best times of my life. It seemed we'd never run out of ideas. Even as I was scripting the issue at hand, I'd be thinking of the next few stories to come and couldn't wait till I could start writing them. As for Jack, the artwork kept pouring out of him as if he'd never stop; page after page, and each one seemingly more exciting and impressive than the one before!

Then came that fateful day.

I distinctly remember the two of us discussing what our next plot should be. As you probably know, the most important thing in any super hero series is the *villain* of the story. An unusual, memorable villain can make a saga unforgettable, while a lackluster, unempathetic villain can make a story sink like the *Titanic*.

Well, that's when I hit upon the idea of the most powerful villain of all. "Forget about mad scientists, or gangsters, or war-like aliens, or wacky fanatics who wanna take over the world," spoketh I, as the excitement mounted within my manly breast. "Let's create the ultimate villain, the most awesome menace of all; someone who can destroy an entire planet without even breathing hard. Let us hoist upon humanity's petard an actual *demi-god*!"

I paused for breath, waiting for Jack's wildly enthusiastic congratulations, or at least a sudden burst of applause. But none was forthcoming. Instead, he had already taken pencil in hand and had nearly finished a completed drawing of Galactus before I knew what was happening. (By the way, did I tell you that ol' King Kirby was the fastest artist I knew? If not, consider yourself told. Greased lightning was a meandering local compared to Jack's express train speed.)

Anyway, it wasn't long before we had worked out all the details of our new story, which would of course feature Galactus, the super-villain with the most ravenous appetite in the known universe! I flipped for the costume Jack had created for our delicious demi-god, and one look at him was all I needed to know that Galactus was sure to be one of our most popular baddies.

I know you're thinking to yourself, "Hey, this is all well and good, but you were supposed to be telling us how you guys dreamed up the Silver Surfer!" See? Even though we're miles apart, I can read your mind! But be ye of good cheer, O impatient one. We'll be getting to the meat of this little fable before you know it. I mean, I've got all this space to fill up—gotta stretch things out, right?

So there we were at the Mighty Marvel Bullpen, doing our thing. After agreeing on the essence of the plot, Jack went home to draw the story, while I went off on a brief lecture tour to some colleges that were probably starved for whatever cultural nourishment a minion of Marvel could bring them. I was serene and relaxed as I brought the momentous Marvel message to campuses far and near, knowing that by the time I returned to the bullpen, Jack would have finished drawing our grandiose Galactus tale and the world would be a better place because of it.

Now hang in there, true believers, because here comes the punch line!

Sure enough, when I returned to the mighty Marvel offices, there was Jolly Jack with the Galactus artwork all complete. And what artwork it was! I felt it surpassed anything he had done till then. I told him it was superb, sensational, spectacular—and then, before running out of "s" words, I stopped. For I saw something I had not expected. Something

3

that nearly knocked me out of my chair!

There, in the middle of the story we had so carefully worked out, was a nut on some sort of flying surfboard!

"Okay," said I, ever calm and reasonable, ever willing to give the other guy the benefit of the doubt. "Obviously your mind was wandering when you drew this irrelevant little bit of whimsy. How long will it take you to erase it?"

Securely ensconsed behind his ever-present cigar, Jack gave me one of his famous Kirbyesque glares. "No, I wasn't kidding when I drew 'im, Stan. I just figured a guy as powerful as Galactus oughtta have his own personal herald, someone to fly around and find planets for him to gobble up. So that's who he is. I gave him the flying surfboard 'cause I'm tired of drawing spaceships!"

Well, the more I looked at the figure on the flying board, the more I liked him. But I realized something that perhaps Jack himself hadn't been fully aware of. I detected a *nobility* in the way Jack had drawn him, a feeling of worthiness, of goodness, of—I might as well say it—of spirituality. As drawn by the genius of Jack Kirby, he was far more than merely some goofy stooge for the main super-villain. To me, he was honor and virtue personified. And that was the way I knew I had to write him!

Now, about his name. I honestly can't remember exactly how he was named or which of us actually named him, but I think it probably happened like this. Jack referred to him as something like the Flying Surfer. But I felt his name should somehow reflect that nobility I was just talking about. To make him really unique (as if a guy who streaked through the cosmos on a flying board wasn't unique enough) I decided to have him colored silver, and after that the name was obvious: the Silver Surfer!

And there you have it. If Jack hadn't decided that a gent like Galactus needed a herald to find him his planets, the world today might be Silver Surferless, a consummation devoutly to be regretted. And, I guess, if I hadn't decided that he should be treated like more than just a flying sidekick, he'd just have joined the endless gallery of offbeat characters that come and go and are eventually forgotten.

Perhaps there's a lesson in all this. Perhaps it shows us the value of collaboration. But even more important, it shows the value of being lucky enough to have collaborated with a talented titan like Jack "King" Kirby!

Excelsior!

Stan

Stan Lee

PART ONE

ORIGIN

THE SILVER SURFER

TOM DeFALCO

BASED ON A STORY BY STAN LEE

Illustration by John Buscema

Under different circumstances, Darrell Walker might have been amused to see his face reflected in the gleaming object. Quick-witted and fast with a laugh, Darrell usually could find the humorous side of even the most depressing situation. The present one, however, taxed even his good nature. The object his face reflected in was a switchblade, and it was swooshing toward his unprotected heart.

Three weeks shy of his fourteenth birthday, Darrell knew he wouldn't survive to see it.

Darrell had committed an unpardonable offense. Instead of directly heading home after school as per his mother's standard instructions, he'd hustled over to the video arcade on 56th Street with Sammy Rosen. The two boys had squandered the hours, along with every cent they had, mastering the finer subtleties of Deluxe Super Combat 3. The sun was still shining when Darrell split from Sammy, but only barely.

That's when Darrell made his first mistake.

Instead of taking the long way home, down 58th for four blocks and left on Buscema Avenue until he hit 70th, he opted to take the shortcut through Kirby Park.

Everybody in the neighborhood knew better than to enter the park after sunset. That's when it became the exclusive playground of the Blazing Ghosts. Darrell was no fool. He usually gave the park a wide berth, even in the daylight hours.

But he was running *real* late. It was almost dinner time, and his mother would be fuming. Darrell didn't want to push her any more than necessary. He knew he'd cave in if she questioned his after-school activities. She'd never been too keen on mixing video arcades with school nights.

With a swagger he hoped was convincing, Darrell jogged into the park. He was fast. He was cocky. He figured he could easily sprint the great lawn, and cross the wooded area that bordered 68th Street long before the Ghosts made their play.

He was wrong.

Darrell was only twenty or so yards from the trees when seven of them came at him, materializing from the woods as suddenly as their namesakes. Ranging in age from late teens to mid-twenties, they all wore the same scuffed leather jackets, ragged jeans, and chilling scowls.

Within seconds, Darrell was surrounded. Rough hands tore at him, brutally yanking him from the open grassy area, and into the shadows of the trees. He was dragged into a small clearing, and thrown at the feet of Handsome Johnny Warwick.

Handsome Johnny leaned against an old oak, his attention focused on his right thumb which was slowly revolving around and rubbing against the remaining four fingers. A ferret-like sneer lit his face, and opaque glasses covered his eyes. A jagged pink scar, starting an inch beneath his left eye, curved around his jaw and disappeared beneath his shirt collar. Some said the scar was the result of a knife fight while Johnny was still in grade school. Others claimed it had been given to him by his drunken father. No matter how the story was told, it always ended the same. Johnny's attacker was found in an alley on 58th, a tire iron embedded in his skull.

From Darrell's perspective on the ground, the leader of the Blazing Ghosts looked as tall and wide as a house. Cool and aloof, Handsome Johnny's gaze never wavered from his fingers.

"What are ya doing here, kid? Where'd ya come from?"

"Should I start with a lecture about the birds and the bees, or would you settle for a description of the last half hour?"

Darrell knew the Ghosts expected him to be terrified (which he was), but figured he might gain a few points by opting for humor.

Mistake number two.

The thumb stopped rotating.

The Ghosts flanking Darrell grabbed the young boy's arms, pulling him to his feet. Darrell watched in mute fascination as Handsome Johnny's right hand slowly closed into a fist and slammed directly into his face.

The young boy saw an honest-to-goodness kaleidoscope of stars against a midnight black background as he fell to the ground. And then, like a bowling pin, the Ghosts automatically propped him back into a standing position.

The fist hit him again and again.

"You're a funny kid," Johnny said. "I don't like funny."

"Your loss." Darrell regretted the words even as they burst from his bloodied mouth. He should have bitten his tongue and taken his beating, hoping that they'd get bored with him and let him be. Instead, he mouthed off at the guy again.

That was his third, and fatal mistake.

"Dumb," Handsome Johnny mumbled, as the switchblade appeared in his hand as if summoned by magic. "Dumb, dumb, *dumb!*"

Quickly noting his battered face on the knife's polished surface, Darrell squeezed his eyes closed. He could hear the other members of the gang snickering at his plight, enjoying his humiliation, but he was determined not to beg or cry. They might see his blood, but he'd never show them his tears.

In his private darkness, Darrell saw his mother. She was calling to him, annoyed because dinner was growing cold. He wanted to reach out to her. He desperately wished he could apologize, and gain her forgiveness for the misery that news of his premature death would cause her.

Suddenly, a jolt rocked Darrell's entire body. Realizing that the switchblade must have pierced his chest, he gritted his teeth in anticipation of the explosion of pain which was surely destined to follow.

But it never came.

And, instead of collapsing to the ground like a sack of dirty laundry, Darrell felt the evening wind ripping at his face, almost as if he were streaking skyward.

That's when he first noticed the pressure under his armpits, and a tightness across his chest.

A quick peek confirmed Darrell's suspicions. He was dead all right. The world was rapidly receding below him as his soul zoomed upward to wherever good souls zoomed.

But then, to Darrell's horror, he detected a shift in direction. He was headed down, down toward that other place!

"Have no fear." A cold voice, with an almost metallic echo to it, whispered in his ear.

Darrell's eyes sprang open. He caught sight of a silver band wrapped around his chest. It looked like . . . an arm?!

Glancing over his shoulder, Darrell realized that it was, indeed, an arm. A rather muscular arm belonging to a silver angel who hefted the teenager as if he weighed no more than a notebook. An angel who glided through the air, gracefully balanced upon what appeared to be a gleaming, silvery surfboard.

Even as Darrell watched, the angel gestured with his free hand. A beam of fiery light flashed toward Handsome Johnny's switchblade, instantly reducing it to molten slag.

Even as Johnny screamed, more in fear than pain, the beam focused on the ground between his feet. It exploded, tossing Johnny in the air like an old rag doll.

Again and again, the beam struck the earth until every single Blazing Ghost was left crawling on his hands and knees, scurrying into the woods with frantic desperation.

With a slight shift in his weight, the angel veered his board toward the tenements on 70th Street. Targeting the rooftop of the tallest building, he gently and expertly coasted to a complete stop.

"You . . . you're the Silver Surfer!" Darrell managed to gasp. "Oh, ma-a-an! I've read about you, seen you on TV, but never thought I'd ever have a chance of running across you. I'm a real fan of guys like you, Spider-Man, Captain America, and Michael Jordan!"

"Are you injured?" the Surfer asked. "Did those human predators harm you?"

"—I'm okay."

A slight frown played across the Silver Surfer's face. "If you insist. Live long and well, my young friend."

"Wait! Don't go!" Darrell shouted as the surfboard, responding to some silent command, slowly began to rise. "I got so many questions to ask, and I'll never get another chance. Who are you? Why do you do the things you do? Where'd you come from? What's your planet like? Are there others like you? Any golden or tin guys?" The questions burst from Darrell's mouth, scrambling over each other in the rush.

The silvery board halted a foot or so above the ground. After several moments during which, Darrell supposed, the Surfer considered his questions, the board lowered gently to the rooftop.

With a gleam in his eyes as bright as any summer day, the Silver Surfer stepped off his board. Glancing upward toward the stars that grew ever-more-visible as night fell, the glimmering man began to speak . . .

I humbly beg your indulgence for the tale I am about to share. It eagerly springs from memory to mouth, without benefit of refinement or rehearsal. Though I have beheld sights no other human eye has seen, been privy to sounds no mortal ear can hear, and experienced sensations no earthly mind will ever grasp, I was born an unexceptional being, who has led an exceptional life. Neither a poet nor a practiced wordsmith, I fear my clumsiness as a teller of stories may bore or discourage you. My phrasing will surely run the gamut from awkward to flowery, without consistency or warning.

My true name is Norrin Radd, though I am better known as the Silver Surfer. Zenn-La in the Deneb system is the planet of my birth.

The people of my homeworld are humanoid. Our outward physical and racial characteristics vary within the same narrow spectra as do the people of this world. I do not know how similar our races are beyond physical appearance, as I have no great understanding of the biological sciences. Still, the only significant physical difference between our races that I have found is in the aging process. We of Zenn-La do not grow old as quickly as you Earth people. Three generations of a human family can pass from infancy to oblivion long before someone from my world has even reached his middle years.

While the greater lifespan may seem an incredible boon, I believe it made a significant contribution to my people's downfall. The longer the life, the more tedious it can become.

Even now, I can recall the early days of my youth, and the yearning, the questioning, the aching discontent which filled my heart. My race had achieved the perfection that is the goal of most worlds. War, crime, illness, all were only distant memories.

We had attained a paradise of sorts, but at what I thought a terrible price. No distant horizons beckoned us. No challenges remained. We had nothing left to accomplish. My people had lost their spirit of adventure. They had no desire to experience the thrill of exploration, nor did they long to see beyond the veil of their current knowledge.

While not actively discouraged, physical exertion was no longer necessary. Why walk, when a mobile conveyor belt would quickly carry you to your destination? Why risk injury at your favorite sport, when you could experience all the sensations, and at an enhanced level of play, while plugged into the virtual reality web? Why work, when every need met with instant gratification and every object you desired could be easily replicated?

My generation had inherited paradise, but I hungered for more. We were meant to strive, to struggle, to yearn. I was not content to spend a lifetime in idleness, pursuing endless pleasure. I longed to live when my race was young and our galaxy aborning!

Daily, I would visit our Museum of Antiquity, drawn like a magnet to its reminders of past glories. Sinn Ott, the ancient member of the Council of Scientists who served as the museum's curator, always had a friendly smile for me. He received few visitors, most citizens preferring to access the museum's files from their homes.

I, however, enjoyed the meaty weight and musky air of ancient objects. Sinn would often indulge me by weaving wondrous tales about every artifact within his care, sharing the little-known facts and bawdy tidbits ignored by more serious-minded historians.

Sinn was an always-inviting font of knowledge. His special field of study was the ten-thousand-century Age of Warfare which had nearly devastated Zenn-La, leaving scars so deep that we renounced the use of personal arms forever. Those dark days were followed by the Golden Age of Reason, which brought learning, wisdom, and peace to our war-ravaged people for a hundred centuries.

My visits often ended with a trip to the museum's virtual reality center, where I would rush into its massive chair to abandon the present and flee to a glorious past.

Within instants, I would find myself in the long-extinct days of my planet's space program, where I would experience the sensations of actually being present at the launching of one of our mighty starships.

That period was the time of Zenn-La's greatest glory, the time when we dared to reach for distant stars. The vast unknown of an entire galaxy beckoned, and we had the courage and will to heed its call.

Our greatest heroes were the astronauts, the time-honored pioneers to whom no journey was too far, no world too forbidding. Traveling to the far corners of our galaxy, they explored, colonized, and brought the blessings of our civilization to every primitive world they encountered, asking nothing in return. The flag of Zenn-La eventually waved over a thousand planets.

Finally, when there seemed to be no new worlds to discover or wonders to experience, even this noble endeavor lost its appeal. Boredom settled in and, as the centuries rolled by, my people gave up their explorations. They abandoned their starships, leaving the spaceways to more aggressive races.

Zenn-La, having scattered its seed to the most distant stars, returned to its mother world, never to venture forth again. We had gone too far, had seen too much. For us, the Age of Space Travel died, never to be reborn. Apathy had claimed another victory.

And yet, for all my discontent, for all my pining for days past, life on Zenn-La was not without its attractions. Chief among these was the lovely Shalla Bal.

Shalla Bal!

Even here, even now, I am haunted by her stunning face. Her eyes twinkling like mischievous stars planning a surprise nova. Her hair as lustrous as the blackest pearl, as soft as the finest silk. Her voice, gentle as the mists of dawn, still whispers within my mind.

And, thinking of her, I am reminded of the fateful day when Zenn-La was rudely shaken from its apathetic slumber.

"Your heart is troubled, Norrin Radd," she had said that day.

"It is nothing, Shalla. Merely a mood that soon shall pass."

With a dismissive shake of her head, Shalla strode to the far end of my living quarters. "I am not deceived, my love. Too long have I sensed the hunger gnawing at your breast. A hunger which will never be satiated on Zenn-La."

Unable to disagree, I kept silent.

Scorching me with a look of disdain, she laughed. "What can it be that you seek? There is no treasure in all the universe that cannot be found here. Look around you, Norrin Radd, see the wonders of this world, enjoy the glories which are ours, merely for the taking."

"No, Shalla. I have done nothing to deserve these riches. A paradise unearned is but a land full of insubstantial shadows! I can no longer bear the sight of my fellow citizens basking in hedonistic pleasures. Even our knowledge is without merit. Who can value a lifetime's learning, when it can be absorbed in minutes by hypno-cubes?"

"You weren't always so serious, Norrin." Her back as erect and stiff as a soldier of old, she glanced at the trophies that lined my mantelpiece. "Whatever happened to the young man who routinely ignored his studies in favor of surfing the lava runs?"

My eyes strayed to the gleaming object in her hand. A graceful figure perched upon a massive surfboard: the evidence of a misspent youth. How many hours had I wasted plugged into the virtual reality web, mentally gliding down the side of an erupting volcano, clad only in a glimmering heat-resistant jumpsuit? How I had loved those days, the wind ripping at my face, my skill commanding ever-increasing speed. But it was all illusion. A manufactured fantasy which I had experienced from the safety of my living room.

And yet, those childhood memories brought a shy smile to

my lips, and a radiant tenderness to Shalla's pretty cheeks.

We were already moving toward each other when the worldwide citizens' alarm sounded for the first time in a millennium.

Within seconds, the entire reality web was tuned to the same announcement, an emergency broadcast from the Council of Science.

"A gigantic alien spacecraft has entered our solar system, piercing our defensive systems as if they were nonexistent! All citizens must be prepared for a possible invasion!"

"It cannot be! We have no space fleet. No weapons!" Shalla cried. It was true. We had been at peace for countless centuries. We had forgotten how to fight. A well-trained enemy could easily destroy us all.

"Never!" I said with far more confidence than I felt.

But, even as I drew her into my arms, I wondered if this taste of danger wasn't just what my people needed. Wondered if this unknown threat wouldn't serve to unite and revitalize them.

Panic soon filled the streets as we learned that the invading spacecraft was nearly half the size of Zenn-La itself, and closing fast. Too many centuries had passed since our government had contended with war, and even then, Zenn-La had never been faced with such a devastating opponent.

No one wanted to take responsibility. None dared make a decision. The fate of Zenn-La was summarily surrendered to machines that had gathered dust for hundreds of years, as the Council of Science raced to get the ancient defensive computers back online, feeding them all the available data.

Even as the mysterious spacecraft seemed to blot out the very heavens themselves, the defensive computers rendered their verdict. Against such absolute power there could be only one response. Without hesitation, a long-forgotten doomsday device from the Age of Warfare called simply the

Weapon Supreme was activated.

While the Council of Science scrambled to find some mention, some description of this ancient weapon, the first tremors from the device began.

Without any warning, the entire planet began to tremble, setting off a string of earthquakes that devastated an entire coastline. The Weapon Supreme had begun to draw power from the very heart of the planet.

By the time the frightened scientists knew what they had unleashed, they were unable stop it.

The great Eastern Sea was instantly vaporized, as an impossibly huge arrow of force erupted from the mouth of Zenn-La, channeling fully half the planet's power reserves into a single lethal thrust.

Neighboring planetoids were abruptly hurled out of orbit, as our Weapon Supreme struck the oncoming invader with the fury of an exploding sun.

But then, to our unsurpassed horror, the force of the Weapon Supreme boomeranged back at us, catching us in a smashing, shattering backlash. In one instant, our homes, our land, our world as we knew it, were rapidly reduced to smoldering rubble.

Skyscrapers toppled! The mobile conveyor belt, which wrapped around the entirety of Zenn-La, collapsed upon itself! Power stations imploded! The virtual reality web crashed, flash-frying every mind plugged into it! Fires blossomed everywhere! Major geological faults clashed violently, as volcanoes vomited in protest! And a vengeful climate, long held in check by artificial means, was suddenly unleashed upon the land!

Over a hundred thousand people perished in that first moment.

The survivors attempted to console themselves with the fact that the enemy was dead.

Or so they thought.

Finding a telescope that was still in operable condition, the Council of Science soon learned that our enormous sacrifice had been in vain.

We had devastated our world, sacrificed thousands of lives, all for naught. Our unknown foe lived. Indeed, his monstrous ship continued its approach to Zenn-La completely unaffected by the Weapon Supreme's onslaught.

At that moment, a once-supremely arrogant race, one that had disregarded fear and discounted want, gave way to despair. The people of Zenn-La ran amok. Looting and howling like maddened beasts, they helplessly awaited their final seconds.

Disgusted, revolted by such unrestrained carnage, I grew even more determined to fight as our ancestors would have done. Believing that we still had a chance, that nothing was impossible to one who refused to accept defeat, I led a protesting Shalla Bal into the street. I thought I could rally our people, and present a united front to our callous invader.

Like a man bereft of reason, I frantically combed the shattered ruins of a once-proud city, desperately seeking an ally, a weapon, anything with which to fight back.

But I could find none who would honor the proud heritage of Zenn-La with a final stand, save the maimed and the mad.

Eventually, avoiding the brutal gangs now roaming in wild packs, Shalla Bal and I made our way to the Museum of Antiquity.

Sinn Ott was dusting a display case of ancient cookware, a nasty gash highlighting his forehead.

"The museum is closed today," he mumbled. "Closed for repairs."

Her eyes brimming with tears, Shalla Bal converted a sleeve

from her blouse into a makeshift bandage, while I led the old man to a nearby bench.

"I have devoted my life to this museum. It is my responsibility to tidy up," he trembled. "Then, and only then, can I die in peace."

"But, Sinn, we know neither our attacker nor his motive." Unbidden, a plan had begun to form. "If I could but reach his spacecraft—!"

"It is useless, Norrin Radd. Our finest scientific minds, our greatest computers, have all agreed our plight is hopeless!"

"Then"—I attempted a confident smile—"we surely have nothing to lose. If you can construct a spacecraft for me, we may confront our enemies, perhaps reason with them."

The elderly scholar peered into my eyes, expecting to find the fires of madness, but discovering only cold determination. His gaze turned toward Shalla Bal who stood motionless, fearing whatever decision he made. Then, he faced his precious ancient artifacts. The guardian of our antiquity was now being asked to help determine our future.

"You shall have your ship," he finally said with the reluctance of a judge pronouncing a death sentence.

Securing the museum from raiders, Sinn led us into the reinforced caverns which ran beneath the great building and had survived the Weapon Supreme's onslaught. He unlocked a cobweb-covered file room and switched on an ancient computer, his wrinkled fingers dancing across the keyboard like playful nymphs.

Within minutes he had accessed the charts for a shuttle from the Age of Space Travel. As Sinn downloaded the necessary information into a nearby materializer, I employed a hypno-cube to familiarize myself with the craft.

My ship was fully outfitted and fueled within the hour.

"I salute you, Norrin Radd. Though you fly to certain doom," Sinn stammered. "A thousand times a thousand of

Zenn-La's finest would have begged to join you in our glory years.''

Unable to speak, Shalla Bal said her farewells with tears and kisses.

I clung tightly to her for as long as I dared. Then, knowing that I would be unable to leave her if I delayed a second longer, I entered my shuttle without a backward glance.

I quickly completed my flight check under Sinn's expert guidance. Then, with a hearty wave and an optimistic smile for my lovely Shalla, who bravely bit back her fear, I fired the ignition, and streaked into the heavens.

My youthful jaunts within the cyber web were not as wasteful as I had come to believe. Instincts and skills learned in virtual reality proved just as reliable in real life. Though I had never actually beheld a true shuttle, the last one having turned to rust long before the birth of my grandfather's grandfather, I recognized the cockpit from countless rounds of the Astro-Pioneer game.

The invader had assumed an orbit above our equator, approximately 350,000 miles from Zenn-La, where his proximity to our planet wreaked terrible havoc on the tides of our oceans, as monumental waves besieged the coastal regions.

My trip through space took a little over an hour, and the alien spacecraft assumed monstrous proportions as I approached. Our scientists had approximated the ship's diameter to be nearly half the size of our motherworld, but that did not prepare me for the sheer enormity of it all.

Even as I attempted to establish contact, I was struck by the utter hopelessness of my mission. Why should the unknown intruders grant us any degree of mercy? Why should they leave us in peace? They had already withstood the onslaught of our Weapon Supreme without apparent injury. They possessed a level of technology as far above ours as ours was above our cave-dwelling ancestors.

And yet, I pressed on.

Buzzing around the mighty Worldship with all the arrogance of an insect presuming to threaten a behemoth, I continued to hail the invader, but my efforts met with silence.

Then, without warning, a massive hatchway opened directly beneath my ship. Before I could react to this unexpected occurrence, a beam of incredible force struck my shuttle, shaking it like one would an unruly child.

The beam was siphoning the shuttle's power. At that rate, my life support systems would be offline within moments. Without power or life support, I was finished. A slow and painful death by either hypothermia or suffocation was all that awaited me.

However, a glance out my starboard portal revealed that the beam, while continuing to drain my energy, was also drawing me into the belly of the great starship. Very curious to learn why I was being summoned, I sat back, silently praying that I would arrive while my shuttle still contained enough heat and air to sustain me.

At least that little bit of luck was with me. To my immense relief, I was eventually deposited into a huge chamber with barely a lungful of oxygen to spare.

I had expected to be welcomed by armed guards, but no one was on hand to greet me. I found no sign of a crew or an invading army. I was completely alone.

The chamber seemed to stretch for hundreds of miles in every direction. Oddly hued lights flashed in the distance, and I could hear the occasional whir of machinery as strange objects streaked overhead.

Who was the captain of this lonely vessel? What were his intentions toward Zenn-La? Where was the invading army? Why had he snatched me from space?

I had no idea how to locate my host, or how to reach him even if I did. My shuttle was without power, and it would surely take a week or more of strenuous hiking to reach even the chamber's closest wall.

Since any action was preferable to standing still, I chose a direction at random, and started walking. I had hardly proceeded a full ten paces when the air before me began to shimmer.

An opening began to form. It matched my height and width, with a foot or so of breathing room on both sides and above my head.

An invitation to the captain's table?

Having no wish to delay our inevitable confrontation, I cautiously stepped into the gleaming entrance.

A vast laboratory awaited me at the other end, along with an almost intolerable glare of light. Within the blaze I could vaguely see a humanoid figure.

He stood as tall as a small building, his height easily surpassing thirty feet. Upon his head sat a massive helmet with giant, protruding antennae. His eyes, when he deigned to gaze upon me, contained a stare which was coldly aloof.

"Do not attempt to speak, puny creature. I know why you have come," he said without preamble. "I granted you this audience in deference to your courage. Never before has a single individual dared confront me. But your efforts have been in vain. You cannot save your world from being ravished by Galactus."

Galactus! The name struck me like a lethal blow. He was a legend throughout a thousand star systems. During the Age of Space Travel, our astronauts had heard tales of this merciless planet destroyer. It was whispered that he belonged to a race that was old before the birth of our very galaxy. Galactus, who strode the starpaths like a demigod! Galactus, the ravager of worlds! Zenn-La had a better chance of surviving a hundred invading armadas than the menace of Galactus.

If the stories about him were true, he sought no wealth, no personal gain, no paltry treasures from our hapless planet. Instead, he intended to drain Zenn-La of all energy. He would convert our once-thriving world into a pitiful husk, leaving behind a planet no longer capable of supporting life.

"No!" I shouted as I envisioned his plans for Zenn-La. "My people will die!"

"It is not my intention to injure any living being, but I must replenish my energy if I am to survive—the energy which only a healthy planet can provide," Galactus said as he resumed his work on an imposing apparatus which stood before him. A device which, I would later learn, was his deadly elemental converter.

"If lesser creatures are wiped out when I deplete a planet, it is regrettable," he added, "but unavoidable."

"There are plenty of other worlds! Worlds which do not support sentient life. Exploit one of them! Even lesser creatures, as you call us, have a right to life."

"Alas, my need is great. The hunger which I feel grows ever stronger." Galactus continued making his adjustments. "I have no time to probe the universe for a suitable planet as rich in basic energy as the one which orbits below."

"Let me do it! I will survey the heavens and scan the spaceways for you!" The words burst from my lips even before I could consider them. "Spare my people, spare Zenn-La, and I will gladly roam the endless cosmos in search of suitable worlds."

Galactus stopped moving.

"Consider well what you have offered," he said quietly. "He who assumes the mantle of Herald to Galactus must do so forevermore!"

I stood silent for a handful of moments, as conflicting thoughts ricocheted within my mind. However, in the end, I had little choice. My own fate was of little consequence if it could save the world that gave me birth.

"If such is my destiny," I said, "willingly shall I accept it!"

The full weight of his impassive gaze fell upon me. I now understood the plight of every insect who must witness the slow descent of the crushing finger. Guided by neither emotion nor a mere desire for expedience, Galactus carefully pondered the ramifications of my offer. His eyes seemed to bore into the most hidden recesses of my very soul. Every treasured secret, every random thought and tawdry shame was laid naked before him. All that I had ever been or known was suddenly exposed to his relentless inspection.

Though he surely found me wanting in countless aspects, I must have held some appeal. Perhaps it was the hunger in my soul, the very desire for adventure which had brought me before him, perhaps it was some other quality. I cannot say. No mere mortal should dare presume to know the mind of Galactus.

"So shall it be," Galactus said.

The glare which surrounded him grew increasingly more unbearable. "You, who have been Norrin Radd, shall be so nevermore!"

Pain ripped through me! I felt as if I were being flayed alive, as layer upon layer of skin was roughly scraped away.

"Prepare yourself, Herald!"

In my mind's eye, I recalled an accident while lava surfing in the virtual reality web. A minute tear in my protective suit had accidentally exposed me to the burning magma. But that was only a fantasy. A quick brush with the illusion of pain, followed by a swift return to the comfort of my living quarters. This was real! By the heavens around me, it was real!

"Prepare yourself to be reborn!"

My knees melted beneath me . . .

"At the command of Galactus, you have fallen."

I squirmed and slithered . . .

"And now, again at my command, I bid you rise!"

Cool and blessed relief washed over me. My infinity of agony was finally over. I opened my eyes to discover that I was balanced on bended knee, genuflecting before the awesome majesty of Galactus.

My body had been completely restructured. No longer was I mere flesh and blood. A silvery substance now encased my entire physique. A substance created by Galactus for the purpose of shielding me from both the frigid, marrow-chilling emptiness of airless space, and the all-consuming inferno of the hottest sun. No longer did I require air to breathe, nor food to eat.

Surveying his handiwork without even the slightest sliver of pride, the grim-visaged Galactus casually opened his right palm. A glittering nimbus of energy slowly began to form.

"To transport you through the endless cosmos," he said, "I shall provide the perfect vehicle."

The glowing cloud took shape, sculpting itself into a most familiar object. An object which had once dominated my youth!

Why did Galactus seize upon this particular image from my psyche? Why did he chose to be heralded by a glimmering figure perched upon an equally gleaming board? I have no answer. I never asked. Even then, I instinctively knew that the will of Galactus was never to be questioned.

Matching my own silvery sheen, the giant board flew to me with the speed of thought. My heart soared, like a playful eagle, as I eagerly leaped aboard. The great adventure I had so long desired was now upon me! Laughter flooded from my lips as I circled Galactus with playful abandonment.

"Go," was all he said. "Find me a world to assuage my gnawing hunger."

Though Galactus possessed immeasurable power and numerous abilities, patience was never among them.

I immediately shifted my weight, and sent the board diving toward the nearest airlock.

Once I hit the freedom of open space, I streaked across the celestial sea like a living comet. Moving far faster than the speed of sound, and quickly surpassing that of light as well, I left conventional physics swamped in my wake.

How can I describe the sheer intoxication of slaloming through the vast void of space? Of riding the waves of escaping gas caused by a recently transformed super-nova? Alas, no mere words could ever allow you, who are bound by harsh gravity, to fully understand the total exuberance that comes from outracing the stars themselves.

But, even as I thrilled to new sights, new sensations, I remained focused on my mission. Galactus must be served!

On and on, I soared! Dodging meteors! Skirting around asteroids! Rocketing from planet to planet, and solar system to solar system!

Farther and farther I traveled, until a mere three star systems away, I finally found a world with the energy and elemental resources so necessary to my master.

Dropping from the heavens, I pierced the planet's atmosphere with the fury of a blazing meteor. Though time was at a premium, I carefully searched for any sign, any indication that this world housed intelligent life. I had no intention of saving the population of one planet at the expense of another.

As soon as I was satisfied, I employed the Power Cosmic which had recently been entrusted to me. Generating a sudden burst of energy, I unleashed a cosmic flare which promptly traveled through hyperspace.

Little time passed before Galactus arrived in his Worldship, a massive universe-spanning sphere which could have comfortably housed a thousand Norrin Radds. Impassive as ever, he sampled the planet's elemental composition, and found it to his taste.

Without a wasted motion, the devourer of worlds quickly set up his mobile elemental converter. I stood transfixed as he soon activated his incredible apparatus by linking its igniters.

The device promptly began to glow, releasing a highly corrosive cloud of unnamed gases into the atmosphere. In a matter of minutes, the sky above the doomed planet was a fiery red, and smelling of bitter ozone. Unable to survive beneath the shroud of gasses which now filled the atmosphere, every sea, every river, every drop of water rapidly began to evaporate, converting to steam before my horrified eyes.

Giant fissures soon began to spread across the land, widening with every passing second, deep veins cracking the surface of this world as if it were glass. The planet spewed molten fury from pole to pole. And, even as the air became clogged with the detritus of a once-living world, the elemental converter reached outward, greedily absorbing every particle of newly-released energy, and transferring it to the awaiting Galactus.

Soon, no longer able to resist the rising tide of destruction, the ill-fated world surrendered to the ultimate cataclysm. In a final release of seething energy, it burst apart like an overfilled balloon.

Where a true planet had orbited only hours before, only shards of lifeless debris and dust remained.

Completely unnerved by the sight I had just witnessed, I turned to Galactus like a child seeking a small measure of reassurance, or some paltry sign of approval.

"More," was all he said. "I crave more."

With a slow nod of acknowledgment, I obediently climbed upon my board.

Ascending upward, ever upward, I realized that a lifetime of such horrors was all that awaited me. But there could be no regrets, no thoughts of turning back. My decision had been freely made. Galactus would keep his part of the bargain. I could do no less. I was determined to be true to my trust for as long as I lived.

But, before I began the longest journey any mortal had ever undertaken, there was one to whom I needed to bid farewell.

Responding to my thoughts, my faithful board cleaved through the vacuum as quickly as a molten spike pierces fresh snow.

I found Shalla Bal in my living quarters. She was attempting to restore some semblance of order after the recent turmoil. Fear flared in her eyes as I entered through an open window. Perhaps she feared I was a costumed looter. But maybe, just maybe, she instinctively recognized the loving heart which now beat beneath silvery glaze.

"Do not be alarmed," I said. "I am he who was Norrin Radd."

"What has happened? What have they done to you?" Hesitantly, Shalla Bal gently caressed my face. She immediately withdrew her hand, shocked by my skin's metallic cold.

"My fate is of little consequence. All you need know is that this planet shall not perish. Zenn-La shall rise again. But our people must never again grow soft and indolent. The spirit of our ancestors must not be lost a second time."

She looked at me with a penetrating gaze. "You do not intend to remain among us, Norrin." It wasn't a question.

"A small price to pay so our world may live." Without another word, I took her into my arms.

"If you must leave," I heard her whisper as I kissed her

for the final time, "take me with you."

A beautiful sentiment, but hardly practical. And yet, when was love ever practical? When did the heart ever bow to the mind? When did emotion step aside for reason?

For an all too brief instant, I considered a life among the stars with Shalla Bal at my side. A life of endless adventure and limitless possibility.

But, even if Galactus would have allowed her to accompany me, I could not. The jagged memory of the planet which I had recently helped to devastate was much too fresh. I could never subject Shalla Bal to such constant atrocities. Where soars the Silver Surfer, he must soar alone!

Sparing her the insincerity of an optimistic smile, I embraced Shalla Bal for the last time. Her eyes were clouded with tears. Mine were not. Even that small token of humanity was now denied to me.

Mounting my board, I streaked into the sky to rejoin Galactus.

Well do I remember my early days as his Herald, when only the endless journeying could mask the bitter ache within my breast. My master's hunger knew no bounds. Though I led him to world after world, he was never satisfied. Never fully satiated! No sooner had he consumed one suitable morsel, than the quest for another began. The search continued unabated.

Staying true to my principles, I scrupulously avoided any world which held intelligent life or the potential for it. But, in every star, in every world, I saw my beloved Shalla Bal. Only with the passing of time did the pain eventually begin to ease.

Or so I thought!

Without my knowledge, Galactus had secretly tampered with my mind. He submerged all memory of my previous life, of who and what I had been. He banished all thoughts of

Zenn-La, all dreams of Shalla Bal, bricking them within the deepest dungeons of my subconscious.

Whether he did it as an act of kindness, a misguided effort to make my servitude more bearable, or merely because he was desirous of the living planets which I deliberately avoided, none will ever know. Suffice it to say that I eventually became as cold and unfeeling within as I was without.

I have no idea how long I served my master in that fashion. In the great void of space, time itself has no meaning. I only know that I witnessed the birth of planets, and the death of even more. I saw star systems crumble, and suns implode.

I blazed my way across the cosmos in my relentless quest, searching, always searching for my master's next repast. No longer did I care if a planet was rich with civilization. No more was I troubled by the annihilation of ancient cultures. My sole mission was to determine if it contained the proper elemental resources. My only allegiance was to Galactus. My single desire was to serve him.

Here is where my story might have ended. I should be attending the mighty Galactus even now. Indeed, still would I be serving him, had it not been for a most capricious whim of fate.

I found myself in a new star system. A young and healthy sun shimmered at its center. Instantly alert, I realized that it was the type of sun which might easily contain at least one planet among its satellites that could appease my master. Galactus was famished. We had voyaged far without success, and the great hunger was upon him.

Whisking among the astronomical bodies moving in orbit around this sun, I found a handful of major planets, along with their various minor dependents. There was both an asteroid belt, possibly the remains of a former planet, and a second region which appeared to be densely filled with space debris. But I could ascertain no world worthy of Galactus.

I spied an advanced society living on a moon which re-volved around a great ringed planet. Curiously, I also ob-served abandoned outposts and other evidence which led me to believe that this system had been regularly visited by such diverse alien races as the Skrull, the Kree, and the Shi'ar.

Why had they all come here? What fascination did this tiny system command? Perhaps it possessed some strategic im-portance due to its great abundance of wormholes, gateways which these star-spanning races could use to journey through hyperspace.

Intergalactic politics held no interest for Galactus. He was above the petty concerns and squabbles of extraterrestrial empires. Impassive and aloof, he was only propelled by his unrelenting appetite.

An appetite which would find no satisfaction here.

I would have normally sped to the next system, but something didn't seem right.

I, who can track a single tear across a great ocean, had spotted a few artificial satellites bobbing in the void. Primitive in design, I had little doubt that they had originated in this system. Which planet had birthed them? Who had sent them adrift?

With renewed purpose, I glided toward the area packed with space debris, determined to give it a closer inspection. The rocks varied in size, but they were uncharacteristically clustered together. Was this really a natural phenomenon?

My suspicions aroused, I attempted to penetrate the bar-rier. Moving in perfect synch, my board and I wove a serpen-tine path through the deadly maze. Swiveling, twisting, and swerving, even one as skillful as I was sorely pressed to avoid the massive boulders which hurled around me.

The barricade extended only a thousand miles in width. The going was slow and treacherous to one who usually flies far beyond the speed of light, but I completed my passage in due course.

Beneath me spun a vibrant globe unlike any I had ever seen. Lush with vegetation, brimming with oceans, and thriving with civilization, it seemed like a veritable paradise. Vague memories echoed within my mind, but I could not grasp them.

Some mysterious force had obviously conspired to conceal this planet from me. Quickly zeroing in on the power which controlled the barrier, I raced toward a towering structure within a great city.

Even as I neared my destination, a flaming humanoid soared toward me. His entire body seemed to be enveloped by a fiery plasma that did not consume him. From the naked aggression in his posture, I had little doubt that he intended to challenge me. But I could not indulge him while Galactus awaited his feast. Instead, I merely slanted my board upward, traversing past the burning man.

Landing upon the rooftop I had sighted earlier, I heard a flurry of shouts behind me even as I unleashed my cosmic flare.

"He is signaling Galactus," someone said to my surprise. "We have failed!"

Galactus? How could the inhabitants of this backward world have learned about my master? How did they know the purpose of my cosmic beacon?

I was still pondering those questions when a gruffer, deeper voice responded to the first.

"Failed nothin'!" it said. "Just let me at 'im!"

A massive fist closed upon my shoulder, and turned me to face a most unusual creature. He stood about six feet in height, and his entire body appeared to be covered with a thick and rock-like hide.

"Forget him, Thing," a man cried behind him. This man

had impossibly long arms that continued to extend in length even as I watched. "He is no longer the problem, Ben. We must prepare for Galactus."

"You do the preparin', pal. I'm more the clobberin' type!" the orange-skinned brute said, as he swung at my face.

Though I could have easily withstood the impact of his blow, I simply glided over the side of the roof. It was the most expedient method for me to depart. I had no reason to battle these poor creatures. Why should I add to their last few moments of misery? Galactus would devour their planet soon enough. Although, to my own astonishment, it was painfully clear that these few planned to deny my master his rightful due.

Such defiance was unthinkable to me now! None may thwart the will of Galactus. Ever-inviolate, he would merely ignore their pitiful efforts.

Rejoining my board, I circled around their building to get a better look at them.

Six figures dotted the aforementioned rooftop. Along with the orange brute, the stretching man and the flaming humanoid whom I have already described, there were two females and a Watcher. One female was clothed in a dark blue uniform which matched the jumpsuit worn by the stretching man. Her hair was the color of a bright sunflower. She seemed to be escorting the other, sandy-haired woman into the bowels of the building. The second woman kept shouting something which might have been a name, because it caught the notice of the orange monster, who quickly raced to join her.

However, it was the Watcher who attracted the majority of my attention. His presence explained much. He was of an ancient and vastly powerful galactic race, who had sworn a sacred oath to passively observe the phenomena of the universe. While many Watchers had languidly observed the feasting of Galactus, none had ever questioned or confronted him. All had honored their pledge not to interfere in the affairs of other races.

Until now.

Arriving without fanfare, Galactus had already established himself upon the very rooftop I was observing. Ignoring the humans as if they were of no consequence, he dignified the Watcher by conversing with him.

Just then, I noticed that neither the orange one nor the sandy-haired woman were among the humans. They had left the roof, only to reappear on the ground below.

At a signal from the brute, a motorized vehicle detached itself from a long line of similar conveyances. With a tenderness which I would have never equated with such a monstrous creature, he tenderly clung to his woman.

Then he quickly ushered her into the awaiting vehicle. His final wave was as hearty as his smile was optimistic. In his naïveté, he was attempting to send the sandy-haired woman to a place of safety.

Safety?! On a world destined to be consumed by Galactus?

To my surprise, I was left oddly unsettled by this parting. Something about it stirred barely remembered thoughts and long dead emotions. I struggled within myself, attempting to force these buried recollections to full bloom. Galactus had done his work too well. My efforts went unrewarded. Nothing surfaced!

My duty was to return to the quest, to seek another suitable planet while my master lay waste to the present one.

Instead, I streaked after the sandy-haired woman. Even now I cannot explain what I hoped to learn. I only know that she reminded me of someone in my past. Someone who had once meant a world to me!

To my shame, I stalked the unsuspecting woman like a hungry vulture. Following her to a large building, I was pleased to discover that she was lodged on the top floor. I saw her through an open skylight.

She appeared to be a very tactile person, touching every object she encountered. Her home was crowded with clay and marble sculptures of various sizes. The orange monster was obviously a favored model, for his brutish features were in great evidence.

But, all of her graceful statues, all of her personal furnishings, would soon be converted into energy for Galactus!

While I watched, she approached a formless lump of clay. Under the magic of her expressive fingers, it began to take form. Before my eyes, the face of the orange monster began to appear. Such was her skill that even he had somehow achieved a rugged handsomeness.

Suddenly, I heard a commotion in the street. Humans were scurrying about, their faces twisted with apprehension. News of Galactus must have reached the masses. Panic was spreading!

Images abruptly blossomed within my mind! I could see skyscrapers toppling, leaving thousands homeless or worse. A strange mobile street tossed even more citizens into oblivion. And the face of a beautiful, but unknown, raven-haired woman suddenly mocked me. Who was she? Why did she haunt me?

A frustrated moan must have escaped my lips.

"Who's there?" The sandy-haired woman had twisted toward me, her fingers accidentally scarring the face on the pedestal before her. "I can hear you, whoever you are," she said as she looked right at me. "And you sound like you could use a friend."

I could have streaked off. I did not. Nor did the woman turn away as I entered her home. Though I could see the fear brimming within her, she stepped forward without hesitation, and ran her hands over my face.

"Your face! It feels very different from any man I have ever felt before."

That is when I suddenly realized that she could not see. I had chosen a blind woman to show me my own heart. "I am more than a man. I am the Silver Surfer, Herald of Galactus."

"Silver Surfer? Galactus? Ben and the others were discussing the two of you earlier. They said you were dangerous. That you intended to destroy us all! You must have followed me from Fantastic Four headquarters. I don't understand why you would do such a thing, or what you hope to gain by menacing the Earth."

"Your lack of understanding cannot alter the destiny that awaits this world."

"I never heard anyone speak so strangely. You seem to be threatening me, and yet, there is a certain nobility in your voice," she said.

Nobility? The word held no meaning for me. I turned to leave, but the woman reached out to me. I later learned her name was Alicia Masters.

"I know I should be terrified, but I don't think you will harm me." Her fingers returned to my face, gently probing. "Perhaps you are hungry? Let me give you something to eat while you explain your mission here."

"The process you term eating is too slow. It is much simpler and more effective to convert your so-called food into pure energy. That is why Galactus has come! He will convert every object on this planet into pure energy."

"The Fantastic Four were right about you! You actually intend to destroy the Earth!"

"Destroy is merely a word. We simply change things," I said without emotion. "We transform elements into energy. Energy which sustains Galactus. For it is only he that matters."

"No! No! We all matter! Every living being! Every bird and beast! This is our world, and we all matter! Perhaps we are not as powerful as your Galactus, but we have hearts. We have souls, we live, breathe, and feel! Can't you see that?" she asked. "Are you as blind as I?"

My hand reached for the shouting woman, as if to silence her. But then, I gently ran my hands over her face, as she had earlier caressed mine. "Never have I heard such words, or sensed such courage."

But I had. I instinctively knew that I had! The images were howling in my mind now like rabid beasts, battering at my subconscious with increasingly greater fury. I caught sight of the misshapen clay face which had been ruined by my entrance.

"You are not just a soulless monster," Alicia said. "You, too, have emotions. I know it. I felt them when I touched you."

"Say no more! Do not build false hopes! I am what I must be. I serve Galactus!" The words seemed so hollow. They sprang only from my mouth, not my heart.

Alicia dragged me to the nearest window. "Look at the city!" she screamed. "Look at the people! Each of them is entitled to life! To happiness!"

I had never bothered to examine any species at close range. I had merely found a planet, judged its worthiness, and returned to the search. The dominant race had been condemned or spared. What could be gained by studying them?

The streets below were crammed with frightened individuals. They huddled in small groups, clutching each other for support. Children cried, and the adults could offer them small comfort.

For the first time since I had become the Silver Surfer, I felt pity.

Alicia gripped my arm. "Our entire planet is in the gravest danger, but I have the strangest feeling that you possess the power to save us."

"I cannot defy Galactus, woman."

"You cannot stand by while our world is destroyed. I couldn't have been so wrong about you when I sensed nobility," Alicia gasped, "when I thought you possessed compassion!"

"Perhaps, human, you were not totally wrong," I said as I mounted my faithful board. Every doubt, every misgiving that had ever flittered through my mind, was suddenly crystallized, molded into concrete form during my conversation with Alicia.

I had to do battle with my master. I could not allow him to consume this world. I had finally found something worth protecting.

I flashed through the concrete canyons of the city, adding to the hysteria which engulfed the population. The sky above this tortured planet still glowed a hardy blue. The elemental converter had not yet been ignited. I still had time!

I have since heard the details of how the Fantastic Four had managed to forestall the destruction of their world. Words such as *monumental* and *courageous* are paltry ones indeed to describe their valiant struggle in the face of seemingly inevitable destruction.

But the hand of Galactus was already moving toward the fatal lever when I arrived on the scene.

"Master!" I cried. "For the first time I realize the dreadful enormity of what you plan to do. You must not tamper with this world. You cannot destroy the entire human race! They are as deserving of life as you or I."

"Would you hesitate to tread upon an ant hill?" His voice betrayed no surprise at my unexpected outburst. "These creatures are of no consequence to Galactus."

"These are not ants, master. They think! They feel!"

"Enough, gleaming one. I reject your plea. You have your duty. Resume your eternal hunt."

"No, master! *No!*"

"You dare challenge me?" Astonishment marred the face of Galactus, distorting his usually implacable features with disbelief. "Have you forgotten the power I wield? I am Galactus!"

I begged him to the leave the Earth. I pleaded with him to spare this world. I did not wish to battle one I had served so faithfully. Though I was only his servant, we had still shared a universe together.

In the end, however, I was compelled to fight.

I unleashed destructive bolts with enough pure force to reduce a towering mountain into smoking rubble.

Galactus stood unmoved and untroubled by my efforts.

I blasted him with sufficient force to obliterate a blazing meteor.

He ignored me, seemingly oblivious to the carnage I heaped upon him.

I attempted to encase him within an unbreakable cocoon of ethereal energy.

He shattered it with barely a shrug.

My power was nothing compared to his. I no more harmed him than the Weapon Supreme had done on Zenn-La. But still I attacked, still I opposed and obstructed him!

"If you do not yield, I shall be forced to slay you," he said simply. "Though such is not my wish."

No matter what my fate, I was determined to face it without qualm! I would find a way to defeat my former master, or die in the attempt. For, though memory of my former life still lay dormant, I had finally remembered how glorious it was to have a cause worth dying for.

"I will tarry no longer. Galactus yields to none! I regret

what I must do. For, of all who live, I have cherished you the most." My former master raised his voice for the first time in my memory. "But now, by my hand, the Silver Surfer shall perish!"

My life would have ended at that very moment, had it not been for the intervention of the Fantastic Four. With the aid of the Watcher, the Human Torch had traveled across the rivers of infinity to the very Worldship which served as the home of Galactus. There, the daring human secured the one device which even the ravager of worlds must fear. A weapon which could destroy a galaxy and lay waste to a universe: the Ultimate Nullifier!

Realizing that no prize could be worth such a frightful cost, Galactus finally agreed to leave the Earth. He relinquished his feast in exchange for the return of the Nullifier.

Never before had the will of Galactus been thwarted.

Though he bore me no malice, Galactus could not depart without one last act. Since I could no longer be his Herald, he exiled me to this planet. A great barrier was erected beyond the Earth's atmosphere which prevented me from venturing back into unexplored space. I, who had journeyed beyond the farthest stars, was now trapped upon a single, lonely sphere.

In finding my conscience, I had lost the stars.

Darrell Walker sat still, patiently awaiting the rest of the story, but his companion remained silent. As the silence lengthened, and the Silver Surfer continued to look at the distant stars, Darrell realized that he had already heard all he would. Darrell said, "I guess your memory returned, huh?"

The Silver Surfer smiled, but his gaze remained on the stars. "Yes, and I eventually managed to breach the barrier which had entrapped me on this planet—but that is a tale for another day."

Darrell climbed to his feet, brushing away the rooftop grime as he stood. His mother would be annoyed enough by his late arrival, no sense aggravating her with smudged clothes. "What about Shalla Bal?" he asked. "You two ever gonna hook up?"

"Perhaps," the Surfer whispered. "Perhaps not."

Turning away from the stars, the Silver Surfer took Darrell by the arm, and led him to the side of the roof. Together, they looked out at the twinkling lights of the city. The Silver Surfer said, "I told you that the people of Earth and Zenn-La were similar. They both have the same promise of greatness, and the same tendency toward weakness.

"Behold! Even in this glorious city, your fellow citizens feel helpless, unable to staunch the rising tide of crime and violence. One individual could make a difference. One willing to muster the neighborhood into a potent force; one daring enough to oppose those would-be Galactuses who consume all that there is."

"Yeah," Darrell breathed, "I'd love to see somebody take down Johnny Warwick and the rest of the Blazing Ghosts."

"He would need help. People he could depend on. Like I depended on the Fantastic Four."

"Yeah." Darrell suddenly snapped his head in the vague direction of his own apartment house, realizing that he'd better hustle. "Oh, ma-a-an! I didn't realize it was so late. I gotta book. My mom's gonna freak. She'll never believe I was so late because I was with you."

"Perhaps this will convince her." The Surfer casually spread his hands. A glowing haze of energy took shape. Darrell half-expected the tiny surfboard which began to form.

He was quite surprised to see the large rose, which blossomed from the board, spreading its petals as if to welcome a warming sun.

A silver rose on a silver surfboard!

With a confident smile, the Silver Surfer willed his amazing board into the air. "Goodbye, Darrell! I wish you luck in whatever quests you dare undertake. Maybe you will be the individual who will eventually banish the Blazing Ghosts from your world."

"Maybe I will," Darrell said.

He watched the Surfer streak across the heavens like a fiery comet. Darrell knew that Norrin Radd was returning to the rolling currents of space, back to the endless adventure he'd always desired.

Darrell glanced at the rose. He knew his mom'd love it, but it wouldn't save him from a scolding. She couldn't be bought off so easily. He'd probably be grounded for the next few weeks, and he would have to do extra chores around the house to get back on her good side.

Still, he wouldn't have missed this night for anything.

Darrell Walker was real pleased to see his face reflected in *this* gleaming object.

PART TWO

EXILE

Following his rebellion against Galactus, the Silver Surfer found himself trapped on Earth. An invisible barrier, which affected only him, held the Surfer within the confines of this single planet. He tried to make his exile on this world as bearable as possible . . .

TO SEE HEAVEN IN A WILD FLOWER

ANN TONSOR ZEDDIES

Illustration by Michael Avon Oeming

Imagine: a silent hurricane of stars, as the galaxy storms and wheels around the maelstrom at its core. Imagine: clusters of suns like fire-flowers, their shells of castoff gases glowing like fallen petals. Imagine: seas of molten gold, and skies of rainbow frost, on worlds of diamond and of coal.

The solitary figure gazing starward has no need to imagine. His vision, like his power, has cosmic range. Nor is sight his only sense. To him the interstellar night is far from silent. He hears the disintegration of comets and the nova's final rage; the hiss of hydrogen and the deep bass thrum that permeates the universe, the final echo of its primal cry. He hears star-songs.

Yet, though he hurls his senses outward to the farthest boundaries of night, he finds no peace. For all he sees and hears is forever beyond his reach. Like a sleekly muscled dolphin stranded on the shore, like an eagle banished from the sky, like a god forbidden heaven, the Silver Surfer stands at the boundary of space, looking outward, and longing.

Imagine: freedom. . . .

His exile had seemed unreal to him at first, just as his transformation into the Herald of Galactus had once seemed unreal. As he had once dreamed every night of awakening in the body of Norrin Radd, free again to walk the green glades of Zenn-La, so he had dreamed each night that in the morning the barrier would be gone and he would be free again to plunge through the starry depths of space. Each day he had imagined, in hope or dread, that Galactus would return for him. Each day he had found the barrier still adamant, and each day he had hurled himself against it till even his transformed body grew weary and sore.

If the power with which he was infused had permitted it, he thought that he might have continued to batter himself against the invisible wall, in despair, until he had extinguished his life. But Galactus had denied him even that final choice. The Power Cosmic within him flamed with maddening vitality. If nothing changed, he would still circle the Earth, bound to its orbit, after it had been reduced to a crusted cinder and all life but his had perished.

That thought had shaken his sanity and had finally driven him from his vigil at the barrier. Self-preservation demanded that he look elsewhere.

The Four who had been his adversaries, then his allies, sought to befriend him in their different ways. Brusquely, he refused their company. They offered him fellowship, but at the price of uniting himself with their petty concerns, their humanity. They were earthbound. How could they understand him? He preferred his solitude.

Even in solitude, there was much to absorb his interest, at first. He circled the planet, grimly determined to see what he had sacrificed himself to save. He had surveyed many worlds in search of fodder for Galactus, but had deliberately dulled himself to their details. Some had been grim, some enchanting, but all would soon be devoured; why concern himself? But this world was different. Grim or fair, it caged him. Every detail now concerned him.

At cloud-height, all worlds were beautiful. He arrowed through thunderheads, dodging lightning bolts, or allowing them to strike him with thunderous shocks that exhilarated him and drove his cares away for a moment. He surfed rainbows and flashed through sunbows, with high-altitude ice crystals tingling against his silver skin. He descended to sea level to cut through the foaming crests of tropical storm waves, and threaded his way through precipitous green canyons where parrots burst from the forest canopy just beneath his feet. In some ways, this world was more beautiful than Zenn-La, because it had not yet been completely tamed. It still held surprises, like hidden gifts.

From human height, the world was not so fair. Norrin soared over farmlands: the vast checkerboards of Kansas and the Ukraine, the crowded mosaics of China and India. He missed the wilderness he loved, but the multicolored patchwork of crops also pleased his eye. Then he descended to the treetops, and smelled the smoke of burning forests and the stench of cattle penned in feedlots. He saw the lazy brown-and-yellow currents carrying wasted topsoil to the bottom of the sea. He saw smoking mountains of garbage, and humans competing with the rats to scavenge a living from the castoffs of their bloated brethren. The gleaming towers of human cities did not have the airy grace of the cities of Zenn-La, but they held a stark beauty of their own—till he saw how their foundations were sunk in human refuse.

"I need not wait till the sun boils away the ocean," he said to a seagull that briefly paced him as he sped through a harbor city toward the clean, open sea. "If I am imprisoned here for only one or two of their generations, I can watch them turn the earth to a cinder with their own hands."

The bird flipped its wings at him indifferently and veered away on its own business, and the Surfer glided on. At first the sharp sea-wind blew the smell of the city away from his face. But when he looked down, he saw a dark slick of oil, studded with floating islands of trash, coating the translucent water. Even the mid-ocean was no longer pure. Far below the surface, long nets drifted, tangled with rotting fish.

The Silver Surfer fled in disgust, but his gleaming board carried him at such speed that the smell of oil still lingered when the dark coastline of another continent appeared on the horizon. At the first sight of human dwellings, the Surfer tilted his board and careened skyward, only to plunge toward earth again.

Enough! he thought sternly to himself. *I cannot flee forever. I must learn to live here among them. I must learn to face their worst. I shall begin now, in this spot, wherever it may be.*

He glided to Earth a little way inland, in a cleared space. Evening was falling. If he had been paying attention, he would have seen that the clearing was not as empty as it seemed. But his thoughts were elsewhere; he did not notice until the shadows began to move and speak.

They crept up to him slowly at first. When he stood un-flinching, they grew bolder, jostling and shoving, hands out-stretched. Their voices swelled from faint pleading moans, like the cries of small trapped animals, to threats and wails. Their clawing fingers could find no grip on his smooth silver skin, but their cries pierced his ears. Their forms seemed humanoid, but he could hardly believe they were the same species as others he had met. They looked far worse than the beggars he had seen in city streets. Their limbs were wasted and bony, their faces hollow and pitted, and it was hard to tell flaccid skin from scabrous rags.

"Get back!" he cried. They shrank back briefly, then surged toward him again. He doubted that they could harm him, yet he could not be sure. He had spent only a short time on their world. His mind was filled with memories of battle, and with the confusion of his fall from the Herald's power to captivity on this isolated planet. He did not know if these beings were dangerous, but he knew their presence filled him with disgust and horror. He knew that he need not endure it. The power his master had left within him was more than enough to deal with this rabble. For a moment he hesitated; was it possible that these creatures were human and should be spared? He could scarcely believe that, even on this wretched world. His outstretched hand began to glow with an eerie light as static electricity gathered around his charged skin. A single blast of raw energy would have wiped the crowd cleanly out of existence.

Instead, the surge of power struck the ground just at their

feet, pulverizing rocks and earth and blowing a trench as deep as a human was tall, and three times as long, between the Surfer and the stampeding crowd. A dust-cloud stilled their shouts to muffled coughing, and sharp fragments rained down from the cloud.

The Silver Surfer's power had missed its aim. Amazed, he glanced down and saw that his arm was tightly gripped by small, surprisingly strong hands. By hanging on with her full weight, the woman who grasped him had succeeded in deflecting his blast.

"What's wrong with you?" she said furiously. "You might have hurt someone!" She glanced left and right. "Quick! Get inside! I need to speak to them. I'll be with *you* in a minute."

She pushed at him. It was impossible for her slender strength to move his powerful mass but, bemused by her intensity, he allowed himself to be guided. He found himself inside a drab canvas tent. A gas-powered lantern swung from a hook on the tentpole, hissing softly as it burned. The Surfer saw chipped, white-enameled folding tables, meticulously arranged shelves, and a boxy shape that he guessed might be a storage container of some sort.

Through the tent flap, he could hear the woman's clear voice above the troubled rumble of the crowd. She tried to calm their fear using, the Surfer noticed, several different languages. Finally, the voices quieted, and the woman entered the tent.

Impatiently, she pulled off a cloth cap and a pair of gloves she had been wearing when she leaped upon the Surfer. She scrubbed her hands with soap till they were lathered to the elbows. She looked around for a helper, but saw no one.

"You!" She pointed her chin in the Surfer's direction. "See that handle? Turn it!"

The Surfer cautiously turned the spigot she indicated. Water rushed out; she rinsed her hands, then scrubbed down the tables with disinfectant.

"I was just setting up for tomorrow's clinic when you interrupted," she said. "Now tell me who you are, and what you're doing here."

"Where is 'here'?" the Surfer asked calmly.

She gave him a sharp look.

"The people outside said you had fallen from the sky," she said. "I can believe that. Have you ever heard of Gambia? We're a few miles from the border. The name of this place probably wouldn't mean anything to you. It wasn't a place at all until a few months ago, when these people began arriving and building tents. It's just a little piece of nowhere for people who have no other place to go."

The Surfer lifted the tent flap and looked out. A huddle of drab tents and shelters of plastic sheet and cardboard sprouted among the rocks like a cluster of dank fungus. Mingled smells of sewage and campfire smoke eddied in the evening air.

" 'People,' " he said. "So these are humans, too."

"Of course they are human!" Her voice was raised; she seemed disturbed by his statement.

"I don't understand," he said. "If these are humans, why are they living here like a pack of vermin? This is a miserable place. Why don't they go home?"

"They have no home," she said. "It was a dry year, and the crops failed. The first lot came wandering in from the countryside, looking for food, and stopped here by the river. Then the famine and the refugee problem led to political troubles, and a civil war broke out. That drove people out of the city, and they ended up here as well. They've been shelled. They don't like things blowing holes in the ground. You nearly caused a panic."

The Surfer studied her. Human ideas of beauty differed

from the standards of Zenn-La, but he thought she would be considered beautiful. The drab, bulky cloth of her garments could not completely conceal a slender, graceful shape. Freed from the cap, her hair rippled in lustrous waves of a rich shade, brown with gleams of russet. Her face showed some of those faint lines that seemed to mark human aging, but her eyes were clear and lively, the color of water. Her speech was precise, her movements self-controlled. She seemed as unlike the animated wreckage outside as the Surfer was unlike his former self.

"What is that to you?" he asked. "They have no home. It seems that no one cares for them. If they have been permitted to sink into such misery, why should you stop me from ending it?"

She swept her arms wide, indicating the pathetically tidy space around them.

"I work for the Society for World Health," she said. "I'm a doctor. I have spent months trying to keep these people alive. Oddly enough, I do not wish to see them obliterated!"

The Surfer shrugged.

"It seems a noble effort," he said, "but pointless. If they cannot look after themselves, why should you concern yourself?"

The woman took a step toward him, examining him more closely.

"A strange comment, coming from you," she said. "I recognize you, you know. We are not so out of touch as you might think."

She rummaged in a file and triumphantly brought out a tattered piece of newsprint.

"THREAT TO EARTH REPELLED," the headline read. Below was a faded but recognizable photograph of Reed Richards and his friends. The Surfer could make out his own

56

shape beside them, and beyond loomed an indistinct, gigantic form. He shuddered involuntarily.

"You are this person they call the 'Silver Surfer,'" the woman said. "You defied your master to save us. The story reached us, even here. I admired your courage. Yet I might ask you the same question: why did you concern yourself? And what are you doing here?"

The Surfer lowered his eyes from her penetrating gaze.

"I begin to wonder," he said. "I was moved to pity for this world by the compassion of a single human female. I thought I saw some spark of greatness in the human will to battle incredible odds without giving in. But now the exhilaration of battle is over, and I must pay the price each day for my rash deeds. I have been traveling your Earth, desperately seeking some assurance that my choice was the right one. The shadow of doubt darkens upon my heart."

"If you have such doubts about us," the woman said, "why stay?" She reached tentatively to touch the gleaming board tucked under the Surfer's arm, and her eyes shone. "If I had the power to soar into space, I would be tempted to leave here, too," she laughed.

"I cannot," the Surfer replied somberly. "That was the price I paid for my defiance. My master confined me to the circles of your world. I must orbit the sun with you forever."

Her eyebrows rose. "That was not in the newspaper," she said.

She turned to a hot plate where a beaker of murky liquid simmered, and poured two cups.

"I sometimes have trouble sleeping," she said, offering one of the tin mugs to him. "Would you like to have a cup of coffee with me, and tell me the rest of the story?"

The Surfer drew back automatically. "I have no need of earthly sustenance," he said.

The woman laughed again. "Good! I'm not offering you any. This is very bad coffee, with canned milk. It's not good for you at all, so if you were looking for nourishment, you'd be out of luck. It is purely recreational—a gesture of hospitality. The correct answer is 'Thank you.' Or, if you don't care for any, a simple 'No, thanks.' You don't have to give me a pompous explanation of your physiology."

A strange sensation tugged at the Surfer's face. Gradually he recognized it as the urge to smile. He wondered if he still could; it seemed like several millenia since he had tried, but it was a pleasant feeling.

"Thank you," he said, and accepted the cup.

"Do you have a name?" the woman said. "Other than this sobriquet from the newspaper?"

"A name has not been necessary," he said stiffly. "I have been the Herald of Galactus. That was title enough."

He hesitated.

"Long ago, I was called Norrin Radd," he admitted.

"Norrin," she repeated, offering her hand. "And I am Jeanne D'Argent. I suppose that makes us cousins, in a way. 'Argent' means 'silver' *en français*—my native language. Shall we sit outside? It will be cooler, if the commotion among my poor friends has died down."

Jeanne sat quietly when Norrin told his tale, sipping at the last bitter dregs of her lukewarm cup. She had accepted the story calmly, as if there were nothing unusual about it. As if he were just another refugee.

"So, somewhere out there, your Shalla Bal is still waiting for you," she said.

"Yes. And I am trapped here."

She set the cup down in the sand and leaned back on her elbows, gazing up at the stars.

"How beautiful they are, and how fortunate you are to have traveled there. It must give you hope to see them every night. Surely you will find a way home someday.''

Norrin threw away the sludgy lees of his coffee, with an angry gesture.

"Perhaps you find that easy to imagine. But I know better. I am trapped, and I cannot take refuge in false hope.''

The doctor smiled. "You remind me of one of my favorite stories,'' she said. "It's about a prince who fell from the sky. It was written by a Frenchman who was the closest thing we had to a star-traveler, in his own time: he was one of the first to fly.

"But Antoine de Saint Exupéry's prince never doubts. On his home planet, he left a single rose, his beloved, and he never loses hope that he will return to her. He says, 'If someone loved a flower who existed only as one example among millions and millions of stars, that would be enough to make him happy when he looked at those stars. He would say, "My rose is there, somewhere. . . ." ' ''

"I find no encouragement in the fairy tales of a primitive race,'' Norrin said shortly.

Jeanne shrugged and seemed about to rise and go.

"Pardon me,'' Norrin said gruffly. "My conversational skills have atrophied somewhat. No one has spoken with me in so long . . . .''

She did not reply. Hastily, Norrin tried to think of a question that would make her stay.

"And what of you? You have not yet told me what brings one like yourself to live among these degenerate creatures.''

At first he thought that something about his question had angered her, but she answered him lightly.

"Nothing so cosmic as your story,'' she said, with a shrug. "When I was fifteen, I became a professional ballet dancer. By the time I was twenty-five, my knees and feet were ruined. Surgery proved insufficient to let me dance again, but I became interested in medicine as I watched the doctors. My family is very wealthy; I could do as I wished. I could have amused myself as a cosmetic surgeon in Paris. I don't know why I came here instead. Perhaps I came to feel that nothing can be enjoyed unless it is truly earned."

The words stirred something oddly within Norrin Radd. They seemed to come from his own past. But the doctor rose and brushed sand from her clothing before he could reflect further.

"I have work to do in the morning," she said. "I don't know if you need to sleep; you are welcome to find a place on the clinic floor. Perhaps you would like to stay and see just what it is that we do here."

The Silver Surfer brooded beneath the starlight when she had left him. This doctor seemed a different kind of female from the beloved of the orange-skinned Thing. She had given him no pity. Yet she intrigued him. True, she was a mere mortal, but rather than admitting this fact and giving way to despair, she strove to improve conditions on this wretched little ball of dirt. He decided that it could do no harm to stay a little longer. After all, he was free to leave at his own will, and he had nothing more pressing to do.

He did not sleep, but he found the sandy hillside a comfortable resting place. The occasional snakes and insects that passed by might have been deadly to a human, but they could not trouble the Silver Surfer. Briefly, he enjoyed watching them weave their little webs of life among the stones and sand grains.

As he shifted a hand to avoid crushing a bright-colored spider, he recalled how he had almost destroyed lives that turned out to be human. For all his brave words to the doctor, he felt bitter shame at that thought. Yet he still felt anger at the creatures who had driven him to such an extreme reaction. He wished that he could simply avoid them all, but they were everywhere on this world. With an effort of will, he turned his mind to more pleasant memories, and roved among them till dawn.

By the time he rejoined the doctor in her tent, she had already eaten breakfast and was washing her dishes in a scant few inches of water.

She saw him looking distastefully at the grey, murky liquid.

"Clean water is scarce here," she said. "It's one of our major problems. People bathe in the river without realizing that contaminated water only spreads more disease. That's why I make every ounce do double duty."

She carefully carried the pan of water around to the back of the tent. Norrin followed, curious to see what she was doing. He saw a small patch of flowers, fenced with wire and staked to let the vines grow without falling over. Jeanne poured the water carefully over the little garden, and paused for a moment to examine the plants.

"Do these plants have some purpose?" Norrin asked. "Are they medicinal?"

She looked embarrassed.

"They are medicine to my spirit," she said. "And I hope they bring some happiness to my patients as well. This place can be so ugly. People need beauty as well as food and water."

She wiped her forehead. The air already blazed with heat. Norrin was no longer affected by extremes of temperature, but he noted that the sun was hot enough to cause discomfort for the average human.

"I forgot last night that you don't even know what a rose is," the doctor said. "That's one. Smell it—if you can smell. Sweet, *n'est-ce pas?*"

The bush she indicated was small, and its leaves tattered by nibbling insects, but it bore a handful of red-velvet

61

blooms. Norrin bent down to them, and discovered that he could still enjoy their delicate perfume. It brought back a wave of nostalgia that almost made him dizzy. He closed his eyes. For a moment, he was walking through the gardens of Zenn-La with a lovely woman by his side.

He straightened, and forced his eyes open.

"I no longer care for such things," he heard himself say. He did not know why he lied.

"A pity," the doctor said. "We have a poem that begins: 'To see a World in a Grain of Sand,/And a Heaven in a Wild Flower,/Hold Infinity in the palm of your hand/And Eternity in an hour.' William Blake, the poet, thought that such perception was a sign of an innocent heart. Perhaps you have lost yours."

She walked briskly back to her tent. Norrin followed, feeling that he had been unfairly treated, but unsure exactly how. The woman had a talent for disturbing him.

A long line of patients had already formed at the door of the clinic. A young boy held back the pushing, shoving crowd. He turned to the doctor with obvious relief when she arrived. To Norrin, he did not look much different from the others. He was thin, brown-skinned, and dressed in rags.

"Norrin, this is my assistant, Ignatius Kaounde. I couldn't get along without him. Ignatius, this is Norrin Radd."

The boy stared. Norrin did not know what to say. He was sure that this youth could not possibly comprehend his identity.

"The Silver Surfer?" Ignatius said incredulously. He reached out and shook Norrin's hand enthusiastically. "I think you're great! I read about you. Will you show me how your surfboard works? We are too far from the ocean now, but I always wanted to be a surfer. Like on the radio, you know. *Wish they all could be California girls,*" he sang.

Norrin looked baffled. The doctor seemed amused.

"I think our guest does not listen much to the radio," she said. "Come now, we have work to do."

Norrin stood back and watched at first as the woman and the painfully thin young man worked tirelessly with the endless stream of the sick and wounded. Wary glances were cast his way, but when he made no threatening moves, he was soon ignored as if he were a gleaming, inanimate statue. The desperate people who waited for help were much too concerned with their immediate problems to worry about the bizarre stranger.

He shuddered at the crudity of the doctor's techniques. She actually pierced the skin of her patients with metal points that apparently were to be cleaned somehow and reused. He thought at first that it might be a religious ritual, for he could hardly believe that such an atrocity could actually have medical value. Soon, however, he realized that it was a primitive method for delivering curative drugs.

He was also surprised by the competence of the doctor's young assistant. He moved quietly and efficiently among the patients and seemed to know exactly what was needed. To Norrin Radd, he looked just like the other human refuse. Norrin wondered what made him different.

Hours passed with no pause in the press of people begging for attention. The doctor paused for a moment to wipe her face with a handkerchief and drink a glass of water, and her eye fell on Norrin.

"You!" she said. "Are you standing there doing nothing? Come here! Ignatius can show you the job."

Norrin drew back. This was exactly what he had wished to avoid—personal involvement in the petty problems of earthlings, problems that were not his to solve.

Before he could refuse, however, a sound of wailing and angry shouting arose just beyond the door. The sides of the tent flapped, and the poles wobbled as bodies careened into the canvas from outside.

A knot of scrawny brown bodies half-fell through the door, while those who had been first in line shoved and struck at the newcomers. Blood splattered across the floor, shockingly bright. At first, the Surfer thought the tent was under attack and moved instinctively to block the doorway. From that position, he could see that the intruders meant no harm. They were merely fleeing the chaos outside, where seemingly random groups of fighters pursued each other, shouting and striking with primitive weapons.

Those who had reached the relative safety of the tent sank to the ground, more blood running from long ugly slashes and trickling down their bruised faces. The noise swelled outside. The doctor glanced briefly toward the door, then back to the wounded.

"Norrin!" she called sharply. "Never mind what's happening out there. Our help is needed here." The Surfer no longer thought of refusing. His first patient had been cut with some sharp implement. Her arms were cut, her hands were cut, two fingers were nearly severed, and an ugly slash had laid open her cheek from forehead to chin. Norrin cleaned her skin and threaded needles while the doctor and the boy stitched the gaping flesh back together. They left Norrin to move her to a cot and place dressings over the wounds. Norrin bit back his disgust at the thought of wrapping bits of cloth over such injuries. He knew they were only trying to protect the wounds as best they could; the sterile fields of Zenn-La's science were far beyond them.

The woman had cried and screamed as they repaired her cuts. When Norrin protested, the doctor told him that the clinic's supply of painkillers was too small to waste on superficial surgery, and there was no time to use them anyway. As Norrin bandaged the woman, she was silent. Her skin had turned an ashy grey. Norrin looked around surreptitiously to make sure no one was watching. Then he placed his hand on the woman's shoulder and allowed the power within him to flow toward her: only the tiniest amount, only enough to ease her breathing and bring a warmer color to her cheeks.

He had assured himself that he would not get involved. But each of the others seemed equally helpless. Each time he shared only a fragment of his power. Yet there were so many that by the time darkness fell, he felt as weary as a human.

At last the doctor turned away the stragglers left in line, dismissed Ignatius with a few words of gratitude, and closed the tent flap. The wounded rested as comfortably as possible. Jeanne shooed most of their relatives away. She allowed a few to stay and watch over patients who were in critical condition.

"They can't do anything to help, of course," she said to Norrin. "But they can come and wake me if they think there's something wrong."

She stepped out into the cooler air, shaking out her sweat-darkened hair.

"I do not understand," Norrin said. "What disaster occurred? I saw the fighting, but I do not know the reason for it. Why were they wounded so brutally?"

Jeanne rubbed her reddened eyes. "One of the relatives told me all about it while I was suturing his brother. I told you there was a civil war across the border. People from both sides end up here, and their enmity is no less because they are now homeless and poor. They carry on the war. Some kind of fight over food started it, I imagine. One clan thought they'd been cheated. So they returned with clubs and machetes to settle it."

Norrin could not believe what he was hearing. He had

thought that he could rise above the random brutality of these primitives, but rage swelled within him.

"Do you mean to tell me that even here, you humans will turn upon each other? They have deprived each other of everything that makes life worth living! They have nothing left—yet they still bite and tear at each other. There can be no compassion for such creatures! They are worse than animals!"

His fists clenched, and the eerie glow of gathering power flickered around them. He did not know what he would strike, but he wished to strike something. He wished that he had wiped the camp's population out of existence as he had first intended.

"For this I made myself a prisoner," he cried bitterly. "For this I lost all hope of seeing my own world. Galactus at least was a great and mighty master. Better to serve him than to be trapped in a cage with rats!"

Jeanne turned to face him, her fists also clenched.

"I am tired of your disdain," she snapped. "Because you have been dipped in stainless steel till dirt won't stick to you, you think you can look down on us? These are not 'creatures.' These are my fellow human beings.

"We have a saying: if one saves a single human life, it is as if he saved the whole world. You think very highly of yourself for having stooped to save our lowly world! Yet each of these 'creatures' is a world unto himself—a world struggling to survive, longing for freedom just as you long, bearing all the possibilities for greatness that you find within yourself. Look at young Ignatius—full of talent, brightness, gentleness, even in the midst of this hell. How dare you decide we are not worthy of your effort?"

Norrin lowered his hands, and the glow around them died.

"I did not mean to include you or your friends," he said

stiffly. "The Four, as well, have noble spirits. But could you not contribute more by working with those like yourself, in a place of civilization?"

"Civilization!" Jeanne laughed. "You still do not understand. Here, they have small wars. You are fortunate, indeed, that you fell to Earth too late to enjoy our latest great war. It was fought with unimaginable savagery by the most advanced and civilized nations on earth.

"And do you know what my so-civilized family did in that war? They became rich in the black market! They profited from the starving, just like those men with machetes. When the war was over, they continued to profit by selling explosive chemicals to poor states, for use in such wars as these. That is the real reason I fled from that 'place of civilization.' I prefer the work that I do here—useless as it may be."

"I'm sorry," Norrin said stiffly. "I did not know."

"No, you could not," she said. "But there is something you know and I do not. How many worlds, do you think, did you sacrifice to your master's appetites before you decided to save this one?"

"I had no choice!" Norrin protested. "I had to serve Galactus. It was the only way to save Zenn-La."

"*Exactement,*" the doctor said sadly. "You put those who were like you first, and let the others die, just as our friends out there have done." She reached across the gap between them to touch his clenched hand gently, frail flesh against invulnerable silver. "I submit, my dear Norrin Radd, that you are all too human." She sighed and let her hand fall to her side. "Pardon me for scolding you, after all the help you gave us today. I am tired and very much worried about things that do not concern you."

Norrin felt buffeted by her words, as if he had ridden storm winds. Yet, as he gazed upon the woman's mortal weariness, he could no longer summon righteous anger. Already he could feel his spent power surging back to fill him with boundless energy. She had no such luxury.

"I would be willing to help, if I could," he offered.

She sighed.

"I doubt it, *mon ami*. I treated four cases of cholera yesterday. Such an outbreak will become an epidemic without a source of clean water. There is vaccine—a medicine to stop the disease—but we can't get it. The trucks that are bringing it are stuck on the road, a hundred miles from here. Between us and them are many angry men, and a great deal of mud."

At the summons of a thought, Norrin's board quivered beneath his feet.

"That problem I can solve!" he said. "Rest without fear tonight. I will bring the medicine you need."

Without waiting for an answer, he launched himself into the sky. It was a joyous relief to feel the cool night wind whipping past him once again! He resolved to find and bring the vaccine. That would more than fulfill any possible obligation. Then he could leave with a clear conscience, before he became yet more involved in earthlings' affairs.

Like everything involving humans, this apparently simple idea proved more complicated than he had imagined. The road was not hard to find. It was the only line anywhere in sight that was even partially straight. Norrin followed it from above, keeping his speed down so he could watch for signs of a convoy.

As he approached the capitol, heavy clouds gathered below him. He had to dive through them and fly close to the earth. Drenching rain annoyed him until he remembered that he did not need to put up with it. He extended the Power Cosmic around himself, and the rain parted and flew away to the sides before touching him.

He found the trucks at a break in the clouds. They were inching their way along the road, which resembled a furrow drawn in the mud by a child with a stick. The truck drivers could not see around the bend some miles ahead, but Norrin could. Puddled ruts disappeared into a morass that looked as if it could easily swallow an elephant. North of the road, Norrin noticed damp wisps of white smoke curling upward, but there was no other sign of human presence.

Norrin glided to a landing within sight of the trucks and waited for them to catch up. He did not want to alarm the people inside by appearing too suddenly. The trucks ground reluctantly to a halt, since he stood in the middle of the road. "I have come to transport the vaccine," he announced. "I can do so more efficiently than these vehicles."

The drivers and guards on the first two trucks frowned at him without replying. Then they spoke with each other.

"What the hell? What is *that?*"

People jumped from the trucks to see what was happening. Norrin heard their exclamations of disgust as they sank ankle-deep in the viscous ochre mud. Driver and guard in the first truck nudged each other.

"Look! The rain doesn't fall on him! He must be a ghost or something."

"Don't be foolish. It must be some kind of pilot suit. He came from the sky, didn't he?"

Slowly, two men in hats dragged their feet through the muck till they stood before Norrin.

"Look, what is this about?" the paler of the two said. "You are holding up an emergency relief convoy." He spoke calmly, but Norrin could detect the usual fear of the unknown in his voice.

"I know you carry medicine," Norrin said. "I have come to take it to its destination. You cannot get there by road."

The man took off his hat and poured the rain off its brim.

"I have no idea who you are," he said, "but you must realize that I cannot simply turn over any of the supplies we carry to a stranger."

The darker-skinned man next to the first man bent and muttered in his ear. Norrin heard him clearly.

"It's the Silver Surfer. He saved the world from a monster named Galactus. I saw a news program. He may be trying to help."

"I don't care who he is," the other man said, slapping his wet hat back onto his head. "We can't let him do this. He has no official authorization. He's just some kind of a freak."

"I have seen the road ahead," the Surfer said. "It is completely blocked. If you turn over your supplies to me, I can assure you they will reach their destination safely and quickly."

"They're not 'my' supplies," the man with the hat said. The fear in his voice had been swallowed up by exasperation. "I'm responsible to the Society for World Health, and I've negotiated agreements with two political parties and three nations to take this convoy through. I personally signed off on every bottle of aspirin on this truck. I can't allow you to touch any of it. If you really want to help, then go back to Nairobi and get some authorization from the SFWH office there. Now will you *please* get out of my way?"

Briefly, the Surfer considered flying to Nairobi. But if one man would not listen to him, it seemed unlikely that he would have better luck with a committee. Furthermore, he had run into problems before when visiting cities unannounced.

"You may continue with the rest of your supplies," he said. "I require only the vaccine."

"He's a loony," the man with the hat said. He waved his arm to the trucks. "Drive on!" he shouted.

"You leave me no choice," Norrin said. "Mine is the Power Cosmic! I cannot allow helpless people to die over a question of paperwork."

He had torn open the rear doors of the first truck when he realized that he did not know which vehicle held the vaccine, or what it looked like. He assumed it would be labeled. He was moving boxes from one stack to another when he felt a shower of small impacts against his shoulders. Annoyed, he wondered if it was raining again. He turned to look and found that the humans were shooting at him.

"Cease," he commanded them. "You cannot harm me. You only endanger yourselves."

He moved to the next truck. That one was filled with heavy crates, but behind them, he could hear something humming. It proved to be a refrigeration unit. The box inside was tightly packed and secured, but the words on the label included "vaccine." Norrin wondered if the medicine could survive exposure to the tropical sun. He decided that he could create a small field around the box and exhaust the heat from it. He could easily maintain such a bubble of cold until he reached Dr. D'Argent.

But the humans had not given up their assault. As he turned to summon his board, a projectile streaked toward him. He was invulnerable, but he feared for the precious box. He deflected the missile into the air, where it exploded in a brief, intense fireball. He rose swiftly, but they continued to fire their futile missiles at him. It no longer mattered. He had only to speed back to the camp and deliver the package. Then he could quit this place that had become so distasteful to him. The disturbance would cease once he had gone, like the bustle of a stirred anthill.

Something checked him in his flight. The sounds were not

diminishing behind him. Instead, they grew louder. He heard a crescendo of gunfire and more explosions. He could not help but think how insignificant the battle sounded. He had listened unmoved while cities crumbled and worlds exploded. This miniature frenzy had already been swallowed by the green forest, by the rain and mud. Still, he hesitated, and the board, in answer to his thought, swerved in a wide, uncertain spiral. He heard cries of pain somewhere beneath the sea of green. He told himself that more lives would be saved by continuing on his flight, yet he found himself returning.

From the northern side of the road, where the faint trails of campfire smoke had showed, thick fumes of rocket exhaust and explosives mushroomed upward. Trees crackled and steamed in fire. Norrin saw trucks overturned in the mire, some of them already in flames.

Heedless of the package he carried, he sped down to confront a scene of horror. Bandits had swarmed out of the trees to attack the convoy, like ants gathering around spilled sugar. Their mines and rockets had already broken all resistance. Men dressed in battered camouflage fatigues without insignia hauled boxes from the wrecked trucks. They scattered everything that was not edible, scavenging only the food and the most basic of the medical supplies. They ignored the moaning, broken figures in the mud.

Norrin swooped down on them like a bird of prey in flames. He was ready to blast the attackers, but it was not necessary. They scattered before him like rats before a blazing torch. He raised his hands to unleash a bolt of power that would obliterate them. Almost too late, he remembered the package he carried. By the time he had tucked it between his feet for safety, the marauders had vanished into the trees. He could still have withered the forest around them with a single devastating blast. His anger demanded action, yet he found he could not strike them.

Instead he turned to the others. He found only a handful of survivors, the man with the hat among them.

"Can I help you?" Norrin asked.

"You've done enough," the man said. "That little firefight you caused gave the bandits our exact location. You can help us put our dead into a truck, if you can find a truck that's running."

"You should have given me the vaccine, as I asked," Norrin said.

The man groaned as he tried to stand up.

"You should have bloody well let us run our own affairs," he said.

"I was trying to help," Norrin said.

"I daresay you were." The man accepted a hand up from Norrin, and did not notice when the Silver Surfer gave him a minor transfusion of force as well.

Norrin forced himself to assist with the gruesome task of piling bodies into the back of the truck. His pride revolted against it, but it seemed only just. They had died attempting the same task he had considered so simple.

"We'll get back all right if it doesn't rain again," the man with the hat said as the truck roared to life. "Next time, remember that you have to understand before you can help."

Norrin sped toward the camp again. The power filled him with strength and vitality, as always, but his heart was weary. He wanted to finish his self-imposed task and go.

But when he arrived, he found the camp in turmoil. Wailing and crying sounded everywhere. Campfires smoldered unattended, and the riverbanks were empty. All the people visible were clustered by the medical tent. Norrin pushed his way through them. They were too sick to shrink from his touch.

"Where's the doctor?" Norrin said. The crowded tent smelled like death. He could not see the woman anywhere. He could not find Ignatius until the boy came to him and touched his arm.

"She is in the back, resting," Ignatius said.

"Get her. Tell her I have brought the medicine."

The boy's eyes shone with renewed hope. Norrin wondered how he could have considered this young man indistinguishable from all the others. His face now seemed unique and welcome among strangers.

When Jeanne emerged from the back of the tent, she clutched at the tentpole to keep herself upright. She wasted no words of greeting.

"Open it," she gasped. She touched the vials as if they were precious jewels.

"Now, Ignatius, you already know how to give the injections. Show Norrin. Start at once, and don't stop till everyone has had a shot. Mark their wrists so you can tell. I will concentrate on those who already have cholera. We aren't defeated yet."

They worked together late into the night, and then Jeanne turned toward the door, said vaguely "Moonrise . . ." and slumped to the ground.

"What's wrong? What should we do?" Norrin asked Ignatius. The boy's face was pinched with fear.

"It's the disease," he said. "I didn't know!"

Norrin tried to lift her from the dirt floor.

"I'll fly you to a hospital," he said. "Tell me where to go."

She opened her eyes with a great effort.

"No, *idiot*," she said. "It is not cholera. I've been vaccinated. It's only my old friend malaria. I'll get through this attack. Just let me lie down for a bit. Leave me some water.

I have my quinine tablets. You must keep working or others will die.''

"I should take you to a doctor,'' Norrin insisted.

This time she did not open her eyes, but her answer was firm.

"No! We cannot afford the time. You are needed here. And I don't wish to leave. This is my place.''

Norrin allowed Ignatius to tuck the blankets around her shoulders.

"She is right,'' the boy said. "We should do as she says.''

Just before dawn, there was a lull in their work. They had finished scouring the wretched shacks for children to vaccinate, and for a few minutes, no more relatives appeared dragging blanket-wrapped patients. Norrin bent to look at the doctor. At first he thought she was sleeping, but the drawn look of her face alarmed him. He turned to call Ignatius, but the boy was frowning as he looked toward the door. Footsteps were approaching, but not the soft, dragging footsteps of the sick. These were heavy and purposeful.

Norrin's quick sight reached out into the darkness and showed him not more victims of disease, but armed intruders. They stood tall and strong, carrying clubs of wood and rusty, vicious blades. They reminded him of the bandits who had scattered the convoy. As Norrin rose from his knees, they burst into the tent. He understood what they were saying.

"Where is the foreigner? Where is the poisoner? She kills our children and lets our enemies live! Kill her! Break her poison needles! Then the sickness will stop!''

Sick people, awakened, screamed aloud in terror. Ignatius threw himself across the doctor's pallet. That was a mistake. It attracted the intruders' attention.

Norrin sprang between them and the boy. But just as he moved to strike, he realized what his power might do in the crowded tent. He cared nothing for these others. He wanted only to save his friend. Behind the first group of marauders, others crowded in, waving rifles as well as knives. The eerie glow flamed around Norrin. He saw no alternative.

"Norrin, no," the doctor said weakly.

It was too late; he had loosed the power. But at the last instant, he turned it aside. The power of destruction would transform matter into scattered energy. The sound of Jeanne's voice reminded the Surfer that other transformations were equally possible. Cold radiance shone like a shining curtain between the intruders and their prey, and as it passed over them, the weapons leaped from their hands. Clubs fell to the ground as a tangle of green stems and metal melted into velvet convolutions. A burst of air, powerful as an explosive blast, swept a sudden scent of flowers through the fetid tent. Knocked flat by the blast, the attackers struggled to their feet and ran, terrified by something truly incomprehensible at last. They left behind no blood, no bodies: nothing but a drift of flowers scattered across the floor, as far as Jeanne's blanket.

"You haven't forgotten about roses," Jeanne said. Her voice was a dry whisper.

Norrin bent to hear it better.

"This is my fault," he said. "I made too many mistakes. I do not understand this world."

"You did your best," she said. "Have some hope for yourself, Norrin. Then you'll see there is hope for us as well."

Her fingers reached feebly and touched the crumpled petals of one flower.

"I'm glad I saw that," she said. "It was beautiful."

Norrin did not understand that she was dead until he saw Ignatius weeping.

Once again he soared in silent vigil on the threshold of space. His sight rested gratefully on the starry vistas, but his thoughts were full of earthly memories. He had not fled that place of death as he had once intended. He had stayed with Ignatius till help was summoned, till the humans came with clean water and food, till the dead were buried and the living cared for. He had even sought help from Reed Richards for the boy, to give him the schooling Jeanne had wanted for him.

Soon he would glide through earthly skies again, and try once more to understand the strange beings who lived below. Perhaps one day he would visit the place Jeanne called the City of Lights, and try to see it through her eyes. Perhaps one day he would again accept friendship when it was offered. Yet before he sped to seek his destiny, he had one thing to do.

One silver hand lightly balanced a globe of imperishable crystal. Safe at its center bloomed a single rose. Its petals were far from perfect, for it had struggled for life in a hard climate. Yet it held a unique beauty. There would never be another like it. For a moment Norrin poised the crystal before his eyes. Then, with gentle but irresistible force, he hurled it from him, past the barrier he himself could not pass, to sail forever among the stars.

Farewell, my friend, he mused. *I no longer despise your people, nor do I pity my own fate. For we are all prisoners of our times and days, yet all may seek the freedom of heart that cannot be taken from us by any power. Yes, my Shalla Bal awaits me, unique among so many million stars, and I know that I shall never again despair as I strive to reach her again. Yet, when I look at those stars, it will also be good to remember a friend found in exile.*

Even after the gleam of crystal was indistinguishable from a grain of star dust, he gazed unseeing through millions upon millions of stars. His heart beheld clearly that which remains forever invisible to the naked eye.

He imagined a future. He imagined hope.

POINT OF VIEW

LEN WEIN

Illustration by George Pérez

The heat of the nearby sun whipped past his face like the hot breath of summer. He shifted his left foot forward slightly on his gleaming board, changing the angle of his flight, picking up speed; the myriad stars that glittered around him reflecting off his seamless metallic shell like so many distant diamonds.

He was Norrin Radd, the Silver Surfer, and today he was trying to outrace a comet.

There was no particular reason for the race, just the sheer exhilaration of the sport. Out here, out beyond the artificial bounds of gravity, out beyond the Celestial Rim, the possibilities were limitless, and so was his power. Thus he bent slightly forward at the waist, as if to cut down wind resistance (though friction was only a concept here), and urged his board onward, ever faster.

Even now, after so very long, it occasionally astounded him how the shining surfboard beneath his feet had become so much a part of him, responsive to his every command, his every whim. The extraordinary entity who had transformed him into the shining creature he now was had made the board a living extension of his body.

The Silver Surfer smiled, and pressed on.

He was closing fast on the comet, its great head of frozen gas and grit leaving behind a trail of star dust that could stretch a hundred million miles. *I could leave a trail of my own,* he thought impishly. *Something to say "The Silver Surfer has passed this way. Bow your heads, you lesser beings, and be thankful."*

He dismissed the thought quickly; such conceit was not his style.

Now he was five thousand miles behind the comet's nucleus, now only a thousand. Now he was neck and neck with the great cosmic traveler, reveling in its majesty, elated and yet somehow humbled. One last impossible burst of speed and now he was ahead.

Grinning, he shifted his weight once more and his surfboard veered sharply left, cutting across the path of the vast juggernaut. He crossed the sixty mile width of the comet's head in less than the blink of an eye, thrusting his fists above his head in a gesture of triumph. Three quick whirling barrel rolls to punctuate his point and at last his race was done.

The Silver Surfer slowed his board to watch the comet depart. "Go in peace, great brother," the Surfer whispered, "until we meet again."

Still exhilarated, the Surfer urged his board onward. In space, the days are forever, after all, and the Silver Surfer still had work to do before he could—

"How fares your quest, Herald? Galactus hungers."

A voice that was not a voice but more like the rumble of distant thunder echoed through the Surfer's mind, jarring him back to reality.

"It goes as well as ever, Master," he said to the void, knowing he would somehow be heard, "I seek new and bountiful worlds to satisfy your need."

"Be quick about it, Herald. Galactus's hunger grows!"

And, with that, the voice was gone, leaving the void more empty than before. No longer quite so joyful, the Surfer flew on, his attention focused on his seemingly endless mission once more; to find suitable planets, rich in life, for his master to consume, to sate his enormous hunger.

Galactus. It was a name to make the universe tremble.

From the moment Norrin Radd first sacrificed his mortality to save his precious homeworld Zenn-La from Galactus's all-consuming need, agreeing to become the great entity's advance scout and Herald, the Surfer had wondered about the truth of his master's origins. There were some who claimed Galactus was the last remaining sentient being from

81

the universe that died so that ours might be born. Others said he was an elemental force, as old as time and as inevitable. Whatever the truth, one fact remained; Galactus hungered, and the Silver Surfer was sworn to find him sustenance.

Onward the Surfer flew, until at last his gleaming board reached a cluster of stars on the outer perimeter of a sprawling galaxy that spiraled like a pinwheel in the darkness. The first few hundred worlds he passed were worthless, huge dead chunks of barren stone, devoid of life or even the faint possibility thereof, bereft of the precious energies Galactus required to appease his terrible appetite.

The 247th world he scanned had once been living, apparently thriving. But the still-glowing radioactive craters that pocked the dead world's surface spoke only too well of the nuclear madness that had brought the planet's inhabitants to their pitiful end.

On the 569th world, the raging winds were sentient, singing songs of unimaginable joy and unbearable sorrow, but the mineral mix beneath the crust would not meet Galactus's needs. For a moment, the Silver Surfer paused to listen to the ancient songs, moved as he had rarely been by their innocent beauty, and he was silently pleased that Galactus would pass this planet by.

On the 1006th world, the air was perfect, the soil rich, the waters that covered four-fifths of the planet's surface a bright copper hue. Hovering over one of the five small continents that dotted the southern hemisphere, the Surfer watched as the first questing crimson shoot of an entirely new species of vegetation forced its way up through the shining soil. In another half-million years or so, the descendants of that plant were destined to become one of the universe's greatest races of scholars and educators—presuming, of course, the species was permitted to survive that long. Reluctantly, the Surfer marked the world as one possibly worthy of Galactus's attention, then he flew on.

Grimly, the Surfer continued to scan the nearby worlds, his extraordinarily heightened senses discerning in an instant whether or not a planet might be ripe for Galactus's harvest. When first the Surfer had begun his ceaseless quest on Galactus's behalf, he had tried to choose only lifeless worlds or worlds where the hope of life someday emerging were astronomically slim. But none of these had truly satisfied his master's needs, and Galactus had threatened to return to Zenn-La if the Surfer did not improve his performance.

After he had located his first populated world, where gentle creatures of golden gossamer floated on the errant breeze, then watched as Galactus consumed the planet utterly, leaving behind only a desiccated husk, the Surfer had wept uncontrollably for days. Since then, he had learned to steel himself, to harden his heart against such overwhelming emotions, and simply do what had to be done. It was the only way the Surfer could preserve his sanity, and while he was not particularly proud of this fact, he had long since come to accept it.

As he approached the next planet in his path, the Surfer slowed his board and paused at the outer atmosphere, astonished by what he saw. Rising from the planet's surface, thousands of feet tall, was a gigantic graven image. Though many of the physical details were wrong, there was clearly no mistaking who it was intended to represent. The great, grim face, the passionless eyes, the sheer physical majesty, were the essence of Galactus.

Soaring in closer to the planet's surface, the Surfer observed a society in decay. Great golden towers that once stretched to the emerald skies now stood tarnished and in disrepair. Vehicles that once slipped through the air controlled by thought alone now lined the cracked and rutted glideways like so many rusting corpses. And everywhere, carved into the statuary, printed on tattered posters, there was the image of Galactus.

The Silver Surfer glided his gleaming board to one of the empty streets, and paused to study one of the many posters more carefully. *He is coming*, read the warning atop the poster. *Prepare yourself for the end.* The ability to instantly understand and speak any alien language was but one of the talents Galactus had granted him as part of his Power Cosmic.

"Are you he?"

The Surfer turned at the sound. Three elderly blue-skinned beings, barely half the Surfer's height, clad in the tattered remains of what had once been brightly brocaded crimson robes, approached him cautiously, their oversized heads bowed in humility.

"Am I who?" the Silver Surfer asked, softly.

"He of whom the legends foretold, the harbinger of the Dark One?" said the foremost figure. "We have awaited your coming for decades."

"I am the Silver Surfer, Herald of Galactus, if that is to whom you refer," replied the shining figure.

"At last," the representative whispered, then all three quickly prostrated themselves at the Surfer's feet.

"Get up." the Silver Surfer demanded, grabbing the spokesman by the scruff of his robe and yanking him sharply to his feet. "I want answers, not subservience."

"As you wish," the spokesman stammered. "We are yours to command."

The Silver Surfer gestured toward the tarnished spires. "Why?" he asked. "This world once held such hope, such promise. Why did you let your dream die?"

The representative glanced up at the Surfer for an instant, then looked down at his sandaled feet again as if suddenly remembering his place. "Why bother?" he mumbled, his voice barely audible. "The Dark One is coming. We have known this for decades. Why build the towers with years of sweat, when he will only tear them down again in an instant? Why waste time building for tomorrow when tomorrow may never come?"

"But what if it does?" the Surfer asked, incredulous. "From the instant we are born, we know we are destined to die, but still that has never stopped us from hoping, from striving, from struggling to make some difference along the way. To truly live while we are able is our one real victory over death."

The Surfer's blue-skinned audience said nothing, but merely scuffed their sandals in the dirt, obviously uncomprehending. Thoroughly disgusted, the Silver Surfer called his shining board to him, and gracefully leaped aboard.

"Why do I waste time even speaking to you?" he asked, as his board swiftly carried him up and out beyond the reach of the planet's gravity. "It appears you are already dead."

And, as the Silver Surfer faded from sight, the inhabitants of the planet went happily to work, preparing for oblivion.

The Surfer flew on, leaving a hundred more worlds in his wake, dead spheres of rock, great balls of gas, all useless for Galactus's needs.

Finally, the Surfer approached the next most likely planet. The atmosphere was rich, the mineral content lush. Here again was a world that could nourish his master, if only for a while.

The Surfer sensed the missiles almost before he saw them, angry red arrows arcing toward him on columns of flame. Casually, he thrust his hands toward the missiles, sizzling bolts of his Power Cosmic leaping from his fingers, disintegrating the projectiles long before they could hope to reach him.

As the Surfer swooped downward, the missile barrage increased. The gleaming skyrider dealt with them all swiftly, blowing them effortlessly out of the skies, as he sped toward the planet's surface. In a matter of minutes, he had circled the globe a half-dozen times and every missile that might have been arrayed against him had been summarily destroyed.

The Surfer glided down to the planet's surface, to verify his earlier readings. Unlike the previous world, the buildings here were crude, utilitarian, serving only as shelter and nothing more. *Here is a world where life is hard,* thought the Surfer, as he glided in for a landing, *and death is a constant companion.* His expression as cold as his metallic face, the skyrider stepped from his board. In an instant, he was completely surrounded by an angry army.

The planet's inhabitants were thick-bodied, huge, with low sloping foreheads and sharp angry teeth. They wore thick armor to protect their shaggy bodies, and yet carried high-powered weapons in their gauntleted fists. Whatever scientific advances had been made here, had been made only in the name of war.

As the Surfer turned to survey the troops surrounding him, they immediately opened fire. Again, the Surfer's Power Cosmic dealt with the weapons easily, their energy blasts ricocheting harmlessly off his gleaming skin.

"Go away, skyrider," shouted one of the attackers, whose superior armor clearly marked him as a leader. "We know what you are, and you are not welcome here." As the Surfer watched, the leader reached down and picked up a large shard of rock.

"Go back and tell your accursed master that we will fight him with every weapon we have, with missiles, with guns, with knives. With rocks and sticks, if we must. With our bare hands and our final breaths." The leader hurled the rock at the

Surfer's head with uncanny accuracy; the skyrider destroyed it with a gesture.

"In the end, Galactus may still devour our world," snarled the leader through clenched and rotting teeth. "But I swear to you, he will choke on it."

"I will give him your message," said the Silver Surfer, as he leaped back on his board and soared heavenward once more. "But I doubt he will bother to listen." And, in the wink of an eye, he was once again gone.

So now there were two worlds to choose from, two planets whose substance might temporarily satisfy Galactus's great appetite. The choice was the Silver Surfer's alone to make.

In answer to the Silver Surfer's summons, Galactus's World-ship hove silently into view, moving into close orbit around the chosen planet like a small, shining moon, every bit as bright, infinitely more impressive. As the doomed planet's inhabitants stood transfixed, horrified by what they were watching yet somehow unable to turn away, a wide hatch slid open in the starship's surface and a ramp as wide as a small island slid out into place. Then, without so much as a whisper of fanfare, Galactus stepped out onto the ramp to survey his next meal.

"I am pleased, Herald," came the great booming voice. "Here Galactus can truly feast!"

Standing astride his board many miles above the planet's surface, the Silver Surfer nodded silently in acknowledgment, knowing what was about to come, long since resigned to its inevitability.

Within minutes, vast machines of extraordinary complexity had been constructed around the planet. As the Surfer watched, Galactus sunk great rods a mile across and thousands of miles long into the world's crust with all the skill of a physician inserting a hypodermic needle.

And the feeding began.

Almost instantly, the ground began to tremble, wide fissures opening in the rutted streets, spewing great gouts of molten magma high into the now-sweltering skies. There should have been panic in the streets, people screaming, fleeing, fighting for their lives; there wasn't. As their once-great towers crumbled around them, the blue-skinned beings simply fell to their knees, lifting their faces to the burning skies as if somehow seeking benediction. All they found was oblivion.

In a matter of minutes, the entire surface of the planet was ablaze, the crust becoming more and more brittle as its energies were extracted by Galactus's machines. Galactus himself stood silent on his ramp, fingertips sunk into the complex console before him, through which he absorbed the very lifeforce of the planet.

Soon it was over. The planet was dead. All that remained was a great charred ember drifting through the void, another grim testimony to Galactus's insatiable hunger.

The Silver Surfer studied the devastated ruin silently, contemplating what he had just done. The choice, when it finally came down to it, was really no choice at all. One world was savage, primitive, seething with life; the other world, despite all it had once achieved, was already long dead at its heart. The Surfer had simply made their grim prophecy a fact.

"You have done well, Herald," said Galactus, as his machines automatically disassembled themselves and returned to their storage units within the Worldship. "But why do you linger? The universe is vast. There are many new worlds to explore. And Galactus hungers!"

"Master, I live but to serve you," said the Silver Surfer, bowing perhaps a touch too melodramatically at the waist. Then he spurred his gleaming board forward and, in less than the space of a heartbeat, he was ten thousand miles away.

Faster, ever faster, the Silver Surfer flew, once again exhilarated. The stars he passed were only pinpoints at first, then, as his speed increased, they became glittering streaks of white. He stared straight ahead, as the bands of white grew wider, brighter. Only here, in the midst of this celestial vastness, was the Silver Surfer truly happy, he thought, as he flew into the heart of the beckoning whiteness.

Only here was he truly free.

"He is gone, Richards," said the Silver Surfer, as he removed the elaborate metallic headband he had been wearing, careful not to disconnect the jumble of wires leading from it to the complex mechanism just a few feet away. "Your friend has found his final peace."

Reed Richards, leader of the Fantastic Four, bowed his head sadly. "Thank you, Surfer," he said, as he stretched a white-gloved hand across the stark white hospital room to take the proffered headband from the gleaming figure's grasp. "You will never know how much this meant to me."

Richards looked down at the frail figure lying in the hospital bed, and removed a similar headband from around the old man's wrinkled brow, barely disturbing the soft fringe of ash gray hair. "Before his stroke, Professor Kurtzberg was one of the most vibrant men I ever knew. He's one of the reasons why I first decided to become a scientist. His is the example I always sought to follow."

Richards paused for a moment, noticing the faint smile now etched forever on his mentor's lips. Struggling to contain his emotions, Richards gently closed the old man's eyes and pulled the starched sheet up over his face.

"By allowing me to link your mind with his through my new V.R. Transducer, you gave the professor the opportunity to die as he had lived," Richards continued, turning to face the Silver Surfer once more. "Not as a helpless quadriplegic, but as the explorer he had always been in his heart, forever charting unknown territory.

"For just a moment, you allowed Professor Kurtzberg to *become* the Silver Surfer, to experience the absolute freedom that only you have known," Richards finished, offering the Surfer his hand. "And that is a debt I may never be able to fully repay."

Ignoring Richards' outstretched hand, the Silver Surfer strode to the window, throwing it open with a gesture, even though it had not been designed to open, and silently summoned his gleaming surfboard from the sky.

"You owe me nothing," the Surfer said, as he leaped to the board, which now hovered in place just below the dusty window ledge. "I doubt I will ever fully understand humankind or all its many quirks. I thought perhaps this experience would help to enlighten me.

"Apparently," the Surfer finished, as he soared away into the blinding light of the afternoon sky, "I was wrong."

Watching the gleaming figure dwindle into the distance, Reed Richards stood silently at the window, his heart filled with a great deal of gratitude.

And more than a little pity.

Maintaining a constant altitude of approximately five miles, the Silver Surfer began to circle the Earth at the equator. He moved slowly at first, then with ever-increasing acceleration, until he was circumnavigating the globe a thousand times a second, so swift that he might have appeared a ring around the world to anyone observing from the depths of space. Then, just when it appeared impossible the Surfer could travel any faster, he arced upward, streaking toward the outer edges of the Earth's atmosphere far faster than the speed of light.

He hit the unseen barrier with devastating force, knocked from his board by the impact. The Silver Surfer plunged, barely conscious, his indestructible body engulfed in flames from the sheer friction-heat, into the depths of the Adriatic Sea. The chill waters revived him almost instantly, and the Surfer kicked his way to the water's surface, to find his gleaming board hovering just inches above the cresting waves, ever faithful. In a moment, he stood on his board once more, battered but unbowed.

So, the barrier still holds.

The Silver Surfer had first come to Earth to make a meal of it for his master, but instead rediscovered his own conscience in the company of Reed Richards and his unique companions. Finding a cause worth fighting for for the first time since he had lost his beloved Zenn-La, the Surfer had stood against his master beside the Fantastic Four in what all thought was a vain effort to save this planet from destruction. And yet, remarkably, they had succeeded.

As punishment for the skyrider's transgressions, Galactus had condemned him to eternal imprisonment on this primitive world, erecting an unseen barrier that the Surfer, for all his awesome power, could never hope to penetrate. Still, that had not prevented the Surfer from trying. If not today, then tomorrow. Or perhaps the day after that. In the end, whatever the cost, the gleaming figure swore he would be free.

After all, he was Norrin Radd, the Silver Surfer, possessor of the Power Cosmic, and thus he could have anything he wanted.

Anything, that is, except the stars.

IMPROPER PROCEDURE

KEITH R.A. DeCANDIDO

Illustration by Ron Frenz and Patrick Olliffe

The Silver Surfer sat on a rooftop in New York City. He was not sure of the exact neighborhood—he was only certain that it was this particular city because of the familiar land-marks of the Fantastic Four's headquarters and the home of Doctor Strange. One accustomed to traveling across galaxies saw little point in trying to distinguish such tiny cities from each other.

The humans called this place "the city that never sleeps," and indeed it seemed that the activity in this metropolis never stopped. A constant stream of humans flitted about, their actions incomprehensible to the Surfer's experiences— but then, his own experiences were likely just as incompre-hensible to them. At best, only the super-powered individuals he had associated with over the years—the Fantastic Four, the Avengers, the Defenders—could come close to under-standing what the Surfer had lost in his exile on this tiny planet.

Then he noticed a human crouching on one of the nearby rooftops, wearing dark blue clothing and a hat with a visor attached. He seemed to be trying to conceal himself—and to other humans he probably *was* concealed—and wielding a large metal object.

The Surfer recognized the object. He'd certainly had enough soldiers pointing them at him. A gun. A quick look around revealed the human's target: another human, a male in a nearby apartment. The male wore a white shirt and shorts, and was speaking on his telephone. The Surfer also spied two women sitting on a couch and a small child playing on the floor.

The one with the gun spoke into a simple communications device. "I've got a clear shot."

Anger boiled within the Surfer. The intent was obvious: the human with the gun would murder the people in the apartment. Not for the first time he wondered, *Is violence the only way they know?*

The Surfer sacrificed everything so these pathetic creatures could continue their existence. He would not stand by and watch one of them kill others wantonly. Summoning his board to him, he stepped on its gleaming silver surface and sailed effortlessly toward the man on the roof.

With but the tiniest fragment of the Power Cosmic, the Surfer blasted the weapon from his grip, also causing some minor pain to the hands that held it.

"Jesus!" the human cried.

"You will terrorize your fellows no longer," the Surfer said.

Lieutenant Vincent Billinghurst wiped sweat off his bald head with the pocket handkerchief his wife had given him for Christmas. He shouldn't have needed it; the temperature had barely climbed above sixty degrees on this April morning. But hostage situations tended to bring out the perspiration in him.

As he stuffed the handkerchief back into his suitjacket pocket with his left hand, he held the phone to his ear with his right. "Look, Hector," he said into the mouthpiece, "we don't want any trouble. If you turn yourself in, I promise nothing will—"

"Don' *gim*me that, man!" Hector Gomez's anxiety was obvious to Billinghurst even through the tinny sound of the earpiece. "They gonna take my Soraya 'way from me! Ain't gonna *let* 'em! Now you get these bitches outta here, an' *leave me alone!*"

Gomez slammed the phone down, preventing Billinghurst from pointing out that he couldn't get the two women from Social Services out of Gomez's apartment because Gomez had threatened to shoot them if the cops came near. The pair had arrived to take Gomez's daughter Soraya away from her abusive, alcoholic father. Gomez had agreed in a court of law to the terms of the remanding of his daughter into the city's care. But on the day he had to give her up, he changed his mind, and held the two women at gunpoint.

An hour later, Gomez hadn't calmed down and had shown no interest in turning himself in or letting his hostages go. Billinghurst's options dwindled with every second Gomez held his prisoners.

He looked over to Eddie DiFillippo, the short, burly lieutenant in charge of the SWAT team, who said, "Roman's the only one 'at's got a clear shot at him without the women'r the kid inna line'a fire."

Billinghurst thought a moment, pulling out his handkerchief and wiping his brow again while he did. Then: "I'm gonna try to talk to him some more. Tell Roman to keep that line on him."

DiFillippo glowered, though the effect was diluted by the mirrorshades he wore. "Vince, you been talkin' to him f'half an hour. It ain't gonna help. An' Roman ain't gonna have that shot forever. We gotta take him out, and we gotta do it now."

Before Billinghurst could argue the point, his attention was drawn to what sounded like an explosion. It came, not from the Gomez apartment, but from one of the adjoining rooftops, where DiFillippo had stationed one of his people. Billinghurst had to avert his gaze at first, as whatever was up there reflected light like a mirror, and the glare from the late afternoon sun hit him right in the eyes.

As he blinked the spots from his eyes, one of the uniforms cried out, "Christ, it's the Silver Surfer!"

Sure enough, the Silver Surfer was attacking one of the SWAT team. *What the hell is that lunatic doing?* Billinghurst thought.

DiFillippo yelled into his walkie-talkie, "Cassalowitz, Jones,

Perez, if you got a shot at the Surfer, open fire!''

"No!" Billinghurst cried, but it was too late. Rifle shots from three different directions pelted the Surfer—or rather, almost pelted him. Before they could strike, they disintegrated, which relieved Billinghurst. He had expected the bullets to ricochet off the Surfer and hit God-knew-where.

Yanking the walkie-talkie out of DiFillippo's hands, Billinghurst bellowed, "Cease fire, dammit, cease fire!" Turning angrily on DiFillippo as the shots silenced, he cried, "Don't you watch the news? Read the reports on the super guys that come in? The Army hit the Surfer with enough shells to bomb out a building a while back, and it didn't do diddly! Bullets ain't gonna stop him, but they'll sure as hell piss Gomez off!''

As if to prove Billinghurst's point, Gomez leaned out the window and shouted, "Whatchoo doin'? You tryin'a kill me? I kill you first!"

Then he started firing wildly.

Billinghurst ducked behind one of the squad cars. DiFillippo crouched next to him and snatched his walkie-talkie back. "Anybody got a shot on Gomez, *take it!*"

However, no shots were forthcoming. Billinghurst looked up and saw why: the Surfer had made a beeline for Gomez's window, and blocked any shot into the apartment.

"Hope at some point someone remembers to fill me in on just what the hell's going on here," Billinghurst muttered.

The Silver Surfer was incensed. He saved the life of this human, who now repays the debt by firing a weapon of his own at a group of humans gathered below. He now recognized that the person he had attacked was a member of some form of human militia—there were so many on this world that the distinctions had proven impossible for the Surfer to keep track of—but that meant little. The Surfer knew from bitter personal experience that these types of humans tended to shoot without provocation.

He streaked towards the human whose life he saved. "You will cease this action at once," he said, and he intended it as a statement, not a question or request.

The human looked up, and his eyes grew wider at the sight of the Surfer. "Get away from me, man, get *away*! I kill you, I kill you *dead*, man, get a*way*!"

"I doubt that."

Behind the human, one of the women, the younger one with the longer hair, started screaming. The older woman seemed to be trying to calm her down.

The human whirled, pointing his weapon at the screaming woman. "Shut *up*, bitch, shut *up*! *Shut up!*"

She kept screaming. Just as the Surfer guided his board into the apartment in the hopes of ceasing this madness, the human shot at her.

The Surfer could have used his power to transmute the gun and its bullets into a harmless substance, but that required a certain delicacy that he had neither the time nor the inclination to indulge in. So he simply blasted the gun to its component atoms.

The human screamed in pain—the blast burned his hands. He collapsed to his knees, still crying in pain, and muttering something to himself.

The Surfer turned to his victim. Blood pooled on her white blouse at the shoulder. The Surfer could not recall whether or not any human vital organs were located in the shoulder. He reached for her, but the older woman blocked his way.

"What're you doing? Who the hell *are* you, anyhow?" she asked, frantically.

"I am called the Silver Surfer."

"Fine, whatever, but what're you doing to Mara?"

The Surfer shrugged. "The Power Cosmic may heal as easily as it may destroy. I will tend to her wound."

"O-okay. You won't hurt her?"

"Of course not." *Do these humans doubt everything?*

"Don' let 'em," the human who shot her muttered. "Gonna take my Soraya 'way from me. Don' let 'em take m' daughter."

The Surfer glanced at the small child, who was huddled, crying, in a corner amidst a pile of papers and children's toys. She looked frightened, which hardly surprised the Surfer.

"Is this true?" he asked the woman. "Do you plan to take this man's child from him?"

"Well, sort of," she replied. "My name's Penny Kitsios. Mara and I work for Social Services. Mr. Gomez here was declared an unfit father, and we came to take his daughter into a foster home. Mr. Gomez *agreed* to this in *court*."

While Penny Kitsios spoke, the Surfer tended to the other one, the one called Mara. Then the door burst open, and several humans wielding weapons came in.

"All right," one of them cried, "everybody freeze!"

"I am unaffected by changes in temperature," the Surfer said.

"Just don't move, okay?"

The Surfer regarded the human who gave the order. But for the dark hue of his skin, he looked almost like a native of his homeworld of Zenn-La in the complete lack of hair on his head. He wore a white shirt and those odd knotted strips of cloth tied around the neck that human males favored. He was followed by several other humans, all of whom were armed.

The bald human asked, "What're you doing to that woman?"

"I am healing her wounds. She was shot by this person."

He indicated the kneeling, whimpering human Penny Kitsios had called "Mr. Gomez."

"Great." The bald human turned to his compatriots. "Get these people downstairs to the paramedics." He turned back to the Surfer. "When you're done laying on hands, you mind talking to me for a minute?"

The various militia escorted Penny Kitsios, Mara, Mr. Gomez, and Soraya out, the latter being carried gently by one of the female militia. The humans all stepped over or onto the Surfer's board, which irked him. He commanded it to rise and move out of the way. This action caught the attention of Soraya, who stopped crying and stared in wonderment at the board's movement as the woman carried her out.

The bald human then commanded the Surfer's attention. "I'm Lieutenant Vincent Billinghurst, NYPD. You got a name?"

"I am called the Silv—"

"I meant a *real* name. Unless you *want* me to call you 'Surfie'."

"I would prefer not." A pause, then: "Once I was called Norrin Radd."

"All right, Mr. Radd, you mind telling me just what the *hell* you thought you were doing out there? Thanks to you, I got an officer scared to death 'cause a guy that looks like an Academy Award blasted his gun outta his hand, and your little attack spooked Gomez enough so that he shot up one of my people—and the lady from Social Services that you just did the glowbug routine on."

"There were no deaths?"

"Despite your best efforts, no, but I don't see—"

"Then *that*, Vincent Billinghurst, is what I was doing. Preventing you humans from killing each other."

"You're kidding. You attacked an officer of the New York Police Department without any provocation—"

"He was attempting to murder a fellow human in cold blood. I could not allow that."

"Gee, how kind of you. It ever occur to you, pal, that he was doing his job? That he was tryin' to prevent this nutcase from shooting his hostages?" Before the Surfer could reply to this indignant human, he continued: "Of course it didn't. You super guys don't give two snots about actual police work, you just wade in, damage a lotta property, and leave us to clean up your messes."

"Is this the only way you know to prevent needless death? By perpetrating more needless death?"

Billinghurst seemed confused by this. "Whaddaya mean?"

"This Gomez human was holding two people hostage. Your only solution was to have your people shoot him down?"

"No, that was the backup plan in case things got outta hand. I was on the phone with him talking, trying to convince him to turn himself in. I might've done it, too, if you hadn't barged in." Billinghurst sighed. "Now we'll never know."

The Surfer realized he had committed a rather grievous error. "I am—I am sorry, Vincent Billinghurst. It would seem I am guilty of the very crime humanity has committed so often against me. Just as humans have attacked me, mistaking me for a threat or menace, so I have done today. My apologies."

Billinghurst opened his mouth as if to reply, then closed it again, then finally said, "All right, I'm impressed."

"I beg your pardon?"

"I gotta admit, I never expected one'a you types to actually apologize."

The Surfer frowned. This human seemed to think the Surfer was anything but unique. "There are, to the best of my knowledge, none like me on this Earth."

"I meant you spandex types," he said with a laugh. "You

know, guys with super powers, like you, the FF, the Avengers, Spider-Man, Daredevil, those guys. I figured you guys'd never actually *care* enough about someone normal to apologize.''

Another human in uniform approached Billinghurst. ''Ain'tcha gonna arrest him, Vince?'' he asked.

''Oh, *good* idea, Eddie. *You* wanna slap the cuffs on him?''

Eddie—who wore the same type of outfit as the human the Surfer attacked on the roof—regarded the Surfer for a moment, then said, ''Well, maybe not. But dammit, Vince, he—''

''Save it,'' Billinghurst interrupted, then turned back to the Surfer. ''Listen, Mr. Radd, uhm—would you mind comin' down to the station?''

The Surfer remembered his previous attempts to interact with humans, not to mention his other encounters with human law-enforcement. None were pleasant affairs. ''I do not believe that would be advantageous.''

''Damn right it wouldn't,'' Eddie interjected. ''What're you, *nuts*, Vince? Only way he's comin' down t'the station house is in cuffs.''

''Your prisons cannot hold one who wields the Power Cosmic,'' the Surfer said.

Billinghurst actually smiled at that. ''Yeah, I heard about what you did to the holding cell down at the Seventeenth. They said you were trying to start a riot.''

''I was trying to halt an alien invasion.'' An attack vessel from the Brotherhood of Badoon had scouted the Earth in a craft invisible to humans, but easily detected by the Silver Surfer. However, his attempts to warn the people of Earth met with resistance, and he was attacked and taken by police into protective custody. The Surfer allowed this, not wishing to harm anyone needlessly, waiting until he was alone in one of their prison cells before making his escape to drive off the Badoon. However, he exited straight through one of the walls of the cell. *Another unthinking act that endangered the humans,* he realized.

"Look," Billinghurst was saying, "it'd really make my life easier if you came along. 'Sides, it might do one'a you super geeks some good to see how *real* law-enforcement works."

At first, the Surfer intended to refuse, but upon further contemplation he decided to accept Billinghurst's offer. It might prove useful to see humans in everyday life. He had tried before, but, with a few individual exceptions, was always rejected outright. Only in the company of other "super guys," as Billinghurst called them, had he found any acceptance. But the Fantastic Four and the Defenders were not the norm of human society. And this time, it was a human who invited him.

"Very well, Vincent Billinghurst. I shall accompany you."

"Good."

The one called Eddie shook his head. "This is a dumbass move, Vince."

To Vince Billinghurst, the hustle and bustle of the Midtown Precinct, North, on 54th Street and 8th Avenue felt like an old coat he'd always worn. Since he first joined the force almost two decades previous, he'd accepted the almost solid wall of sound that was a police precinct as part of the natural order, in much the same way he accepted the noise of the elevated train right outside his bedroom growing up in the Bronx.

The Silver Surfer seemed to have a bit more difficulty with it. *Well, maybe not "difficulty," exactly,* Billinghurst thought, *but he sure don't look comfortable.* Then again, this guy used to travel around space. No way that space was this crowded—or this loud. It had to be unusual for the Surfer.

No, not the Surfer, Billinghurst reminded himself. *Norrin. Think of him as Norrin. The Silver Surfer is some super guy with a lotta power and an attitude problem. You think of him as Norrin, then he's just another witness.*

Then he looked again at the man striding confidently next to him. Though of average height, the Surfer seemed to tower over everyone else in the room—an impression aided by the shiny surfboard that followed obediently behind him like an airborne dog.

Just another witness. Sure, Vince.

The room grew unnaturally quiet as they walked in farther. While the noise never actually ceased, several of the other cops turned and gazed quietly on the sight of Billinghurst walking with the Surfer—with Norrin. Most of those gazes were angry ones.

"Hey! Hey you! The Stupid Surfer!"

Billinghurst put his head in his hands. It was Grossman, the partner of Caggiano, the officer Gomez had shot. He moved to intercept the uniformed officer. "Lay off, Grossman."

"Like hell, Lieutenant, this scumbucket got my partner shot!"

"My apologies," Norrin said. "I did not intend that anyone be harmed. In fact, my intention was to prevent violence, not cause it."

"Oh, really? Well, lemme tell you somethin', you—"

Billinghurst interrupted. "I *said* back off, Grossman, do I make myself *clear*?!"

Grossman glowered at Norrin a moment longer. Then he walked backwards, continuing to stare at Norrin as he moved away. "You're lucky, you alien bastard. Jeanne was wearin' her vest, so she just got some busted ribs. If she got hurt bad or killed 'cause'a you, you'd be a *dead man*, you hear? A *dead man*!"

Billinghurst grabbed Norrin by the arm and led him toward the door marked, "CAPTAIN K. GROBÉ." "This way."

"I fear coming here was ill-advised, Vince. I have done a grievous wrong, and my presence at this facility has only made things worse."

"Maybe, maybe not. But you're here now, so let's make the best of it."

The captain, a tall man with short, jet-black hair, burst out of his office before Billinghurst and Norrin could enter. "What the hell is *that* doing here?"

"Mr. Radd is a—"

"Mr. *what?*"

"Mr. Norrin Radd is a witness to the hostage situation, Captain, he—"

"Why the hell hasn't he been arrested?"

Billinghurst suppressed a smile. The captain hated it when people smiled in his presence, but having already gone through this with DiFillippo, Billinghurst couldn't help but find it amusing. "'Cause I'm not stupid. Sir, if we could even process him, we couldn't hold him. Remember what happened at the one-seven?"

The captain glared angrily at Billinghurst, then turned his gaze to the Surfer. Finally, he turned on his heel and said, "Come into my office, both'a you."

Billinghurst loosened his tie. As usual, the windows were all shut and, since the captain preferred to leave the door closed, it was about a million degrees and stuffy. He pulled out his handkerchief to stave off another onslaught of sweat. He *hated* meetings in the captain's office.

He looked over to Norrin, remembering the Surfer's comment about how he wasn't affected by changes in temperature. Billinghurst would pay a small fortune to have that ability right now.

"Okay," the captain said, "now tell me, slowly, just what happened."

Billinghurst proceeded to explain the situation in detail,

aware that the captain knew most of this, but also aware that the captain preferred complete accounts.

The captain turned a frowning face on Norrin. "So you—" He averted his gaze. "Jesus, I can't look at this guy. 'S'like lookin' in one'a those damn carnival mirrors. Why'd you attack Roman?"

"I thought he intended to murder Hector Gomez in cold blood."

"Didn't the uniform clue you in that he was there for a *reason?*"

"The nuances of human clothing are not something I've studied in depth."

The captain regarded Norrin for a moment, then said, "Yeah, I guess you wouldn't've. Okay, now that you managed to make a hash outta my hostage situation, whaddaya want *now?*"

"To make amends, if I may. Your Lieutenant Billinghurst requested that I come to the station and give you a full account. And also, as he put it, to see the intricacies of your work."

The captain picked up a pencil and started fiddling with it and staring at the eraser intently. Billinghurst knew what that meant: he had an idea.

"You wanna make amends?" the captain asked, gaze still fixed on the eraser.

"If possible, yes."

Still looking at the eraser, he asked Billinghurst, "Lieutenant, where we at on that gun shipment?"

"It's supposed to go down tomorrow night."

"Gun shipment?" Norrin asked.

The captain glanced at Billinghurst, an obvious cue to fill the Surfer in. "We've been setting up a big buy-and-bust for a shipment of M-16s due to come into the 79th Street Boat

Basin tomorrow night. We're hoping to nail the shipment when it comes in."

"The problem," the captain explained, "is that we been rushin' this. See, the guns're Army issue. One'a these guys stole 'em from a depot, so the Army's *real* hot to get 'em back. So're a coupla senators. Me, I just wanna keep those damn guns off the street. In fact, that's the only thing that really matters, 'cause if this shipment gets through, a lotta people are gonna be a lotta dead. I don't like that."

"What is it you wish me to do?" Norrin asked. Billinghurst wondered if the Silver Surfer understood or cared about the political ramifications; the only thing he seemed to directly respond to was the captain's casual reference to multiple murders.

The captain continued to stare at the pencil, but replied, "See, what I'm worried about is that things'll get ugly. Anything goes wrong, we got us a primo shootin' match. Means a lotta cops're gonna get hurt. I don't like that, either. So I'm thinkin' maybe I can get myself a nice, shiny ace-in-the-hole, and then there won't be nothin' I don't like." Finally he looked up at Norrin. "Whaddaya think, Shiny?"

Norrin frowned. "I am not sure what, exactly, I can contribute."

"The lieutenant here said that you stuck your silver butt into my hostage situation 'cause you wanted to save lives. I wantcha to keep an eye on things, from a distance. If it *does* get ugly, you remonstrate."

"Remonstrate?"

"Get involved," Billinghurst explained. "Do the same kinda thing you did this afternoon—keep people from gettin' killed."

Norrin seemed to be contemplating the offer. At least, Billinghurst assumed that to be the case, since he remained quiet for several seconds before finally saying, "Very well,

Captain. I will be happy to assist your officers in this endeavor."

"Great. Lieutenant, you take care of it. When this is over, I want a shipment'a impounded M-16s, and this guy outta my life, got it?"

"Got it," Billinghurst assured.

Billinghurst introduced Norrin to the officer who had done most of the real work setting up the bust, a newly promoted sergeant named Vance Hawkins. The three of them coordinated the endeavor. Norrin had to repeatedly assure Hawkins, who was understandably skeptical, that despite his appearance, the Silver Surfer was more than capable of being incognito.

When that was all completed, Billinghurst asked, "So, you, uh, you got any plans for the evening?"

Norrin frowned. "Not as such."

"In that case, how'd you like to attend a good old-fashioned family dinner?" Billinghurst asked with a grin.

"I do not require sustenance in the same manner as—"

"Sustenance has nothin' to do with it. Look, you wanna know what normal people are like? Then come to dinner with me and the family. Ain't no better way to see us."

Norrin seemed to consider this request, then finally said, "Very well. It might be—educational."

Billinghurst was about to say something in reply, when a thought occurred. "Hm. Dunno if riding the subway's such a hot idea, though. I mean, we get a lotta weirdos on the 2 train, but still—"

And then the Silver Surfer did something Vincent Billinghurst never thought he'd see him do.

He smiled.

"I believe that will not be a problem, Vince."

* * *

Vincent Billinghurst was not the first passenger to ride on his board, but the Surfer couldn't remember anyone being quite so taken with the experience. Vincent did not experience the disorientation and vertigo some humans felt when riding virtually unfettered through the air—he explained to the Surfer that he'd gone hanggliding a few times, but that this was "a thousand percent better." They flew north past Manhattan and over the Bronx, the northernmost of New York City's five boroughs. Until this moment, the Surfer had not realized that the city's boundaries extended beyond the one island.

"This is great!" Vincent bellowed, struggling to be heard over the wind. "It's like lookin' at a map! There's Park Avenue," he said, pointing to a street that had a train track bisecting it. "Betcha didn't know Park went into the Bronx, huh? There's Van Cortlandt Park, Woodlawn Cemetery," he added, pointing to two large parks to the north. "You'd better get down closer! See that street with the elevated train?"

The Surfer in fact saw several streets that could be so described, and said as much.

Vincent smiled. "The one just to the right of the cemetery!" he yelled.

Eventually, Vincent was able to direct them to the front entrance of the building on E. 235th Street, near White Plains Road, the street where he and his family rented an apartment.

Vincent had phoned his wife Ayesha to inform her of their rather infamous dinner guest, so the Surfer's presence was expected. According to Vincent, Ayesha hadn't planned on cooking anything after the travails of her day—she worked as a nurse at a hospital in a place called Bronxville which, to the Surfer's confusion, was not actually in the Bronx—but said she'd cobble something together for the Surfer. For his own part, the Surfer did not see the need for her to do so.

109

As he explained, he did not take his sustenance in the same manner as humans.

In addition, he was more than a little apprehensive. Too often he had expected the hand of friendship from humans, only to find fear and loathing.

They walked up one flight of stairs to the Billinghurst apartment. When Vincent opened the door, a voice came from within: "If you say 'Honey, I'm home,' Vince, so help me I'll pop you one."

Vincent laughed. "Wouldn't dream of it, darlin'."

The front door opened to a small hallway that connected to two other rooms, one of which was obviously the kitchen. From that kitchen came a woman of the same height as Vince, but stouter, rounder, and with a full head of hair braided in an intricate fashion that fascinated the Surfer. Zenn-Lavian women tended toward simple hairstyles.

Vincent kissed Ayesha, then indicated the Surfer. "Ayesha, this is Norrin Radd. He's helpin' us out with a case."

The woman reached out a hand, which the Surfer shook. "Pleased to meet you," she said, unflustered by either the Surfer or the gleaming board. "What kinda name is Norrin?"

The Surfer hesitated, unsure how to answer the question. "It's—It's Zenn-Lavian."

She frowned, said, "Oh," then smiled again. "Why don't you come in and have a seat in the living room? Dinner'll be on in a few minutes."

"I thank you for your hospitality, Ayesha Billinghurst."

"You're very welcome."

Two small children ran from the other doorway into the hallway then, one male, one female. The male collided with the Surfer's leg. After picking himself up off the floor, he stared up at the Surfer with large brown eyes. "Whoa! You're that super hero guy, right? The Super Surfer?"

"Ma!" the girl bellowed. "Alex's botherin' me!"

"She started it!" the boy bellowed back.

"No, I didn't!"

"Yes, you did!"

"Hey!" Vince interjected. "We have a *guest*."

The kids quieted down.

"Norrin, these are two of our kids, Leigh and Alex. Kids, this is Norrin Radd."

"*Wow!*" Alex said. "It's, like, okay?"

The Surfer frowned. "Is what okay?"

"That we know your *secret identity*?"

"I don't understand. I have never made a secret of my name."

Vince interjected, "Never mind. C'mon, let's get out of Ayesha's way. I'll give you the nickel tour."

The Billinghurst apartment was small and cramped, nothing like the spacious residences belonging to the Fantastic Four and Doctor Strange. To one used to flying unfettered, the limited floorspace and narrow hallways were somewhat unnerving.

Upon noticing two items prominently displayed in the room where Vince and Ayesha slept, the Surfer asked their purpose. Vince replied: "Those're our diplomas. When we completed our educations, we got these certificates that say we're qualified to do our jobs."

"Fascinating. So—"

"Dinner's ready," came Ayesha's voice from the kitchen, cutting off the Surfer's query about the certificates.

They entered the kitchen, which also served as a dining area. This surprised the Surfer; other human dwellings he'd been in had a separate dining facility. Vince asked, "Where's Kenny?"

Ayesha simply shrugged as she, Leigh, and Alex put several platters on the table. "He's late again."

The front door opened, and a young man—older than the

other children and as tall as Vince and Ayesha—came in. The Surfer assumed this was Kenny.

"Where you been, son?" Vince asked.

"Out," Kenny replied. Then he noticed the Surfer. "Whoa. Aren't you that Surfer dude?"

"Yes, I am called the Silver Surfer."

"Whoa," Kenny repeated, then looked at Ayesha. "What's he doin' *here?*"

"Having dinner," she replied, "which is what you should be doing. Sit down."

Kenny obliged his mother. "This is *cool.* He helpin' you with a case, Dad?"

"Mhm," Vince said while chewing his food.

As Ayesha sat down, she asked, "Aren't you going to eat anything, Norrin?"

The Surfer hesitated. "I do not require sustenance the way you humans do. I tried to explain this to Vince, but—"

Ayesha held up her hand. "That's okay. I wasn't sure you were gonna be able to eat, anyhow, being an alien and all."

The Surfer remembered that Ayesha was in the medical profession, so she obviously understood about the differing biologies of two different species.

"Hey," Alex asked, "you carry a gun like Dad?"

"I do not carry any weapons, no."

Alex frowned. "How you fight the bad guys, then?"

"I do not 'fight the bad guys,' as such. I attempt to stay the forces of chaos that ravage this world, and when I do, I am assisted by the Power Cosmic."

"I don't get it. I mean, whaddaya *do?*"

The Surfer hesitated. *How do I explain the Power Cosmic to a child?* He barely understood it himself.

He was spared this necessity by Vince, who said, "That's enough, Alex. Eat your food and stop pestering our guest."

"I do not feel pestered, Vince. The child's questions are legitimate—it is simply difficult to explain the Power Cosmic."

"Whaddaya need the stupid surfboard for?" Kenny asked.

This question took the Surfer aback. "Without it, I could not travel the skyways." *Or navigate the depths of space,* he added wistfully to himself.

"Don't you control it?"

"Of course."

"Then whaddaya need it for?"

"*Stupid,*" Leigh said, rolling her eyes, "'cause he couldn't *fly* otherwise."

"So you got all this power," Kenny said, "and you can't even *fly* without some dumb surfboard?"

"Son," Vince started.

"Well, I wanna *know!* I mean if he's so damn powerful—"

Ayesha interrupted, "Don't you swear, Kenny."

"You are *so* dumb," Leigh said, shaking her head.

"Please," the Surfer said, and that quieted the table for the moment. "I am afraid, Kenny, that I do not know why I need my board. My power was granted to me by Galactus. I would not presume to guess at his reasons. I know only that it was his decision that I should only be allowed to transport myself by means of my board and that there is little that can change the will of Galactus once he has decided upon a course of action."

Kenny didn't have an answer to that, at first. Then he finally said, "Well, I *still* think it's dumb that he can't fly."

By the time 8:30 rolled around, Norrin announced that it was time for him to leave. Billinghurst was disappointed by this. "You sure you can't stay a little longer? I mean, Leigh and Alex have to go to bed, so it might be a little quieter."

"I mean no disrespect, Vince. I have enjoyed the company of your family and have experienced many things I might never have encountered had you not invited me into your home."

"You sure you won't stick around?"

Norrin hesitated. "You must understand that I find my confinement to this planet almost unbearable. I am afraid that, if I should remain in a space this enclosed for much longer, I will go mad."

The proverbial light bulb went off over Billinghurst's head. "Oh hell, I hadn't even thought of that. But yeah, I guess it makes sense you'd be claustrophobic."

"Claustrophobic? There is no fear involved, Vince—simply what I am accustomed to."

"Whatever. Look, I'm really glad you came. For one thing, you've probably given my kids the thrill of their lives."

"I am happy to have given them pleasure. And I am glad to have had this opportunity. My direct experiences with humans have not always been the most cordial."

"I know," Billinghurst said, remembering the hostility at the precinct house. "Now remember, you hover near the boat basin 'round nine tomorrow night, got it?"

Norrin nodded. "I will be there, Vince."

"Good," he replied, hoping and praying that he would not see Norrin at all the next night, since he was only supposed to show up if things got hairy, and Billinghurst did *not* want things to get hairy.

This made him realize that he may never see Norrin again at all, so he added, "Listen, Norrin, in case I *don't* see you tomorrow night—" He hesitated.

"Yes?" Norrin prompted.

"Take care of yourself, okay? And try to get all the facts of a situation before you go wading in with both barrels?"

"I will endeavor to do so, Vince. Thank you."

Then Billinghurst reached out his hand for a handshake. Norrin frowned at first, then smiled and returned it. "Be good, pal."

With that, Norrin Radd stepped through the open window to the fire escape, his board hovering behind him. Then he stepped on the board and soared southward, following the path of the elevated train.

Only after he left did Billinghurst realize that the window had been closed only moments before. *Damn super guys . . .*

Twenty-four hours later, Vincent Billinghurst sat in a car just off the traffic circle that serviced the 79th Street exit on the Henry Hudson Parkway. Next to him in the passenger seat was Sergeant Stephen Drew. Both wore earjacks that allowed them to listen to Sergeants Acevedo and Hawkins, who awaited the arrival of the gun shipment at the boat basin itself. Both were wired, their transmissions going to every unit parked near the basin.

"The boat's coming in," came Hawkins's whisper.

Acevedo added, "Time to bake the donuts."

As the two undercover officers prepared for the boat's arrival, Drew turned to Billinghurst. "Hey, Lieutenant, where's Oscar?"

Billinghurst frowned. "Who?"

"Y'know, the Surfer guy. We been callin' him Oscar."

"Uh-huh. Well, as it happens, I haven't the foggiest. Let's hope it stays that way. He's only here to step in if things go bad, and I do *not* want things goin' bad."

"No, sir," Drew said, shaking his head so emphatically his blond hair shook. "If y'don't mind my askin'—whose idea was it to get Oscar involved?" There was a hint of criticism in Drew's voice.

"The captain's."

"Oh."

"And mine. You have a problem, Sergeant?"

"Yeah, I got a problem. Caggiano got let outta the hospital today. She's gonna be stuck at a desk 'til her ribs heal. And it's that guy's fault. A lotta the guys think—"

"Sergeant, I don't give a hoot in hell what a lotta the guys *think*. Let's try some facts. Fact: the Surfer screwed up and he knows it. Fact: he's sorry for what happened to Caggiano, and he's helpin' us out tonight to try to make up for it. Fact: he coulda just flown off on his surfboard and forgotten all about us, but he didn't."

Before the conversation could continue, they heard voices in their earjacks.

"You got the money, Acevedo?"

"Naw, I jus' like standin' on docks after dark. 'Course I got the damn money. You got the shipment?"

"Ain't mangoes in them boxes."

"Yeah, well, I'm *sure* you won't mind if I take a look first?"

"First, let's see some cash."

The only thing they heard then was the clicking sound of a briefcase opening. Presumably Hawkins was showing them the cash.

Acevedo then said, "You get the briefcase after I see *all* the boxes."

"Send 'em down!" the contact shouted.

Several tense moments followed. Drew fidgeted in the passenger seat next to Billinghurst. Some clunking noises—the boxes being thrown down from the boat to the dock—followed by the sound of a crowbar opening four boxes in succession.

"All-*right*. Gen-yoo-ine Army-issue M-16s. And a full set'a ammo. *Very* nice."

"Just like I said, Acevedo."

"Hey, I never doubted, m'friend, never doubted. Just gotta

be careful these days, am I right? These guns will *definitely* let me be all that I can be.''

That was the signal. Billinghurst started the car and drove down the incline to the basin. Drew said into the radio, ''All units converge, repeat, all units converge!''

Just as the car reached the basin, Acevedo's contact cried, ''What the hell is *that?*''

A bright light blinded Billinghurst just as he stopped the car. When his vision cleared, he saw the Silver Surfer flying straight towards the dock.

What the hell is that lunatic doing? Billinghurst wondered. The bust was going down smooth as silk. There was no reason for the Surfer to interfere.

Gunfire ricocheted off the Surfer's body, but the alien showed no sign of noticing it. Instead, he simply made a beeline for the four crates that sat on the dock. When he was within a few feet, he thrust his hands forward.

The four crates then exploded.

Bizarrely, the wooden planks did not catch fire and, while the force blew Acevedo, Hawkins, and several others back a bit, the explosion hurt no one. Billinghurst blinked; he didn't realize Norrin had such tight control over his power.

Then the Surfer flew off.

Drew stared up after him. ''Lieutenant—how'd he do that?''

Billinghurst said nothing in reply at first. Then he shook his head and said, ''C'mon, we got a bust to finish.''

The next morning, Vincent Billinghurst loosened his tie as he entered the captain's office.

''Close the goddamn door,'' the captain said. Sighing, Billinghurst obliged, pulling out his pocket handkerchief to hold in reserve.

The captain stared at Billinghurst for several seconds before finally saying, "This is a goddamn disaster. I got the commissioner and the mayor callin' me givin' me crap. I got three generals, two senators, an' a guy from some government department I never even *heard* of bitchin' at me 'cause a lotta government hardware went poof! And I got an angina attack comin' on, an' it's all 'cause'a your silver friend."

"Sir, if you don't mind my—"

"*Shuddup*, Billinghurst, I ain't finished. I also got a buncha suspects that I'm gonna haveta kick 'cause there's no evidence t'back up the busts. The D.A.'s ready to hang me by my little toe, an' these garbanzos got some hotshot lawyer that's threatenin' t'sue the city. None'a this is makin' me a happy person, Billinghurst."

"Sir—"

"I said I ain't finished."

"*Sir*, if I can just say one thing?"

"Fine, say your goddamn thing."

Billinghurst took a breath, then wiped the sweat from his bald head. "Sir, you yourself said to the Surfer that the only thing that really mattered was keepin' those guns off the street. You told him that *nothin'* else mattered."

"I never said that."

"Yes you did, sir. You told him that the only important thing we were trying to accomplish here was to keep those M-16s off the street. Well, he did that. I mean, c'mon, he's an *alien*. You think he gives a hoot in hell about senators and evidence and government hardware and the D.A.'s office? All he cares about is keeping people alive. That's why he let himself get trapped on this planet when Galactus showed up, and that's why he got involved in the Gomez situation, to keep people alive. And he did it again last night."

The captain stared at Billinghurst for almost a full minute before finally speaking. "I just got two things t'say t'you, Billinghurst. Any crap this precinct catches, you're catchin' right alongside me. This was your operation, and you brought that shiny sonofabitch in here. That's the first thing. The second thing is, I see that bastard in here, I don't care how goddamn powerful he is, he gets busted for interferin' in a police operation, got it?"

Billinghurst knew better than to argue the point any further. "Got it."

"Now get the hell outta my goddamn office."

He rose and left. He passed Caggiano's desk on his way to the men's room, but stopped when he noticed the flowers. They looked sort of like roses, but he'd never seen such a deep color of indigo on roses before. "Who sent those?" he asked the officer, who was typing up a report.

"I dunno. I never seen flowers like this."

Sergeant Hawkins wandered over. He was renowned in the precinct for his vast knowledge of trivia. He said, "Those are Panther Roses. Can only get them in Wakanda."

"Well, I got 'em yesterday morning. The card just says, 'Granting you a quick recovery. —N.R.' "

And then Billinghurst laughed. He wondered if the Surfer—if Norrin—had gone straight to Wakanda after leaving his apartment.

Instead of going to the men's room, he went to the roof of the precinct. He saw a few helicopters in the sky and spied Thor of the Avengers flying past at one point, but caught no sign of the Silver Surfer. *Of course, Norrin could be in Outer Mongolia right now*, Billinghurst reminded himself.

Still, he looked up at the bright New York sky and said, "Good luck to you, pal."

DO YOU DREAM IN SILVER?

JAMES DAWSON

Illustration by Gary Frank

Jennifer Ambrose flitted past a cooking show devoted to Louisiana cuisine, a soap opera, a commercial for dog food, a weather update on an upper atmosphere disturbance, a rock video with unintelligible lyrics, and a black-and-white movie with unidentifiable stars.

She wasn't looking for anything in particular. She was just channel-surfing. Her thumb stopped jabbing the remote when she saw Angie Evangalia's instantly recognizable face.

". . . celebrities, but those fantasies usually involve movie stars or rock singers," the talk show host was saying into her hand-held microphone. A video screen behind her was filled with the colorful *Everything's Angie* logo. "However, some women set their standards for the perfect man a little higher—and I definitely mean higher. Today's topic: Do you dream in silver?"

As she said it, the show's title logo dissolved into archival footage of the Silver Surfer stepping onto his board and flying off into a deep blue sky. But Angie's technical crew had tinkered with that famous piece of news video. Instead of disappearing into the distance, the Surfer was plunging into a silver, sky-filling valentine.

Jennifer leaned back against the left arm of her sofa and put aside her remote. "I guess this means I'm not the only one, huh, Norrin?"

Her silver-furred cat did not deign to reply.

As the applause and theme music died down, Angie stepped away from the studio video screen to stand behind several seated women. Their chairs were arranged in a semi-circle facing the predominantly female studio audience.

"Our guests today are six ladies whose ages range from sixteen to sixty-seven, but these gals all have one thing in common." Angie rested her hand on the shoulder of a twentyish blonde. The lapel of the woman's short jacket was accessorized with a gleaming, three-inch-long silver surfboard.

"Their ideal mate isn't some hunky coworker down at the office or a good-looking friend-of-a-friend," Angie continued. "Instead, these women are all ga-ga over that special skyrider of the spaceways, the Silver Surfer. Today, we'll hear all about their devotion to this cosmic catch. We'll also open up the phone lines to hear about your own high-flying fantasies and daydreams. So stick around, and we'll be right back after these messages."

The camera panned the applauding audience, the shot faded to black, and a bra commercial started.

"Lunchtime!" Jennifer said, hurrying to the kitchen. She went into a skid when her white cotton socks slipped on the vinyl floor, but she grabbed the refrigerator handle without losing her balance. Norrin acknowledged her graceful recovery with a lazy twitch of his tail.

Jennifer snatched a bottle of Evian, a loaf of bread and a half-empty jar of strawberry jam from the fridge. As she was hastily preparing a sandwich, two white flashes of light appeared outside her window. The underside of a cloudbank on the horizon was glowing. A second later, a muffled boom gently rattled the plates in her cupboards.

"Oh great, more rain on the way. Just what we need," she muttered sarcastically. When she heard the *Everything's Angie* back-from-commercial music from the other room, she grabbed her sandwich and bottle and hurried—carefully— back across the slippery floor to her sofa.

Above the clouds, the Silver Surfer readjusted his footing on his hovering board. He was less than a third as tall as the massive humanoid suspended in midair before him. The stranger wore a red cape, and his skin was marred with what appeared to be burn marks—which perplexed the Surfer, as the humanoid had attacked with a fireball that emitted from his hands.

"There is no reason for us to battle," the Surfer said. "I know not why you assaulted me in my flight and nearly toppled me from my board. But I am none the worse for the encounter and would gladly hear your explanation."

The stranger appeared both skeptical and mildly amused. "Are you saying that you would overlook both my attack and my challenge?"

"I say only that I am disposed to extend the hand of friendship, if you will but take it."

The red-caped giant appeared to consider this, scowling dramatically and rubbing the scarred, patchwork flesh of his chin. "I already have enough friends," he replied, abruptly extending one arm. A bolt of flaming electricity leaped from his palm to envelop the Surfer's gleaming body.

Within the glowing field, the Surfer raised one of his own arms. A burst of cosmic energy shot from his fingertips, tore through the static nimbus, and hit the giant square in the chest.

Knocked backward, his foe instantly ceased his attack. The two adversaries looked at each other appraisingly. The Surfer waited in a half-crouch on his board, ready to loose another thrust of the Power Cosmic. The giant made a show of brushing at his costume, as if flicking away the residue of the Surfer's effort.

"What purpose is served in continuing this pointless confrontation?" the Surfer asked. "I know nothing of your origins, your name, or your intentions."

The stranger thrust out his jaw. "You can call me the Red Giant. My origins? I'm the mutant offspring of an unwitting gene-research guinea pig. I am the attacking vanguard of a dying alien race that bears a grudge against more fortunate lifeforms. I am the last son of an ancient Antarctic civilization that wants revenge for the ozone hole. Take your pick, it doesn't matter."

He hurled a boulder-sized fireball. The Surfer flexed his knees to let the flames roll under his board like a red-orange wave. They dissipated behind him in a brilliantly white cloud-bank.

Instead of retaliating, the Surfer made another attempt at appealing to reason. "Why do you persist in actions that will surely result in your defeat?"

His adversary threw two huge fistfuls of liquid fire at the Surfer's head. "Maybe I just woke up on the wrong side of the bed this morning," he shouted.

"We're back, with ladies who'd like to wake up every morning next to everyone's favorite former Herald of Galactus," Angie Evangalia said. She had taken her microphone to the left aisle of her studio during the commercial break, so she could work the crowd better.

"Our first guest is Heidi, a twenty-six-year-old who works as a cosmetics clerk at a department store. Heidi, you've had a recurring dream about the Surfer, isn't that right?"

The platinum-blonde at the far left of the raised platform reddened slightly. "Well, yeah. About once a week, I dream that I'm alone in bed in my apartment when I hear a tapping on my window, from the outside. Did I mention that I live on the tenth floor? Anyway, when I go to see what's making the sound, I see the Silver Surfer. I mean, you know, *Norrin*. He's in midair, standing on his board. When I raise the window, he tells me he's been watching me at night. Now, this should probably make me feel kind of funny, but instead it makes me get really hot."

"I think our audience is getting pretty hot just hearing about it," Angie said, to scattered chuckles.

"So he asks if he can come in, and I say, 'Sure.' When he starts to climb through the window, I reach to help him. The way his hand feels is hard to describe. It's cool, but not cold, and almost slippery because it's so smooth."

The woman sitting beside Heidi spoke up. "That's the way I imagine it, too. Almost like a soft metal that's been chilled slightly." A couple of other women on the stage nodded their heads in agreement.

"So he steps into my bedroom, and that's when I realize I'm only wearing a really sheer nightie, with nothing underneath," Heidi continued. "And even though I can't be sure exactly where Norrin is looking—you know, because he has those weird eyes—somehow, I'm certain that he's staring at my body, and—"

"And that's where we have to break for a commercial," Angie interrupted, theatrically fanning herself as if she were overheated. "Hold onto that thought, folks."

In her living room, Jennifer threw a pillow at her TV. "Just when it was getting good," she muttered. But when Angie's toll-free number appeared onscreen, she forgot her frustration and scrambled for a pencil.

Sunlight glinted from the Surfer's bright body and board as he hurtled toward the Red Giant, who was pummelling him with fireballs that seemed to materialize in his palms. Because the giant's hands were close together, the Surfer was able to place both of his own palms directly against the giant's much larger ones to halt the attack. Wisps of red fire sputtered around the Surfer's outstretched fingers, which were barely big enough to cover the center of his foe's hands. The intense heat made the Surfer grimace.

"What manner of fire is this, that can pain one who has flown through the flames of stars?" The Surfer was determined not to take his hands away, despite the searing pain. "It can have no natural origin . . ."

"A very perceptive observation," the Red Giant hissed from between scarred lips. "I found this fire on another plane, where what is natural to us has little meaning. As you can see from my own badly healed flesh, harnessing its power exacted a terrible cost. But now I am its master, and I will use these fires of my obsession to destroy you."

The backs of the Surfer's hands were glowing red from the excruciating heat emanating from the Red Giant's palms. He felt as if the thin, silvery skin that covered his body might actually melt and run if he tried to hold on much longer. Still, he gasped out two words: "Why . . . me?"

"Because you fascinate me, with your great melancholy and your much-vaunted noble soul. You've become an icon on this planet, Surfer: a symbol of purity and determination and selfless martyrdom. I happen to think that you're just too damned good for this world."

Gathering his strength, the Surfer shouted, "You leave me no choice then, madman!" Shifting his hands to grip the Red Giant's thumbs, he repositioned himself on his board to swing his foe in great circles around his body. When he had built up sufficient momentum, he released his grip and flung his enemy high into the stratosphere.

Before the Red Giant could recover his balance, the Surfer was speeding toward him. The giant was windmilling his arms in the air, trying to right himself, when the dull edge of the Surfer's fast-moving board caught him full in the stomach.

"I don't know about the rest of you, but I'm still trying to catch my breath after that last segment." Angie pantomimed the act of wiping sweat from her forehead.

In her apartment, Jennifer had her phone in her lap and the receiver wedged between her shoulder and ear. She heard her call connect, heard the busy signal's buzz, pushed down the disconnect, and hit the redial button for the fourteenth time. She knew the odds of getting through to *Everything's Angie* were slim, but what the heck—it wasn't like punching "redial" was strenuous exercise or anything.

"Okay, let's hear from one of our home viewers," Angie said from the screen. "Caller, are you there?"

"Hello? Angie?" The voice sounded like it belonged to a woman in her late twenties, right around Jennifer's own age. Jennifer sighed with resentment. *It could've been me,* she thought.

"Yes, go ahead, caller."

"Oh, okay. I just wanted to say I love the Surfer, too, and that my whole apartment is decorated in a Silver Surfer motif. I had the walls done in silver foil wallpaper with black pin-stripes in the middle that run horizontally around the room, just like on his board. I've always wanted to meet him, and I'm a charter member of both the American and the international fan clubs. I can't imagine what it would be like to, you know, to make love to him."

The studio audience went "Wooooo." Angie cocked her head to one side and said, "Tell me something, caller: What would you say to the Surfer if you *did* meet him?"

"*Say* to him?" the caller asked, flustered.

"That's right. What do you think you could say to him that would make him interested in you, as a woman?"

Yeah, why the heck would he want anything to do with a fanatic like you? Jennifer thought.

The woman on the other end of the line paused. "Gosh, I don't know. I'm really just sort of average. I guess I might tell him how much I appreciate all the good he's done for people here on Earth."

"But what about you, personally?" Angie said. "What would you do or say that would attract him to you?"

I can't wait to hear this, Jennifer thought. When she heard another busy signal, she disconnected and pushed redial automatically.

"I could tell him how faithful I am to him, and how devoted I would be," the caller said. "I could show him all of the scrapbooks I've filled with news stories about him, or my shelf of news videos that show him in action. Guys like that kind of attention, don't they?"

Jennifer disconnected and hit redial again. *This lady is pathetic,* she thought. *If I get through, I'll know exactly what to say.*

Onscreen, Angie had the jokingly frustrated look of a schoolteacher who is trying her best to get a good answer out of a slow student. "Now, come on, you can do better than that. Anybody can keep a scrapbook. What would you say to get him to appreciate special, individual you?"

Another pause. "I guess I could tell him what a good person I am, and how I love kids and animals. I've got a lot of pets, and I do volunteer work at the animal shelter. I've even got a cat named Norrin."

Jennifer's hand froze in midair above her redial button. All of a sudden, she couldn't think of a thing she wanted to say.

There were no more words above the clouds, only the deafening noise of fireballs crackling against metallic skin and cosmic bolts exploding against invulnerable flesh.

The Red Giant mouthed an incantation without making sounds. Heedless of the Surfer's attack, he turned his back and spread his crimson cape. The Surfer paused in curiosity.

All at once the Red Giant spun to face him again. Behind his cape he had created a fireball as tall as his twenty-foot body. It hurtled toward the Surfer now like a miniature yellow sun with a glowing red core.

The Surfer's cosmic energy blasts had no effect on that boulder of alien starfire. When it hit the Surfer, he plummeted backwards through the clouds and fell dazed toward New York, a half-mile below.

As if possessed of its own will, his board swooped beneath

him and carried him out of harm's way. The Surfer shook his head and regained his senses in time to see the Red Giant flying toward him. One of his gargantuan fists was drawn back to strike.

Before the Surfer could raise his hand to ward off the attack, the blow sent him arcing toward the Statue of Liberty in the harbor below.

Angie was asking another of her on-stage guests about what she thought it would be like to "do the nasty," as she put it, with the Silver Surfer.

"Well, it would certainly have to be an out-of-this-world experience," replied the middle-aged brunette. "With that Power Cosmic of his, let's just say that I'm sure it would be one heck of a Big Bang if any girl ever got him to get down."

The Surfer plunged to Earth at an angle intersecting the drapery at Miss Liberty's knees. His whole body ached, but he'd managed to keep a three-fingered grip on his board. Just before he would have crashed through the Statue of Liberty's green-patina gown, he pulled the board hard right, missing the structure by inches.

A fireball caught him in the back before he could pull the board up. Distracted and nearly unconscious, he could not keep his board from flying toward the city and its cluster of tall buildings.

"I just wanted to say that I think your guests and callers today are a little wacked-out," said a male caller. "Don't any of you remember how the Surfer helped that creep Galactus destroy whole planets before he came to Earth? How do we really know that none of those planets had life on them? And maybe the only reason he's helping us these days is because he's trapped here himself. Ever think of that?"

Some members of the *Everything's Angie* audience were booing and making thumbs-down signs. Angie put out her hand in a calming gesture. "Now, hold on, everybody. Maybe this guy is onto something."

"You're darn right I'm onto something. These women don't know a thing about the Surfer. Nobody does, except maybe the Fantastic Four and some of those other super-types. These fanatics you've got on your show today are just starry-eyed over him the same way people get all goofy about movie actors and rock singers."

"Why is that so bad?" Angie asked.

"Because maybe they should all grow up and stop being obsessed with becoming 'Mrs. Silver Surfer.' There ain't no Prince Charming on a surfboard that's gonna take them all away to Fantasyland. But there's plenty of real guys out here who might like their company."

The studio audience and the women onstage were all trying to talk at once: "You don't understand," "Pig," "It's guys like you . . . ," "You're so wrong." Some were shaking their heads, and a couple were shaking their fists.

Watching them, Jennifer put her phone back on the end table and looked at her cat. "Am I one of them, Norrin?"

Her cat looked up at her from the rug.

"Maybe I should get out more," Jennifer continued. "It's not like I'm going to meet the Silver Surfer or anybody else just sitting around this dumpy apartment."

Norrin looked toward the window and jumped onto the couch a millisecond before the Silver Surfer crashed through Jennifer's wall in an explosion of brick, wood, and glass. The Surfer lost his grip amid the destruction, slipping from his board with enough momentum to crush Jennifer's television set into splinters and shards. His board embedded itself in the far wall without going through it.

He rolled onto his back at Jennifer's feet.

"Norrin?" she said, meekly.

Her cat meowed.

The Surfer slowly turned his head toward Jennifer from where he lay on the rug.

"What can I do to help you?" Jennifer said, crouching beside him. Without thinking, she grabbed her bottle of Evian from the end table. "Would some water help?"

She was so nervous she dropped the plastic bottle onto his chest. The water splashed out across his broad, shining pectorals and down across his gleaming abdomen. The Surfer got up on one elbow. The thin rivulets of water looked like mercury streams trailing down his silver skin.

Far beyond the gaping hole that used to be Jennifer's outer wall, the Surfer saw the Red Giant hovering high above the harbor. Waiting.

"Yes," the Surfer said, his voice as pure and clear as a note from a silver bell. "Yes, I think water is exactly what I need."

He got to his feet and glanced at his board, which immediately detached itself from the wall. He stepped onto it and briefly touched Jennifer's shoulder. "Thank you," he said, and then he was off. The slipstream behind him fluttered Jennifer's clothes.

"You're . . . welcome," Jennifer whispered. Then she promptly passed out on her couch.

The Surfer bolted back across the Manhattan skyline like a quicksilver slash through the blue. The Red Giant had both arms extended in his direction. Balls of red and yellow flames boiled in the giant's scarred palms, waiting to explode toward the Surfer again when he tried to make another stand.

But things were going to be different this time.

Instead of stopping, the Surfer picked up speed. He leaned forward, tucked his head close to his leading shoulder, and slammed into the Red Giant's massive chest with enough force that shockwaves echoed off buildings on either side of the harbor. The giant toppled backward through the air with a shout of angry surprise. He clutched at the Surfer with hands as fiery and hot as exploding suns, but the Surfer kept pushing him down, ever down.

Their plummet lasted less than three seconds, but for the Surfer each moment was filled with mind-shattering agony. The giant was squeezing him in a hellish grip, and the Surfer was burning. He opened his mouth and screamed, and kept on screaming, but never stopped pushing.

The Red Giant had just pulled back his hands to focus two concentrated beams of fire on the Surfer's back when they hit the water.

The supernova heat of the Red Giant's flames evaporated twenty-five million gallons of water on contact. The resulting steam cloud instantly fogged over the windows of every boat, car, and skyscraper on both sides of the river. The rest of the water in the harbor bubbled and boiled furiously. Even the biggest cruise ships and cargo tankers docked at shore rocked dangerously on the unnatural tide.

The Red Giant flailed in helpless anger as the Surfer pushed him backward in ever-tightening underwater circles around the harbor bottom. The sheer mass of water surrounding them was starting to affect the giant's power. Whatever its metaphysical origins, it was still fire. And it was going out.

Now it was the Red Giant's turn to scream.

His back hit castoff cars, sunken sailboats, rusting cans, broken bottles, unexploded fireworks, mossy rocks, rotting logs, Mafiosi skeletons, unmarked oil drums, and centuries of other debris as the Surfer relentlessly shoved him around and around the harbor mud.

The Surfer's blinding speed was causing a massive waterspout to rise from the surface of the water above them.

Thousands of fish were flung from that whirling, half-mile-high column like glittering sparks from an out-of-control generator.

The resulting change in the vicinity's air pressure sucked every nearby cloud into a single downward spiral that crackled with chain lightning. Its tornado-shaped tip touched the top of the waterspout like an ominous mirror image in the sky. The hurricane roar of wind around the water column and the deafening thunder from the roiling cloud funnel above it shattered windows in three states.

When he could see that the Red Giant's flames were completely doused, the Silver Surfer used the last of his strength to fling his unconscious foe up through the center of the waterspout itself. The Red Giant bobbled at the top of that spinning, gargantuan fountain like a limp doll.

Adding insult to injury, the grey spiral of clouds above him chose that moment to let loose with a remarkably heavy downpour of rain.

Two network newscasts used Jennifer's encounter as "human interest" sidebars that night to their stories about the Surfer's battle. Jennifer had to move in with a friend until repairs on her apartment were finished, but she was happily surprised that her renter's insurance check arrived in just three days. She used the money she got for her smashed TV to buy some new clothes.

She was wearing one of those outfits tonight. She'd taken a coworker up on his offer to take her to see the new David Mamet play.

"Hey, look, the Surfer story made the covers of both *Time* and *Newsweek*," Tom said, reaching for copies of each. "Maybe they mention you."

Jennifer grabbed him by the arm and playfully pulled him

from the newsstand. "We'll check them later. Come on, we're going to be late."

"You're a hard lady to impress," Tom said. "I guess I should feel pretty fortunate that you worked me into your social calendar these days, huh?"

"A gal can't sit around waiting for the Silver Surfer to show up every night," Jennifer said, smiling. "He's kind of unreliable that way."

"Lucky for me," Tom said.

Jennifer took him by the hand. His skin was warm.

INCIDENT ON A
SKYSCRAPER

DAVE SMEDS

Illustration by Steve Leialoha

I'll always be sixteen.

That's the thought that came to me just before I jumped. No growing up and turning into an old hag. Suicide has its bright spots, right?

The street was so far down, each of my goose bumps got as big as that zit I had on my forehead last Christmas, the one that looked like Mt. Pinatubo. I knew if I didn't step off the edge right away, I'd chicken out. So I launched off.

You wouldn't believe how fast you fall when you've got the length of a skyscraper to pick up momentum. The windows flipping by reminded me of a TV that's lost its vertical hold— I don't know how I managed to see that one lady, her mouth dropping open as she saw me whiz past. She was screaming, I think. I know *I* was.

The cracks in the sidewalk were getting as big as canyons by the time a pair of arms wrapped around me. A flat shining thing cut off my view of the concrete, and the brakes grabbed. Talk about precision antilock.

We didn't actually stop falling until we were even with the first floor awning. By that time I was face-up, looking into a reflection of myself—jeez, was I pale!—captured in the mirror-skin of the guy who was holding me.

It took me a second to figure it out. I know it sounds pretty unbelievable to say I didn't recognize him, but my brain wasn't exactly working normally just then. Sure, I had heard about him and seen the news coverage and everything, but it's not like he's a local guy, you know? I might have expected Spider-Man or Daredevil to be patrolling that part of town, but not him. He plopped us on the rooftop of another building, out of sight of all the rubberneckers who'd watched me fall, and only then did it sink in that I wasn't dead. The old gray matter in my head slapped a label on the flat shining thing that said "surfboard" and he—

Well, he was him. You know who I mean.

Saved by an alien. Who would've thought? I sure hadn't planned on it. Of course, if he hadn't shown up, I would've been a very messy spot on a curb, but what did I care?

"Why does a child your age wish to end her existence?" he said.

A *child?* Oooh. Tact was *not* his strong point. And his voice was downright spooky, like something pumped through a microphone. Sort of stereo. Sort of in my head, not in my ears. Does that make any sense?

"It seemed like a good idea at the time." I winced as I said it. What a cliché. I had definitely watched too much TV in my time.

"Your actions were intentional?"

"You could say that."

"Then," he said, tossing me up on the board again like I weighed, oh, four pounds, "I will deposit you on the surface of the planet, where you cannot make such an attempt again."

I had to laugh. "Well, that would slow me down, I guess. I'd have to find another building with a roof access door I can unlock."

He stared at me. I guess you would call it a stare. It's hard to tell with a set of eyes that don't have pupils. "If you are determined to commit this act, you will surely succeed."

I got the feeling he'd known other people who'd killed themselves, and he didn't like dealing with the memory. Up till then I admit I'd been a little ticked at him. It wasn't like I could whip up the courage to jump off a building every day, no matter what I said out loud. But I hadn't meant to make him feel bad. He was just doing what those super-guys are supposed to do. Even if it was a case of butting in, I suppose I should've acted a little grateful.

That's when I began to realize what was happening. Here I was, nose to pecs with the Silver Surfer. How many ordinary people ever got a closeup of him like this? He didn't do Letterman or Larry King. He was a mystery dude—popping up in the middle of some disaster or battle-for-the-world or some such, and then disappearing again. What was I doing acting like I wanted to get away from him?

The board began carrying us off. "Wait!" I said. "Couldn't we, like, talk or something?"

He frowned as he parked the board in midair about four hundred feet above the asphalt. If gravity had been working right, we would've become some taxi driver's fare of a life-time. "If you wish to speak with someone, surely there are people in your life who would serve that function better than I."

"Can't think of anyone," I said. "Look, I'll make you a deal. If you stay and talk awhile, I promise not to kill myself until next Tuesday."

"One who rides the skyways will not be a target of base coercion, child."

"Candace. My name is Candace Weldon. Look—forget I asked. Obviously you don't think I'm good enough to waste your time on."

He bowed his head. That lowered his chrome dome, let-ting me see my reflection better than ever. I wished he wouldn't do that. It's hard to watch yourself talk to somebody, especially when you feel all chicken-choked.

"If you were not worth the expenditure of attention, I would not have rescued you." We floated back to the rooftop and touched down. Was I ever glad of that—I may have been ready to jump a few minutes earlier, but having to hang out there above the street was giving me Jello knees. "What do you wish to speak of . . . Candace?"

I hadn't thought that far yet, so I said the first thing that came to mind. "What are, um, what are you doing in New York?"

He stepped over to the lip of the roof, standing where the sun blazed off him like a hood ornament on one of those limousines down below, the kind that chauffeurs spend every day polishing. A few blocks away, Four Freedom's Plaza, the headquarters of the Fantastic Four, stuck up right in the direction he was facing.

"I came to ask old acquaintances for advice. Certain behaviors of ordinary humans have been puzzling me. Sometimes I am so mystified by psychological matters that it is as if I had never been a man, but always the creature Galactus made of me."

The Silver Surfer used to be human? Hah. And his plan was so dumb I laughed. "You expect the Fantastic Four to have any idea what ordinary humans are all about?"

You know, I think he blushed. Except on him, that meant the sheen of his cheeks shifted toward white. "What would you suggest?" he asked.

"I can tell you about people," I said. "They're all the same. Never dependable. Always looking out for themselves."

"You obviously believe what you say. But you are incorrect. There is a wealth of diversity to the human experience. The species is replete with surprises, and I have witnessed dramatic instances of altruism."

"You always look on the bright side?"

He walked to the shade of the utility shed and sat down. Until then, I'd thought he hadn't realized how close he was to blinding me. I'd left my dark glasses at home. Didn't think I needed them to attend a suicide.

"No." He said it so softly the stereo effect almost disappeared. "I am well acquainted with despair."

A little shiver ran down my spine, bone by bone, like kisses of a ghost. He meant what he said. But that didn't make any sense. He was a super-powered dude. What did *he* have to complain about?

"Sure," I said. "You don't know what it's like to be in my shoes, though."

"Show me."

I took a step back. If it had been anyone else, I would've known they were using a figure of speech. But I had the distinct impression the Surfer meant it literally, and that weirded me out.

"How? Can you read minds?" I asked.

"What I propose is telepathy only by the broadest of definitions," he said, which sounded suspiciously like he was dodging the question. "My cosmic powers can duplicate and amplify the electrical activity of your brain. If you were to remember scenes as vividly as possible, I would be able to project the memories into the air atop this very building. In so doing, I would be able to witness the experiences as if they were occurring for the first time, and share in the emotions you felt then."

I gulped. It was like he had asked me to strip off my clothes. "I . . . I hardly know you. You know, like, we just met?"

"Does that mean you would find it easier to reveal yourself to someone who knew you?"

"Heck, no. That'd be even *more* embarrassing."

"Then I am the best possible witness. Show me why you have so little faith in your fellow Terrans, Candace."

He had a point. He was about as close to a neutral party as I was ever going to find. I could never have opened my skull to my friends, or worse, my family. Every single one of those bozos would have blabbed everything they learned to the whole world. But who was the Surfer going to tell?

"All right," I said. "Let's try something simple." I sat down and tried to clear my mind. It wasn't hard to think of an example of being let down.

I'd hardly let the memories collect in one place when

everything around me shifted. The rooftop faded out. I couldn't even feel the tar paper and gravel under my butt. The Surfer *almost* faded. I couldn't actually see him, but he was, like, somewhere in the background, you know? A presence.

I felt like I was littler. I was wearing a party dress. I hadn't worn anything on my legs but pants or shorts since I turned thirteen, and it almost knocked me out of the . . . the spell, the illusion, whatever-you-wanna-call-it. I wasn't just *seeing* it happen. I was *there*. I was exactly ten years old, having a birthday party.

Mom's apartment wasn't as ratty as it is now. Not only was the place newer back then, but we'd only been in it six months. Not enough time had gone by to really mess it up, and Mom had actually straightened up some stuff before the party. I wanted to do a freeze-frame number and just look at everything. It was like time-traveling. Had Mom really had that Central Park poster on the wall that long ago? (Since we couldn't afford a place with a view of *any* park, Mom figured why not pretend to have the best?) But I was sucked into the magic. In another couple of seconds, I wasn't sixteen-year-old Candace Weldon looking back, I was ten-year-old Candy, in the moment.

"When's he going to get here?" I demanded. My friends had all arrived. They were running around screaming. Bobby was jabbing Dorie in the ribs. Monica was sucking her helium balloon and making Donald Duck voices. Dad had promised to swing by, drop off a present, and give us all piggyback rides. He was supposed to do it before we got all stuffed with ice cream and cake.

"Have a little patience, Candy. You know he's usually late."

"But he said he'd be *early*."

"Yeah, I know. He's a creep, honey. What can I say?"

I hated it when Mom talked like that. Just because she and

143

Dad were divorced didn't mean she had to be nasty. I especially didn't like it on my birthday.

I kept looking at the door between every bite of sweet stuff. Pretty soon it was time to open presents. The best one was the squirt gun from Bobby. He was trying to be a smartass, but it backfired, because I *preferred* boy stuff. Tearing open the packages distracted me for a little while, but then it was over.

One by one, the other kids left. Mom heaved a big sigh and went to crash in her room without cleaning up. I sat by the phone until it got dark. I didn't bother turning on the lights.

The phone never rang.

"He forgot," I said as the dark apartment was replaced by the brilliance of the top of the skyscraper. "He hasn't remembered the right date of my birthday since he and Mom split up. He even got the month wrong one time."

I turned to the Surfer and was surprised to see him hunkered down, head to his knees. He looked like he had cramps or something.

This business was really getting to him. It wasn't exactly a roller coaster ride for me, but it was a kind of pain I was used to. I didn't know what to think. Wasn't he, like, next to invulnerable and all that jazz?

"You want to stop or something?" I asked.

"No. Go on." His voice was tight, like he was gritting his teeth. "Bring forth the memories, Candace. Show me another incident."

"All right," I said, still confused. "You've pretty much got a handle on me-and-my-dad. There was a time when I was twelve that's classic me-and-my-mom."

The transition was faster this time. So long, skyscraper.

Hello, motel room in Atlantic City. I was sitting on a so-called queen-sized bed that wasn't even as wide as a double. The racket of the cheap air-conditioning unit under the window was almost drowning out what Mom was saying.

I'd heard the lecture so many times I'd memorized it. It wasn't like this was our first trip here. It wasn't like she hadn't ever come back from the casinos and announced that she had a date with some guy she'd met an hour back. It was the "Stay in the room and don't whine about being left alone, I'll be back in the morning" speech. The one that always ended with, "I'm entitled to a social life, aren't I?"

"No," I said. I was shaking in my socks. I'd said no to Mom before. Ten million times. But not about something like this. Not this kind of "no."

"What?"

I grabbed the keys to the rental car off the nightstand and tightened my fist around them. "No way, Mom." It was six o'clock and she was already drunk. This guy she'd met might have been a Greek god for all I knew, but I didn't figure he was worth getting behind a wheel in her condition.

"Give me those keys, young lady."

Her voice had a growl to it that reminded me of a mountain lion I'd seen at the zoo, the one with the scars on its muzzle. I scooted back as far as I could on the bed. I'd never heard Mom like this before, and I'd been around her at her worst.

"You can't have the keys!" I shouted.

She came at me so quickly I didn't know what to do. I'd thought she was too fat to pounce that way. She slapped me on the side of the head, injecting a dial tone into my ears and turning my grip to putty. She snatched the keys out of my hand and had slammed the door shut behind her before I could choke out a word.

Tears rolled down my face, stinging where her ring had scratched my cheek.

"I hope you get in a wreck and die, Mom," I whispered.

When the memory video stopped, the tears were there again, dribbling over the little scar. "It got worse," I added. "Mom's date stood her up. She blamed me. Sometimes I think it would have been better if she had never brought me home from that trip."

The Surfer was lying on the rooftop, head in his hands. If this session had been bad for me, it seemed to have been five times worse for him.

"Are you okay?" I asked.

"Show me . . . one more thing." Again it sounded like he was having to squeeze the words out. "Show me the event that made you decide to jump today."

That made me dry-mouthed. No way did I want to go along with *that* idea. It was too personal. But the memory was so fresh, so "on my mind," that it bubbled right to the surface and the silver guy did his thing with it.

I was walking down a corridor in my high school between classes. I was just thinking how a few parts of my life were going okay for once. I might only have been an average student with nothing in the bank, creeps for parents, and knees that were too knobby, but I had finally been accepted by *some* cool people. Then I saw those very people standing near the stairwell.

One of the group was my boyfriend, Nick. At least, I'd been thinking he was my boyfriend. We'd gone out just the night before. But here he was, with his arm draped over the shoulders of Melanie Lange. The *best* thing I could say about Melanie Lange was that she was an airhead.

"What's going on?" I asked. I kept staring at his arm,

146

thinking maybe he'd take the hint and lift it away from her. But if anything, he seemed to be leaving it there on purpose. The rest of the bunch kept glancing back and forth from Nick to me as if they were in the front row at a boxing match between the Hulk and the Thing. My stomach began to feel as if the eggs I'd eaten for breakfast had been full of salmonella.

"What's going on?" I asked again, this time more loudly. "I thought you meant the things you told me last night."

"Did you mean the things you said to me?"

I should have smelled the trap. He wasn't behaving at all like the Nick I thought I knew. But I didn't stop to think, because I knew exactly what I believed. "Yes. Of course," I replied, as truthful as I'd ever been in my life. I was crazy about him.

He laughed. Every last one of them laughed.

I was shaking. "What's so funny?" Stupid question, Candace. You don't want to know.

"Me and Jason, we made a bet. He said I couldn't fool you. And I won."

"Fool me?" I was shrinking. I was down to about the level of his shirt pocket and rapidly turning into a puddle of grease on the floor. I had never been so humiliated in my life. "Then you don't . . . ?"

"Who'd want *you?*" he said. Do you know that scorn can sometimes feel just like a fist in the face? I've had both of those. Trust me, they're the same. "You're a nobody, Candy. Now get lost. The contest's over."

I turned and ran. No way could I hang around this school ever again. The laughter chased me out of the building and into the streets.

The echoes of all those giggles and guffaws bounced off the windows of the nearby skyscrapers long after the visuals had dissolved. I didn't think I'd ever be able to get that sound out of my ears. Not as long as I was alive.

"Nick was right," I said. "I am a nobody. At least if I'd gone splat on a downtown sidewalk, I would have been somebody for a day."

The Surfer was curled up on his side. He was quivering. If I hadn't been so blown away by the vividness of the replayed memory, I would have tried to lift him up. It scared me to see him like that. He was *hurting*. Why?

Then I figured it out. He was super-strong, super-fast, super-everything. That meant he was super-*empathic*, too. When he amplified what I was feeling in order to project it onto the rooftop, the emotions must have been amplified *into* him as well. He could have put up walls, I suppose. Protected himself. God knows I had steel-reinforced concrete barricades in my heart by now. But that probably would have interfered with the gimmick. He had no choice but to go through the pain.

He was feeling all my baggage more than I ever had. Was that an eye-opener. I'd always thought super heroes could take poundings better than regular folks. It had never trickled into my diet cola brain that their *vulnerabilities* might be boosted, too. The Surfer was proving that dudes like him had tender spots worse than a normal chick like me.

What a jerk I was. How could I ask him to do all that for me? Rude, Candace. The best thing right then was for me to get away from him as fast as I could.

"Sorry to mess up your day," I said. "Thank you for trying to understand. I really appreciate it." Trying not to trip over my feet, I rushed toward the roof access door. But naturally, it was locked.

There was always the edge of the roof. I had promised not to jump until Tuesday, but maybe there was a more direct way down.

"Stop," the Surfer called before I'd made it to the first seam in the tarpaper. Something in his tone made me freeze so instantly that I halted in midstep, too intimidated even to put my foot down. It was awesome just how compelling his voice could be. Here he was looking almost crippled by the intensity of what he was feeling, but he was still the Silver Surfer.

He stood up. "You have given me something, Candace Weldon. I would like to offer you something in return. I can show you glimpses of my life, as you showed me yours. It may be of some benefit to you."

I could tell we were heading into a new phase. He had this look about him that said he was done being an observer. No more Mr. Passive. Now *that* was scary. He was standing so straight now, being so much . . . so much *himself* that I nearly fell back on my bottom.

And at the same time, I was enjoying it. In sixteen years, I'd never had anything happen to me that compared with seeing all that power up so close. Truth be told, I didn't want it to end yet.

"Yes," I said. God! To look at an alien's memories! I was insane.

When the rooftop disappeared, it wasn't the slow dissolve it had been the other times. It felt like the skyscraper dropped away beneath us. We raced upward through a mist and into a black tunnel, and when we came out a heartbeat later, we were under a sky that I knew couldn't be found anywhere on Earth. Between scattered clouds peeked a shade of blue I'd never seen over my head, not even that time that I visited the Rocky Mountains.

The rest of the illusion settled in. Candace Weldon became a shadow off in a corner, one ounce shy of being forgotten. I was now a man named Norrin Radd, and I knew plenty about the planet underneath my boots. It was called Zenn-La.

"I" was walking through a garden between two tall, magnificent buildings—museums that I knew were filled with a dazzling collection of artwork, historical artifacts, jewelry. I glanced up at a footbridge connecting the seventh floors of the two structures and waved to a pedestrian. Not because I knew him, but merely because I was in a friendly mood. He waved back.

A woman walked beside me. Her name was Shalla Bal. I loved her, and she loved me. Today was a special day, because it was one I was allowed to share with her. We were doing nothing out of the ordinary. You might say we were "working" in the garden. But it was all I could ever ask of an afternoon.

Shalla Bal was entering programs into a computerlike interface she was carrying in her hand. Every time she coded in a set of instructions, some part of the garden changed. New plants sprung up in less time than it took to inhale and exhale, built molecule by molecule at her command. She changed the position of the shrubbery ahead, manufacturing a path of flat stones in the gap she'd made. Tree branches rearranged themselves to allow a little more sun on one of the flower beds.

I accepted a turn with the device, using it to alter a fish pond into a new configuration, finding a shape that complemented the greenery perfectly. From our vantage, the reflection of leaves and sky on the water's surface was enough all by itself to make us pause and sigh in satisfaction at what we had done.

I was content. Shalla Bal was my prize, and the beauty and technological wonders of Zenn-La seemed endless. I had every reason to hope this would never change.

* * *

I was crying when the Surfer and I withdrew to the rooftop. I've cried a lot in my life, but I'm not sure I'd ever cried from happiness before. I didn't want to move on to the next round. I wanted to just stay like that, live in that mood, forever.

"Was it . . . was it really like that?" I asked.

"Remembrance is a molten process, constantly toying with the mind," he said. "That was my home and my mate as I recall them. Whether there was ever a time so perfect, I can no longer say. If not, then I will keep the illusion, not the reality."

He let me drift for a few moments, then waved his hand. "Let us move on."

Suddenly we were riding the skyways, deep in interstellar space, on his—on *my*—surfboard. I wasn't Norrin Radd anymore. I was the Silver Surfer, Herald of Galactus. Zenn-La was a faded memory. Shalla Bal—who was she? I didn't care anything about the past, or about the hopes and ambitions of mortal beings. My existence had one purpose: to search for living planets to assuage my master's appetite. It was a task I performed faithfully and well.

At this particular moment I was far from my master, deep in a region of space I had never before explored. As I passed a star that burned with warm glows of yellow gold, it triggered remembrances of things normally forgotten. The realization of all that I had lost washed over me, leaving me and my board adrift. So much gone. So much of myself sacrificed. I had no choice if I were to save my homeworld, but when I had made the bargain with Galactus, I had not realized that the transformation to this body of coalesced cosmic energy would alter my inner self as well as my outer self.

I forced the images of my mortal incarnation and of Shalla Bal and Zenn-La back into the niche in my soul from which they had emerged. It was the only way to bear the lack of their presence. A faint melancholy remained with me, but I ignored it. The stars were singing, calling to me in etheric voices, recognizing me as their sibling. I sensed the worlds ahead of me, awaiting the caress of my board and I. Beautiful worlds—whether they were doomed to die by the hand of Galactus or whether they would remain unchanged for billions of years more. I felt the tug of neutron stars, tasted the kiss of cometary dust. None experienced the universe as did the Silver Surfer.

At least, no one *had* experienced it like him, until then. I collapsed onto my knees as the replay ended, confused to be back in a soft, weak, five-foot four-inch human body. All that infinity, all that cold, inhuman perspective. It made me feel smaller than an amoeba.

"Stop," I said. "I can't do any more."

"That is not true," he answered. "You have strength inside, Candace Weldon. One more simulation of the past, and it will be done. Be resolute."

He had a lot more faith in me than I had. But I nodded, and the rooftop fogged over again.

This time we didn't zoom off through a tunnel to some other part of the galaxy. As I drifted into the background, once again losing track of who I was, the mists cleared to show me an airplane-style view of New York City.

A jet followed me as I detoured out over the ocean. A fighter, judging by the rockets hanging from the wings and most of all by the bullets and tracers pouring out of it in my direction. Metal slugs slammed into me and the board, stinging me and knocking me sideways.

Recovering, I swooped, came around behind the jet, and melted its gun barrels and the trigger mechanisms of its rockets. Then, deciding that the pilot deserved chastisement, I fragmented the craft and let the pieces fall into the sea, leaving only the man and his seat intact. His emergency parachute opened as I departed.

Within moments I was on the other side of the globe. Below me a gun battle was in progress. Disgusted, I turned my board to find a new locale, but my enhanced senses brought to my hearing the frightened cries of a child. I darted downward. The child, no more than three, sat in front of a burning building. I sensed no living beings within the structure, so I picked up the little girl and deposited her in the company of a group of unarmed people huddling behind a partially demolished wall.

I raced around the planet again, coming to a stop in a range of high mountains. Among the rocks grew luxuriant expanses of green grass. Sheep grazed just below me. Here, I thought, I can sit and have a moment's respite.

But a shepherd appeared from the other side of a boulder. At the sight of me, he raised his fist and shouted. I could have translated the words as I do those of any other sentient being; but there was no need. As they echoed off the walls of the gorge beyond me, the message was unmistakable: "Go away. You do not belong here. You are frightening my animals. You are frightening me."

I rose up, aiming at the top of the sky. But as I approached, I felt the presence of the barrier left by my master when I betrayed him. I pulled up before I slammed into it. The previous time I had tested it, I had knocked myself unconscious. No point to do so again. So I floated, draped across my surfboard, gazing down at the planet to which I was exiled.

Shalla Bal was gone. Zenn-La was gone. And now even the expanses of the galaxy were denied me. I had no purpose left, not even to search for worlds so that Galactus could suck them dry of life. I was trapped in the company of an immature and emotionally volatile race, without a place among them, always a stranger.

Death would be better than this.

Coming out of the replay was like coming back from the grave. When I was able to get my muscles to work, I reached for the Surfer's hand. He clasped mine in his. Do you know that he's warm? Not hard and cold like metal at all, despite appearances.

"Do you still feel hopeless?" he asked.

"Not like . . . that," I whispered. "Not like what you went through. How did you ever make it?"

"I don't know. Perhaps because of friends. Perhaps because of enemies."

"Enemies?"

"Yes. Antagonists who saw me in my weakness and tried to destroy me. Nothing makes one cling to existence more than when another tries to snuff it out. In any event, I survived. Life . . . went on. If it had not, there are many wonders I would have missed."

"Yeah." Not the most witty comeback, but I was still getting used to the idea of knowing—really, really *knowing*—that someone else knew what it was like to be down and out. He'd said it, but now I believed.

"Do you still feel nameless?" he asked.

"Still feel like a nobody, you mean?" I started to laugh. Of *course* I was still a nobody.

Or was I?

Earlier that day I had been just another unwanted American teenager. But now I was someone who had seen other worlds, someone who had outraced comets and basked in the photon breezes of stars. Nobody at my school could make a claim like that. I was more than I had been. And the best thing was, I didn't even need to tell anyone about it to make it real. It was inside me, and no one could ever take it away.

"No, I'm not a nobody," I told the Surfer. "Thank you."

"Thanks are unnecessary. It was a trade."

"It was?"

He nodded. "Your struggles loomed as large to you as mine did to me. We are kindred spirits. You have reminded me of an essential fact: I am not so alone in the universe."

So it had happened to him, too. What a kick. What a wonderful kick.

"Will you try to take your own life again?" he asked.

"Maybe," I said. "Who knows?"

He scowled.

"All right, all right!" I said. "You're so literal sometimes. The answer is no. I'm not going to kill myself." I grinned.

My problems hadn't disappeared. I might have some hard times ahead. But my attitude was totally, like, realigned. The Surfer had shown me that as long as life continues, any number of possibilities might turn up. Some of them might even lead to happiness. Why not check some of them out? I might never catch a glimpse of the cool stuff he was bound to surf into, but then again, I wouldn't have to save the cosmos or fight super-villains. There are some benefits to being just plain old Candace Weldon.

I could cope with a lot more than I'd thought. No one else could have shown me that the way he had. He was an angel. A Herald. The savior of Zenn-La. The world needed more guys like him.

Speaking of which . . .

"Could you do this with anyone?" I asked.

He stared at me with those pupilless eyes. "The power lies within me. But tell me, would *you* go through the process a second time?"

I thought about the costs of going through it all. I'd come out okay, but my arms and legs were still shaking. I was reminded of that car accident I'd had with mom. The car had been totalled, but we came out of it with just a few scratches. When I'd realized I'd survived, the rush was incredible. But it took some time before I was comfortable riding in a car again.

"I guess not," I said. But I was me. He was made of different stuff. "Does that mean that in the future, if you see someone leaping to their death, you won't rescue them? You won't ask them why they did it?"

"I believe you already know the answer, Candace Weldon," was all he said. "Farewell." Stepping onto his surfboard, he was gone—shrinking to a glimmering speck in the sky, bypassing Four Freedom's Plaza and heading up, up, up.

He was right; I knew the answer. I knew what he would do if he ever met someone like me again. Some people you can depend on to be there in a crunch.

ON THE BEACH

JOHN J. ORDOVER

Illustration by Colleen Doran

Every kind of person shows up on the Los Angeles beaches at one time or another. Presidents and kings, scientists and movie stars, mutants and aliens from outer space.

That's why David Smith liked it there, especially at night when the chance of meeting someone outside the norm went up by a factor of ten or twelve.

It was after eleven on a warm summer night, and David came out to the beach for a late night party some of the guys from his office were throwing. Pretty much everyone was plastered by the time he got there, and since that didn't really interest him, his opportunities for interesting conversation were limited. Not that he would have felt comfortable with the office crowd, even if they weren't drinking. They just weren't his type of people. If the party wasn't at the beach, he wouldn't have shown up at all.

He got himself a can of soda and sat down to watch the others go crazy. They were laughing and dancing and skinny-dipping in the ocean—not a good idea, David thought, what with the sand and shells and who-knew-what-all-else—and he resigned himself to sitting alone.

Eventually he had to answer nature's call, and when he asked Bob from accounting where the nearest rest room was, Bob just pointed a shaky hand toward a patch of sea grass over a dune.

David wandered out of sight of the party and made his way to the dune. He was about to give up on the beach for the night when he saw a silvery light coming from a sandy hilltop across the way.

From where David stood he couldn't quite make out what the light was, but it was a slow night, and there was nothing waiting for him but an exceptionally dull party, so he headed lazily up the hill.

As he got closer he could see that the silvery light was in the shape of a man sitting with his head against his knees, his back against a large, silvery surfboard that was stuck in the sand behind him. The board was shining with the same light the man-shape was.

For a moment David thought it was just a neon sign advertising Surf's Up! or some other chain, just another piece of commercial junk cluttering up the beaches. But in another second he saw that it was a man, a man glowing with a silvery light.

David walked over to him. Up close he could see that the silvery light came from a coating that covered the man's skin from head to toe, leaving only blank white spaces for his eyes. The board behind him, which looked a little old-fashioned even to David's untrained eye, was either coated with, or made out of, the same substance that covered the shimmering man.

Wherever he's from, David thought, it's nowhere around here.

"Nice night," David said to the silver man, keeping his voice open and friendly. "How's it going?" At first David thought the man wouldn't answer, that he was too wrapped up in whatever was troubling him. Then the silver man lifted his head up and gave David a look so filled with sadness and longing that David almost turned away.

Instead, he steadied himself and asked, more quietly, "What's the problem? Can I help?" As he spoke, David sat slowly down on the sand.

"That is unlikely," the silver man said at last. His voice was smooth and musical and elegant, and filled with sorrow that seemed to shine from him as brightly as his silvery glow. "You could not understand."

David could guess what the silver man was thinking. "You think I can't understand," David said, "because I'm only human. Maybe you're mistaken. I've been around, seen a lot. Maybe I can help."

159

The silver man almost smiled at that, but caught himself and sighed deeply instead. "The problem is," he said, "that I am trapped here, on this small world, while my life and my heart lie—out there." He gestured upward, toward the stars.

"I know how you feel," David began, then, seeing the silver man's quick, doubtful look, added, "Well, maybe not exactly. But everyone feels out of place from time to time." David thought a minute, then continued. "Look at me," David said, "do you think my life's anything like what I had in mind? Anything at all? Not even close." David sighed. "But I'm stuck with the hand I was dealt. Just like you are."

The silver man gave David a look of sincere sympathy, as if despite the agony tearing at his soul, there was still room enough inside him to feel for another's problems.

"I am afraid," the silver man said after a time, "that it is not the same thing."

"It's more than that," David said quickly. "There are times when I feel like life is a big trap. I feel like the whole universe is a box I've been put in by someone with a dark sense of humor. It's like I'm playing some kind of nasty, cosmic game, and no one will tell me the rules."

That made the silver man thoughtful. Again, he almost smiled. "It is not much better," he said, an almost-smile on his lips, "when you know what the rules are. It means only that you can be certain there is no path to victory, no reason for hope."

"You don't say?" David smiled cynically. "Well, listen, rule book or not, I figured the hopeless part out years ago."

"Really?" The silver man was genuinely curious. "I had thought that ignorance was, in part, the reason for the joyousness I see so often on this planet."

"I know," David said nodding, " 'everyone's having a good time but me, there must be something wrong with them.' Look," he said, "we all know the score: Universe 1, Us 0. But at some point you just have to pick yourself up and get on with it. Just because you can't win in the end doesn't mean the game doesn't give you a few good rounds. So your life won't be what it might have been. So what? You look around, figure out what you've got, and do the best you can." David suddenly felt like a *Saturday Night Live* sketch: Samurai Shrink meets the Man from Space. He kept going. "If you don't like where you are, change it. If you can't change it, deal with it and move on."

The silver man said nothing for quite a while. Then he stood, no sand sticking to the backs of his silver legs, and turned away from David, his gaze flowing upward to the stars. After a while he turned back.

"Perhaps you are right," he said. "Perhaps I will make one last effort to free myself from this world-prison, and if that fails, I will tear the stars from my heart and begin life anew."

"Hey," David said, "you don't have to go through it alone. You have friends, don't you? Maybe they can help, if you ask them."

"Perhaps they can."

"And if there's anything I can do. . . ."

The silver man smiled, a genuine, full smile this time. "You have done much already. I will think about what you have said." The silver man raised his hand and his long glimmering board pulled itself from the sand and hovered near him, a foot above the ground. As he stepped up onto it, he said, "Perhaps we will meet again if I fail. But if I do not fail, I will think of you as I travel among the stars."

Then he did the last thing David could have expected: he held out his hand. David took it, and felt his palm tingle as it met the silver man's.

"One question before you go," David said. "How did you wind up here anyway? What did you do?"

Sadly, but with a voice full of pride, the silver man answered, "I did what I thought was right, rather than what I was told to do."

David laughed and nodded. "Same here," David said, "same here." He let go of the silver man's hand, and faster than David could follow, the man and his board were gone.

David walked slowly back to his car. Down the beach, the party was still going strong as he sat down behind the wheel. He reached up, tilted the rear-view mirror down and took a good, hard look at himself. For just a moment he let his human shape fall away, and stared into the green Skrull face that seemed more and more alien to him with each decade he spent exiled on this small green world.

Well, he thought, *I'm pretty good at giving out advice. Let's see how good I am at taking it.* He put his human face back on, got out of his car, and walked down to the party.

PART THREE

FREEDOM

*With the help of the Fantastic Four, the Silver
Surfer eventually found the freedom he had
yearned for, as he at last penetrated Galactus's
barrier. Now he roams the spaceways, a cosmic
defender of justice . . .*

DISTURB NOT HER DREAM

STEVE RASNIC TEM

Illustration by Scot Eaton

A point of light in infinite space.

Of what does the Silver Surfer dream? His failures and triumphs? Hopes, fears, the events of the day? Rarely do the expected subjects intrude upon his cosmic sleep. For the Surfer—in suspension on his board in the darkness just beyond some major star cluster, reposing below the natural spires of some mountainous planet, quiescent beneath the dumb gaze of another world's primitive inhabitants—soars the invisible pathways of space even in his sleep. Even one endowed with the Power Cosmic must sometimes rest, but his rest is like no other's, for it is landscaped with lines and arcs and exquisite curvatures, studded with points of light both brilliant and dim whose real-world significance may be known only to the Surfer and a handful of other voyagers through these infinite vistas. For creatures such as the Surfer, those destined to travel unhindered through boundless space, astronomical realities have both an external *and* an internal existence. Any change in the universe is likely to disturb their sleep, provoking immediate, personal concern.

Such is this singular point of light. Rationality suggests it should be indistinguishable from all others of the cosmos, but it is not. This star has come to him every night in his dreams, and it seems to have been inevitable that he would eventually undertake this voyage, that he would call his board to him and fly as if pulled toward this distant, ethereal light.

The Silver Surfer races through the darkness of the deepest well of space at immeasurable speed, the solar winds streaming past him like the spectacular yet insubstantial flowing hair of some god, hidden warps and eddies pulling at his thoughts, shaping them into the dreams that will fill his head the next time he submits to sleep. It is at times such as these that the Surfer feels most at peace, his every effort pushing him through the infinite. He does not think, in particular, of his destination during this voyage, his reasons for making

166

this trip, or the obvious lack thereof. He simply travels, and *is* his travel. The vastness he leaves unmarked by his passage.

In time he nears his destination, the field of stars that once surrounded him now reduced to one star, one light, which gently unfolds, expands, the edges softening, a softness drifting to the center of the great object as if a vast veil had been drawn. Startled, the Silver Surfer suddenly realizes the star that had drawn him through dream after dream and an eternity of space is in actuality an enormous, luminescent face.

The floating face is that of a woman, the most beautiful woman he might imagine: a mosaic, an amalgam, a sad recollection of all those women he has loved, recalled from death, disaster, the price of duty. Shalla Bal, Nova, Mantis, his own mother: their faces blend, morph into this vision of beauty on a celestial scale.

Closer still, drawn by the gravity of her countenance, clouds of stellar debris part to reveal the rest of her body whose measures might be commensurate with those of a solar system: her limber arms and supple torso seemingly as insubstantial as a cloud of cosmic dust, her long legs receding into the dark between stars. She is far larger than Galactus himself. Indeed, the Surfer realizes she may be the largest creature he has encountered in his travel through the stars.

What is this? The Surfer soars into the veil of particles that swallows her waist and hips like the most delicate of fabrics, and discovers there a great chain of spherical forcefields surrounding her like an enormous belt, each sphere containing an entire planet. Flying closer to the spheres, skipping his board from point to point off the shimmering glow trapping their atmospheres, he sees that each of these planets is populated.

"This is an outrage!" he shouts at the enormous woman, gliding up to her face. "You would use *these* for your *decoration?*"

But she is asleep, her eyes the size of moons closed, the pale flesh of her lids rippling softly in dream. Her chest swells and subsides almost imperceptibly. The Surfer can't help but feel that her peaceful slumber is fortunate for the billions of lives trapped inside the baubles studding her belt. *Or is it a chain?* he thinks, and sails down and around the string of planets. At the edges of several of the forcefields he sees that the inhabitants are using every available airborne weapon to pierce the shimmering barrier, but to no avail. At one such forcefield, giant dragon-like creatures beat their wings futilely against the walls of their prison. At another, large wailing faces are projected against the sky. At still others, the planets appear to be dead, or asleep.

The forcespheres are equal in diameter, not taking the size of the individual planets into account, so that the largest of the planets almost fill their shimmering jails, the surface of the fields just above the rooftops of the tallest buildings, permitting little room for adequate atmosphere. Gliding close to one of these worlds, he sees ruin after ruin on the continents below, the cities ravaged as if madness had swept the globe, the inhabitants moving listlessly if at all. The Surfer can see his own anguished reflection in the polished field above one such destroyed city, a reminder of his own exile on the planet Earth years ago. Enraged, the Surfer hurls himself at the field, intent on freeing those trapped inside. He bounces harmlessly away. He turns and raises his hands toward the globe, sending out one cosmic blast after another, the forcefield glowing brighter with each repetition, trapping the energy of his blasts, so that astronomers of distant worlds must think a new sun is forming.

Suddenly a great shriek fills his hearing, and the Surfer hurtles away from his own blasts, gripping his head to ward off the sound assaulting him. A huge hand passes through space in front of him, and in his distraction he is unable to avoid a collision. The hand knocks him several light years away. Without pause, he streaks back toward that singular point of light, that beautiful and terrible face.

The Silver Surfer returns to peer into the enormous woman's face, seeking some clue as to her purposes here, her intentions. The two moon-sized eyes gaze at him coolly, her pupils like craters filled with inky black. The Surfer feels he might fall into those eyes against his will and is compelled to turn from her direct gaze. "I am sorry," he says to the space around him, "I meant you no real harm. But you *must* let these creatures go!"

I do not keep them. A voice like a solar wind fills his head, a thrill to the edges of his thoughts. *It is they who keep me. They are not my captors, but they are my chain.*

"But who would have the power to do such a thing? This is not the way of Galactus, nor do I see the will of a Thanos here. Surely not Mephisto . . ."

My own have so enslaved me. One great eye blinks, and its aspect appears suddenly more brilliant, as if the surface of the eye contained more moisture than before. *It is They-Who-Remain-Invisible. I was once a part of the One. And now I am Alone.*

"And quite visible, I should say."

And visible. Having lost the purity of Being-In-Thought, and the pride that comes from existence without form.

"And yet your physicality . . ." The Silver Surfer feels himself drifting dangerously close to the eyes of monstrous size. "Surely you must know . . . what a beautiful creature you are."

I was a foolish creature! The Surfer's form shakes from the force of her booming voice working its way from inside him, as if her words might fill his belly and explode from there out his own mouth. But then the woman's voice suddenly shrinks, as if she understands the discomfort she has caused.

I was always prone to . . . longings, obsession with the physical, the realm of forces, appetites, the touch of the Other. I deserved punishment—this came through the One. It was just. They brought me out into the Visible, into this gross physical manifestation. They punished me. They made me alone.

"But these worlds, these billions . . ."

A chain of the many worlds They-Who-Remain-Invisible deem guilty of the major crimes of the flesh. On each of these worlds there have been dramatic, socially-sanctioned instances of violence, appetite, and acquisition.

"Such arrogance!" he cries. "Their audacity equals that of Galactus himself!"

I have no understanding of your concepts. I understand only the hideousness of my physical form, and the justness of my punishment. My own have evolved over the ages into beings of pure thought. My desires were a perversion—I know that now. They judged me unstable—I was unstable. My punishment is just.

"Such power your people must possess, matched by such arrogance! Surely you might access some small portion of it to help these beings who have joined your imprisonment?"

The wind, the voice created in the Surfer's head by the woman, flutters now, rubs lightly against the tissues of his brain, suggesting unnameable thrills. The Surfer at first considers this a mild seduction, the playful flirtation of a creature isolated too long from her own kind. But then he recognizes the timbre and form of her response and knows it for what it is. Laughter.

"Surely this is no time . . ."

It is your own arrogance that amazes me, tiny silver man. You, who have the freedom to travel wherever your heart might lead you, wherever your dreams might tell. Powers may be given and powers may be taken away. When they brought me down into this form, this repugnant devolution, I lost those powers that go beyond the physical, those powers to move and create merely by thinking. I possess only minor telepathic abilities in my gross form, barely strong enough to create those ripples in space that might affect the dreams of some would-be rescuer such as yourself.

"Make no mistake, my lady—it is these innocents whose rescuer I would be. I know nothing of your race, or its principles, although from what I have seen they take no account of other beings and their needs. But you said your punishment was a just one—if so, what need might you have of rescuing?"

The wind in his head grows still and empty, until the Surfer can feel no presence, a sensation greatly at odds with the gargantuan vision looming before him. But then there comes a stirring out of the dim recesses of his mind, and a soft, sighing utterance. *If you freed these worlds, and as a result my chain were to dissolve like some thought long past, I would not object.*

"I must admit, my beautiful lady, that I am as pleased to find your self-loathing has its limitations as I am appalled by the audacity of your race." The Surfer drops to the worlds surrounding her torso, gliding over each shimmering sphere in search of weakness or even subtle variation. But the spheres are as perfect as the skin of this goddess of his dreams.

Goddess of his dreams.

"My lady," he says, gliding across one of her cheeks, "do you, can you make contact with any of the beings on these imprisoned worlds?"

As with you, I may speak to them through their dreams. I may plant ideas in their heads and nourish them. I have suggested to them that they do everything within their power to break through their spherical containments. But as you can see, they have failed themselves as I have failed them. For all the time I have spent within their dreams I know very little about them.

"Learning requires some modesty, of which it appears your race has short supply. Can you enter their dreams while still maintaining telepathic contact with me?''

I believe that can be done.

"Then do so, and perhaps we both shall learn something of freedom, in dream."

Into her pale flesh of stardust and a wind that wraps galaxies he fades, so quickly he cannot protest. He immediately finds himself spinning inside a great and violent gust, his board gone, his silver form flashing with fragmented colors, fractal patterns, and the transient emotions of millions of sentient beings sheeting off his body like rain.

"Stop!" he screams, and he does.

The Surfer floats inside a storm the likes of which he has never seen before. And yet above him, through spaces between the wind and debris, he can see the shining inner curvature of one of the forcespheres. *I am inside!* he thinks, but something nags at him, something he should know but cannot quite grasp.

Suddenly a body passes through him. Another. Another still. Blue-skinned, with scarlet-edged gills, their mouths gasping for air. One of the creatures turns inside out in front of him, trailing its inner organs as the wind whips it away. Another below him explodes. Several creatures fly by clinging desperately to some sort of aquatic vehicle. Another spins through him as if he were not there. Another still. And another. And yet another.

Ah . . . of course. I am in their dream. Their communal nightmare. The thoughts are the Surfer's own, but he can hear echoes of the enormous woman's thoughts within them.

. . . they have such fear . . . they are in such pain . . . The woman's thoughts come through, heavy with sadness.

Locomotion in this state is no easy matter, he discovers, as direct movements have no effect, or an effect opposite to that intended. Sometimes it appears as if someone else is in control of his passage through this place, dreaming his journey through a dream. *Look . . . look at this . . .* the woman says inside and about him, and he is suddenly moving out of the storm and out over this largely ocean-covered planet, and from there he can see the full extent of the storm: the arms of it, the long legs, supple torso and looming face all made of turbulent shadow. The storm that terrifies these ocean dwellers in their worst nightmare is a doppelgänger of the enormous woman herself.

I have seen enough, she rumbles inside him, and he feels himself being pulled out of this world, through ghostly flesh and glistening barrier . . .

"Wait!" he cries, and once again the nightmare snaps into focus, and he is staring into the darkly beautiful form of the storm, with something silver tangled in it, passing through it.

What is it?

"I do not know," he replies, seeking to move back into the storm, but with each movement there is struggle, and he must content himself with glimpses: a silver form struggling with the storm, tearing off bits and pieces, redirecting its terrible force, the glad shouts of the sleeping millions.

So you have a twin? she says, and he shakes his head, trying to glimpse the face, but it comes no clearer. Or is it his eyesight failing? For this world, this dream is fading all around. *I believe their awakening comes . . .*

But where one dream ends, another must surely begin, as the Silver Surfer floats down out of the high clouds above a procession of great winged creatures—dragons—whose blue and gray hides glisten in the fiery light given off by the barrier that imprisons their world. For all their bulk they are among the most graceful beings the Surfer has ever seen, their wings tilting their huge forms just so, synchronous in their turns as they make tight spirals down toward the open volcano below them.

They seem content, she says inside him. *I see no anguish here.*

Out of the volcano rises the very image of the enormous woman, stained with soot and lava streaming down her hair. The dragons appear startled, caught off guard, but so inbred is their discipline that only a few veer from the downward spiral.

"No!" the Surfer screams as the woman throws back her head and opens her mouth as if to laugh, instead erupting a tall column of flame from deep inside her which burns the dragons to cinders. By the time they float gently around her face, clinging to forehead and cheekbone, they are of the lightest ash.

The enormous woman smiles and wipes the flame from her lips.

More dragons descend from the clouds and begin their precise spiral down to the destruction she holds in her mouth like a kiss withheld until the proper time.

Why? When they know . . .

"They are true creatures of habit," he replies. "Even knowing what awaits them, they have no choice in the matter. *This* is *their* nightmare."

And their rescuer?

Something silver drops from the clouds, so quickly the Surfer cannot make out a face or the exact specifics of form, only that it descends upon the woman at appalling speed, and the woman is alarmed.

And inside his head, the original of this dream woman screams . . .

I am sorry, she says, more softly than he would have imagined possible. *I did not expect to feel so.*

He is in a bedroom, a luxurious bedroom similar to the

finest bedchamber he might find on his own Zenn-La. The woman's voice seems at home here—he can almost imagine her reclining behind one of the floor-to-ceiling curtains. He imagines her voice to be that of his own Shalla Bal. "You apologize?"

My scream. I cannot remember when last I . . . I have never screamed.

"That is because you have never dreamed, my lady. Never known nightmare. Not until now."

The Surfer pulls back one of the sheer curtains, half expecting to find the beautiful, alluring image of her, reduced from cosmic size to something more understandable, graspable. But there is only a bed, its coverings light and full as clouds.

Pull back the sheet . . . It is not exactly a command he hears in her voice this time, but more a fear asking for its own confirmation. He does as she requests.

And finds hundreds of pale, wailing, alien faces, trapped within the bed, staring upward at . . .

The Surfer looks above him to where a ceiling should be, finding instead the open top of a dream, the enormous woman's face looking down, descending, her hungry mouth opening, something silver caught between her teeth, struggling, unable to save any of the poor creatures below.

I am a monster to them, she says, having retrieved the Silver Surfer from the last dream. *To all of them.*

The Surfer floats around her, more secure to be on his board. Dreams or not, he would have much rather traveled those strange realms with his board beneath his feet. "You misinterpret," he tells her. "Indeed, you were a monster, but a goddess and a lover as well."

And what is the difference, when all bring terror?

"A monster would not free them, which you and I are about to do."

You have a plan, little silver man?

"Indeed, my lady. To free them all, with you as goddess and lover, even monster, myself as champion even as you seek my aid. We shall free them all, even those my perceptions tell me could do well with more imprisonment, for it is not our place to judge. Take that wisdom back to the others of your kind, if your freedom also results."

There is some question?

"Nothing is ever settled, my lady, particularly not in the dreams of billions."

Explain your plan.

"In each of their dreams we will bring the silver champion out of shadow, demonstrating to all that he is one of them, but no weaker for it. He, with the aid of a tamed monster, goddess, or lover will move their planets through space and out of the control of the force fields. What happens in dreams shall happen in fact."

What power might possibly accomplish this?

"The power to dream, my lady, the power to imagine, and be. Even your diminished power, magnifying the raw power of billions of these dreams, should be adequate to bend the surrounding space sufficiently for these planets to return to their original locations."

And the forcefields?

"I must tell you . . . they may be so fixed in place you might still be chained here."

I think you are the dreamer, little silver man. Not simply from the evidence of this outrageous plan, but also that you would depend upon my aid, when it might not result in my own freedom. I may deserve such punishment, but I am still of Those-Who-Remain-Invisible, so what are these other creatures to someone of my race? Dreams, silver man, no more than brief, quickly forgotten dreams. If your plan works, and I see the planets escaping, these forcefields must dissolve as the worlds are removed from them in order to ensure my full cooperation. Else I swear I will take them back myself, and wear them throughout eternity.

In the dreams of the millions of aquatic beings of a planet virtually covered in ocean:

The silver one flashes his scarlet-rimmed gills and slaps his fins as he instructs his people in herding the dark storm around the center of the planet, stretching it, guiding it, until it is a belt of turbulence binding the planet pole to pole. The ocean creatures are both alarmed by the storm's force and amazed by its pliability, its willingness to be moved where needed. With guttural clicks and gill-snappings the creatures compose songs of praise in its honor, in *her* honor, for they have decided the storm is their mother, in its fierceness, in its love. They all came out of the storm and one day will return there, and now they sing and watch in amazement as the vast belt of storm pulls their planet out of its orbit and into the light.

In the dreams of the millions of dragons flying a dance of spirals in currents across the surface of a desolate, volcanic world:

The great silver dragon drops out of the sky with jaws full of crystal. He circles the volcano where the great woman sleeps, and when she opens her mouth in hunger he drops the crystals down her gullet. Dragon after dragon follows his example, until the sky is black with their numbers, each holding the shining crystals that they drop down the gullet of the goddess whose hunger knows no end. They do this again and again, going to the distant mines on other parts of their world, then flying to the great volcano to feed the ravenous hunger of the goddess who sleeps there. They cannot help themselves. They are creatures of habit and they are easily led. Suddenly the goddess screams. Led by the silver dragon they retreat to the other side of their world. From out of the great volcano of the goddess on the other side of their world a dazzling light erupts, slowly pushing their world through the dark skies and to another place within the night full of eyes.

In the dreams of millions of two-dimensional faces, their passions evident in their pale, drawn features, as they seek a strange comfort in the rooms they dream exist on other worlds:

The silver face floats above them and they are calmed. He brings to them the face of a beautiful woman, and when she kisses each of them in turn, they are moved.

The Silver Surfer returns to where the space both inside and surrounding the forcefields has distorted, the planets shifted out of their fixed positions, vanished from their imprisoning spheres, doubtless reappearing somewhere beyond his ability to see.

But the series of bead-like forcefields remains intact, in place, at least as strong as before.

The woman remains, held in place by her empty chain. "I am sorry," he says, to her, to those freed worlds she will seek and imprison again. Even if she cannot force them back into their spheres, he thinks, they surely must break apart when once again they are compelled to move.

But nothing happens. She does not stir. The spheres remain empty.

I shall be in their dreams for all time, shall I not, little silver man?

"Surely."

Those-Who-Remain-Invisible would be amazed, and outraged, at what I am feeling.

"I am sorry."

You will visit me again?

"You have my vow."

Do not waste your sadness on me, silver man. Is it not better to be a constellation a billion others might see, and take with them into dream, than so many stray thoughts floating through an infinite dark?

"I am not the source for such wisdom, my lady."

Then dream, little man. Dream.

THE BROKEN LAND

PIERCE ASKEGREN

Illustration by Paul Ryan

The Silver Surfer approached Earth's atmosphere from above the ecliptic, effortlessly gliding past the former boundary of Galactus's great barrier and entering at slightly more than twice the speed of sound. Once, twice, he circled the blue-green globe in a lazy circumpolar orbit that let most of its surface pass beneath him. The world's features were plain to his star-born senses, even from his great height. He could see the great urban enclave where first he had challenged Galactus, ending his term of service and beginning his imprisonment. He could see the mountain castle where an armored monarch had stolen the Power Cosmic and been driven nearly mad by the feat. He could see the site of his great battle with the Stranger, a desperate struggle to save an unknowing world from celestial judgment. Earth held many memories for the Surfer. Few of them were pleasant, but memories of prison seldom are.

As he guided his board downward, the air became denser. It caught and tugged at him, then heated and threatened to ignite; without conscious thought, he slowed his descent as he cut through the progressively heavier strata. The Surfer, at home in the airless expanses between the stars, sometimes forgot the quirks of planetary existence. For all its beauty, for all its infuriating and contradictory extremes, Earth was in many ways a typical world. It held the seeds of greatness. Those seeds drew the Surfer to it again and again, even after he had gained his freedom.

The Surfer had never troubled himself to learn the geographical labels that Earth's natives had imposed on their world. To one who held the Power Cosmic, such things were inconsequential. He knew his first goal, even if he did not know the place's name. Somewhere on the northeast quadrant of a major land mass, beneath six feet of good soil, lay the remains of his friend, Al Harper.

He touched down just outside the cemetery, stepped off

his board and strode silently between the graves and tombs. Years had passed since his last visit to this site, years filled with adventure and challenge, but not enough years to let him forget. Now, it was time to pay his respects once more.

Harper had been one of the few to befriend the Surfer— first by attempting to help the Surfer circumvent Galactus's barrier, then by sacrificing himself during the battle with the Stranger. The Surfer had won in that particular conflict; or, rather, the Stranger had lost. Al Harper had perished, a minor but key participant in a battle beyond his comprehension. The Surfer had marked his grave with a memorial beacon, a flare of cosmic energy. It would burn as long as the world Harper had helped save endured.

But now, the Surfer was enraged to discover, that beacon had been stolen.

Many miles away and deep beneath the earth, in a vaulted chamber carved from a mountain's heart, Enoch Matthews stared grimly at the console before him. It was a patchwork assemblage of new and antiquated components, adapted to meet unique requirements. For the thousandth time, he tried to assess the data presented. The basic radiation counts—alpha, beta, gamma, pi mesons, muons, positrons— were especially puzzling. Individually, the values were acceptable, but taken together, they were contradictory, even senseless. He knew the reason; his instruments were attempting to gauge energies that they could not actually measure. The elemental force imprisoned in his experimental containment vessel was absolutely unique. Since he had first discovered the power source he had spent countless hours studying it, coaxing it to release its secrets, however grudgingly. Still, its full properties were a mystery, and would likely remain so. Matthews tapped a command sequence into the keyboard and waited for the results.

There was a humming noise as hidden motors opened the crucible he had anchored to the lab ceiling. Superdense metal shields slid back to reveal the beacon he had discovered, by chance, in a lonely graveyard. Coruscating waves of energy pulsed forth, lighting the darkened lab and filling it with the harsh tang of ozone. Channeled and directed by the vessel's circuits, the released radiance surged down to bathe its human target, strapped to a lab table below.

Despite the anesthetic Matthews had administered, Jimmie Shipplett shrieked and struggled against his bonds as the first bolt struck him. He screamed again as his body began to melt and flow, as flesh and bone and sinew found new, different shapes. Proportions shifted, extremities reshaped and transformed, and even the features of his face rearranged themselves.

Five seconds passed, then ten. Matthews stood silently, his hands poised above the controls, watching as Jimmie writhed and convulsed. For a brief moment, he thought success had come at last—then Jimmie's eyes darkened and closed. Matthews cursed and initiated shutdown, but it was too late; before the crucible had sealed itself, his console's life sign monitors made their final, grim reports. One by one, breathing, heartbeat, brain activity, and cellular respiration all dropped to zero as life fled. Jimmie's body, still shrouded with a lingering nimbus of power, was left only partly transformed, a twisted caricature that looked only half-human. Another failure, another re-genesis betrayed by the weakness of the underlying flesh.

"Poor Jimmie. He was too weak for this, too close to death already." Rebecca Shipplett's slurred voice was a whisper as she stepped from behind another console. Already in her late teens, she looked much older. She walked slowly, dragging her bad leg. She touched her brother's face, the three fingers of her deformed left hand gentle as they traced his

twisted features. "He wanted so badly to be your first success."

"Yes, he did," Matthews said. "I wish—"

His words were interrupted by a harsh klaxon, a loud alarm
that echoed through the complex's cavernous interior. Matthews looked again at his console, but he knew what he
would see: the same senseless, contradictory readings. This
time, however, they weren't from the containment vessel,
sealed and dark, but relayed from exterior sensors studding
the mountain's surface.

"What is it?" Rebecca's words came in a rush and would
have been unintelligible to any but Matthews's practiced ear.
"What does it mean?"

"It means I was right about where the beacon came from,"
Matthews snapped. "Tell the others the Silver Surfer is here.
Get them to shelter."

"No. No, they can hide themselves. I want to help you."

Matthews had already stepped to another equipment
bench, donned an armored vest studded with electronic components. "Fine, fine," he said, angry beyond reasoning. "If
you want the rest to end up like Jimmie, stay here. But I'll
face the Surfer alone."

Rebecca Shipplett watched as Matthews attached one piece
of equipment after another to the vest he wore. She had
helped him build the suit, knew its every feature almost as
well as he did. Only as he added a visored helmet did she
bow her head in obedience. "I'll tell them," she said. "I'll
help them hide."

Matthews did not hear her. He was already in the elevator,
sixteen seconds from the surface.

At another time, the Silver Surfer might have chosen to feel
the brisk mountain air and enjoy it, or rejoiced in the harsh
sunlight that filled the cloudless sky. He might have

noted the region's ragged beauty, more of the dangerous but natural grandeur that made Earth so unique. He might even have pondered the comforting solitude, not unlike that of the cosmos where he made his home. Now, however, other matters attracted his attention.

He could feel the Power Cosmic calling him, sense the fragment of his own power that someone had stolen. It was here, in these mountains, beneath the ancient, weathered stone maze he now traversed. But his was not the only energy alien to this place; he could also distinguish elevated levels of basic radiation, too high to be natural. Even here, he thought, the Earth people have tainted their own environment, soiling their nest with atomic energy. To the Surfer, the power levels present were minor, inconsequential; to the humans, he knew, they were dangerously high. One valley held the remains of a small, abandoned village, overgrown and decaying. Humans had lived here once, but surely no more—and if they did, what could they want with his beacon?

Then the Surfer rounded another mountain, and saw the solitary figure standing on an isolated ledge, aiming what looked like a very large weapon at him.

The express elevator took Matthews to his stronghold's north face. In the quarter minute it had taken him to make the trip, he had booted up his suit's operating system and run its diagnostic software. Now, as he stepped out onto the ledge, the massive remote unit he wore on his left arm abruptly became feather-light. The servomotors had kicked in. This was it. He was as ready as he would ever be.

His helmet was lined with LED readouts and digital displays that fed him information without obscuring his vision. What concerned him most was a proximity gauge set to respond to the Surfer's unique energy signature. This one wasn't as sensitive or responsive as the lab version. It could take as much as three seconds to get a fix on its target—and Matthews wasn't sure he had those seconds. Then he knew he didn't have them, as he glimpsed the Surfer, gliding silently between two weathered peaks.

Since discovering the beacon and first deducing its origins, Matthews had analyzed every scrap of data he could find on the Silver Surfer, reviewed every inch of videotape available to him. None of it had done the Surfer justice, and now he wondered if any human instrument could. Perfect beyond human measure, flawless and gleaming, the Surfer's shining form caught the sky's pellucid blue and threw it back. Otherworldly, inhuman in its grandeur and grace, the Surfer's actual presence far transcended any recorded image Matthews had seen. For a split instant, he stood transfixed by what he beheld. Then his visor's targeting cross-hairs found the Surfer, and he squeezed his trigger.

Instantly, the displays surged to life. The readings for alpha, beta, gamma and the rest were the same as he had seen earlier, but multiplied by a factor of ten and still increasing. Matthews could feel his suit's backpack computer hum as it strained to process the incoming data flow. He was getting more information than he had dared hope for, countless bytes of essential data that threatened to overwhelm his processing capabilities—but he knew that these were only fragmentary clues in an infinite mystery. Distantly, he wondered what kind of being could fully control such terrible forces, how a creature like the Surfer would view the world to which Matthews had been born.

A sudden burning odor interrupted his reveries. One of the LED displays had overloaded. As he watched, another followed suit, then a third. He looked past them, through the visor. The Surfer had turned to face him. Blank eyes that had seen sights beyond Matthews's wildest imaginings met his. Then the Surfer's hand rose and gestured.

The remote unit went first, overloading and heating until the automated safety interlocks activated and released it, to fall on the ledge at Matthews's feet. He barely noticed; by then, a nimbus of cosmic energy had encased him and begun to lift. Even as Matthews's feet left the ledge, his suit's systems continued to overload and fuse. The backpack computer was smoldering scrap by the time Matthews stopped rising and hovered, helpless, before the Surfer.

The Surfer gestured again. In response, Matthews's computer and helmet tore free and fell. He could hear them bounce and break against outcroppings, as they plummeted more than a mile to the canyon floor. Countless hours of toil and sweat went with them, but all that Matthews regretted losing was the information trapped within their circuits.

The Surfer spoke, his voice a resonant thunder. "Who are you?"

"E-Enoch Matthews."

"That instrument was not a weapon, was it?"

"N-no." Matthews stared at the Surfer's impassive, mirrored face. He saw his own features superimposed on the reflecting skin, contorted in terror. With almost inhuman effort, he composed himself, forcing his own expression into one of studied calm. "No," he said. "It was a full spectrum remote analyzer, with associated processors."

"It is unwise to peer too deeply into the secrets of the infinite."

Matthews didn't say anything. For a long moment he hung in mid-air, silent and helpless, but meeting the gaze of a being whose presence could herald the death of entire worlds. Then the Surfer gestured again, and set Matthews down on the mountain ledge.

"You have something of mine," the Surfer said. "Take me to it, so that I may leave this place."

*   *   *

188

Matthews didn't bother to tell the Surfer about the elevator. Instead, the two trudged down flight after flight of stairs, through raw and unfinished passages that had been blasted from the ancient stone. For long minutes neither spoke, and the silence was broken only by the sound of their footsteps on dusty concrete. As they descended, he wondered desperately about Rebecca and the others. He had sent them to the stronghold's bottom-most levels, to bunkers hardened against nuclear strikes. Now, however, Matthews realized grimly that they wouldn't last an instant against the Surfer. His sensors had told him that much. The glistening figure behind him, brilliant even in the stairwell's dim lighting, held within his humanoid form a greater potential for destruction than all of Earth's weapons combined.

They had almost reached their destination when the Surfer spoke. "What is this place?" he asked.

"It's called Omega Keep," Matthews replied. "It used to belong to the Army, but it's mine, now."

Neither spoke again, until they stood before the reinforced blast doors of the main lab. Once there, Matthews turned to the Surfer and said, "Look, your problem's with me. I'll give you what you came for. Just take it, and leave. Leave the others in peace."

"Others?"

Matthews didn't have a chance to reply. The lab doors slid abruptly open, revealing Rebecca Shipplett, teeth bared in a feral snarl, cradling an antique shotgun in her withered arms. Framed in the doorway, stunted and twisted, quivering with anger and fear, she startled even Matthews. "You're not going to hurt him," she hissed at the Surfer. "Leave him alone!"

Things happened fast then, but Matthews managed to act faster. Rebecca Shipplett's trigger finger tightened, turned white with strain as the Surfer raised one hand in a reflexive, defensive gesture.

"Rebecca, no!" Matthews yelled as he leaped at the Surfer, throwing his full weight into a single frantic effort. It was futile; the Surfer's flesh was as unyielding as steel. Even as Rebecca's shotgun roared and Matthews spoke, the Power Cosmic struck its target. The lead pellets belched out by the gun disappeared instantly, transmuted into a cloud of white smoke. Matthews could feel the hot wind of transformed particles as they dispersed into the cavern air. After a single dazed instant, he realized he was still alive. Neither the shotgun blast nor the Surfer's bolt had struck him. Rebecca, rocked by the gun's recoil, fell back against the door frame and slumped to the bare concrete floor. Tears flowed like blood down her ruined face.

For a long moment, the Surfer gazed impassively at Matthews and at the sobbing girl who still clutched her useless weapon. "I would not have harmed her," he said, his voice gentle, but wondering. "She could not have hurt me. But you risked all to save her." He stepped past the two of them, into the main lab chamber.

Matthews turned to Rebecca. "The others?" he asked. "Are they safe?"

"In there," Rebecca said. "They're in the main chamber. They wouldn't go below, wouldn't desert you." She paused, gasped for breath. "They're in there, with him."

The Silver Surfer took no note of his surroundings as he strode into Matthews's laboratory. The instruments, the equipment, the dank gloom meant nothing to him. All that mattered was the fragment of his own power that languished in a metal chamber fixed to the lab ceiling. Effortlessly, he called it to him, made it burst free from its prison and flow through the cool, still air to rejoin him. Only after that did he take note of the vaguely human body strapped to the lab table. He stepped closer to examine it, drawn by a residue of cosmic energy lingering in the lifeless flesh. As he did, he became aware that he was not alone. Matthews and the woman had joined him in the lab, but others were there, as well.

They were clustered in one corner of the huge chamber, away from the light, but mere shadows could not hide them from eyes accustomed to the infinite blackness of space. Rebecca's brethren, by the look of them. Nearly a hundred and nearly human, men and women and children who had been twisted and distorted into cruel parodies of Earth's dominant species. Silently, they stared back at the Surfer as he surveyed them, taking in the full measure of their deformity. Some quailed as the Surfer's impassive gaze took in their twisted limbs and ravaged skin, bald scalps and ulcerated faces. Most met his eyes with a certain dignity, however, staring back at his chrome perfection with mingled awe and fear. Each was unique, but all were similar. The Surfer had seen this kind of damage before.

He looked back at the figure strapped to Matthews's lab table, looking at it with new eyes. The deformities did not seem so great now, not in contrast with those of the others. The dead man's face held a puzzling expression that the Surfer now understood. A look of peace.

"Not a pretty sight, is it?" As Matthews spoke, sighs of relief erupted from the huddled group. He gestured for them to remain silent.

"No, Enoch Matthews, it is not. It does not please me." The Surfer looked somberly at the scientist. "I believe you have much to explain."

"Right after graduate school, I tried to conquer the world," Matthews said. "Literally." He smiled at the memory. "Those were the days. All you needed was a gimmick and an attitude, and I had both. I invented an ionic destabilizer coil that suppressed valent potentials—"

"A weapon."

"More than a weapon. It was the key to my utter domination of human society." Matthews shook his head ruefully. "Or so I thought."

"What happened?"

"A member of the super hero community took me down, in about thirty seconds flat. I had overlooked something, of course. I wasn't as smart as I thought. I had some time in a federal penitentiary to correct that situation. When I got out—" Matthews looked at the Surfer. "Are you sure you need to hear this?"

The Surfer nodded. "Continue."

Matthews had kept his nose clean in prison, he explained, spending much of his sentence in the library. A passing reference to a shuttered Army installation in West Virginia caught his eye; diligent use of online database services provided a few more details. He'd always been good at puzzles, assembling seemingly unrelated pieces into an unexpected whole. Omega Keep was mentioned in federal budget documents three times before 1970, and never again after that date. An entire sequence of Army telephone numbers allocated for the mid-Atlantic region remained officially unassigned. A Freedom of Information Act request yielded an inch-thick sheaf of shipping invoices, with specific delivery sites deleted—but tax-stamped by West Virginia. Even the indirect clues petered out after 1975, except for a flurry of apparently unsuccessful salvage bids. The implication was clear: whatever the Army had put in Appalachia was still there, waiting for someone smart enough to use it. Waiting for Enoch Matthews.

"I came here after I got out," Matthews said. "I was looking for equipment, tools, weapons. Something I could use or sell.'' He paused, gestured at Rebecca Shipplett. ''Instead, I found Rebecca, here. She was just a little girl then. I found many more like her. They were very happy to see me.''

Rebecca nodded. ''Yes. You saved us.'' She spoke to Matthews, but stared at the Surfer. Her eyes burned with fear and envy as they took in his shimmering perfection. The shadowed figures behind her nodded and murmured in agreement.

''I've seen such damage before,'' the Surfer said. ''Radiation. It burns within her still. What happened here?''

''A spill. It may have been deliberate. It's why they closed this place down, almost twenty years ago.'' Matthews sounded deliberately detached as he continued his story. ''The Army scientists were working on a powdered aerosol of radioactive material. They wanted to sterilize entire countries for a generation or two, but they didn't want the more extensive damage associated with atomic blasts.'' He paused. ''I don't think they had all the bugs worked out.''

Matthews continued to explain that he had found Omega Keep easily enough, but he'd also found the remnants of Creighton, a small isolated mountain town poisoned by radioactive dust. The last members of the previous generation were sick and dying, eaten alive by cancer. He'd also found the children and adolescents who'd survived their parents, marked by the terrible scars of birth defects and deformity. Twisted and misshapen, unable to comprehend what had been done to them or why, they lived in complete poverty and despair. Many were unable to care for themselves. When the last of their parents died, he had realized, the children would be helpless.

''I buried Rebecca's father a week after I found Creighton,'' Matthews said. ''I've been here ever since, leaving only to get supplies and equipment. I found your beacon on one

193

of those trips, by sheer coincidence. My father is buried in that same cemetery. I'd heard of the power you wield, thought I could use it to help Rebecca and the rest." He paused. "Experiments on animals have been promising, but I've had no success with humans. That may be because I've tried it only on the weakest, on the dying. That's all of them, of course." He gestured. "Like poor Jimmie, there."

"You are clever, Enoch Matthews, as clever as any of your race I have met. But the Power Cosmic is beyond such as you, and these troubles are beyond even that," the Surfer said. Gently, he reached out and traced the lines of Rebecca Shipplett's face. She trembled as his metallic fingers touched her. "They are as nature and radiation made them. Any attempt to remake them so late in life is doomed to failure."

"No," Matthews said, his voice hard. "I don't believe that, I can't. There must be some way to save them. If it takes the rest of my life, I'll prove you wrong."

"Why is that?"

"Why is what?"

"Why do you labor here? Why did you not take what you came for, and leave?" the Surfer asked. "The world is still out there, and you do not rule it yet. Why did you stay?"

"They need—" Matthews glanced at the Surfer, at Rebecca Shipplett, at the huddled figures standing silently. "They needed somebody, anybody, and I was here. I could not—I cannot abandon them," he said. "Now, get out of here. I have work to do."

For the first time since Matthews first saw him, the Surfer smiled. "No," he said. "*We* have work to do."

It took the Silver Surfer hours of flight and observation to measure fully the crime that had been committed against Creighton, and to realize that he would never understand it. Radioactive isotopes had infiltrated the entire ecosystem for miles around, carried by the wind and ingested by members of every species. Countless unstable atoms were locked within the bone and tissue of every living being, emitting their deadly radiation as they collapsed into new forms. Even if he cleaned the land, or took them from it, Rebecca's people would ultimately be poisoned by their own flesh. Each cell of their bodies held their doom, decaying isotopes trapped in complex organic webs. Given a thousand years or so, the Earth would clean itself—but by then, Creighton and its people would be long dead.

Matthews was contaminated, too, though not to so great an extent. Every day he stayed here, every day he breathed Creighton's air, he took another step towards death. Not even Omega Keep's sophisticated filters and circulation system would save him, and Matthews surely knew it.

He baffled the Surfer. The man personified the unanswerable riddle that had confronted him since his first visit to Earth. Matthews had labored tirelessly to better the lot of his charges, but still waxed nostalgic when he spoke of his days as a would-be conqueror. Aloof and even peremptory to the Surfer, his arrogance fled when he spoke with Rebecca or the others. The people of Creighton saw him as a combination of savior and ultimate parent, but to the Surfer, he was the quintessential distillation of humanity, a combination of selflessness and savagery unlike any other race.

The Silver Surfer found himself wondering what Matthews would do if freed of his responsibilities, what unpleasant goals the man's remarkable ingenuity might once more pursue—but he drove the thought from his mind as he continued to orbit Omega Keep, probing the ravaged land.

Finally, he was done. He glided toward the mountain ledge were he had first encountered Enoch Matthews, and found the scientist there once more, ruefully examining the remnants of his remote analyzer. As the Surfer landed, Matthews pulled one module from the unit's fused housing and shook his head ruefully. "A total loss," he said. "You sure know how to hurt a guy."

"The Power Cosmic can destroy," the Surfer said, "but it can also restore."

"You mean you can heal the villagers?" Matthews's voice held a note of hope as he casually slid the component he had salvaged into his pocket.

"No, I cannot heal them. But I can drive the poisons from their land and their bodies. I can enable them to live out their lives in relative ease. Come, there is much we must do."

Dusk had arrived by the time they had made their last preparations. The Surfer stepped from the elevator as the last sliver of sunlight disappeared beneath the western horizon, its reddish rays turning his skin copper. He turned to face Matthews. "Return to your shelter," he said. "I must do this alone."

"Are you sure you're ready?"

"Nothing can ever be certain, Enoch Matthews. But, yes, I am prepared. The data you gave me was quite comprehensive, especially the biological information. It will help me in this."

"It was the most current I could find," Matthews said. "And I'm pretty good at research."

"Yes. Now go. You will be safer inside."

The elevator doors closed behind Matthews, leaving the Surfer alone. For a long moment, he stood motionless, preparing himself for the task ahead. Then night gave way to a false day, as the Surfer released the full fury of the Power Cosmic and lit the landscape.

Creighton's miracle had begun.

It was fantastically difficult, a feat that only the Surfer or Galactus himself could even consider. The power radiated from him, creating a zone of transformation that embraced every atom, every molecule within its boundary. Rock, air, animal, plant—all were the same to him now, constructs of varying complexity, but all composed of the same essential particles. Gently, he extended his consciousness into the energy field, seeking the unstable elements of the great matrix that surrounded him.

He began at the stone beneath his feet, with a single clinging lichen and the atoms within it. A moment's concentration, a gentle nudge from the Power Cosmic, and the plant surrendered its poisonous burden of radiation as specific atoms abruptly found stability. Their nuclear fires had been extinguished.

A bat flitted into the zone's boundaries, squeaking its protest of the sudden, untimely glare. The Surfer's power reached out, touched it; the winged mammal flew away, unaware that it had been cleansed, unaware even that it had needed cleansing.

Mere hours before, the Surfer had turned lead to vapor, reflexively neutralizing Rebecca Shipplett's shotgun blast. That feat of atomic restructuring, though infinitely complex by human standards, was child's play compared to what he now intended: effectively transmuting all poisoned atoms in the surrounding land into more stable isotopes, without damaging the structures that held them. It called for power levels far greater than he had ever before unleashed within Earth's atmosphere, and carried with it the potential for almost unimaginable devastation, should something go wrong. It also called for complete concentration, including ignoring any potential threats. He would be utterly vulnerable until his work was done.

For the briefest of instants, the Surfer considered Enoch Matthews again. Then he refocused his will and extended the transformation field another fractional increment.

* * *

Rebecca Shipplett was at Matthews's side as he monitored the process from within Omega Keep. She had no inkling of the scale of power being unleashed above her, of course. Even Matthews could only wonder at the complexity of the task the Surfer had set for himself.

"He's helping us, isn't he?"

"Yes. Yes, he is," Matthews replied, staring at his console.

"Why? I thought you were scared of him."

"I don't know why. Only he knows that," Matthews said. "But, yes, I'm scared of him. I'm very scared."

"What happens when he's done? Will we all be like you, like Mama and Papa?"

"I don't know what happens when he's done, Rebecca," Matthews said. "But you won't be like me, ever." He kissed her gently on the forehead. Her skin was dry and cool beneath his lips. He wondered what her life would have been like without him. "I'm sorry."

"That's okay, I guess," Rebecca said. "Just don't leave us."

Matthews, transfixed by his monitors, made no reply. The Surfer's zone had expanded a third and fourth time, and now extended a mile from the boundaries of his body. Already, background radiation levels had dropped by more than a third. Matthews wondered precisely where the Surfer's work was being done now. In his body? In Rebecca's? Inside the hundred or so twisted forms that slept, unknowing, in the bunkers below? Unanswerable questions, he knew; the Surfer was working at levels far too fundamental for measurement by the human nervous system. That required more subtle instruments.

He continued to stare at the monitors before him, watched as they steadily accumulated information relayed from the detectors he had placed on the neighboring mountain faces. His pocket still held the onboard processor he had retrieved from his remote sensor. The information it held was unique, because he had gathered it at close range during an un-guarded moment. He wondered how it might complement his new data.

The mystery of the Power Cosmic might be solvable, after all.

At dawn, Matthews found the Surfer slumped on the ledge where he had stood, completely spent and comatose. At some point during the long night, the mountain's granite had yielded to his power; now, as the sun rose, Matthews could see that the Surfer's feet and body had sunk into the softened rock, like a man might sink in mud. But the silver-skinned being was unscarred, completely unmarked by the incredible energies he had unleashed, then contained once more.

He was too heavy for Matthews to move. As the sun rose, the scientist tended to him where he had fallen. Matthews had no idea when or if the Surfer would wake. He showed no life signs that Matthews could measure. If he had lungs to breathe with, he was not using them. If he had a heart, Matthews could not detect its beats. He could not even tell if the Surfer's blank eyes, metallic like the rest of him, were open or closed. All he could find was the same unique energy signature, weak but slowly building.

One hour passed, then two, with the two of them alone on the scarred ledge. Matthews looked out across the moun-tains, at the day's first birds as they kited and dove through the cloudless sky. Something had changed during the night, something no human eye could see but which he, impossibly, could. The sky, the air, the very stone on which he stood, all were subtly cleaner now, washed of their invisible poisons.

Rebecca was below, he knew, looking to the needs of her fellows. Matthews had examined her carefully before emerg-ing to find the Surfer. She was clean, absolutely free of the toxins she had accumulated during her short but very hard life. She still bore her scars, but all of her life signs were improved, as if her vitality had been subtly boosted by a caress from the Power Cosmic. Even without checking, Matthews knew that the others were the same. He understood enough of the process to know that it was beyond his full comprehension. Anyone who could re-create the Surfer's power on even a fractional basis would, quite literally, have a world at his feet.

He heard a noise, something like a sigh. The Surfer had awakened, his power regenerated, and was struggling to stand. Matthews turned to help him, but the Surfer was already stepping out of the indentation his body had left in the rock.

"You did it," Matthews said.

"Yes."

"They'll live out their full lifespans now. We don't have to worry about the cancer, about contaminated water or crops. I can even move them back to the village. They won't have easy lives, but they'll have good ones."

"I but did what I could," the Surfer said. "I could do no less."

"I—thank you. You saved them."

"No." The Surfer had stepped onto his board, readying himself to leave. "I only helped," he said. "You saved them. And, I think, they saved you, as well. Farewell, Enoch Matthews. I am pleased that I met you."

Then he was gone, silently gliding through the cool morning air. Matthews watched as the glistening form grew smaller in the distance, then disappeared. For long minutes, he stood alone on the ledge, pondering the Surfer's parting words. Then he reached into his pocket and pulled out the processor module.

He considered the possibilities it held. With its secrets, he might conceivably re-create some portion of the glory he had seen this night. His researches suggested that others had tried to do so and had even succeeded to some small extent. Who knew what remarkable feats he could accomplish with such power at his command?

With a shrug, he threw the processor away from him, out into the chasm below. He did not hear it hit bottom. By the time it did, the elevator's doors had already closed behind him.

He had work to do.

Later, the Silver Surfer stood again at Al Harper's grave, gazing at the new memorial beacon he had created. Only his eyes could see the changes that he had made in it, subtle safeguards that would keep the Power Cosmic from falling into unworthy hands. He had been fortunate—Earth had been fortunate—this time, but he could not risk the beacon being taken again, by someone less scrupulous.

For the thousandth time, he considered the baffling human race. Never in all his travels had he seen such compassion and hunger for conquest bound so closely together. Enoch Matthews had sacrificed his life as thoroughly as had Al Harper. Once a predator with petty dreams of conquest, he now slaved in total obscurity for a tiny enclave of forgotten souls. But the survivors of Creighton loved him completely. When death came for him, his people would mourn him with every fiber of their beings. The Silver Surfer wondered if anyone else on Earth was so blessed.

Then, alone, he took to the skies. The stars were calling.

WHAT'S YER POISON?

CHRISTOPHER GOLDEN
AND JOSÉ R. NIETO

Illustration by Amanda Conner

When the Silver Surfer stepped into Rankor's Ditch, the first thing he noticed was the smell, a shocking mixture of sweat, ammonia, and oily smoke. The fact that anyone would voluntarily bear that stench—slouching on awkward riveted stools, guzzling mug after mug of intoxicants—puzzled the Surfer. Not that he had the time, or inclination, to consider such questions. He had come to this "dive," as his old friend Ben Grimm would have called it, at the urgent request of a friend, and a tenuous friend at that.

As the Surfer walked to the bar, jittery conversations hushed, revealing the lilt of a Rigolletian pipe melody. All at once, a rowdy throng turned away from the holo-projector and craned their necks to follow the Surfer's progress. Even the bartender, a bored-looking Shi'ar half-breed, stopped buffing a stained tumbler and stared.

So remote was the planet Keffelix that the power beings of the universe were relegated to the most tentative myths, stories passed down from one generation to the next. A visit from a being such as the Surfer was, for many, a once-in-a-lifetime experience. Before today, the Surfer had known Keffelix only by reputation; armpit of the Mattei system, a place of quick tempers and violent consequences. These people, the Surfer suspected, liked nothing better than a fight. He would have to be wary while in Rankor's Ditch. To meet the hardened stare of any number of these beings could lead only to battle and destruction. The Silver Surfer was not afraid of these things, but he understood the wisdom of not inciting them.

The bartender regarded the Surfer with slit eyes. Behind him, nailed to the wall, hung twelve disembodied heads, every one of a different species, their mouths held open by round frames. Each grossly distended mouth held a glass bottle, as if consuming one final, eternal drink. Under the grisly display hung a large sign: "All accounts will be settled before leaving the premises."

"What's yer poison?" the bartender drawled in a gruff voice. He seemed unimpressed by the Surfer's gleaming skin, stately poise, and determined brow. The Shi'ar were a proud race, and the Surfer knew that the bartender, an extremely tall and burly male, must have done the empire an egregious wrong to be exiled (or have fled) to the Nacite mining colonies of the Mattei system.

The Surfer lifted his chin and scanned the room, which had settled back to its usual din. In the far corner, the holoprojector strobed dimly, showing the hideous aftermath of an illegal death-pike match. A heavy Vordon female pushed her way through the crowd, yanking lost wagers from the hands of grumbling losers. In the confusion, the Surfer could not find the man he was supposed to meet. He was answering a summons from the former Avenger Starfox, whom he'd always known as Eros of Titan.

Trust had always been hard to come by in the grudging association—perhaps friendship was too strong a word—that he had developed with Eros. After all, his only brother, Thanos, was one of the galaxy's most despicable villains. But the Surfer had always looked up to Mentor, their father, and so gave Eros the benefit of the doubt. It wasn't easy, considering Eros's flighty, unpredictable nature. Plus, he had the ability to stimulate the pleasure centers of the brain, a skill the Surfer found unnerving.

"Hey!" the bartender growled. "Pay attention, friend. What'll you have?"

The Surfer almost smiled. The Shi'ar knew, of course, who he was, but had chosen not to acknowledge him by name. Any high-born Shi'ar, which the half-breed clearly was by his markings, would be appalled by such manners. The Surfer considered chastising him in the high tongue of his people, but let the insult pass.

Slowly, he turned to the bartender.

"Rankor," the Surfer said in the Shi'ar high tongue, causing the man's eyes to soften. Rather than admonishing him, the simple act of naming had at once shamed and honored the man. It would not be lost on him that the Surfer had recognized him as the owner of the Ditch; an unusually perceptive people, the Shi'ar had little patience for those who failed to see the obvious, or those who wasted precious words.

"What can I do for you, Norrin Radd?" Rankor said with dignity.

"I'm meeting someone here. A humanoid. With red hair. Do you know who I mean?"

"In the back," he said. The Surfer nodded and turned away from the bar. He headed for the smoky shadows at the rear of the room, sliding past loud, gesticulating patrons. If his own visit was a tale for Keffelixians to tell their children, how much better the story if a second power being had come into the bar the same day? And yet, would any of them know Eros of Titan on sight? He thought not. Eros would find it much easier to remain inconspicuous than the Surfer.

Eros sat at a private booth, sipping a green elixir the Surfer could not identify by sight. The overhead lights deepened his perfect eyes; made him look haggard, even sinister. Once again the Surfer felt unsettled. He and Eros had been allies, yes, but how had he ever thought them friends?

"Ah," Eros said, nodding in greeting as he stood. "Thank you for coming, Surfer. I was certain that I could count on you."

The Surfer found himself missing the Shi'ar's terseness. Eros's every word was meant to influence. "Of course, son of Mentor," he said formally, "though I cannot understand why we are forced to meet in this place. Spatial coordinates would have sufficed, I believe, and been more convenient for both of us.''

"Hear me out, Surfer, and I believe you will come to understand the necessity for such inconvenience,'' Eros said grimly. The Surfer's brow furrowed, distorting a hazy reflection. Eros, Cupid of the cosmos, was rarely grim, or even out of sorts.

"You have my full attention,'' the Surfer said, touching his jaw and resting his elbow on the table.

"Surfer,'' Eros began, then paused and lowered his gaze. "Norrin, I know you respect my father greatly. It is for this reason that I come to you. I believe that Mentor is in great danger. Not, as you may be inclined to conclude, from my brother Thanos, but from himself. And you, my dear friend, are the only one who can help him.''

The Surfer narrowed his eyes. "I am honored to be of any assistance to Mentor, Eros,'' he said, "but it would be best if you disposed of this vagueness and spoke plainly of what ails your father.''

Before Eros could answer, a piercing cry rose from the death-pike tables. A bestial thing—three meters tall, golden fur matted across its back, head shaped like an anvil—struggled with the Vordon female. They seemed caught in a feverish dance, hand and talon clamped above their heads, pounding anyone or anything in their path. Within seconds a large space had cleared about them.

"You made the bet!'' the Vordon screamed, her voice a painful shrill. "You raised your cursed claw, you made the bet!''

The beast was in no mood for an argument. In one smooth motion, it lifted the blubbery female over its shoulders and threw her into the holo-projector. The Vordon crashed through the poly-glass casing. Blood-stained shards clattered against the floor.

"We must put a stop to this insanity!" the Surfer said, tensing his legs under the table. Eros grabbed his wrist.

"Pay attention," he said quietly. Strange words, even if they came from someone as whimsical as Eros. Did this brawl have anything to do with Mentor's plight? The Surfer doubted it. Still, how else could he account for Eros's request, for the intensity of his stare? The Surfer would comply, for now at least.

Alone now, the golden-coated beast spread a set of gleaming claws and began to spin. Its manic wails echoed in the cavern-like room. Across the hall, a Badoon pilot, thin even by the standards of his people, jumped behind an upturned table and opened fire with his stunner, to no effect. Caught in its war ecstasy, the beast had become a force majeure, a whirlwind of razors and fur.

Then, just as suddenly as it had begun, the creature's rampage stopped. Its face froze in a shocked grimace; eyes wide open, jaw clenched. Where its chest had been, there now was a hole, half-a-meter in diameter. Through it the Surfer could see the diffused light of the ruined holo-projector. After a moment the beast tumbled forward, landing with a wet thud.

At first the Surfer could not discern what had happened. Then, as if reading the Surfer's mind, Eros cleared his throat and pointed at the bar. In his burly arms, Rankor cradled a steaming Nacite borer.

"Show's over!" yelled the Shi'ar. He patted the mining tool, then stored it under the bar. Almost immediately, most of the patrons righted their tables and chairs and settled back to their business. A few walked out the door, grumbling and shaking their heads; the gambling den was, in effect, closed.

During the lull, a strange being ambled through a sliding panel by the rear tables. At first glance it looked like a war robot, with pistoned legs and thick metallic arms. A plasma cannon protruded from its shoulder. The robotic illusion would have been complete had it not been for a triptych of faces that peered from its burnished helmet. One was mousy and greasy-bearded, another blue and reptilian. The third possessed a single eye, wedged in the middle of its scaly forehead. In all his travels, the Surfer had never seen anything like it.

"Jajuga! It's time to earn your pay!" Rankor snarled. "The Vordon's out of commission."

"I'll take care of it, boss," Jajuga said in a bizarre chorus of voices, three mouths offering widely varied tones. It scanned the room with all five eyes. "Who among these shall I punish?"

"Never mind that!" the bartender said and turned to serve a drink. "Just clean up the mess!" Then, as an afterthought, he looked over his shoulder and added: "And save the head! That mug'll look great under the new Skrull liqueur."

The Surfer watched Jajuga as it pulled the slumped body of the Vordon female from the holo-projector. He was fascinated by the creature: it moved fluidly, with obvious determination, and yet, their combined consciousness seemed to be in control of the robotic appendages. It functioned like a well-rehearsed choir—every turn a harmonious phrase, every shift a startling fugue.

"Eros," the Surfer began, turning to his companion, "what manner of being . . . ?"

"That," the former Avenger said, "is the reason I brought you here."

A piercing screech erupted from behind him.

"It's you!" came a sonorous wail. "After all this time, it's you!"

Eros smiled thinly. "I believe that you are being addressed."

"Norrin Radd of Zenn-La! Our name is Jajuga. You killed

our planets, and now we are going to kill you! Prepare to die!''

The Surfer's eyes widened. "Is this what ails Mentor?" he asked his comrade, and Eros merely smiled. Huffing out a long breath, the Surfer stood and faced the armament-sheathed Jajuga.

Without another word, the guardian of Rankor's Ditch started across the bar, hate burning in its features. Before it could reach the Surfer, though, Jajuga's armored shoulder slammed into a pair of Dalvian mercenaries. The thugs splashed Badoon swamp-mead on one another and turned, fuming, to find the culprit. Without a thought to Rankor's Nacite borer, the two tackled Jajuga, driving it to the sticky floor. More than a dozen patrons followed suit. Apparently, Jajuga was not well-liked at its place of employ.

His frustration growing, the Surfer waded into the melee, tossing aside aliens three times his weight. He wanted only to end this and be off, away from Eros, away from the stench of Rankor's Ditch.

When he was finally able to extricate Jajuga from the fray, he lifted the thrashing being by the harness of its exoskeleton and put it down on the shattered remnants of the holo-projector.

"You thirst for vengeance, and yet we have never met," the Surfer stated calmly. "I know nothing of you, or your people."

Jajuga's mouse-face scowled and spit on the Surfer's shining cheek.

"Of course you know nothing of my people!" This time it was the cyclops who spoke. "You never came close enough to dip your hands in the blood of your victims, you coward!"

The Surfer wiped the spit from his cheek and lowered his hands. An aching chill rose within him.

"Was your race a victim of Galactus?" he asked.

"Not of Galactus," said the reptile face, "Kyjael may have served as feed to the devourer of worlds, but it was *you*, Norrin Radd, Herald of Galactus, who guided his plow. It was *you* who doomed my people to extinction!"

"Who are you?" the Surfer demanded. Behind the bar, Rankor stared and stroked his cheek. This time he did not intend to interfere.

"Nothing but survivors!" Jajuga said in a melodious scream. "After Galactus destroyed our planets, Kyjael, Basooga, and Tartom, fate tossed us into the same stellar transport, chained together as slaves. Jarelg, Junmant, and Garalon were separate beings then. Powerless, measly, insignificant. As we sped to the Nacite mines we learned that the three of us shared an unquenchable hate, a seething desire for justice. We craved your blood, Norrin Radd! But we knew that on our own we would never achieve vengeance."

"So you became . . . this?" the Surfer asked, motioning at the creature.

"*You* turned us into this! We should have perished when the escape shuttle exploded over the Nacite mines. Only our hate for you kept us alive—even as we drifted through the cosmos, our bodies fused to the ship's bulkhead, and to one another. We endured for you!"

"I did not—" the Surfer began to explain.

"Now you will listen!" the creature screamed. "We promised ourselves that before we destroy the Silver Surfer, he shall know the full extent of his crime." And then Jajuga smiled. It was a terrible sneer, choked with loathing. All three mouths curled in unison. "Ahh, I see that your are curious, Norrin Radd. Even as you face extinction, you want to know. The answer is simple: Mentor found us. Yes, your old friend Mentor, he discovered the wreck of our ship when it was pulled into the gravitational field of Titan. But the damage to our flesh was too extensive; he couldn't separate us. And so he built this body for us—" its robotic arms spread with a pneumatic whir "—this abomination!"

As punctuation for his last word, Jajuga's exoskeleton erupted in a hail of plasma bolts, all aimed directly at the Surfer's chest. Norrin Radd was blasted the length of the room. He crashed into the mirror above the bar and landed hard, shattering bottles and alien skulls beneath his impenetrable skin.

Despite his power, and the durability of his physical form, the Surfer was in pain.

The Surfer let loose with a blast of the Power Cosmic, moderated so he would only stun the fused cyborg. As he attacked, he cried, "While pursuing me, did you never hear the details of my own life? Did it never occur to you that I, too, might be a victim of Galactus?"

The Surfer's blast had been deflected by a force shield emitted from its exoskeleton, but Jajuga was knocked off its feet nevertheless. It rose immediately, the Surfer's words apparently having even less effect than his blast.

"We've heard it before, Surfer. You were only following orders! We're told that you're a hero now, the sentinel of the spaceways. But the spirits of our three peoples cry for justice. It ends now, assassin. One way or another."

Jajuga fired on the Surfer again, even more force behind the blast, every ounce of energy its exoskeleton could muster focused on a single goal. But the Surfer would not be taken by surprise again. He unleashed a bolt of energy that met Jajuga's blast in the center of the bar. The explosion blew out the roof and buckled the floor of Rankor's Ditch. The fusion of the opposing forces was not static, however. As the Surfer increased his power, the tiny supernova moved toward Jajuga, carving a trench in its wake.

A distressed grin cut across Jajuga's cyclopean face as fear filled the eyes of its "brothers."

"The humorous thing is, before this fateful evening we had all but surrendered our quest," the merged aliens said with a cynical, unified laugh. "We traveled back and forth across the galaxy searching for you, missing you by weeks, days, once by a matter of minutes."

Jajuga had to squint, so close had the supernova come.

"It isn't fair!" it screamed.

The pain of its words overwhelmed the Surfer's rage. His temper was extinguished. In his time as Herald of Galactus, he had led the world-devourer to innumerable planets, many of which had been populated by sentient beings. The Surfer had felt little compunction about his duties until he was shaken from his walking nightmare by the tenderness and courage of a handful of Terrans: the Fantastic Four of the planet Earth. Only later did he learn that when Galactus had bestowed upon him the Power Cosmic, his master had also tampered with his conscience.

He was not at fault. And yet, that could never assuage his feelings of responsibility. Nor would it quell the fire of hate that burned within his accuser, within all the souls he had helped condemn. *It isn't fair,* Jajuga had cried.

"You're right," said the Surfer.

He put his hands in the air, a gesture of acceptance, and was overtaken by Jajuga's beam. Driven to his knees, the Surfer was buffeted by wave after wave of force, as his amazed executioner drew gradually closer.

(No! Fight back!) A voice filled his ears. No, not his ears, it was his own voice, hissing in the chaos of his mind. *(You were but a pawn, not responsible for the actions of Galactus. These creatures must be made to understand. They cannot challenge the Power Cosmic!)*

Yes, the Surfer thought, *how dare they judge, those who would murder to avenge murder?*

(Precisely! You are the Silver Surfer, protector of the universe. You

are needed. Who are these who challenge you, who dare to be your jury and executioner? Mere insects! Beetles on this dungpile of a planet! Creatures who should have died with their people those many years ago!)

But should it be I who takes their life?

(Yes, yes! Don't you see? End their miserable existence and your burden shall be lifted, your guilt assuaged. With them gone, who would remember Kyjael, or Basooga, or Tartom? Who would mourn such pitiful rocks?)

I will remember, the Surfer thought, *I will mourn.*

(You will forget, eventually. Just as you had before you met this metal monstrosity. And then, your crime shall be expurgated. What remains of the past, after all, but memories? One blast and you will be as pure as when you sacrificed yourself for Zenn-La, for Shalla Bal. One blast and you will kill that gnawing beast inside of you! One blast and . . .)

"No!" the Surfer shouted, just as reality fixed itself around him. Jajuga lay prone, its energy dissipated. The Surfer stood over the creature, hand clenching its shoulder, fist pulsing with a killing charge.

"One blast, monster!" Jajuga wheezed. "Just one blast and your genocide will be complete!"

"Never again!" the Surfer screamed. He raised his fist and released the burst of cosmic power through the wrecked ceiling. The blinding light rose into the night sky.

"The guilt is mine," he said, "mine to carry all of my days. But as long as my will is my own, as long as my soul is my own, I will not kill!"

At that moment, the bar transformed itself into a seething, foul, fetid pit of carnage, its clientele a mass of slobbering demons. Across a flaming chasm, Eros stood with hands on hips, a sickening smile playing about his lips.

"As long as your soul is your own, Norrin Radd?" Eros mused, and his utterance was the same, insinuating voice which the Surfer in his fugue had mistaken for his own.

And then he changed. His red hair lengthened, his jaw stretching to accommodate a mouthful of fangs and a forked tongue. His costume burned away to reveal flesh the color of blood, a pallor now reflected on his gleefully laughing face.

Mephisto, the master of deceit, stood revealed.

"What an interesting choice of words," the demon said. "Did you like my little mystery play? I found it quite amusing, myself. It's been said I have quite the flair for the dramatic. Ah, but it seems that perhaps you sensed my hand at work here? Everybody's a critic. No matter. With each temptation, each new blow to your oh-so-noble conscience, we grow closer to the day of my victory."

"So all of this has been nothing more than a hellish illusion, a tissue of lies from the Lord of Lies, another gambit in your campaign to claim me?" the Surfer said, shaking his head in disgusted disappointment.

As the Surfer spoke, the impish humor fled Mephisto's demonic countenance. There was no amusement left in his sneer, only the purest hatred.

"Nothing so simple," Mephisto answered, gesturing past the Surfer. "Your sins are no illusion."

The Surfer turned, and was sickened at the sight before him. Jajuga lay in a pool of liquid fire, impaled on a bone-white stalagmite, the flaming, skeletal hands of the damned clawing at its faces.

"Free him, Mephisto! I demand it! This contest was never meant to include others," the Surfer shouted, unable to avert his eyes from Jajuga's suffering.

Mephisto appeared suddenly, as was his custom, crouching by the cyborg.

"You promised me the Surfer, Mephisto," Jajuga screamed

now, the words merging with its cries of agony. "You swore that his life would be mine!"

"I guaranteed you the opportunity, not the kill," Mephisto said, the most reasonable of barristers. "But now you must pay my fee."

"No!" Norrin Radd screamed as Mephisto plunged his hands into Jajuga's breast, claws passing through metal and flesh without making a wound.

When Mephisto withdrew, three gossamer, shimmering forms struggled within his fists. The trio of souls that lived within Jajuga were now his.

"Never!" the Surfer screamed, blasting Mephisto with an enormous dose of cosmic power, which threw the demon backward and into the flames. Jajuga's essence slipped from Mephisto's grasp, and shot back toward its host.

"I will not have a single innocent soul damned on my account!" the Surfer declared, as Mephisto rose to face him.

A torrent of hellfire flew from the demon lord's talons, blinding the Surfer momentarily. He unleashed another cosmic blast in return, but was well aware, from their many previous encounters, that they were too evenly matched. Any physical battle between them must end in stalemate.

Jajuga cried out in ecstasy as its souls returned. Mentally summoning his board even as he buffeted Mephisto with wave after wave of power, the Surfer knelt and slid Jajuga's broken form from the stalagmite that had speared it. His board appeared and he stepped on, holding the cyborg. With a final blast, he flew toward the ceiling of flame that capped Mephisto's lair.

The Silver Surfer knew that by saving Jajuga, he guaranteed that the being would continue its vendetta. Someday they would face one another again, and who could be certain of the outcome? But what other choice did he have? These souls, which had once been innocent, were tainted in part because of his actions.

The board thrust through the infernal barrier, and as he emerged, the Surfer heard a mad, shrill cackling at his feet. Looking down, he saw that the last illusion had been torn away. Jajuga was no longer. In its place was a minor demon, who burst into flame and dissipated into the ether of space.

"Damn you, Mephisto!" the Surfer cried. Then, like venom, the voice of Mephisto seeped into his mind.

(Slowly I poison your soul), Mephisto laughed. *(It is a game for me, Norrin Radd, more of amusement than consequence. For you see, it is a game that I'm destined to win. I can play it forever. Can you?)*

"Ah, Mephisto," the Surfer said aloud, shaking his head with a sudden, comforting realization, "you have soothed me more than you know. My guilt remains, as I believe it always will. But a part of me will always know that I am not responsible for my actions as the Herald of Galactus. Otherwise my soul would be tainted already, of no interest to a purist such as you."

In his mind, the Surfer could feel the chill of the demon lord's fury.

(You may run as long and as far as you like, Norrin Radd. But one day, your path will lead you back to my domain.)

(I shall be waiting.)

GODHOOD'S END

SHARMAN DiVONO

Illustration by Jordan Raskin

The Silver Surfer felt the cosmic pulse of boundless space with his whole being and knew that something was wrong.

Only a moment before, he'd thrilled to the pleasure of his solitary cruise toward the center of a particularly beautiful stellar cluster with its suns burning with youth and vitality. Many were orbited by planets already formed and cooled for tens of millions of years, and by gas giants in vibrant colors which identified the contents of their upper atmospheres.

But his enjoyment—and his peace of mind—had been destroyed, abruptly, by the dreaded sound of an irregular beat of a nuclear heart. A stellar arrhythmia.

It was a terminal condition.

The Surfer easily pinpointed a blue-white sun, one of a cluster of young stars near the center of a graceful spiral arm, as the source of the sound. Premature death was tragic for a star so young and full of promise, he thought. This was an impending tragedy that merited closer examination.

In the time it took the thought to form, the surfboard beneath his feet responded, crossing the vast interstellar distance to the sun. In mere moments, the Surfer was maneuvering deftly through the powerful eddies and currents of its solar wind.

He counted five planets in the system; five lesser siblings born of the same mother of explosions as the star itself, and which, from his angle of approach, were spread out before him in a magnificent and colorful array. Each was a sovereign in its orbit and lord over multiple moons . . .

. . . and each was also a hapless, doomed prisoner of the defective star, destined to suffer a grim and predictable fate, the Surfer reminded himself, though it might take anywhere from a few thousand to a few tens of thousands of years for the end to finally come. The end for the planets, that is, not the star. Its end would come in a few million years.

The three inner planets were little more than globs of

heavy elements with outer shells of dried mud. They were worlds baked barren in their infancy, and the Surfer looked past them and was attracted by the spectacular deep blue color of the fourth planet which testified to its thick atmosphere of methane gas. It possessed moons, but it also had intricate rings of sand and rock, the remains of asteroids and moons pulled apart and pulverized by powerful, wrenching gravitational and tidal forces. The Surfer looked down through the atmosphere of the gas giant to its pockmarked surface, scanning for signs of life. Finding none, he turned his attention to the fifth planet, a harlequin by comparison with the others because of its multicolored bands of atmospheric ammonia, methane, oxygen, hydrogen, and hydrogen sulfide. The board, again obeying his thoughts, took him down to the surface.

Upon entering the atmosphere and descending through the gaseous layers to find certain concentrations of gaseous hydrogen and oxygen at the lower altitudes, the Surfer was not surprised—nor was he disturbed—to find the rocky surface of the planet and the waters of its oceans teaming with organic life. However, he was disturbed to see the kinds of hand-fabricated structures, widely scattered over the land masses, and the types of coast-hugging sailing vessels that attested to the presence of *intelligent* organic life.

Indeed, the scars on the land from the open-pit mining of coal and copper and the clouds of smoke-polluted air testified to primitive smelting techniques practiced on a planet-wide scale. The civilizations of this world had learned how to exploit some of the planet's natural resources. It appeared that, independently of one another, they had developed a measurable degree of metal-working capability. They were at a period of development in which primitive city-states ruled geographic areas and went to war with each other using crude bronze weapons in brute physical contests where bloody hand-to-hand combat decided victory or defeat.

Ruins in the high mountains below him were evidence that such an incident had recently taken place, and a feeling of anxiety welled up in the Silver Surfer. Time was slipping away for these people! If only they could be made to realize what a waste of valuable time, resources, and life wars were.

He swept low for a better view of the complete destruction of what had obviously been a great city, and he noted with surprise how the solid stone blocks of the casmate walls and battlements had been shattered as though by extreme heat. The stone shards had been through a firestorm. Something was wrong with this picture, and the incongruity temporarily pushed all the Surfer's other thoughts aside. Every weapon of destruction had its grim signature, and the scars left by the discharge of plasma and laser weapons were clearly out of place here.

Rann of the people of Kteris-Aken, the great walled city of the Kteris Valley, held the polished metal hand mirror up so she could see the reflection of her back in the large mirror propped up behind her. She watched her attendant apply the last dabs of the paint made from the powder of the soft yellow metal to the elaborate, multicolored design rendered on her shoulder and upper dorsal plates. She was nervous and, despite all her efforts to relax, the hand holding the mirror was trembling. Today, of all days, her makeup had to be perfect. Every part of her natural facial, head, and body armor not hidden by an accessory or a garment had to be so decorated. For her to appear otherwise in public was unciv-ilized, especially now that she was married to the God.

A pang of anxiety accompanied the thought, and she took a deep breath to calm herself. When the attendant looked at her questioningly, she managed a wan smile and made an impatient gesture to the woman to finish her work. A glance at her reflection in the mirror showed her that the sharp intake of breath resulted in several bad brush strokes, but overall it was a satisfactory job. Unfortunately, the lighting inside a military camp tent was not the best for applying makeup. She couldn't help comparing her current crude nomadic living conditions with her family's quarters in the eastern wall of Kteris-Aken, where she'd felt secure in the privacy of her own room, among her own possessions.

She had to suppress such nostalgic thoughts, however. They only served to fuel her anxieties about the present and the future. Everything was different now. The people had always worshipped the gods of the rain, the gods of the wind, and the gods of the soil, but one day this God had come down from the heavens and had quickly proved that he was God over all the others. He was now among the people as a living God. She was a sacrifice to him, dead to her family, and she too thought of herself as dead. Even the impending siege of Gataris-Aken was merely another adventure in her grim new afterlife. It had been thus since the year began.

This year would go down in history as the year of the three miracles: the appearance of the God was the first; the second was that the world was now the guardian of seven moons instead of the six it had shepherded through the night sky since the people could remember; and the third miracle was that the people still existed at all.

The God had appeared first at Obaisis-Aken, the city of the far mountains. Though she had not been a witness to the city's destruction and the annihilation of its people, the tales brought to Kteris-Aken by the first newscarriers of the conditions in which the corpses were found made it clear that there was a new and excruciating form of death in the world.

Still, after hearing such tales, the city leaders had not yet been afraid. Was not Kteris-Aken the most technologically advanced civilization in the world? Their war machines could accurately deliver an impressive variety of lethal projectiles on distant targets, thus preventing the high number of war casualties that had been of concern since the discovery of metalworking and the invention of weapons capable of piercing natural armor.

Bsiris-Aken, the great trading city on the coast of the Bsiris Sea, had been next. Again, the New Death had been used to cut the inhabitants down as if they were no more than blades of grass before a scythe.

When the God had appeared before the gates of Kteris-Aken, the city leaders had marched out at the head of an army of three thousand of the best warriors. They had had the best possible weaponry, backed by the city's own formidable defense system, but they did not get the chance to fight. The God destroyed them with a wave of his hand. Nothing could harm him. He beat the city into submission in a matter of a few moments.

Yet the God had spared the people of Kteris-Aken. Try as she might, she could not fathom the divine whim that led to this action.

Her chief obligation now was to avoid making any mistakes that would humiliate or endanger her people. If only she knew for certain how not to displease or anger the God. If only she could get over the initial terror she always experienced at the sight of him. He was not repulsive to look at, but he was more massive and stronger-limbed than even the largest warrior males of her race. His skin was a pale pinkish yellow, and he was without natural protective armor of any kind—though he needed none, it seemed, for no weapon could penetrate his flesh.

She heard a flourish of trumpets outside the tent and the sound of running footsteps. Then came the clatter of weapons and armor of a thousand warriors hurrying into their battle formations, followed by the ponderous groan of the catapult, and the battering ram and siege tower being pulled forward.

However, it was all for show. The might of the soldiers and their war machines was nothing compared to the power the God wielded with a slight flick of his finger on the device he always carried in his right hand. The purpose of the war machines and the soldiers was to carry out the actual work of sacking the city. The God had a fondness for the yellow metal and the colored stones used to embellish clothing and jewelry. If that's what pleased him, the people were more than happy to give him all he wanted. It was easy enough to obtain more.

The attendant pulled open the flap of the tent and Rann stepped out into the melee. She took a few steps toward the gilded chair which would carry her to the battlefield on the shoulders of twelve attendants. However, when she raised her eyes and saw the God watching her, her courage deserted her. Her knees buckled, and she sank to the ground and prostrated herself. So intense had been the rush of fear that she now felt physically weak. She needed those few seconds with her body pressed to the ground to recover her composure.

"Arise, woman," she heard the God say to her in a bored tone; then, in a louder voice he shouted, "Everyone arise, for you are the chosen people of your God, and today you will behold his power!"

Rann could not mistake the sarcasm in his tone when he said the words, and it sent a feeling of dread through her and stiffened her resolve. Under no circumstances must the God become displeased with the people of Kteris-Aken.

From the air, the Silver Surfer saw the glint of gold as the sunlight struck the massive gates and the battlements of the walled fortress city which was the only sign of civilization on

the broad plain below him. What drew his attention, however, was the activity before the gates, for an army was laying
siege to the city. The soldiers on the city's battlements were
operating huge cauldrons of boiling oil, and near them, archers in hard leather armor which protected the upper parts
of their bodies stood ready. Other soldiers held long poles
to push away any scaling ladders that might be used against
them.

The attacking force was surprisingly small. No more than
a thousand troops were marching against the main gates of
the city. The soldiers wore ornate gold and silver helmets
with jewel-encrusted grotesque face plates, and their bodies
were protected by burnished armor that reflected the sunlight. They carried a statue depicting a person—presumably
a ruler, perhaps even a deity—before them. Next to the
statue, atop a golden throne resting on a bed of flowers and
carried by a dozen attendants in white toga-like garments,
rode a beautiful native female, semi-nude and bedecked in
colorful body paint, precious metal, and jewels. Behind them
rolled an impressive array of siege weapons.

The city's defenders cursed and shouted insults from the
battlements while the attackers shrieked and screamed in return. The pattern was always the same, the Surfer observed
grimly: destruction and death would follow, and in the
cosmic scheme of things, in one hundred of the planet's
years, it wouldn't matter which side triumphed. Both the
dead and their cause would be forgotten.

There was something odd about the statue, the Surfer
noted. It was the costume. Unlike the garb of the others, it
resembled the type of uniform worn by space travelers to
protect them from the harsh vacuum of space. Suddenly, all
his suspicions were confirmed as the statue moved and directed a beam of plasma energy towards the city's gates. The

ornate metal barriers disintegrated amid a flash of light, heat, and smoke.

Interstellar space had its scavengers, its buzzards and carrion-eaters—aliens that homed in on doomed worlds. This alien was no fool, and certainly no weakling. He was alone on the surface because he needed no others to help him conquer and plunder it. Where was his spaceship? The Surfer hadn't spotted it on his way to the planet's surface, but it had to be nearby.

Before the alien and his forces could move through the opening in the wall where the gates had stood, the Surfer glided in front of them and blocked their way. Standing stabilized and motionless on his board a few feet above their heads, he held out his arms to arrest their forward motion, and said simply, "Hold."

Awestruck, the native warriors fell to their knees and touched their foreheads to the sand. The bearers of the alien and his consort also lost their nerve, and quickly and unceremoniously lowered their burdens roughly to the ground. The Surfer could hear their murmurs, "a statue of silver that walks like a man," and "he must be a God, too . . ."

The Surfer frowned at the sea of bowed heads before him. In view of the situation, he should have expected this reaction. However, it still annoyed him. The irony was that these people would perish on the spot from fright if they ever beheld the awful splendor of the mighty Galactus—and Galactus was definitely not a god. The alien and the native woman were looking at him, and he smiled back at them, satisfied that, for the moment, his "miraculous" appearance had foiled the alien's plans.

"I recognize you, Silver Surfer, though I have not met you till now," the alien said, rising from his chair, and the Surfer detected the crackle of energy from his forcefield body armor as he straightened to his full height and stepped to the ground. "We are both space wanderers and should be friends," the alien continued. "There are enough riches here to satisfy the most hearty of appetites, so let us now join forces."

"Where are you from, and who else knows of your visit here?" the Surfer asked, keeping a watchful eye on the alien's movements and, in particular, on the hand holding the plasma gun.

"I am alone," the alien answered smoothly. "In my wanderings, I detected the signature of a foundering star and came here to investigate, as you probably also did. I chanced upon this planet, rich beyond my wildest dreams in gold, silver, and other precious metals. These will make me very rich back home." The alien burst out in a hearty laugh and walked over to caress the young female at his side, possessively. "Though, there is much to be said for remaining here." His expression became crafty as he added, "I have told no one of my rich find, so why should we not share our good fortune together in peace?"

"It's obvious that you have been posing as a deity, my friend. It is among the oldest con games in the universe," the Surfer said.

"In a place like this, it works every time," the alien responded. "I didn't start out to use it. At first I just took what I wanted. These people are doomed anyway. But, I got bored after awhile. I needed an amusing pasttime, so I decided to employ a little showmanship. I like the feeling of power. It's exhilarating. I'm even thinking of taking the female with me when I leave."

"And, when you grow bored with her, you'll desert her on some faraway planet," the Surfer said matter-of-factly.

The alien shrugged. "You have it all figured out."

"It is an old story."

"Then, what more can I say except that . . . God happens,"

the alien said, shrugging. He displayed a wide grin which the Surfer knew was meant to be cleverly disarming, and waved his plasma gun for emphasis as he added, "Don't be fooled into thinking that my generosity is a sign of weakness. I'll do battle and kill you if I must."

The Silver Surfer stepped down from his board and walked toward the alien. "If you know who I am, you must know that, not only will I not avail myself of your generous offer, but I cannot stand idly by and allow you to plunder this planet and exploit these people."

Beneath the theatrical grin, both anger and fear registered on the alien's face, and he stepped back until he was in the midst of his warriors. However, rather than leaping to their feet to shield him, they remained on their knees with their heads in the sand in supplication. "Arise, you worthless cowards, and help defend your God," he growled at them.

"Put your weapon away and prepare to leave this planet," the Surfer said.

The alien answered the threat with action, bringing the plasma gun into position and firing off a lethal salvo of concentrated energy. However, as fast as he was with the weapon, the Silver Surfer was faster. He'd anticipated just such a reaction and he erected a shield which absorbed the blast and dissipated the plasma energy harmlessly.

It was as if the blast was a signal to the warriors, and, much to the Surfer's annoyance, they scrambled to their feet and ran in all directions, allowing the alien to take advantage of their confusion and to use them as a shield. The Surfer defended himself against another salvo from the plasma gun, then he got an opportunity for a clear shot at the alien. He channeled the energy from his body and directed the beam at his assailant, striking him in the torso. For the first time, fear showed on the alien's face as sparks sizzled and leaped from the beam's impact point followed by a visible surge of current that traveled across the surface of his body armor. The burst of energy had exceeded the armor's capacity.

Again the Silver Surfer fired a burst of energy, and this time the armor's energy field collapsed for a few seconds, then sputtered on again. Then the Surfer had to defend himself, as the alien fired a series of rapid pulses from his plasma gun to cover his retreat.

Suddenly, a shadow fell over the plain and the Surfer looked up to see that it was caused by a large misshapen object that was now descending through the clouds. It looked like—and was—a small asteroid, but its controlled descent indicated that it had been hollowed out and fitted with maneuvering rockets and a stardrive.

An inexpensive way to build a spacecraft, it was an identifiable technology, and he knew from whence it had come. It was not a product of the alien's home planet, but had instead been borrowed, purchased, or perhaps stolen. Most importantly, he knew that it was incapable of long-range interstellar travel at practical speeds. It was a fighter ship, and it had to have come from a mother ship somewhere in the immediate area.

The alien's "bride" was staring up at the descending craft with an innocent wonder that might soon prove fatal, if he did not act quickly. Grabbing her firmly but gently around the waist, the Surfer leaped onto his silver board which sped them quickly out of the craft's landing zone.

However, when it was but a few feet from the ground, the craft stopped its descent and hovered.

"I'll get you for this, Surfer," the alien shouted as a tube of red light descended from the underbelly of the ship and enveloped him. His body seemed to come apart and disintegrate within it, then the tube of light was withdrawn back inside the ship. The craft rose rapidly upward and disappeared into the clouds.

When the board again touched ground, the Surfer released his hold on the female. But, instead of running away as he expected, she lingered, regarding him with a mixture of curiosity and awe. He looked around and saw that they were alone on the broad plain, and, when he glanced up at the walls of the city, he saw that the defenders had also fled in terror.

He wondered if he should try to explain about the alien. "Each of the points of light you see in the night sky is a sun," he said. "Many of the suns have planets—worlds like your own world. The alien . . . the 'god' . . ."

To his surprise, the woman nodded in comprehension. "I will be forever grateful to you, Silver Surfer—if that is really your name—for the people have suffered at the hand of that being who came not from heaven, but only from the stars," she said.

Impressed with her poise and intelligence, he said, "Let that be a lesson to you in the future. A true god has no need of plasma guns, or spaceships, or other such devices."

The woman looked at the silver surfboard thoughtfully, then she smiled, and the Surfer was struck by the beauty of her face and form. A humanoid, she carried herself gracefully and athletically upright. Her head was well-shaped, the facial features had a symmetry which he found attractive. Her brain case was protected not by hair, but by an intricate mosaic of mottled brown patches or "plates" of a type of hardened, callused skin that served as natural armor. This same armor extended across her shoulders, down her arms and along her spine, and, he suspected, over all her vital organs, though her skillfully draped and pinned garment hid most of her torso and her lower body from his scrutiny. A split in the floor length skirt revealed the powerful thigh and calf muscles of her legs and her small four-toed feet, and these, too, were protected by armor, as were her delicate hands.

Four long fingers and an opposing thumb meant ample capability for rapid technological advancement—if these people were given the proper time to develop and were not extinguished in their prime!

The light tan skin between the armor plates was supple, but tough and not easily scraped or pierced. When the nictitating membranes passed lazily over her half-closed eyes, it gave her a sultry, sensual look. By certain standards, she would be considered very attractive.

"If you are not a God," she asked, "what are you?"

"A space traveler. A wanderer."

"I am Rann of Kteris-Aken. I was the bride of the God. You drove him away, but for me, nothing can be as it was. I think that now I would like to go with you."

The last thing the Surfer wanted or needed was a bride. "He's gone for now," he said, "but we haven't heard the last of your god, I'm afraid."

"Yes, he has vowed revenge upon you. What will you do?"

"I have not yet decided. I have a more important reason for coming here. After that, I may go in search of him."

"Perhaps you will find him on the seventh moon."

"Why there?"

"Until the God came, there were only six moons."

"Of course," the Surfer responded, annoyed with himself. "I should have realized. That should prove to you that I am not a god. I am neither all-knowing nor omnipotent."

The woman reacted with an amused chuckle. The warmth of it touched the Surfer. He did not want to be involved with these people, yet now he was involved. By coming here and intervening in a bad situation, he had rescued them from their own ignorance, so he felt responsible for them. It was an emotional trap that he'd fallen into many times before, and he was feeling the familiar anxiety that went along with it.

The concept of time was meaningless in the universe, except to intelligent, sentient organic life forms, who needed some means by which to measure their all-too-brief existence. How many orbits would the harlequin planet complete around the star before its nuclear "beat" changed to a terminal rhythm and all life on the planet's surface began to die?

Having been the Herald of Galactus, he was forever burdened with memories of the destruction of countless worlds. Thus, when he visualized the beginning of the end for the hearty residents of the fifth planet, a representative of which was now regarding him with a mixture of attraction, curiosity, and awe, he shuddered.

They would have to move or perish, that was certain, but to where? It had been the Silver Surfer's experience that habitable planets were already inhabited. Uninhabited planets would be that way because they were inhospitable—because nothing could live there. Therefore, they must take over a planet from another life form and, in doing so, destroy it or be destroyed in the process.

Intelligent life was by nature nomadic. Groups of beings on a single planet always pushed others from territory to gain living space for themselves. They were, in turn, pushed by the next wave of territorial invaders. It had always been thus since the beginning of time, not necessarily by the physically strong, but by the mentally alert and knowledgeable.

Rather than his trying to bring these beings bad tidings, it might be better that they not be made aware of what would happen to them a few thousand years hence, until they were in a better position to do something about it. However, by then, it would be impossible to move the entire population. The responsibility weighed heavily on his shoulders, for he alone was in the position to plan a strategy that would determine whether these people would survive or not.

It had been to save his own planet from destruction that he had been forced to become the Silver Surfer; to save another that he allowed himself to be imprisoned for many years. Though he thought it odd that he should feel such angst over the predictive and prophetic fate of this planet, he realized that as long as some part of his life on Zenn-La was still within him, his compassion, his sense of values, his soul, would not die. He would remain vulnerable to the plight of the less fortunate.

This included the humanoid beings occupying this planet who were, unfortunately, engaged in uncooperative pursuits against each other, blissfully unaware that in the long run their efforts would be useless, unless they learned to become civilized and to cooperate for the common good.

Notwithstanding that, he had succeeded in stopping an advancing horde in their tracks and averting a bloody battle. Perhaps, if he just sowed the first seeds of cooperation to develop a nucleus for the direction of the future development of the planet, it would be of some help. He could seize this opportunity to turn them from the plundering psychology of their alien god and set them on the paths of cooperation and survival.

Even as he entertained the thought, the Silver Surfer knew that would not be enough, and he felt the weight of the monumental task he was undertaking. How could he instill into these people the necessity for advancing their civilization, to develop advanced forms of space travel so that their progeny could continue to exist by finding another planet, orbiting another sun? For these beings to grasp that concept now was beyond their comprehension.

He was also mindful that, even if one or two of the civilizations could develop the capability to visit the nearby planets during the succeeding centuries, it would take half a millennium at least, after that, for all the peoples on this planet to think of themselves as one people with the common goal of salvation. Then, before climatic conditions began to change because of the faltering star, it would take hardy souls with infinite courage to leave the womb of their birth and venture forth into the unknown, knowing that they could never return.

Were these people up to such a monumental task? If there was no chance for them to save themselves, would it be more merciful if they didn't know of their impending doom?

Even as he pondered these questions, something inside him would not let him give up on them.

Remembering the scattered enclaves of civilization that he'd passed over during his initial survey of the planet, the Silver Surfer pondered to whom, and how, he should give his warning. He could tell the woman and her people, but if he selected only one settlement, would all of the other civilizations on the planet eventually get the message and pass it on to subsequent generations or, after many generations, would it become mythologized and lose all meaning?

How could he leave an important message for an entire planet that was meant to be picked up and acted upon by future generations in a few thousand years?

The woman's excited voice interrupted his reverie.

"Look, Silver Surfer! A delegation comes from the city. They are expecting to meet with the leaders of Kteris-Aken—the leaders of my people—but there are no leaders. The God saw to that."

"That could be a problem."

"Will you talk to them?"

"I am simply a passer-by. You should greet them."

"Me? But I have no authority."

"You were the wife of the god. You have the stature and the authority, if you choose to exercise them."

Before she could protest further, he turned towards the

approaching natives again, and noted that a female, settled on a bower of flowers within a golden chariot and pulled by a group of young males, had been included in the party.

Everything had happened so quickly, he wasn't sure what these people from the city had seen, but there had been no bloodshed and very little violence in this sudden change of command. He hoped that, with his help, the woman beside him could cement a peace between their two warring tribes before the alien returned to take his revenge.

When they were in vocal range, the leader of the delegation, an elderly male, approached with arms outstretched and hands held with open palms. The Surfer smiled in welcome and indicated for the woman beside him to do the same.

"Oh powerful lord and God of Kteris-Aken, this is our most precious gift to you," the leader called out to the Surfer as they drew closer. "She is my most treasured and beautiful daughter. Take her for your wife, and let us join the people of Kteris-Aken in worshipping you."

"Do not call me god," the Surfer answered. "I am a mortal who serves the Queen of Kteris-Aken."

To the Surfer's surprise, the old man frowned. "In what way do you serve the Queen? Are you her mate?"

"I am Rann, leader of the people," the woman said, regally. "The Silver Surfer comes here from another world. The false God whom he has chased from this planet is also from another world. He wanted the riches of our planet. He cared nothing about us except to fuel his selfish ends. Because he was evil, he caused us to attack you. We now ask you to embrace us as sisters and brothers and let us each return to out separate cities as friends."

The old man nodded sagely. "We desire a hereditary bond. A symbol that will ensure that future generations of both our peoples will become a new people." He turned and motioned to a tall warrior in his prime to step forward. "This is my son, great Queen," he announced proudly.

The old man was thinking of future generations. He did not know of the disaster hanging over them—and yet there was an inherent wisdom in his words, the seed of an idea that the Surfer hadn't considered before.

"I wish to think over your proposition," Rann said.

"We will return to the city and await your decision," the leader replied.

As they watched the delegation head back through the destroyed gates of the city, the Surfer said, "I came here out of curiosity, but I stayed because I wanted to save future generations of your people."

"The God said we were doomed. Is that the nature of your message?"

The Surfer nodded. "I bring a warning of a disaster that will strike your world several thousand years in the future, when your sun begins to die and thus ceases to be a source of life."

"The leader of the city wondered if you were my mate. You could stay here and rule with me as my consort, Silver Surfer. Together, we could spread your message of warning to all the people in the world."

"Staying with you would not be . . . displeasing, but in the end, it would be a selfish act on my part, and your people would suffer for it. However, the old one's words have given me an idea, and I know that it is the only way to deliver my message, but we don't have much time. We must gather all of the women in your camp, and as many of the women and female children from the city as we can bring to this spot quickly."

"It will be night, soon, and it will be difficult to gather the people, then."

"It is necessary, so that I may . . . counsel you." He grasped her and pulled her onto the board with him. "Let us make haste, as I'm certain that the alien will return for his revenge. I want to complete my mission before then."

The near side of the seventh moon filled the asteroid fighter's main view screen as, seething with pent-up rage, the alien strode onto the bridge and pulled the craft's pilot out of his seat. He took over the controls and checked the instrument readings.

"B-but, m-my lord, we're perfectly aligned with docking bay five, just as you ordered," the pilot stammered fearfully.

"I can see that, you gibbering sack of tentacles," the alien fired back at the creature, who was one of the motley band of cutthroats, pirates, and adventurers he'd recruited from throughout the galaxy to serve as his crew.

Initially, he'd chosen to put his moon in a high parking orbit around the planet, so as not to attract the attention of any passers-by—especially any of his fellow scavengers—to his real source of treasure. But, in the end, the Surfer had blundered into the situation and had spoiled everything, anyway.

He blessed the day he'd purchased the big "moon ship" and its complement of asteroid fighters from the people whose specialty was the technology to quickly and cheaply tunnel into a small moon or an asteroid and fit it with a stardrive. The surface rock served as the perfect form of shielding for deep-space travel in or out of hyperdrive, and the ships were impervious to micrometeoroid strikes.

The asteroid fighter descended past the rim of the number five crater, and the alien checked the telemetry and assured himself that it was still properly aligned for the docking bay. He'd been kicked off his planet and humiliated by the Silver Surfer, and he wasn't going to take it.

"What are you going to do, now?" the pilot asked, as if reading his mind.

"As soon as I disembark, prepare for launch turnaround," he answered. "I intend to take us out of our present orbit."

Yes, the Silver Surfer was going to pay for the humiliation he'd suffered, and the inhabitants of the harlequin planet were shortly going to be terrified out of their wits. He would put the giant spacecraft into a low orbit, so they would suffer the earthquakes, tidal waves, and other natural disasters on the planet's surface from the wrenching tidal and gravitational forces caused by the moon's proximity. Then, he would launch the fighters and annihilate every living thing. They deserved it.

It was twilight when the Silver Surfer completed his work on the structure of his "genetic time capsule." Once he had established in his own mind that the only sure way to guarantee the survival of the people on the harlequin planet was not through indoctrination, but through instinct—call it desire, ambition, drive, or whatever—to leave their solar system, the next step had been to design a working model. He was now satisfied that he had made no errors in the encoding of his customized gene.

Uppermost in his mind since conceiving the whole idea had been the thought that the alien had taken over this planet to plunder it, and he would be back to claim what he considered his prize. How much time the Surfer had before this would come to pass, he could only guess.

As the number of people that he would be able to implant was limited, he could only consider implantation of the females because of technological conditions. He was counting on their sense of responsibility as the childbearers and nurturers to be a dominant characteristic among the group as compared to males, whose more hazardous activities and irresponsible pasttimes resulted in much higher mortality rates.

From what he'd seen of their war technology, he had a strong faith that, well within two thousand years, the inhabitants of the harlequin planet would develop a space technology and achieve a rudimentary orbital capability. That was a baby step on the path to interstellar travel and the means for escaping from this doomed planet and saving themselves, so he needed to inculcate within them the desire to fulfill that need for survival. They would have the innate desire to leave this place and not look back.

He and Rann had rounded up nearly three hundred and fifty women and female children from the camp. There were prostitutes among them, the kind that always followed an army, but they were of childbearing age. They had coaxed another five hundred females into venturing out from the city and to the spot on the plain he had chosen. However, new complications were threatening to make the execution of his plan difficult. A windstorm was blowing across the plain, and, during the last hour, a series of earthquakes had made the ground shake with increasing violence. The sudden onset of these planetary disturbances gave him an uneasy feeling, and he found himself glancing frequently up at the darkening sky for the answer to what was happening. The planet's thick atmosphere diffused the light from the stars, but he could count the moons, and he was reminded of what Rann had told him about the seventh one. Indeed, each time he glanced up, one of the pale orbs had moved a little further in the night sky, as if under its own power. Too, it was perceptibly larger than it had been just an hour ago.

Rann had to employ her most persuasive words to keep the women from dispersing to seek shelter from the blinding wind-driven sand and the shaking ground beneath their feet. Now, they were waiting for him in a restless and disorganized group as he approached and addressed them.

"I've gathered you here because I want to do something

to improve your lives and the lives of your progeny. Please stand where you are, and close your eyes."

When he was finished, he said, "At present your numbers are few. In the future, there will be millions of your descendants roaming this planet who will benefit from having you as their ancestors . . ."

Suddenly, a streak of plasma energy hit the ground near him. The women screamed and ran as other blasts hit in quick succession nearby.

The Surfer noticed Rann trying to reach him in the chaos. At that moment, an asteroid fighter became visible as it descended through the atmosphere to make a second strafing run, and the Surfer struck it with a well-placed burst of energy that caused it to disintegrate in a ball of orange fire.

Sweeping Rann up in his arms he said, "The alien is back. It's me he's after, so I must go now. Remember—and pass on the memory of this battle to your children and your children's children—that this is not a contest of the gods. It is not a product of the supernatural, no sorcery or magic are involved. It is science, and someday your people will also have that knowledge."

He released his hold on the woman, but she threw her arms around him in a tight embrace to hold him back. "Will you come back when you have defeated him?"

"I am afraid not," the Surfer said, stroking her cheek. With that, he mounted his board, and departed.

Once in outer space, the Surfer saw eight more asteroid fighters massing for an attack. Behind them was a small rogue moon, and he identified it as both the alien's ship and the source of the planetary disturbances. It was spheroid, and approximately ten kilometers in diameter. Technically speaking, it was a giant asteroid, but it had enough mass to wreak havoc with the planet's gravitational equilibrium if it got much closer—and it was definitely being guided into a lower orbit around the planet.

He maneuvered to reach the moon by outflanking the fighters, but they broke formation and surrounded him. Suddenly, the Silver Surfer was enveloped in the white hot flash of their simultaneously fired plasma beams. The galactic glaze covering his body absorbed much of the lethal power of the beams, though he was stunned, momentarily, by the sheer force of the plasma field. When he recovered, he saw that the fighters had left him for dead, and were speeding toward the planet ahead of their mother ship.

The Surfer swiftly overtook them. Sailing directly into their midst, he fired randomly at them, destroying his targets in balls of orange fire, and leaving their group in disarray. The surviving fighters, four in all, broke off their attack on the planet to pursue him. They had obviously been ordered to divert his attention while the moon, the alien's deadly juggernaut, relentlessly closed in on its target.

He did not fall prey to their strategy. As the asteroid fighters sped towards him, he wove a tight net of pure energy directly in their path. With no time to veer off their course, all four ships hit the barrier with the full force of their momentum. The rock that served as the outer hulls survived the barrier, but not so the artificial controls inside them. The ships hung lifeless in the net and, when the energy of it dissipated, they remained as hulks drifting in space.

Suddenly, every nerve in the Surfer's body cried out in agony as he was blindsided by a powerful plasma beam. He collapsed onto his board, and held on while it sped him out of range. Looking in the direction of the harlequin planet, he saw the moon leaving orbit to pursue him like some crazed behemoth. His eyes also beheld the sun—the very star whose missed "beat" had first lured him here.

In that same instant, he thought of a way to use the star's

power to destroy the alien. He turned the surfboard so that its mirror-smooth surface caught the sun's light and reflected it in a tight beam upon the surface of the oncoming moon. It took only milliseconds for the solid rock at the impact point to melt, and a few seconds more for the moon to become a red ball of molten magma hurtling through space. The Surfer watched as droplets and streams of liquid rock were blown away by the force of the solar wind until there was nothing left, and, when he could see the stars clearly once more, he looked back toward the harlequin planet, and thought of Rann . . .

. . . and felt the familiar ache of loneliness that always came from leaving.

S A M B A T Y O N

DAVID M. HONIGSBERG

Illustration by Tom Morgan

The name was known by every wanderer, every pilgrim who had ever sought the desire of his or her innermost heart—Sambatyon. Its precise location varied, tale by tale, yet all said that the River Sambatyon could be found only in the Holy Land and only by those who were prepared to find it.

Norrin Radd knew the stories as well as anybody for he, too, had searched out that legendary place. It was not an obsession for him, as it was for some. Nevertheless, he longed to find it, for it was said by many that those who crossed the River Sambatyon could truly atone for their past transgressions.

He thought back on his quest as he soared through the vastness of space, the surfboard he rode upon an extension of his mind, his silver skin glinting with the light of the stars around him. He had followed scattered leads, journeyed through miles of desert, in the hopes of stumbling across the river. He had gazed down upon the remains of caravan routes and dried-out river beds, hoping that he would find the one which was, or had been, the Sambatyon. Trying to prevent himself from becoming too anxious, he had walked over trace after trace with no results at all. He could do no more than conclude that the legends of the river were just that—legends, spun by rabbi's and kabbalists throughout the ages, just one more dead end laid out for the unwary spiritual traveller.

With a thought, he turned his gleaming surfboard towards an uninhabited star system, a place he sometimes journeyed to when feeling contemplative. There was nothing to differentiate it from other, similar systems. To the Silver Surfer, though, it had a particular feel, an essence which he could not define. He had found in the past, however, that it was a place where he could let his mind wander, a place of true peace and solitude.

Following his usual path, he crossed the planar rim, gliding past the fifth planet towards the gap which lay between it and the fourth, some distance away. As he approached the midpoint between the two spheres, he stopped and sat down upon the board, dangling his feet off of the edge as he took in the grandeur of the expanses around him.

A glimmer caught his eye and he turned his head towards it. The glimmer grew brighter, became a definitive point of light not too far distant from him. As he watched, the light expanded, shifted, took on more definition. The Surfer realized that he was watching the appearance of a planet in a place where, on earlier voyages, there had never been one.

Within minutes the transformation was complete. A planet hung in space orbiting the system's sun at a distance conducive to carbon-based life. A burning desire to explore this new world consumed him. He rose to his feet, turning his thoughts, and his board, towards the shining planet.

The Surfer cautiously entered the oxygen/nitrogen atmosphere, knowing full well that any advanced civilization might have means to detect his intrusion. He remained watchful of indications that he had been noticed, that those below were working towards his destruction. He was surprised, therefore, when he passed beneath a layer of wispy clouds without sensing any alarm from the city he saw in the distance.

With a thought, he headed toward it. The city was bordered on one side by an ocean and on the other by a desert. Soon he descended close enough to make out a number of smaller cities and villages nearby, many of which were also situated on the coast.

An airship of some sort rose from the outskirts of the city, moving swiftly in his direction. It appeared to be weaponless, but Norrin Radd knew from experience that did not necessarily mean it had none. Still, he made no movements that could be interpreted as hostile, and continued his approach to the city. He watched as the airship passed him, then turned to match his speed, remaining no more than one hundred yards' distance to his right.

It soon became obvious that the ship had been sent as nothing more than a guide, an escort. When he was directly over the city he came to a complete stop and hovered a mile in the air. The airship did the same, leaving only when he allowed himself to slowly drop the remaining distance into a park in the center of the city. A wide, grassy area in the park had become filled with people. As he grew closer, he saw that the crowd consisted of both men and women, but that the women were greatly outnumbered.

He remained on his board, a few feet above the ground, still on the lookout for anything that would warn him of danger. Those gathered remained a respectful distance from him, but he could see them whispering to each other and knew that he was the cause of their guarded glances and hushed tones. He waited to see what would happen. Before long, the crowd parted to admit a man dressed in robes of gold, blue, red, and crimson. A breastplate hung from the robes, set with twelve stones of varied colors. Without a hint of hesitation, he strode toward the Surfer, the crowd parting further as he approached.

When the man reached the Surfer, he bowed in greeting. "Shalom aleichem," he said. "Peace be with you. I am Elisha, son of Malachi, of the tribe of Ephraim. In the name of the One, I welcome you to this world."

The Surfer bowed in return, but did not make any motion to get off of the board. "Thank you for your welcome, Elisha, son of Malachi. I am Norrin Radd, once of the planet Zenn-La. I am also known as the Silver Surfer." There was a stirring in the crowd, an excited murmuring. "What is this place which has appeared without warning? And what position do you hold?"

Elisha looked at him directly and said, "It is a place called Sambatyon. I am the High Priest of these people."

"I had begun to believe that Sambatyon was no more than a story, Elisha. A legend of a boiling river beyond which could be found the lost tribes of Israel. And I thought that there was no longer a need for the position of High Priest."

A wide grin spread across Elisha's face. "As long as there is a people, there is need for a High Priest." He gestured toward the crowd. "And since many people have gathered here for a very holy day, my services are required. As for the rest of what you say, you can see, Norrin Radd, that we are anything but lost. If pressed, we would have to admit that Judah and Israel are the true lost tribes. For some reason, there was no trace of them when we found ourselves here. As for myself, I can follow my lineage all the way back to our ancestor Aaron, may his name be blessed forever."

"Then you and your people were once from Earth?" the Surfer asked.

Elisha nodded. "The chronicles say little about this, I am afraid. I have been taught, though, that many years ago a priest from each of the 'Lost Tribes,' as you call them, was visited by strange dreams. They were interpreted as portents that something quite profound was to happen to those tribes and, to their credit, the priests bade their people prepare, even though they did not know what this preparation was for. One morning, all those sleeping in the camps of those ten tribes awoke to find themselves on the shore of an ocean. The priests assured everybody that this sudden transition was an act of God and, although there were those that doubted, it was soon apparent that wherever they were, it was not Earth. The city of New Jerusalem was built first and, from there, other cities and villages were founded. We now know no other home but this one. All ties between here and Earth are broken."

"But where is 'here'?" the Surfer asked. "Why have I never seen this planet before today, during all of my wanderings in this system?'' He stepped off of his board and walked toward Elisha.

Elisha stepped closer to his guest. "You are full of questions, my friend. This is as it should be, on the afternoon before the holiest of days. There is much that we all deserve to reflect upon. There are many crimes which we must answer for.''

The Surfer stepped away from Elisha, wondering how the man knew of his history. "Crimes? I have committed no crime here.''

Elisha spread his arms wide. The breastplate glittered in the afternoon sun. "We all have crimes upon our conscience, Norrin Radd. There are always things which must be atoned for. That is why this eve and the next day have been set aside. As it is commanded in the most holy books of the Law, 'On this day you shall have all your sins atoned, so that you will be cleansed. This is a law for all time.' ''

"A day of atonement,'' the Surfer muttered to himself. He looked at the High Priest, beginning to understand.

Elisha continued, "We do not desire that this planet be easily found. We have developed the means to make it entirely invisible to all who search for it. Only on this day do we drop the shields which render us undetectable, in the hopes that one or more precious searchers will have discerned our secret to join us in the rituals of purification and atonement. You are one of a small number who have found us. Whether you understand the reason or not, you have a need to be with us on this holy day.''

"What do you expect of me, then?''

"We expect naught but that you respect our traditions, Norrin Radd, and that you participate as best you can. Though you be a sojourner here, our laws regarding this day apply to you as well as to anybody else. Only those who cannot travel to New Jerusalem are exempt from the main ritual.

All, however, are commanded to observe this day as they see fit, with prayer, reflection and fasting."

The Surfer thought for a moment, then nodded to the High Priest. "I can see no reason for my refusing to join you. Besides," he added softly, "I am sure that you are right. There is no one who has not committed a crime, of some sort. Some transgressions, however, may be much more severe than those of others."

"This may be true," Elisha replied in tones which matched the Surfer's, "but there are no sins which the Lord cannot forgive if, of course, one truly desires to atone."

"In my life," the Surfer told Elisha, "I have done much which would leave my soul irreparably harmed. I have, however, been forgiven by those I have wronged, as difficult as that forgiveness was for me to ask."

"That is the first step only, Norrin Radd. You have repented for the things you have done, whatever they might be. It is important that those you have wronged have forgiven you, more important than being forgiven by the One. Tomorrow, you will be more than forgiven. You will be cleansed."

The High Priest turned to those who were gathered. "This man," he announced, "is a visitor from afar. As we have always done with strangers on this solemn day, we will welcome him into our midst so that he, too, can benefit from the blessings which the Lord will bestow upon us tomorrow. Go now, each one of you to your homes, and prepare yourselves for the ritual. I shall see to it that Norrin Radd receives as much hospitality as this poor servant can afford him."

The people nodded in response and slowly dispersed, many of them talking amongst themselves and casting glances at the Surfer as they did so. Finally, Elisha and the Surfer were alone in the park. The sun was beginning to set as Elisha indicated that his guest should follow him and led the Surfer to a conveyance which waited just outside of the park.

The next day, the Surfer was summoned by Elisha's wife, Miriam. She informed him that Elisha had left very early to prepare for the ritual and that he was to meet the priest at the northern edge of the city when he was refreshed. He thanked her and, within the hour, his surfboard floating of its own accord above and behind him, began to make his way towards the place she had indicated.

The way was not easy, as the streets were packed with pilgrims who, in accordance with the law, had come to New Jerusalem from all over Sambatyon to witness the ritual. News of the arrival of a rare traveller had been broadcast throughout the city and, as he walked, he was greeted by many who encountered him. He noted that nearly everybody wore plain white robes and that those who didn't were dressed in simple clothes. Many went barefoot.

The crowd grew thicker and thicker as the Surfer got farther north until, much against his initial wishes, he had to resort to an aerial approach, lest he find himself lost in the throngs.

From the air it was easy to find the High Priest, as there was a great deal of activity going on in a tremendous lot to the north. It was filled with a great number of vehicles, each one large enough to comfortably hold hundreds of people. Instead of using wheels, they hovered two feet above the ground on powerful but silent engines. Farther out from the city he saw what he recognized as broadcast antennae.

When he finally set down, Elisha rushed over to greet him. Unlike the previous day, when he was dressed in finery which could have befitted a king, he was clad in a white robe similar to those which the majority of the populace wore.

"Greetings, Norrin Radd. I trust that you slept well?"

"I have no need of sleep."

"I see. Well, everything here is in readiness. I am very glad that you are able to join us. I would like very much if you would ride with me when we begin."

"Ride with you? Where are we going?"

"Just outside of the city is a great desert. I'm certain that you saw it when you arrived, didn't you?"

"I did, yes."

"In accordance with the law, all who are able will travel to the desert, to the Tent of Meeting, either by foot or in one of these." He gestured to the rows of vehicles. "There they will be absolved of their sins. There shall the sins of all the people be sent to Azazel."

"I would be honored to travel with you, Elisha. There are most certainly things which I feel the need to reflect upon. If, as you say, this is a day conducive to that, I hope to find some small amount of peace through your rituals."

Elisha nodded, as if he were aware of what the Surfer spoke of. Two younger priests approached and informed Elisha that all was prepared.

"Let the people know, then," he told them. "We shall leave at once."

Speakers the Surfer hadn't noticed before came to life, solemn music breaking through the hubbub of the pilgrims. "Shalom aleichem, New Jerusalem," a rich baritone voice announced. "Greetings on this Day of Atonement." Those gathered stopped what they were doing to listen. "Our esteemed High Priest, Elisha ben Malachai, has declared that all is in readiness. The procession to the Tent of Meeting is preparing to depart from New Jerusalem. All those who intend to walk to that sacred place should begin their journey now. Any who do not wish to walk, or who are unable to do so, should make their way towards the vehicles at this time."

253

"The event is broadcast?" the Surfer asked.

"It is. There are many who are not able or, in some cases, willing, to make the journey to New Jerusalem. It is for their benefit that all of the proceedings are broadcast. I would prefer otherwise, but I am sure that those who watch from their homes feel that they are doing as much as they can to partake in the rituals."

The crowd began to move again, many bypassing the vehicles entirely, to start their walk into the desert. The doors on the vehicles opened up to accept the citizens and pilgrims who needed their services.

Elisha motioned for the Surfer to accompany him to a private vehicle located at the front of the procession and which, like the vehicles, hovered just above the ground. As they neared it, two people, a man and a woman, separated from the crowd and approached, one holding a recording device, the other a microphone. Like almost everybody else, they were dressed in white. When they reached the Surfer and the High Priest, the woman took a position between them. The speakers blared to life again.

"As reported last night, we are pleased and honored to have a visitor joining us on this holiday, the Silver Surfer. Miriam bat Nathan is with him now. We take you live to New Jerusalem. Miriam?"

"Thank you, Amos." Her words echoed over the speakers so that all could hear what was being said. "I am here, just outside of the city, with Elisha ben Malachai and our esteemed guest, the Silver Surfer. As you can see from the activity surrounding us, the procession to the tent of meeting is well under way." She turned to the Surfer. "Could you tell our viewers what brought you here yesterday?"

The interview was unexpected, and the Surfer mused that perhaps they hadn't cut as many ties with Earth as Elisha believed. He turned to face Miriam. "My appearance here is accidental, to say the least. Until yesterday, I was not aware of Sambatyon's existence. But Elisha believes that my being here is important, both to me and to the citizens of this planet, and I can see no reason to argue with him in this matter. I would also like to thank Elisha ben Malachai for his hospitality and that of his family."

"Thank you." The woman faced Elisha, who seemed uncomfortable with her appearance. As he listened to her question, he continually glanced towards the car which awaited. "Rabbi Elisha, do you have anything which you would like to tell the citizens of Sambatyon?"

Elisha smiled at Miriam and looked into the recorder. "As has been our tradition for generation after generation, we gather today to think about the past year. We think about those we have wronged, the promises we have made and broken, the things we did that we should not have done, the things we did not do that we should have done. It is my wish for all those who are here today, and all who watch from home, that the next year be for all of us a good one, a year of health, a year of good fortune and, above all, a year of peace. Now, if you will excuse me, we must be on our way."

"Of course." She faced the recorder. "This is Miriam bat Nathan outside of New Jerusalem."

The priest turned back to the vehicle as the reporter and her camera operator moved away and into the throng of pilgrims. The voice of the reporter in the desert could be heard over the speakers, but the Surfer paid little attention to what was being said.

"Open," Elisha said. Three of the four doors opened, revealing a comfortable space within. "There is more than enough room in here for your board," he told the Surfer, indicating the rear section. "You will sit up front with me, please."

The Surfer carefully placed his board into the vehicle and then sat in the seat which Elisha had offered. As he settled in, both of the doors on his side of the conveyance gently closed. Elisha walked around to the other door and slid into the remaining seat. When the door closed he spoke towards the array of instruments before him. "The Tent," he said, and the transport began to glide away from the city.

The priest leaned back in his seat. "The trip should take no longer than half an hour or so," he told the Surfer. "When we arrive, I will have to go into the tent. That is the one place that you cannot go. I have arranged for you to stand with the notables of the city, if that is acceptable to you."

"Again, I thank you. However, I may wish to stay with the pilgrims. Don't forget that I am one of them."

Elisha smiled and nodded. "Whatever you wish to do, Norrin Radd, is fine with me. If you would be more comfortable with the masses, that is where you should be."

The priest grew silent as they progressed and the Surfer sensed that his thoughts had turned inward, towards the ritual he was about to perform. Not wanting to intrude upon those thoughts, he watched as they grew closer and closer to the Tent of Meeting, taking note of the activity surrounding that place. White-clad men tended a fire which burned under a large brazier while others busied themselves with the handling of a number of animals nearby.

Elisha noticed the movements of the men, too. He nodded towards them and told the Surfer, "They are also priests. Their tasks on this day are simple, compared to mine. They need to make sure the fire burns and the sacrificial animals are properly readied. My mission, on the other hand, is nothing less than to atone for all the sins of this sometimes

stiff-necked people; and for myself, of course." He smiled
and faced the Surfer. "Don't misunderstand, my friend. I
love these people the way I love my family. Sometimes I feel
that their dedication to the Law is considerably less than my
own." He sighed. "That is to be expected, I suppose. If we
were all perfect, then this ritual would be unnecessary."

He lapsed into silence again and did not say another word
until they arrived a few hundred yards from the tent. As the
vehicle came to a stop, the doors opened, allowing both men
to exit. The Surfer retrieved his board and glanced towards
the city. The vehicles were still some distance away, as were
the pilgrims who had left on foot.

Turning back to the tent, he noticed that two enormous
video screens stood on either side of it and that there was a
great deal of activity taking place at other vehicles.

Elisha looked up at the screens and sighed. "One day,
perhaps, all of the people of this planet will come to New
Jerusalem. I doubt that this will happen in my lifetime,
though."

The priest looked at his watch. "It will be another hour or
more before we begin," Elisha informed him. "I will speak
to you after all is complete." He left the Surfer, walking deliberately to the tent. The Surfer watched as he spoke to the
priests who tended the fire and then walked to the back of
the tent, out of sight from the Surfer's eyes.

The sun climbed higher in the sky as the hour progressed.
Vehicles from the city arrived and disgorged their passengers,
who then walked the remaining distance to a place close to
the tent. The Surfer joined them, finding a place near the
front of the crowd where he would be able to watch all that
commenced. Although he could still feel the energy and anticipation of the pilgrims, they were quiet now, solemn, each
one alone with his or her thoughts.

The Surfer stood alone, too. He remembered his encounter with Adam Warlock and of his audience thereafter with Galactus. The world-devourer allowed as how he had submerged the Surfer's guilt and compassion while he served as Herald. At the Surfer's request, Galactus had restored his soul to its former condition, though the feelings of pain and guilt that accompanied that transformation nearly rent him in two. He recalled his journey through the Hall of Absolutes where he was forgiven by those closest to him for that which he had done while still Herald. He silently wept as he recounted the myriads of planets he had given into Galactus's hands, the millions of souls which his actions had snuffed out in the blink of an eye.

How, he wondered, *can any ritual erase these stains? How can any ceremony truly cleanse me?*

As if to answer his question, Elisha appeared before the opening of the tent. At the same time, his image filled the screens. He was still clad in white, but had changed his robes. Where he had worn a simple robe earlier in the day, he now wore an outfit consisting of a tunic, pants, a sash and a turban, all of the purest white linen. He held his arms to the side and the throng pressed closer together.

One of the other priests led a bull forward, and Elisha placed his hands on the bull's head. "This bull shall be my sin offering," he intoned, "so that before the Lord I, and my family, may be cleansed of all of our sins." Although the Surfer could not see any means of amplification, his soft voice carried clearly over the speakers.

The priest led the animal away while another brought two pure white goats before the High Priest. Yet a third handed him two stones which Elisha cast down in front of the animals. The Surfer watched as the goats were taken away to different places near the tent.

Before Elisha could say another word, his image on the

video screens was replaced with that of a blue-skinned alien. It wore a black tunic upon which was pinned a golden triangle and a helmet which covered its forehead. Its nose was broad and flat, its eyes the color of a red-hot forge and its grinning mouth was set with a myriad of small, sharp teeth.

"People of Sambatyon." The voice which emanated from the speakers was deep and gravelly. "I am Commander Gark Dur of the Shalran strike team. Our glorious leader, Cavor Sar, has decreed that this entire star system, including your planet, is to be placed under Shalra's beneficent rule. We have been waiting for Sambatyon to become visible for some time. Today is the day you shall know the might and power of the forces of Shalra. In order that you do not again vanish from our sight, I have ordered attack craft to disable the cloaking generators of New Jerusalem. When this has been accomplished, I will announce the conditions of your surrender."

The sound of an explosion rocked the masses. All present turned to see what had caused it. They were greeted by the sight of New Jerusalem being attacked by a fleet of spaceships. One of the ships turned and flew toward the tent. As the Surfer summoned his board to his side, he looked to see what Elisha would do. At that moment the priest's face reappeared on the viewscreens. The Surfer could see the fear in his eyes, the hesitation on his face.

"How can this be?" The priest's whisper carried over the speakers. "How can this be?"

"What shall we do?" somebody shouted.

"We must . . . must . . ."

The advancing ship released a burst of white-hot energy at the back of the crowd. The screams of the wounded and dying filled the air, adding an unholy counterpoint to the sounds of the city being destroyed.

As the Surfer's board carried him into the air, rage filled

him. Those near him scattered in all directions, trampling others who were too slow or too infirm to move quickly enough. The ship released another blast, which seared the desert floor itself. Another glance at the screens showed the Surfer that Elisha had still not moved to protect himself or his community.

How dare intruders disturb these proceedings and massacre innocents, he thought to himself. Remembering the hospitality he had been shown, the Surfer continued his ascent, racing to meet the attacking ship head on.

A burst of red-orange energy speared towards him, but he returned it with a bolt of his own power. The forces met and exploded with a brilliant flash. The pilot, not having expected any resistance, banked to the right in an effort to evade the source of the counterattack. The Surfer, not content to allow the ship to escape unscathed, unleashed yet another bolt of his Power Cosmic, which hit the intruder amidships. The power of the energy split it neatly in two. The pieces flew apart, hurtling into the desert floor below.

With one of the enemy fleet destroyed, the Surfer turned his attention towards the ships that were blasting the city. Smoke billowed from scores of buildings. The sound of sirens rent the air and many of the citizens who had not travelled to the desert filled the streets leading out of New Jerusalem. The pilots of the ships, however, were more intent on the destruction of the generators and left those on the ground to cope as best they could.

Anger coursed through the Surfer as he blasted another ship out of the skies. Momentum carried him past the city and out over the water. He spun around only to find that the remaining six ships had broken off their attack and were converging on his position.

As one, they fired tight beams of deadly force at the silver man in their viewscreens. The massed attack drove the Surfer off his board and he plummeted towards the ocean below. With a splash he hit the surface. The cool waters closed over him.

The attack served only to anger him more. He called his board, which shot out of the water a few yards away. Driven by the urgency of its master, the gleaming board sped to the Surfer who clambered aboard and again rose into the sky.

The fleet had returned to their task of leveling New Jerusalem. With the crews of the ships single-mindedly at their tasks, the Surfer found it easy to knock out two more before being noticed again. As before, the remaining ships turned and approached him, ready to combine their attacks.

This time, the Surfer anticipated the tactic. He led the ships until they were all over the ocean, then raced purposefully to the water. He entered just as the ships released their deadly rays, and felt the water bubbling overhead. Summoning all the speed he could he flashed through the water until he reached a place he surmised would bring him safely behind the ships. Only then did he burst out of the waters to renew his attack.

As he had thought, the ships were once again turning towards the city. Before they were able to get any closer, yet another had begun a fiery spiral downward. The remaining three ships, finally seeming to understand that the forces they battled were stronger than their own, tilted upwards and flew away. The Surfer followed them until they were well away from Sambatyon. After passing the outermost planet in the system, they vanished into hyperspace. He took careful note of the direction they were heading, in the event that he decided to pay a visit to Shalra in the future.

He guided his board back to Sambatyon's surface, shaking his head, hoping that the remainder of the day would be uneventful. As he sailed over the city he saw that many of those who had fled from the congregation were gathering again and that the majority of those who had escaped New Jerusalem during the attack were making their way towards the Tent of Meeting. He returned to the tent and, though the area was swarming with emergency vehicles and medical personnel, he sought out Elisha.

He found the priest near the spot he had last seen him, sitting in front of the entrance to the tent. The High Priest's eyes were wild with emotion. The Surfer put a hand upon Elisha's shoulder. "You shall be bothered no more today, Elisha. The danger is past."

"How did they—"

"They must have hidden behind one of the nearby planets. I chased them off and they have now left this system."

"I have never known such fear, Norrin Radd. I have never felt so helpless to do anything for my people."

"Elisha, we all have doubts and fears. That is what makes us what we are."

"Words cannot express what my heart feels, Norrin Radd. It must be as I believed. The Lord has sent you to us on this day so that our people can be saved. I cannot thank you enough."

"Thanks are unnecessary. The only thing which I believe is necessary is that you finish what you started here. If what you have told me is true, these people are depending upon you. They still wait for you to take away their sins."

"I cannot finish this ritual, my friend. It is too much for me, I think."

"You must finish. It is your responsibility, Elisha. You have no choice."

The High Priest rose to his feet and straightened his tunic. "You are right, of course. I fear, however, that the amplification devices are functioning no longer."

"That will not matter. Speak louder than you usually do. At least one person will hear."

Elisha sighed and signalled for the two goats to be led forth. "There has already been too much bloodshed today. My own fear will suffice as a sin offering to the Lord. This goat, which was chosen before, will bear the sins of this people."

A few men in the front of the milling crowd heard Elisha's words. They turned and called for quiet, a call which was picked up by others until the call for attention rode through the multitude like a wave riding into shore. Above the throng the Surfer rode, watching the scene unfolding below.

He saw the aimless motions of the crowd cease as all eyes were directed towards the activities of the High Priest. Although no sound could be heard, the cameras which broadcast the proceedings had, miraculously, not been harmed. The assembly watched as Elisha tied a scarlet ribbon around the neck of one of the goats and laid his hands upon its head. He closed his eyes and spoke words that nobody could hear, then motioned to one of the other priests. A young man approached and, without a word, led the goat out of the area, away from the city, into the heart of the desert where, the Surfer knew, it would surely meet its death.

His heart was filled with a feeling he had not known for years, one of true peace and contentment. He thought back on all of the reflection he had done earlier that day, all of the discussions he had with Elisha. He understood what Elisha had told him, that being forgiven was just the first step. For the first time that he could recall, he felt cleansed, fresh, as if a tremendous weight had lifted off of his shoulders.

Elisha motioned yet again and the younger priests began to disperse the people. Some filed into those transports which had not been destroyed in the attack, others began the walk back to their wounded city. The Surfer floated down to Elisha.

"The sun is beginning to set, my friend," the priest said.

"If the generators which cloak us are still in operation, we will soon vanish from sight."

"I know. And I will now take my leave of you."

"You could stay if you wanted."

"Thank you, but I cannot. I must return to the depths of space. It is the only place that I feel truly at home."

The High Priest nodded in understanding.

"Thank you, Elisha, for allowing me to view this ritual. I am not sure that I can find the words to describe what I feel, but I do know that I am at peace with myself."

Elisha grinned. "I am glad to hear that, very glad."

"Shalom aleichem, Elisha ben Malachai."

Elisha blinked in surprise, then replied with a smile, "Aleichem shalom, Norrin Radd."

The Surfer rose higher and higher, the air thinning around him, the sky deepening from blue to jet. Below him, he knew, people were tending their wounded, but he also knew that many must feel as he did.

He floated above Sambatyon, watching the clouds making arcane patterns in the atmosphere. The planet shimmered, then twinkled, then began to fade from sight. Within moments there was no trace of it, nothing to suggest that it had ever been there at all.

Norrin Radd smiled to himself. *Perhaps,* he thought, *I shall journey here again next year.* Turning his back on the empty space where Sambatyon had been, he flew away on his silver board.

THE LOVE OF DEATH OR THE DEATH OF LOVE

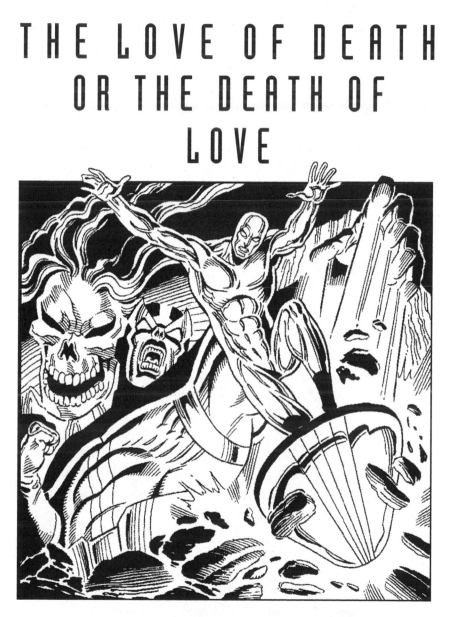

CRAIG SHAW GARDNER

Illustration by Grant Miehm

The universe was largely filled with emptiness.

They were still trying to kill him, but Thanos had other things on his mind.

It was a joke. All of existence was a joke. It might even be amusing, if Thanos still had a sense of humor.

Thanos looked at his hand, thick-fingered, powerful, chords of muscle ascending from his knuckles to his wrist. He had been born to conquer, his skin the color of granite, like a great stone statue that even time could not touch. Born on Titan to a race far superior to most of those puny species who dared to call themselves sentient. And even his birthright had not been enough, for he had soon left his family and fellows behind, killing those of Titan who got in his way—family member or no—in his first bid for power.

That had been so long ago. Thanos had been so naïve. As if power—simple, pure, absolute power—could ever be enough.

Thanos looked past the puny warship that came for him now, out to the stars. There were billions upon billions of stars in the cosmos. There was a time when he had ruled this realm, and he swore he one day would wield the power to rule it again. When the realm is infinite, all things are possible. And in the infinite, even a being like Thanos could find love.

An image of Death, the only woman Thanos had ever cared for, flitted through his thoughts. Sweet Death, so cold, so unattainable. He had died and returned to life for her, served as her lackey until he could bear it no more, and then conquered existence to be by her side.

Only Thanos, who had spent his lives pushing the boundaries of reality, could understand her beauty, her hair the dark of the void, her smile the white of bone, her dear face a perfect skull with the lightest coating of pale flesh.

He had longed to be one with Death. But even with all the power he had gathered around him, he had not been high enough, important enough, for her to even notice. So he had captured the Infinity gems—one of the great powers of the universe—and the laws of nature were his to shape and command. For a glorious moment, he contained *everything*. He rushed to Death's palace, her equal at last, eager for her to have a throne at his side.

She would not speak with him. He had miscalculated. They were no more equal than they had been before. Her minions informed Thanos that, if he were infinity, Death was one mere strand of that infinity. Someone as small as Death could not address the all-powerful directly.

He could have possessed Death, but he could not have her love. The only thing that had ever mattered to him would be forever beyond his grasp.

He would not think of it again.

Thanos had come to this place in order to not think of it. He had come perhaps to destroy a world and gain another prize of power, but mostly he had come to not think of it.

The great starship rushed towards him above the horizon, the pride of the fleet of the planet called Heart's Desire. Thanos always made sure to study the competition before battle. He knew the ship was full of their finest fighters and jammed with state-of-the-art instruments of destruction. The Deathship—for that is what they called it—could demolish a dozen suns with the push of a button, implode a black hole with the flick of a switch. Quite impressive, in a way; almost worthy of Thanos's skills. The great engine of catastrophe rushed towards Thanos's own craft, a hundred different weapons turned toward the Titan.

Thanos pushed a button of his own with one great, grey finger, and blasted the warship from the sky, evaporating the vessel's outer shell so that the hundred-member crew would fall to the planet's surface like drops of rain. He could hear their screams as they fell. The ship was no more, and all they had left was death. Thanos allowed himself the slightest of smiles. It was diverting for an instant.

Thanos did not want to think, so he fought. He fought because love was beyond him. He fought because without love all he had left was anger.

He fought because he was angry with all of existence. And perhaps the end of existence as well.

No. He did not want to think again of Mistress Death.

"Thanos."

He looked up toward his viewscreen at the single, spoken word. Apparently, the warriors of Heart's Desire were not finished yet.

They had changed their tactics and sent a lone warrior. He was a massive individual, great knots of muscles showing about the edges of his uniform; a fine specimen, both tall and broad, and almost as large as Thanos. Furthermore, Thanos was certain that that impressive build was specially enhanced by some hidden energy, like one of the Heralds of Galactus or those super heroes from the planet Earth.

The warrior waited for Thanos upon the surface of the moon below; the last great hope of Heart's Desire. Thanos could press another button and turn that hope to dust. That, of course, would be murder. Not that Thanos hadn't murdered, now and then.

But this was a challenge. The wise heads of Heart's Desire were depending that he would have honor, and accept their challenge.

Thanos cared nothing for honor, but he did care for diversion. Battle was his last great satisfaction, and a one-on-one confrontation was always the most satisfying of all.

Thanos steered his vessel to the surface of the moon. He would allow himself to be diverted for a little while longer.

He stepped from his craft and faced the puny last hope of Heart's Desire.

"I am Thanos," he announced. It was more satisfying when he exchanged words with his opponent. If they didn't talk, the battle was over far too quickly.

The warrior held a sword, a great curved weapon decorated with a line of runes, made of some metal that seemed to glow with a light of its own. No doubt it was some ceremonial weapon of great significance, perhaps even a source of power itself. "You cannot take the Orb of Niesta."

"I most certainly can," Thanos replied casually, as if he could barely be troubled with this conversation. "Why else would I bother with an insignificant world like yours?"

"We cannot allow that." The warrior shifted his weight, gripping his sword with both of his hands. "It will leave us worse than dead. It is the reason why we live. It gives us everything."

Thanos looked at the warrior and laughed. Thanos had had everything and let it slip from his grasp. And Thanos still survived, after a fashion. So he searched for new powers, new ways to gain all he had lost and all he never had.

"The Orb is father and mother, lover and child," the warrior continued, allowing desperation to creep into his voice. "The Orb will not let you take it away."

Thanos had heard of this planet called Heart's Desire—a name both totally innocent yet filled with tremendous conceit. Yet this fabled Orb of Niesta intrigued Thanos. It was a source of unlimited power, the rumors said, and the planet's deepest secret. A secret, that is, to all but a few. Thanos allowed himself a smile. When so many feared you, it was easy to obtain information.

The warrior lifted his sword before him. The battle was about to begin.

"It will destroy us," the warrior added, his voice little more than a whisper. "Without the Orb, Heart's Desire will cease to exist."

Thanos shook his great head. The gold of his armor shone coldly beneath the stars. "What happens to your world is no concern of mine. I long only for the Orb, and a new form of power. They tell me the Orb draws its energy from certain dimensions not our own."

That was what had interested him most about this mysterious Orb, that its powers came from sources both new and strange. If the rumors were true, it was a power based on different rules, perhaps even a power without limits. But the poor fools of Heart's Desire never realized what they had in their hands. A power like that would only reach its full potential in someone such as he: one with strength and vision, and need. The possibilities were intriguing. In an infinite universe, there were infinite ways to conquer.

"I will tell you no more about the Orb," replied the champion of Heart's Desire. "I must stop you, even if I have to destroy you."

So the battle had come at last.

"You must certainly try," Thanos agreed. He stood, legs apart, waiting for the hero to come to him.

He easily sidestepped the first swing of the sword. But the champion was remarkably quick, shifting his weight and thrusting before his opponent had quite regained his balance. Thanos had to use some power of his own to deflect the second strike, a power that seemed to be drawn within the rune-filled blade. The sword metal glowed brighter than it had before.

So Thanos's own power might be used against him? Perhaps he had found a worthy opponent in this warrior.

Thanos barely avoided the champion's next thrust, but he was beginning to notice a rhythm to the warrior's movements; a pattern that might allow him to anticipate his opponent's next blow.

Yes! Thanos pushed back the sword with an energy blast;

energy that the weapon again absorbed. But Thanos had expected that strike. He stepped away from the arcing sword an instant before the blade would have met his flesh. The champion stumbled, carried forward by the force of the blow.

Thanos stepped past the sword arm and hit the champion full in the face with his fist.

The champion fell, the glowing sword falling upon his chest. The great-muscled body arced as the blade touched his flesh, as though electrocuted by the power in the metal. The sword dimmed, and the warrior was still.

The hero of Heart's Desire was dead. Thanos found himself a trifle disappointed. This was far too easy a victory against a people who held an object of such power.

The inhabitants of Heart's Desire must have depended far too much upon the powers of the Orb of Niesta; it had made them soft. Once Thanos had claimed the Orb for his own, he would have to be careful not to follow in their careless footsteps.

He looked back to the fallen champion. Something was wrong with the body. As Thanos watched, the proud face crumbled; muscles cracked and fell away. In a matter of moments the body had turned to dust.

The dust blew away in a sudden wind, a wind that vanished as soon as its job was done. But the wind left something behind: a glowing, milky globe the size of a fist.

He recognized that glowing sphere from all the tales he'd heard. It was the Orb of Niesta. The Champion of Heart's Desire had hidden it upon his person—to keep it safe, perhaps, or to give him strength? Why had the people of Heart's Desire not protected their greatest prize from their enemy?

Thanos would never know. Not that it mattered now. He knelt and picked up his prize. A shock went through his body as he touched it. The sensation was nearly overwhelming, far beyond the raw power he'd found in the other items of power he'd obtained over the years. With the Orb in his hand, he was filled with a feeling of well being, and a feeling of limitless possibilities.

He looked in the cool whiteness of the globe, and saw a face. It was the face of Mistress Death. Her image looked boldly out at Thanos, almost as if her gaze met his own. And she was smiling.

Surely this was some illusion. But the globe, and the feelings that now filled Thanos, told him otherwise. No matter how she tried to hide within her cold domain, this image showed the truth. Mistress Death waited for one who was worthy. She waited for Thanos to prove himself.

This was the secret of the Orb of Niesta. It gave its owner power not just over matter and energy, but emotions as well. Thanos felt an almost overwhelming joy. With this new source of power, he could show sweet Death his love at last.

But he had to prove himself. He had felt that very strongly. He could not go before her empty handed. He needed to make a proper offering, a love-token to his cherished one.

What would Death want? Destruction, perhaps. But it had to be a very special destruction, the termination of someone or something that would normally be beyond Death's grasp. Thanos thought about those other beings with power, the super heroes of Earth and the Heralds of Galactus. They were the sort who cheated Death over and over.

What if Thanos were to destroy all the Heralds of Galactus, and then perhaps go before Mistress Death to destroy Galactus himself? He looked back at the Orb of Niesta. The image was fainter now, but he could swear he saw Death smiling fully now, eager for the tokens of his devotion.

For Mistress Death, Thanos would make murder an art. He would make a gift of the Power Cosmic. He and the Orb in his hand would change creation!

Then, together, they would change Thanos's life as well.

Thanos would begin his new work immediately. He had certain equipment aboard his spacecraft. And he had the incredibly powerful Orb. One way or another, he would let the Heralds know they were needed.

The universe was filled with worlds, ready for the taking.

He was Morg, Herald to Galactus. Once, it seemed now very long ago, he was mortal. He was a soldier on a world torn by civil war, a rebel beneath a general whom he thought had the strength to win. But the rebels were defeated, and all became prisoners to be tortured and killed—all except Morg. Morg had allied himself with the victorious Queen— now there was strength—and had been sent to torture and kill those that he had fought beside. Why not? They were useless to Morg. Their strength was gone.

Then Galactus came, to sate his great hunger by devouring Morg's world. Galactus came, and Morg had challenged him. And, in his battle with Galactus, Morg finally saw real strength for the first time.

Galactus had tossed Morg aside—pitiful mortal that Morg was—and devoured the planet's ecosystem. But Morg had been saved, and as his world had died he was born again, filled by Galactus with the Power Cosmic, so that Morg might become the servant of the greatest strength he had ever known. What did it matter that the planet and all he knew upon it were gone? Now Morg had real power. The strength of Galactus and the strength of Morg were one.

One thing had not changed for the new Herald of Galactus: both before and since being filled with the Power Cosmic, Morg was a good soldier. He lived for the orders of others. He served best as the instrument of their thoughts.

He was the Herald Galactus had been searching for. He would serve Galactus forever, seeking out worlds to satisfy his master's hunger. Whether the planets were inhabited, whether they held intelligence, did not matter to Morg. He was pleased to follow his master's dictates. Galactus had his Herald and Morg had finally found his true purpose.

There was a planet nearby, he could sense it. It was a place that had lost its reason for being, a place that would look at the coming of Galactus as an act of mercy.

Worlds without hope were hard to come by. Morg was pleased to find one so close to self-destruction. He rushed to investigate, eager to tell his master.

Morg would be the good soldier once again.

The universe was filled with life, but sometimes, the Silver Surfer grieved for what was gone.

He was the first Herald of Galactus, first to seek out worlds for that entity's never-ending hunger. It was a bargain he had made, to spare his homeworld and his beloved from Galactus's annihilation, a bargain that had doomed a thousand other worlds and a hundred billion souls.

Galactus had given him great power, turning him into something close to a god. But with that power Galactus had also twisted the way his new Herald thought, so that the Silver Surfer only sought new worlds to plunder, and could not hear the screams of the dying as Galactus had his fill. The Surfer had been blind to the carnage he brought until a great battle on the planet Earth had freed him of Galactus's bondage, and shown him the truth. A truth he would have to live with for the rest of time.

He still retained the power Galactus had bestowed upon him, but to what end? No matter how quickly he could fly, or how well he could fight, or how many wonders he might see, the past was always with him. Should he live a thousand years, he could only begin to right the wrongs he had done before.

The Surfer paused in his never-ending flight between the stars, both him and his board glowing a dull silver beneath the cold light of the stars. Somehow, he knew a world was dying, quite close to this corner of the galaxy through which he flew. He had to find this planet on the edge of destruction, and help to make things right. It was one more sacrifice, one more attempt at atonement.

It was his quest, his purpose, his vision, the reason why the Silver Surfer still soared the spaceways. And he had to be true to that vision, even though the quest might never end.

Morg was not pleased with the chaos before him. The planet seemed to be destroying itself. Great cracks had appeared toward both of the poles. Rivers ended in geysers of steam, while monstrous tidal waves rocked the oceans. Morg would have to summon his master quickly if Galactus was to get his fill.

The scene shifted violently as Morg heard a voice in his ear.

"The world is yours, if you kill me first."

Morg found himself standing on the planet's moon. And there, motionless before him with arms crossed, was a being he had met before: the self-important Thanos.

Morg laughed. This single being, this Thanos, would try to stop him? Sometimes, Morg thought, he could take real pleasure in his work.

"If you insist," Morg agreed. He raised the battle ax he always carried for these occasions.

"So you will fight?" Thanos smiled in return. "Of course, you might have to make some choices."

Morg frowned. Where one Thanos had stood, there were now two, side by side.

"You are not simply fighting me, Herald," Thanos explained. But the words came out of four different mouths. "You are fighting the power of the Orb of Niesta." Sixteen images of Thanos threw back their heads and laughed at Morg. "Why don't you make it simple for us all, and use that ax to slit your throat?"

Morg would not be mocked. With a cry for blood that exploded from his throat, he leapt forward, his great weapon swinging before him. The first image of Thanos was illusion, the ax whistling cleanly through it.

But the second image gushed crimson, far too much, as if this Thanos was nothing but a great mass of blood. The third shattered at the battle ax's touch, as though it was nothing but brittle bone.

"Ah, yes," Thanos said. "There are so many ways to die. Let us find a new one for you, shall we?" The thirteen remaining Titans beckoned him forward with a mocking smile. They chuckled together.

Thirteen versions of Thanos, and Morg wanted to kill them all. Morg would find the real one, and put an end to his laughter, and then let Galactus feed upon this moon that held the Titan's corpse.

Morg rushed forward again, his voice hoarse with the call of battle.

The Surfer saw the battle beneath him, and recognized both who fought. But the battle itself seemed somehow unreal.

Morg seemed to swing at phantoms, ghostly outlines that the Surfer could barely see. Meanwhile, at a very safe distance from Herald and ax, Thanos held a glowing orb above his head and laughed.

The Surfer supposed this had something to do with the planet just beyond. But he had no time for petty squabbles, not until the planet was safe.

There were limits to the Power Cosmic. It could not create whole new worlds, nor bring back life that was truly gone. But, in the Surfer's hands, it could nurture and heal, and make right what had gone astray.

The Surfer looked down at the suffering world and called upon all the power within him: power to calm the roiling seas, power to seal the great rents in the earth, power to calm the rumbles beneath the surface and the storms in the air.

So the Surfer worked, flying above the planet, putting it back together piece by piece, until the Power Cosmic all but drained from his body, and he could fly no more. He let his board settle to the planet below. He stumbled from it onto the now quiet ground, and fell to his knees.

He hoped his work would succeed. He had nothing more to give.

"You've done this, haven't you?" An old man, leaning heavily upon a cane, approached the Surfer.

The Surfer looked up at the bent and shriveled mortal. His body was old, but his gaze was intense. The Surfer nodded. "I have helped to calm the turmoil that troubled this place."

"It was once called Heart's Desire," the man explained. He looked around him at ruined buildings and uprooted vegetation left over from the planet's near destruction. "The name may have to change."

Others followed the old man, calling out to both he and the Surfer.

"The Orb!" one of the newcomers shouted in a voice filled with despair. "The Orb is gone!"

"They speak of the Orb of Niesta," the old man explained. "But this planet was already dying, overwhelmed by years of the Orb's fantasy. You see, this gem has the power to change reality—or so we thought."

The Surfer nodded. He had seen other instruments of

great power in his travels, dangerous instruments desired by dangerous beings—like Thanos.

"But did the Orb truly change reality, or only the perception of reality among those who have owned it?" The old man nodded at the destruction about him. "I have come to my senses. I am old, and remember a time before we gained the Orb. A time not too different from this."

The others were coming closer, a mob full of misery, calling out their sadness.

"The Orb! We must have the Orb!"

"We will die!"

"Life will be empty!"

"How can we live without it?"

They reached out as they approached, their hands grasping the air, as if they might grab the Surfer and force him to do their bidding.

The old man stepped before the mob, raising his cane like a club to fend them off.

"I have come to my senses," the old man repeated. "The others will have to follow." He glanced back to the Surfer. "You have saved our world. That is enough. Now leave before my fellows embarrass me further."

The Surfer stood, and found that the power was beginning to build in him again. He stepped upon his board, and angled it up into the sky. Cries of agony and curses of rage followed him for as long as he could hear the mob below.

"Be careful of the Orb!" the old man called as the voices faded with distance. "It will fulfill your every fantasy. But they are nothing but dreams, phantoms of the imagination."

The Surfer flew on, longing now for the silence of space. While he might save worlds, the minds of mortals seemed always beyond him.

*   *   *

Thanos sensed another. A former minion of Galactus responded to his call. And the newcomer was perhaps the one Thanos despised most among all the Heralds of Galactus, the Silver Surfer.

Thanos chuckled as he watched Morg perform his exhausting battle-dance, chasing phantom Titans across the surface of the moon. The Surfer would join them soon. The Orb would draw all the Heralds here. They would fly to him, nothing more than insects caught in a trap.

Perhaps Thanos could destroy both Morg and the Surfer together. Two at once. *That* would get Mistress Death's attention.

Thanos was overcome again with that fierce joy. The Orb shone too brightly now for Thanos to gaze on it directly. But he knew there was a face that watched and waited within.

Surely, Mistress Death was laughing with him!

Morg did not know where to turn.

The images of Thanos were everywhere, and ever-changing. His ax sliced through a Thanos with two heads, then gutted another with six arms. All illusions, surely. But how could Morg tell what was real?

"Herald of Galactus!" another voice called. "I have come to join the battle!"

Morg looked aloft and saw the hated Silver Surfer, streaking down upon his board. Morg had very little use for his predecessor, but against Thanos he was glad for the assistance. "So be it!" he reluctantly called back.

"No!" Thanos called. "I do not like these odds."

Only one of the half dozen Thanoses currently in existence raised a glowing globe above his head. A beam of light shot from the globe to the Surfer's chest. And the Surfer screamed.

*   *   *

Thanos laughed as the Surfer clutched at his chest and fell from his board. He lay still upon the surface of the moon.

Using the Orb in such a violent fashion might not be as subtle as Thanos would like, but it would have to do.

He was still learning to use the Orb, the intricate ways in which this globe shaped his thoughts. With the two of them together, they might have been able to defeat enough of the false images to make him temporarily vulnerable. He needed to fell the Surfer—though he was careful that it wasn't a killing blow—while he decided what torments to visit on both of the Heralds now.

And yet, the globe felt so natural in his grip, as though it were an extension of his hands, like it had always been a part of him. Death was in his hands. Death was everywhere. She would come to him soon.

All things were possible with the Orb of Niesta. True bliss would be his forever.

Morg turned when someone called his name.

"This way," the Silver Surfer beckoned.

But hadn't Morg seen the Surfer struck down by Thanos? For the first time since he had come to this moon, Morg was overcome, as if two Surfers on top of limitless Thanoses were far too much for his mind to handle.

He stared at the second Surfer. But he walked to join him behind the jagged outcropping that would hide them both from Thanos.

"Thanos is busy playing with his reality," the Surfer explained. "I saw no reason for him to play with ours. If he wants to fight using replicas of himself, I can give him a replica of myself to complete the battle."

Morg poked his head past the outcropping to look back at the field of battle. One of the many Thanoses walked over to examine the fallen Surfer.

Morg turned back to the Surfer. "But how can he believe such a thing?"

"He will believe it because he wants to believe it. That is the power of the new gift in his hand. The Orb gives him what he wants, even if it is only in his own mind." Quickly the Surfer explained how he had used the Power Cosmic to create his doppelgänger.

Somehow, to Morg, the battle did not feel complete. "So, we do not defeat our enemy?"

"No, we circumvent him. We go where we will, while he stays here perhaps till the end of time, doing battle with our doubles."

"We eliminate Thanos from our lives." The warrior-turned-Herald smiled at that. "I can consider that a victory." He hefted his ax, and turned to finish his work. "I must prepare the way for Galactus."

But the Surfer held up his hand. "The world is whole again."

Morg turned and looked toward the planet spinning above. What was once a planet half torn asunder was now a whole globe, healthy and alive.

"Your duties and my destiny lie elsewhere," the Surfer insisted.

Morg stared at the former Herald for a long moment, his fury at the Surfer snatching this world away from Galactus warring with a maddening gratitude.

"Very well, Norrin Radd," he said at last. "You freed me from madness, I spare the world. It seems a fair exchange—this time."

Morg grabbed his battle ax and was gone.

Thanos and the Orb were one. He would fight half a dozen of the Heralds at once, bringing them all ever closer to death, and none could do a thing to resist. They had all come now, Terrax, Air-Walker, Destroyer, Firelord, even Nova, whom Thanos had thought to be dead. Oh, how his mistress would be pleased when Thanos returned Nova to Death's cold embrace!

It was an inspired act of violence, draining all of the Heralds of their power, a killing by slow degrees. And the spirit of Mistress Death hovered by his side, approving of every nuance of his performance, whispering how soon they should be together. Already, he thought he saw her in the distance, walking to embrace him across the surface of this wonderful barren moon.

And still he tortured his foes, and still he waited for his mistress. Thanos laughed, fulfilled at last. He would know no mercy, and sing to Death forever.

The universe is vast. There are millions of worlds for the taking. There are millions of worlds to be saved.

Thanos, though, had found a world of his very own, a place to lose himself forever, a reality as small as his mind and as large as the universe. In a way, Thanos had found peace.

Perhaps Thanos would break free of the Orb. Perhaps Thanos and the Surfer would fight again. Or perhaps Thanos would continue his own private battle for the rest of time. The Surfer would leave him here. It was the only merciful thing to do.

The Silver Surfer turned away from the moon, back toward the stars, and another peace that was much more elusive.

THE TARNISHED SOUL

KATHERINE LAWRENCE

Illustration by Scott McDaniel

An empty, wandering planetoid on the fringes of the galaxy is the perfect place to indulge a severely introspective depression. Or so it seemed to the Silver Surfer.

The distant stars reflected off his silver form, or as much of it as was left. That was the problem. For some time now he'd noticed dark spots on his silver skin; spots which grew slowly but steadily.

At first he took them for shadows and ignored them. But as they increased in size and even spread to his silver board, he sought out Reed Richards of the Fantastic Four on Earth. Reed did all the analyses his brilliant mind could conceive, including building a new form of microscope, capable of looking at particles far smaller than electrons.

The tests showed the molecular structure of the Surfer's skin to be unchanged, except for its color. Reed did not make any jokes about the Silver Surfer now being tarnished, but Johnny Storm, a.k.a the Human Torch, was not so generous.

The Surfer had his own ideas as to the cause of the darkness, ideas he desperately wanted to refute.

He next sought out those like him: the other Heralds of Galactus. Firelord wondered why it bothered him since his ability to wield the Power Cosmic was unchanged. "If as Richards said, you are unchanged physically, what difference does it make?"

Air-Walker was less kind. "You worry about stupid things, Surfer. I wonder sometimes why Galactus chose you. You lack the proper attitude for a Herald."

The darkness on the Silver Surfer's skin continued to grow. Again the Surfer sought for a reason other than the one his heart knew to be true.

Galactus had recently fed and was in a relatively patient mood. "Why do you come to me, my former Herald? Your power is as it was when I gave it to you, as is your silver skin. Leave me."

Unable to bear his thoughts, the Surfer fled to the farthest reaches of the galaxy, to this small planetoid. It was much like his skin: dark with glimmerings of starlight. Dark as his soul was dark.

No one else to ask; nowhere else to flee. Each bit of darkness had a name: some belonged to friends, others to strangers, others to entire planets. All the failures, large and small. All the times he had failed to uphold justice, as his heart demanded.

"Silver One?"

The time he nearly destroyed thousands of innocent lives in a rage. The mechanical bureaucrats of Dynamo City, an artificial satellite deep in space, had captured and enslaved him, robbing him of his power and his freedom.

If a fellow slave, Zeaklar, hadn't gotten himself teleported out of the City with the Surfer, he would have attacked the City, seeking revenge against the bureaucrats. It was Zeaklar who stopped the Surfer, forcing him to remember that any battle would likely breach the dome protecting the city, killing thousands as their air streamed into space. Something the Surfer should have remembered.

"Silver One."

The moment when he realized that without the accident that caused him to enter Alicia Masters' studio, he would have caused Earth, and all those who would someday befriend him, to become an appetizer for Galactus.

Galactus's manipulation of the Surfer's memories was no excuse. His soul had still been his own. He should have known better.

"Silver One!"

Someone was shaking him, drawing his attention back to the outside world.

"Silver One, welcome to Moerae." The voice was soft, but powerful.

The Surfer turned and saw a beautiful young woman with long, dark, curly hair flowing over her shoulders, and over the silver gown she wore. He rose to his feet immediately, and bowed over her offered hand.

"My apologies for the preoccupation which kept me from noticing your arrival. I am the Silver Surfer."

"Yes, I know." Her laughter was vibrant, like the ringing of small bells. "And I am Clotho. Come, it is time to meet my sisters."

Bewildered to find others in this place, others he had inexplicably not sensed with the Power Cosmic, the Surfer let himself be led around the rock he'd been leaning against, and into a cave lit by flickering firelight.

Two other women were seated by the fire: a mature woman in white whom Clotho introduced as Lachesis, and a small, stooped-over, aged woman in black, introduced as Atropos.

"You have found him. Good." The voice of Atropos was as wizened as her form, and sent a chill up the Surfer's back. He recognized the three women from childhood stories of Zenn-La. They were the Nornir, the Three Fates for which he was named.

"Come join us, Silver One." Lachesis gestured to the other side of the fire, opposite where she sat with Atropos.

"So, we finally meet." Atropos looked him up and down with a calculating look as Clotho continued around the fire and sat down next to Lachesis.

"You're not quite what your name led us to expect," Lachesis said as soon as the Surfer sat down.

He found himself unexpectedly blurting out the truth. "My skin reflects my soul. It is tarnished with failures and deaths. I fear the *Silver* Surfer will soon disappear, leaving only a Dark Surfer."

"Let us see." Clotho reached into the darkness behind her and pulled out a segment of silver thread with no visible beginning or end. Atropos reached out and ran a gnarled finger along it.

The Surfer shuddered in pain greater than any he had yet known.

"And the other?" Atropos demanded.

A second thread appeared in Clotho's hands, a dark one, appearing to be spun from the air as the Surfer and the sisters watched.

The Surfer moaned in agony, feeling as if his soul was being ripped apart. Not even receiving his silver skin and all that went with it had caused pain such as this.

As he collapsed backwards onto the cave's stone floor, the darkness started to swirl and reshape itself, taking on a humanoid form. That form began to claw its way out through the Silver Surfer's chest. After a moment, the Surfer found himself to be silver again, but also facing a jet-black doppelgänger, a Dark Surfer.

"Now we have a new Surfer. Dandai, for another of our names, the Danaids," Clotho said, naming him as was her right.

To his amazement, the Surfer was still alive. His silver skin glittered in the flickering firelight, all darkness gone. He looked at his dark twin. The only difference between them was their color.

Dandai looked at the Surfer, then called forth the Power Cosmic until his body glowed. Refusing to give in to the fear that the Power had disappeared into his twin along with the darkness, the Surfer too called it forth, and for a brief moment, before the two Surfers let it fade, the cave glowed as if lit by Earth's sun.

"Twins, alike in all but color," Lachesis said. "And who shall say which thread shall be the longer?" She pulled on the silver and black threads in Clotho's hands, lengthening them, measuring them, without finding an end.

"Go!" Atropos ordered.

The Surfer rose to his feet, grateful to the sisters for solving his problem, and turned to leave the cave.

"No. Go deeper. Continue into the cave, past our fire. Both of you." Atropos defined her order.

The Surfer turned back, but stayed where he was. "To what purpose? Until I learn to embrace my own darkness? Until we end up challenging each other and fight until one dies? I have been the tool of Galactus. I will never again follow another's orders."

"You are afraid." Dandai's voice was deeper than the Surfer's, and softer.

"Yes. Only a stupid man would not be. The legends of the Nornir are many, and few of them show kindness to mortals."

Clothos' laughter echoed within the cave. "You may be a hero, Silver One, but you are as foolish as every other mortal. Do you not remember the journey that brought you here? All the attempts to avoid this meeting? What choice do you now have?"

The Surfer glared at them. His freedom was almost as important to him as his need to see justice done. Yet he was indeed trapped, as legend said even the gods were by these three.

The Surfer strode towards the darkness at the back of the cave. "Come on," he ordered Dandai.

Dandai hesitated, letting the Surfer know he was going voluntarily, not because the Surfer ordered it, then followed his silver twin.

The Surfer called forth some of the Power Cosmic to illuminate the cave so he could see where the tunnel took him. Dandai was close on his heels.

The tunnel angled downwards, at first shallowly, then more and more steeply. As they got deeper, the Power Cosmic dwindled, requiring more and more effort from the Surfer to light their path. He considered returning to the surface, but Dandai's footsteps behind him reminded the Surfer why he was on this journey, and he kept going.

Then the tunnel split into two.

"Which way?" Dandai asked.

The Surfer could detect no difference between the tunnels. No fresher air from one than the other, no light, nothing. But it had to be a test. That's what the Nornir did, when they weren't cutting life threads short.

"I refuse to let them force us to a single path. There's no reason we need to stay together, is there?"

Dandai looked down both tunnels, then nodded. "Splitting up seems the optimum choice. So, which of us shall take which tunnel?"

The Surfer was standing on Dandai's left, and without hesitation headed down the left tunnel. He heard Dandai's footsteps moving down the one on the right, then fading away.

The Surfer's light, and the Power Cosmic, continued to fade. Within a hundred yards the Surfer was in total darkness. He stopped, knowing the wrong step in the darkness could, without his Power, lead to certain death.

As his eyes adapted, he saw a faint yellow glow in the distance, and carefully moved towards it.

The tunnel turned a corner, then came to an abrupt end, dumping him into a huge, furnished chamber. A raised dais sat at the far end, with lower seats on either side, a small row of benches perpendicular to the dais, and a much longer row of benches opposite it. The Surfer realized that it was a courtroom, more specifically a courtroom from Earth!

Before he could puzzle out this anachronism, a bewigged, older man in a black robe hustled up to the Surfer, a black robe and more elaborate white wig in his hands. "Hurry, Your Honor. Court is almost in session. The defendant is awaiting your pleasure."

He didn't wait for the Surfer's permission; he plopped the wig with its rolled curls onto the Surfer's head, then dressed him in the black judge's robe, as if the Surfer were a child.

"What is this?" the Surfer asked.

"Your court, Your Honor." The older man tugged the Surfer towards the high judge's bench at the far end of the room. "We have the witnesses ready to testify, and the defendant is in custody. It only remains for you to hear the case and render a decision."

Reminding himself that he was still within the Nornir's power, the Surfer climbed the steps to the bench and sat down.

The older man straightened the Surfer's wig, and picked up the waiting gavel, striking it against the wooden block next to it. "Hear ye, hear ye! The case of the Universe vs. the Dark Surfer is now in session." He handed the gavel to the Surfer, then descended the steps, to take his place as bailiff.

The witnesses filed in and sat down to await their turns. The Surfer recognized most of them.

Then Dandai, the Dark Surfer, was brought in wearing chains by two black-garbed and masked guards. Dandai's chains were attached to a bolt in the floor in the middle of the open area between the judge's bench and the seats for the witnesses.

"What is going on?!" Dandai demanded of his silver twin.

The bailiff answered. "You're here to answer charges brought by Norrin Radd, the Silver Surfer. Crimes against humanity, against the universe, and against Norrin Radd himself."

"He has no right to judge me."

The Surfer turned to the bailiff and agreed. "How can I be the judge, when you claim I brought the charges against him?"

The bailiff sorted through his various stacks of paperwork as he answered. "It's your universe and you set yourself up as judge and prosecutor. This is your court, Your Honor. However, since you need to stay up there, I will act as prosecutor."

The bailiff found the paperwork he wanted and called out, "I call Zeaklar of Pyrofax!"

Zeaklar moved forward to the witness stand. He looked puzzled as he looked back and forth between Dandai and the Surfer.

"Tell us what happened at Dynamo City, Zeaklar," the Bailiff requested.

"Surfer and I were slaves there, along with lots of other folks. Then he came up with a plan to escape, but it didn't quite work, and we were spaced. But that's what we wanted anyway, because he got his Power back, and we were free."

"What happened after you escaped?" the Bailiff asked.

"I returned to Pyrofax. No idea where Surfer went."

"No, no. Immediately after you escaped. Didn't the robot guards come after the two of you?"

Zeaklar's forehead acquired even more wrinkles as he tried to remember. "Well, I remember him blowing up three of those bullies who wanted to take us back to the City since space hadn't killed us."

"How did Surfer react to that?" the Bailiff asked.

"He was angry. I mean, first they took his power and humiliated him, then when he didn't act as a proper slave, they tried to destroy him. Good thing they didn't know all it took was getting out into space for his Power to return."

The Bailiff took a deep breath. This was apparently what he'd been waiting for. "Angry? In what way?"

291

Zeaklar gave a short laugh. "He wanted to go back and take out all those mechanical guards and bureaucrats. Vermin, that's what he called them."

"And did he?"

"No, no. I reminded him that as much as I'd like to see something done about that place too, any battle with them would take so much power that the City's dome would likely crack, and that would kill lots of the slaves still stuck there."

The Bailiff smiled. "So, if you hadn't stopped him, the Surfer would have destroyed thousands of innocent lives in revenge for slights to his ego?"

"Well, I wouldn't put it quite like that."

"Please, answer the question."

"Well, yeah. Sort of." Zeaklar looked upset. "But as soon as I mentioned it, he knew I was right. I didn't have to say anything more than that."

"Thank you. You're dismissed."

The Bailiff turned to the Surfer on the bench. "And what, Your Honor, should the penalty be for forgetting the prices paid by the innocent? If this person from Pyrofax wasn't there to stop the Surfer, how many lives would have been lost?"

The Surfer was appalled. It was one thing to castigate himself for that lapse, but quite another to have this Bailiff/Prosecutor put it in those terms. He looked across at Dandai, who refused to meet his eyes.

"Call the next witness," the Surfer told the Bailiff. "I want to hear all the evidence."

The next witness was one of the Elders of the Universe, Obliterator. The Surfer couldn't understand why this member of the universe's oldest race was there. Obliterator had assisted the Surfer once long ago, when he sought out another Elder, the Grandmaster.

The Bailiff asked the witness to state his name, then asked

why he was there as witness against the Surfer.

"The Surfer destroyed me, turning five billion years of work into nothingness, condemning me to an eternity of helplessness."

"And how did he do this?"

"I'm the Obliterator! I destroyed every other member of my race, and billions more. That was what I did. Then the Surfer turned my devastating weapons into toys that shot only visible light, not destruction. The devices that allowed me to travel the universe were also transformed. They never worked again. I was a prisoner on a planet far from anywhere, unable to escape, unable to defend myself. I want to see him as helpless as I was."

"He didn't kill you, did he?"

"I wish he had. But . . ."

"That's enough. You're dismissed."

The Obliterator returned to his seat and the Bailiff turned to the Surfer. "An eternity of helplessness. What penalty should be paid for that?"

"Next witness," the Surfer demanded.

One by one they came up. Some declared crimes that the Surfer knew he was guilty of, such as the tall man with glasses and silver-streaked dark hair and mustache from Earth, who knew even more details than the Surfer did about what happened when the Surfer led Galactus to Earth.

There was Doctor Doom, cursing the Surfer for not warning him about the barrier Galactus had erected around Earth, when the doctor "acquired" the Surfer's powers.

Mephisto was there with his lies about what the Surfer had done while imprisoned on Earth, ignoring what he'd done to the Surfer. Ganymede was there, to complain that the Surfer had misled her as to his powers when they took on Tyrant. Even Shalla Bal was there, telling of how Galactus had drained Zenn-La after the Surfer betrayed Galactus and

293

stopped him from devouring Earth.

Dandai was hunched into a ball on the floor, crying. The Bailiff asked him if he had anything to say for himself.

"No," he sobbed. "It's all true. I betrayed my word, my honor, my home, and my friends. Do with me what you will."

The Bailiff turned back to the bench. "It's your decision, Your Honor."

The Surfer stood, tossed off the wig and black robe, and descended the steps. He walked over to Dandai, and pulled the Dark Surfer to his feet.

"Some of what was said was true, but what of the planets you saved? The evil you ended, the friendships you made? Are you going to tell me Alicia Masters was mistaken? No one here has accomplished anything without paying a price for it." The words came from the Surfer's heart.

Dandai looked at his silver twin. "Then why do I exist? You created me because of the criminal activity the witnesses reported. The Danaids merely gave me my voice, finishing what you began."

The Surfer released Dandai as if the contact burned. It was true. He'd condemned himself just as much as these witnesses had, and demanded the same penalty—an end to his life as the Silver Surfer.

From nowhere a mighty blow struck him on the side of his head, and he went flying. He slammed into a rock wall, and would have lost consciousness if his Power Cosmic hadn't abruptly returned.

He was back in the cave with the Nornir. Atropos was standing near the fire, one sleeve rolled up revealing a surprisingly muscled arm and a clenched fist. "Feel sufficiently punished, Surfer? I can do that again, if you want." The old woman cackled at his look of amazement.

The Surfer got to his feet, wincing at the bruises. "You have made your point." He looked around the cave. "Where is Dandai? What have you done with him?"

Lachesis mimed measuring out a thread and holding it for Atropos to cut. "His time is ended," she said.

The Surfer looked down at his shimmering silver form. "Then . . ."

"As others will tell you, lighten up," Atropos said with another of those cackling laughs.

Clotho came up to him, took his hand, and led him out of the cave into the starlight. "You're still the Silver One," she said as the distant flash of a quasar reflected off his skin. The darkness was gone.

"Thank you."

"And now I suppose you want to know how long your life-thread is," she said. "That's the one question everyone asks."

He didn't hesitate. "No. I dwell too much on negatives. I'm alive now; that's all that matters."

"A hero indeed," Clotho said, and disappeared.

The Surfer searched, but couldn't find the cave. His Power Cosmic showed the planetoid to be empty, as it had when he'd arrived. Too empty. It was time to return to his friends, and not just the labor of redemption his life had been, but meeting the challenge of new opportunities to serve justice.

He called his board and headed back toward the center of the galaxy. There was still much to be done before his time was ended.

A GAME OF THE APOCALYPSE

STINER

DAN PERSONS

Illustration by Ernie Stiner

"*Kediera han* *t'docid*," his father had called him, "A shadow amongst the trees." The ability had come unbidden, a trait of blood passed on from one generation to the next: to meld as one with rock, soil, foliage; to pass unseen, unheard through the heart of the forest, as if born of the living heart of his world. Such agility would be treasured in any society. In the forests of this world, where a well-balanced knife was valued more dearly than gold, and a village prospered or faltered in equal measure to the skills of its hunters, stealth was a blessing beyond compare.

Almost from infancy, Linnel Jen had dreamed of the night of his ascension, when he would at last run with the hunting party. Almost from the time he was first able to wrap fingers around a knife's handle, he ached for the moment when his tribe would feast on flesh felled by his hand. Time only heightened his desire, a passage of days that saw his father instilling in him the arts needed to swiftly drop his prey, a progress of years that witnessed his fur gradually assume the gradients of reds and browns needed to blend perfectly with the surrounding forest. He had believed the time drew close when he would fulfill his life's purpose. But that time would never arrive.

They had come in the night, a team of Aroyu warriors, an assemblage that numbered fully three quarters of that village. They were led by a priest who could mesmerize with but a few words, dressed in raiments the likes of which the depths of the forest had never seen. The cleric spoke of a fearsome enemy that even now readied for war: godless creatures whose goal was to slaughter all in their path. He spoke of the holy unity that had led the Aroyu to abandon longstanding enmities (for, indeed, their recent past had been too-well littered with skirmishes over hunting ranges), seeking allies where once had stood only foes. And he spoke of the great god Cirremon, He of unbounded power, under whose

298

protection the blessed would overcome all unbelievers.

He spoke about all of this, and more. And if he spoke of the fact that the "godless enemy" were actually the Moriya, a peaceful tribe that lived a day's journey to the east, if he spoke of the trail of blood he and his Aroyu warriors had already left behind, or of how an unsettling number of those slaughtered had not long before considered themselves allies in the Great War, none heard these words, so captivating was the priest's passion.

And the one who could will himself amongst the trees, the one who had dreamed the life of a hunter, did not find himself immune to the cleric's entreaties. He had presented himself before the priest, demonstrated his unique skills. The priest had watched, had smiled, had at once proclaimed him anew: "*Kedeira han n'rima.*"

"A shadow amongst our enemies."

The hunter had rejoiced, had felt his blood quicken at the touch of the priest's hands upon his shoulders, at the sound of his voice entreating the beloved Cirremon to bestow his blessings upon this latest recruit to the holy war. So blinded was he by the lure of war's purpose, so seduced by the thought that, at last, his knife would taste the blood of prey, he did not think to ask for what gain these lives would be sacrificed, what profit would his people see from the conflict.

Only when it was too late had he found answers. Only then, on the night of his knowledge, could he curse fate for the blessing of his stealth.

Linnel Jen, the assassin, grasped the tri-bladed knife, and willed himself into the shelter of the foliage. It was a full-moon night, and bright, too bright for the task at hand. There was nothing he could do about that.

In the clearing ahead, the Aroyu raiding party went about

their business: laying out their beddings, attending to the fires, stretching hides out onto tanning racks. Jen tilted his head towards the wind, sniffed, caught the scent of those skins. He had to force himself not to think about their source.

Before him, the Aroyu prepared for sleep. Behind him, the people of his village slept as well, but a sleep from which none ever rouse. For a moment, his eyes refused to continue their watch; the image of his village's remains superseded all. If his people were capable of tears, Jen's would have flowed then. For him, though, only the slight tremor of his fingers as he adjusted his grip on the knife remained as testament to his grief.

He had been a fool; he knew that now. Only his zeal in serving Cirremon had saved him, had compelled him to linger in the remnants of the Moriya village after the battle was over; to spend two days and half of one more seeking out those who had fled the slaughter. He had been swift, and thorough; he had adhered to the hunter's creed and assured that those dispatched by his blade did not suffer needlessly. With those deaths, with the time it took for Jen to confirm that the Moriya bloodline was terminated once and for all, did he save his own life.

He had anticipated a hero's welcome upon his return. The first sign waking him from his reverie was the taste of smoke upon the wind: dark, bitter, and carried from the direction of his village. The next was the scent: of fires recently died, tainted with the stench of charred fur. Last was sight: a ruin where once family lodges and storehouses stood, paths where footprints had been erased by the umber tracings of spilled blood. No ranking of corpses rested at the village's outskirts, as there would have been had defenders tried to protect their homes from attack. The betrayal had come without warning, the murderers permitted into their victims' midst before the act commenced.

Most had been slain where they stood, then casually abandoned. Some had suffered mutilations—the contortions frozen upon their faces suggested that their skinnings, impalements, and dismemberments had occurred before the mercy of death was granted. His father, once leader of the hunt and also elder of the village, had been accorded the honor of being bound to a makeshift rack and treated to some grotesque game involving the scoring of knife cuts and the application of flaming brands.

And now, Jen's former battle-mates prepared for bed, within scenting distance of their atrocity. That pleased the assassin, for it meant that the priest had not been present for the massacre, had not known that his treasured assassin, his *Kedeira han n'rima*, had survived the slaughter. Had he but known, he would have pulled camp immediately. He would pay for that error.

Linnel Jen surrendered himself to the cover of night, and waited. It would not be long before the Aroyu had bedded down. The task, then, would be simple: the swift and silent dispatching of the guards, the extermination of a few, token soldiers. Finally, entry into the tent of the one who had orchestrated his people's murder. Seconds after, Jen would vanish into the night with his trophies: the still-beating hearts of the priest of Cirremon.

The moon continued its journey across the sky. Activity in the camp dwindled, stilled. Jen felt the moment, sensed the time when the murderers' sleep was its deepest, when even the lookouts struggled against dozing. With all the stealth of his birth-gift, he moved from cover, blended his footfalls with the natural shift of the forest's growth, willed his body to blend into the variegated shadows cast by the moon's light. A guard sat by a tree, not more than three arm-spans distant.

Jen could feel the soft, rhythmic thrust of the Aroyu's breath as the soldier fought sleep, could feel the heat of his blood as it pulsed beneath fur and flesh. Jen smiled, moved forward, rejoiced in the knowledge that soon the tree's roots would nurture themselves upon that blood.

The knife was drawn, wielded as if it was a part of Jen's own hand. Without thought, it reached out, keen stone blade seeking of its own will the soft flesh of the throat, and the vital artery shielded beneath. The guard did not stir as Jen approached from behind, his hand moving as the knife had its first kiss of receptive flesh.

And then the world was chaos.

The ground had vanished, dropped away in a span of breath. He was borne aloft, flying with no control over his trajectory and no comprehension of this sudden gift. The darkened forest streaked into a tapestry of grey and black. He seemed to sense his waist engirdled, as if seized by an entity of incomparable strength.

He'd had a vision of his captor then, there in the cold light of the moon: a man, but larger than any who had ever walked the surface of this world; a man, but one whose un-furred flesh captured the blue light of night and cast it back pure and unmodulated. Only a glance, then, but a glance was enough. The sight, combined with the sudden accelera-tion of his flight, was more than Jen's forest-bound mind could assimilate. In the next second, he ceased trying alto-gether, and allowed oblivion to claim him.

His world was still in night when he roused. Whether this meant he was unconscious for minutes, or for a full cycle of the sun, he wasn't prepared to say. For a moment, he listened to the movement of foliage, took a cautious sniff of the air, was able to divine that he had been carried at least a half-cycle from the camp. A vague hope formed: that his abductor had been a hallucination, that his dream of flight masked his triumphant escape from the Aroyu camp. But a search of the surrounding ground found no sign of the priest's hearts, and an examination of his knife—which he found lying not far from his side—showed no trace of the blood of his enemies.

Further confounding hope that his flight had been fantasy was Jen's realization that *he* was still there, the abductor whose flesh caught and returned light more perfectly than the stillest of waters. He had waited silently during the assassin's recovery and now hovered over his prone body . . . quite literally, as it turned out: the stranger's feet were planted, not upon the soil, but upon a platform that floated not two handsbreadths above the surface, a platform whose looking-glass perfection rivaled that of its owner.

Jen regarded his captor, restrained himself from crying out as the creature knelt to bring his face close to the assassin's own. "There may be a reason," the creature said—his voice, raised no higher than the whisper of the trees, bespeaking a strength that no mortal creature could possess—"why you feel justified in sacrificing the life of one who has not raised a hand against you. There may be a reason why war rages across the whole of this world, but with no coherent plan, and no obvious goal. I do not know these reasons. Perhaps you do."

His flesh reflected the moonlight filtering through the foliage that netted overhead. The forest wrapped around this creature, rested as easily upon his shoulders as a cloak spun from the soul of the world.

And the assassin at once knew him: God of the Forest. He had been present all along, had watched Jen as he had forsaken his destiny as hunter to serve at the feet of the vile god Cirremon. Jen had sinned against the delicate balance of his world, and now the One who watched over all had retrieved him to extract His justice.

Jen fell forward, clasped hands together, dared to press them at the edge of that moon-kissed platform. "Forgive me, Lord," he sobbed. "I have broken Your law, stolen lives that weren't mine to claim. Take me, if You wish—I offer my soul to Your service. These hands can never rebuild in life what they have destroyed. In death, they will serve Your will, gladly, to the end of eternity."

A moment's silence. Then he felt the creature move, felt him draw near. A part of Jen cowered at the imminence of his death, trembled within as does the child who has come to understand the true nature of mortality. He steeled that child still, soothed it with the knowledge that the fate about to befall him was justice reaching out to restore what he himself had fouled. Death still frightened him, but death was all he now had to offer. With that understanding, peace enveloped him, and he awaited the moment of his judgment.

A hand seized his wrist, drew him to his feet. He readied himself for the blow, prayed silently that the pain would be brief. But seconds passed, and no blow fell. A few more seconds passed, and he felt only the movement of the forest around him, heard only the whisper of the breeze. After a moment, he dared open his eyes, turning his face up to his judge.

The creature knelt upon his platform, his glance meeting Jen's. He regarded the assassin not with hatred, nor with fury, but with something Jen had once seen, something the assassin realized had been lost in the mad days of the god Cirremon. Something he had not realized he had missed until this very moment. Something like mercy.

"I am no god," the spirit said. "I am not here to judge you. Tell me your story."

It was a Field Evangel's most cherished skill: the sleep that wasn't quite sleep, the ability to rest without fully succumbing

to the night's comforting embrace. In a time of war, when
assassins ruled the darkness, such talent could mean the difference between seeing the next dawn, or finding oneself
consigned to a premature judgment upon the grinding stone
of the blessed Cirremon. Field Evangel Liss Tavah had developed this skill, had seen it save his soul on more than one
occasion. On this night, though, it would deliver him to the
very mouth of Hell.

The panic had started at the edge of camp. From his tent,
Tavah listened in the dark, traced the bark of barely coherent
orders, scented fear and confusion carried on the wind.
Throwing off his bedclothes, the priest rose, used a flint to
light the stub of a taper, and quickly donned his robes.

The camp was fully possessed by the time he emerged from
his tent. Soldiers busied themselves adjusting what meager
scraps of armor they had, readying their weapons, hurriedly
seeking out their place in formation. The captains moved
between the ranks, struggling to spin order from chaos,
and—Tavah noted with relief—generally succeeding.

One of his captains, Fein Nehst, passed by, and Tavah
beckoned to her. The girl—not many years beyond her ascension, but already one of the priest's best leaders—rushed
to him, dropped to her knees, pressed forehead to ground.
"All victory is held in the hand of Cirremon," she said to
the dirt.

"Cirremon watches over his soldiers this night," Tavah replied. Then, as Nehst rose, "Why has the alert been
sounded?"

"Something entered the camp, my father."

"Enemy or beast?"

"Neither, my father."

"Neither?"

The girl swallowed, and Tavah could almost see her struggling for words. "On the north perimeter," she said, "on

Lessom's watch. Something came from the woods. Fast, it was, and Lessom said it caught light like polished stone. It passed within a handsbreadth of him, and was gone.''

What little sleep still clouded Tavah's mind fled upon hearing Nehst's words. He looked down at the girl, judging carefully how fully she believed this tale. Nothing in her eyes, the set of her mouth, told him she doubted any of what she'd conveyed.

Tavah glanced around at his soldiers, now ranked and awaiting orders, then again regarded his captain. "A disturbance occurs at the edge of camp, prominent enough to put the troops on alert. What could be the enemy's motive?''

"Diversion, my father,'' Nehst replied without hesitation. "They wish to draw our strength away from the point of attack.''

"Good soldier. Put Nehko in charge of your troops, make sure all perimeters are well guarded.''

The girl bowed her head. "I serve the will of Cirremon.''

"By His grace, our enemies shall be dust. Go.''

The captain moved to carry out her orders. Tavah watched her disappear, then struck out for the north perimeter, weaving his way between the troops. As he walked, he considered the tale Nehst had conveyed to him, deciding for the present to reserve judgment. He had heard Lessom's name before, knew him to be an adequate watchman, but one with a reputation for dozing. If the sleep of Tavah's troops had been disturbed by the dreams of a slothful guard, Cirremon would have yet another soul to feast upon this night.

Tavah knew his route, knew also it would be slowed as his soldiers sought his attention. It came to him as no surprise that those who would willingly sacrifice their lives for the cause of Cirremon now craved the word of His chosen. Tavah was not inclined to disappoint them. The voices called, and he responded: imparting a glance here, a smile there, slow-ing his stride for the length of time it took to touch the brow of a kneeling supplicant. It was, in his mind, an exchange of strength: soldiers drawing courage from the passage of their leader, the priest cementing within himself the resolve of Cirremon's power through the presence of these impassioned warriors.

He looked at his troops, studied their faces as they awaited their futures. Had these once been the savages who had known little of Cirremon's strength, who had satisfied themselves with the confines of their own village, and the spoils of their meager skirmishes? It was Tavah who had shown them a greater glory, who sensed the spark of Cirremon within their souls and fanned it until the flames burned brighter, hotter than those stoked in the depths of any furnace. He looked into their eyes, regarded their stances. Their fur lacked the gold-and-silver mottling that marked the muzzles of the higher castes; they faced their battles half-naked, armored only with whatever scraps of bone and leather they could tool themselves. Yet within these ragged souls Tavah saw another nobility, that of hearts surrendered fully to the will of Cirremon, ready to carry His might to the farthest reaches of their world.

He wondered whether he himself would see the day that this world would be united under the hand of Cirremon. He prayed it would be so. The wars were hard, and Cirremon's own dictates—proclamations that abruptly turned ally to foe, that compelled his charges to slay those who had, not several suns prior, fought by their sides—extracted an enormous, emotional price. He had never doubted his Lord's will, yet nights such as the one recently passed—during which an entire village was judged apostate and promptly dispatched—put his faith to the greatest of tests. He had prayed silently for those lost allies, had entreated Cirremon to guide them in their next existences to the glory of His rule. He believed that only when he himself had been gathered into Cirremon's arms would the outcome of those prayers be revealed.

Had he been blindfolded, he still would have been able to detect the approach of the north perimeter. The stench of fear was heavy upon the air, so dense it could impede the forward movement of a less determined soul.

With one glance, he knew there was no need to question the watchman. The invader was here, traveling the length of a cordon formed by the troops' bodies, moving with a speed and silence that Tavah had thought only the night wind possessed. This was no native creature, this figure whose flesh caught and reflected the faces of the startled warriors, whose feet needed no contact with the soil to achieve their swiftness. Tavah struggled to recall whether any of Cirremon's messengers took the form of a silver apparition, borne upon a slender board. He could remember no such reference.

The creature reached the end of the cordon, turned, and retraced his path back along the line. There was stern intent upon his face, less the look of an enraged invader than of one enmeshed in search, concentrating to match faces to a template only he knew. The priest had by this time reached a spot just behind the front rank of his troops; he watched as the creature passed no more than two man-lengths before him. Tavah could see the change in the creature's glance as their eyes met; instantly the invader glided to a stop, turned to confront the row of soldiers. "You are the priest," he said.

The voice startled, so quiet that it seemed sourced in the wind itself, yet so possessed of authority that no one could doubt that there were powers within this creature that no mortal could attain. Instinctively, Tavah's soldiers closed ranks. The priest tasted fear crest upon the air, shared briefly in the emotion. He then steeled his soul: this demon had summoned him out; though the creature's visage was such that it might inspire a weaker individual to deny all that had led him to don the robes of his Lord, for his soldiers' sake and his own, Tavah would not allow such frailty to show. Whatever this creature's intent, he acted as the priest himself did: by the grace of Cirremon. Any outcome that followed had been foretold by His decree.

And so Tavah drew himself to his full height, gathered his robes about him, and spoke in a voice that betrayed no fear, "I am the priest."

"You will come with me."

As one, the soldiers raised their spears, placing a barrier of weaponry between their leader and his would-be abductor. As the marksmen fixed aim, Sehr Burra, captain of these warriors, said, "Come try to steal our priest, devil. We wish to see if your blood casts reflections as true as your flesh."

If the threat had startled the creature, no trace of the emotion played across his face. His sole reaction was to shift balance, allowing his board to carry him backward to the forest line. "I do not wish to hurt you," the creature said, "or your priest. But he must come with me."

Burra's response was a signal to his soldiers. Tavah could hear a few whisper, "By the will of Cirremon," before unleashing their weapons. Beyond that, the air was stirred only by the sound of spears in flight.

The captain had chosen his marksmen well. Of the half-dozen spears loosed in the first barrage, not a one would find its mark anywhere but in the demon's breast. The second-line marksmen already had their weapons raised, ready to release at the next signal.

The creature raised a hand. For a second, day bloomed in the forest.

Where once had flown spears, only cinders drifted, marking a spot half the distance between the troops and the devil. The creature betrayed no exhaustion for having eradicated six weapons in flight. A wind—dry, hot, and smelling of scorch—kissed Tavah's face, and was gone almost immediately.

Tavah could feel his people stir, feel a tentative wave of panic pass through their ranks. The hesitation dispelled as quickly as it had arisen, but by then it was too late. Even as the second-line marksmen targeted their prey, even as the surrounding soldiers readied their knives for hand-to-hand combat, the creature approached, hand extended. Fire leapt from those outstretched fingers, fire that arced towards the wall of men.

The light seared. Tavah, witnessing the approach of what he knew to be his death, threw his arms over his eyes, dropped to the ground. Face pressed into the dirt, he silently consigned his soul to Cirremon's keep, and awaited his end.

He heard the cries of soldiers, heard a sound not unlike that of red-hot iron plunged into cold water. A stench of burning came to his nostrils, and he knew the time of his death had arrived. But seconds passed, and the hand of death refused to touch him. In those seconds, all he could sense of the surrounding world was a taste of ash upon the air, and a preternatural silence.

He dared to look up, dreading the tableau that would greet him. What he saw was not the burned and twisted bodies of soldiers who had bravely resisted the demon. Instead, his troops—still breathing, still alive—had assumed positions much as himself: dropped to ground, hands or arms shielding eyes from the searing light. Before the prostrate bodies of those soldiers had been drawn a line of burned earth, a line as true as any engraved by straightedge. This had been the stink that Tavah had breathed, and he realized at once that the precision with which that line had missed his soldiers' bodies was no failure of marksmanship. The demon had kept his word: not harming those who opposed him, yet managing still to clear a path to his prey.

And there he hovered, staring down at the prone soldiers with a look that seemed stirred less by contempt than some rarefied form of pity. In the next second, his eyes rose, met the priest's. Again, he glided silently, swiftly forward. The priest had time to draw breath, to attempt a hastily composed entreaty to his Lord. Before the cry could be completed, he had been gathered in the demon's arms, which assumed their burden as if it were no heavier than an infant. In seconds, the priest had been borne surely and swiftly away.

The sun rose on the embattled forests. The sun rose on lush growth and creatures who knew nothing of the horrors of war. The sun rose also on soldiers who had spent their night in search, fruitlessly seeking out signs of their vanished leader.

Kilometers distant, in a clearing so remote that it had never felt the tread of sentient feet, the sun rose on a repentant assassin, a lone priest, and the silver entity who struggled to sift sense from their tortured stories.

Tavah, Field Evangel, had not hesitated to confirm the words of the assassin Jen, describing for the stranger the glorious arrival of the god Cirremon, and his initiation of the Jihad. He explained the rigors with which Cirremon judged each society, and how upon one cycle of the sun friends could be judged enemies. He recounted myriad nights in which he had seen unbelievers dispatched, assassins sent first into the enemies' villages to slay the leaders, followed by a flow of warriors to eliminate the demoralized populace.

"Allies one day," the stranger said, "enemies the next. Can't you see the madness in this? Can't you see the decimation that the caprice of one god has spawned?"

"We are the servants of Cirremon," the priest replied. "He has but to command, and we obey, the faster to see the rise of His kingdom upon this world."

The assassin reared back and cried to the skies, "I no

311

longer seek Cirremon's pleasure! He is no less a murderer than I. And you, priest, share in his evil!"

He drew his knife, but his hand was stayed by a grip of warm silver. A voice that no native throat could utter said, "Death travels this world, and you would aid its spread? Is this how you renounce your past, assassin?"

The boy locked gazes with the stranger, whose shining visage remained imperturbable. Awakened finally to the horror of his own hypocrisy, Jen allowed his knife to fall, his knees buckling so that, in remorse, he followed the weapon's descent.

For long seconds, the silver creature did little but allow Jen to cry out his grief. Then, turning to Tavah, he said, "You, priest, follow the dictates of Cirremon. And how does Cirremon convey these blessed words to you?"

"I am no more than a Field Evangel," the priest replied. "I have not yet been deemed worthy of hearing the voice of Cirremon himself. I carry out His will as it is imparted to me by messengers dispatched directly from His tabernacle at the foot of Mount T'hurein."

"And at this tabernacle, does Cirremon speak?"

"At the tabernacle dwells the one to whom Cirremon confides his will."

The creature turned towards Jen, whose body had ceased its convulsions, whose face now turned up to behold the two surrounding him. "Assassin," the visitor said, "leave your knife here, you will have no more need of it." Then, addressing the two: "We will make a pilgrimage to the tabernacle of Cirremon, to seek an audience with the one who receives the confidences of your conqueror god."

High Evangel Moss had come to believe that no time existed before the raising of these stark, white columns. She had come to believe that—before Cirremon's hand had moved over the polished floor of this hallowed cathedral, engraving

312

it with the great map—this world had existed only as a dream, a shadow-world yet awaiting His touch to draw it towards reality. Now, the dream was ending, and she was the one who would summon her people to wakefulness.

She sat upon the dais, looked down upon her sentinels as one by one they entered the tabernacle to prostrate themselves before her, to deliver their news. "By the blessed hand of Cirremon," one would say, "Field Evangel Rashiss reports that resistance from the Erais villagers was greater than anticipated, and the lives of many holy were lost. But with our Lord's blessing, we have overcome their forces, and their blood now enriches soil newly sanctified."

"By Cirremon's grace," another would proclaim, "we have made little progress against the blasphemers of Tinalss. In his wisdom, Field Evangel Darrah has imparted the spirit of our Lord upon the souls of those who dwell in the neighboring village of Hierae. With their aid, the footsteps of the unholy will not long foul the soil."

Across the map scribed into the expanse of the hall's floor, the subalterns would move, placing markers to indicate the progress of the holy battle. Moss would close her eyes, summon to mind her most recent audience with the blessed Cirremon, and impart His will upon these messengers. "Our Lord smiles upon Evangel Rashiss's victory," she would say. "His forces shall now turn east, where the inhabitants of the village of Quetast defile Cirremon's word with their very presence."

Or, "Evangel Darrah has moved wisely to seek this alliance, but should act in care. Lord Cirremon has decreed that within the inhabitants of Hierae flows the blood of the unholy. Use them, if they are willing, but know that once they have helped rid this world of the Tinalss, the Hierae themselves must soon follow."

And the messengers would kneel, press lips against the bottom-most step of the dais, and rise to carry unquestioning the decrees spun by the lips of Cirremon. So had the days and nights passed for High Evangel Moss. So had she imagined they would always pass.

On this night, she would discover her error.

She heard the cries first, filtering up from the hall's stone steps, echoing across the arched breadth of its ceiling. She recognized the voices: those of her guards, issuing a call to arms, challenging the approach of some intruder. There followed the sound of archers loosing their weapons, accompanied by another sound, one she could not describe, one like a force of wind condensed into a filament no thicker than a hair. The floor of the temple—a floor hewn of solid rock—shook. And then, silence.

Moss sat upon her dais, and waited. Flight was not an option for her. She was High Evangel, and lived in the shelter of Cirremon's might. Whatever force sought to defile this temple would soon perish by His hand.

The entrance to the hall lay twenty man-lengths away, yet Moss had no trouble identifying the invader as he entered the hall. He glided silently forward upon a board of gleaming metal, his flesh reflecting the flames cast by the surrounding wall sconces. Behind him followed two pilgrims. One, Moss recognized as a Field Evangel, an especially talented one named Tavah. The other was obviously a villager, dressed in little but crudely cured leathers and lacking the markings of the high-caste carried by the Field Evangel and herself. Moss had no knowledge of this one, nor the reason for his presence here, but she could breathe the scent of the primitive even from this distance.

She allowed the intruders to reach the halfway point between the entrance and the expanse of engraved map. Then she rose from her seat. "You have defiled ground blessed by our Lord Cirremon," she said. "Say your peace and ready your souls for consignment to His hands. You will not leave here the way you entered.''

The creature's response was to raise a hand and gesture to the map before him. A fire unlike any she had seen before leaped from the extended fingers, striking the map at its very center. From the point of contact, rock began to glow, the color of live coals spreading until the whole of the chart's surface had been engulfed. Moss could see the image within blur, distort, then vanish as it was subsumed by a sudden bloom of white-hot light. Overwhelmed, the priestess fell back into her seat.

The assault ceased as abruptly as it had begun, and the creature moved forward, heedless of the molten pit his board traveled over. "The hand of Cirremon moves across your world," he said, "and this is all that will be left if its progress is not stopped. You have been claimed by madness, priestess, incapable of telling friend from enemy, piety from bloodlust. Your Cirremon seeks to destroy you all."

"Blasphemy," Moss hissed. "For such words, Cirremon will doom you to Hell."

"Let him send me there himself," the creature replied, reaching the foot of the dais. "I seek an audience with your god."

In the face of such power, in the face of this demonic messenger, Moss still could not resist allowing one corner of her mouth to turn up. "He will not see you, devil."

"Does he so fear his challengers?"

"They are nothing to Him."

"Then my intrusion will be a waste of no one's time but my own," said the creature. "Take me to him, priestess. I promise you"— and he now allowed his own mouth to mirror the sardonic curl of the High Evangel's—"if he wishes to ignore me, I'll find a way to survive the slight."

* * *

315

What ego had carved this hall, hollowed out of the very summit of Mount T'hurein? the Silver Surfer wondered. Whose hand would dare to fashion a throne of such baroque grotesqueness—an entanglement of serpents, demons, and gargoyles frozen in the midst of battle—and place it at the very center of the cavernous space? Whose mind would wish to inscribe the vaulting walls with images of war and slaughter, of lands consumed in flame and worlds torn asunder? In the depths of his heart, the Surfer believed he possessed the answer, but would not admit it even to himself until he'd seen the proof with his own eyes.

Behind him Moss, Tavah, and Jen followed his path. He could sense their fear at daring to set foot upon the domain of their lord, could feel their hesitation, even after they had heard his suspicions about the one who had proclaimed himself their god. As the trio lingered within the entryway, the Surfer moved forward, gliding to the center of the cavern, to the vacant throne that rested there.

A voice echoed across the space. Deep, malevolent, it seemed to rise from the very bowels of this world, was caught and reflected by the walls' every curve: "Is this all it takes? Does a condemned race need only to cry out with its last, dying breath, and Norrin Radd descends to assume their cause? How generous you are!"

The source came from somewhere above, its exact position blurred by the cave's acoustics. The Surfer glanced up, scanned the shadowed depths, and spoke towards the ceiling, "This, then, is the voice of the Lord Cirremon? You will excuse me if I do not prostrate myself at its mere sound. I prefer my deities to be just slightly more tangible."

The chuckle was soft, threatening. "Have you ever bent your knee, Radd, to one who was your superior? That is not your history, at least not the part that we have lived."

He could sense the direction: the farthest wall, high overhead. "To one who tempered his power with wisdom and mercy," the Surfer replied, "I would defer without hesitation. But those who wield their power with hatred, who dominate their supplicants and feast upon their fear, such gods win only my contempt." He stopped by the throne, focused his glance upward. "And those gods who conceal themselves from my sight are not worthy of even that."

Another laugh. "You place great value on your respect, Radd. You flatter yourself. I've never had need to win your regard. Indeed, I would be far happier if this universe were freed of your presence, once and for all. You have no taste for reticent gods? Very well. Behold Cirremon, and behold your death."

It was a cunning hiding place, the ledge whose presence was concealed by a fortuitous conjunction of shadows, and the stairway that led down from it, circling one-quarter the perimeter of the cave's wall and similarly hidden in darkness. Now that the Surfer had found this aerie, he glanced up, saw movement on the precipice, within the shadows. As he watched, the creature concealed there stepped forward into the light, revealing what the Surfer had known all along.

How long ago had he confronted those eyes, eyes that blazed like red-hot coal? How long had it been since that mottled, brown body towered over his, silver hair streaming as an ax poised to slice him in two? What time had passed since he'd seen those lips part, curling back to emit a bestial cry in anticipation of the Surfer's demise? Not long enough, he knew. And now, it started again.

The Silver Surfer stared up into the darkness, and watched as Morg, present Herald to the world-devouring Galactus, stepped to the edge of the precipice. "This is no pleasure, Radd," said the Herald, smiling down at him and propping his ax on one shoulder. "I have labored long to ready this

world for my master, and here you are, once again determined to foil my plans."

"You should not be here," the Surfer replied. "Nahl 3 is
home to sentient life. It is not a fit offering for the likes of
Galactus."

Morg nodded. "Home to sentient life, for now. Not much
longer. Have you witnessed my handiwork? Have you seen
how close I am to cleansing this globe of its annoying inhabitants?"

"So," the Surfer said, allowing himself a bitter smile, "the
spread of madness was a goal in itself. Wage wars without
bound, shift alliances at random, allow hatred and suspicion
to overtake all who participated. Let it run unchecked, and
your victims would do your work for you."

"Are you surprised?" said Morg, approaching the stairway,
beginning his descent. "Did you think that I would stand to
one side and allow Air-Walker to guide the Worldship to
whatever arid rock he saw fit to offer? Did you think that my
hunger could be so cheaply staved? You did not consider fully
the one to whom Galactus has entrusted the task of Herald-
ship, or the reasons for my selection. My Master did not summon me to labor under the restraints of Air-Walker, or
Firelord, or even yourself, but to find ways *around* them. And
here, I have succeeded."

He stopped upon the stairs, turned to face the Surfer.
"The Worldship approaches, Norrin Radd. Even as we speak,
it enters the Nahl system. You've seen the results of my efforts; would even Air-Walker argue that these creatures are
not irretrievably set upon the path of their extinction?
Wouldn't he agree that, at this point, surrendering this
sphere to the hungers of Galactus would be nothing less than
a mercy?"

"This was *your* doing, Morg," the Surfer said softly, as he
watched the Herald resume his descent. "You cannot claim

the sanction of mercy for an atrocity that you yourself have created.''

Morg reached the foot of the stairs, drew his ax forward, began to approach the Surfer. "Mercy or not, this world is doomed. Galactus will feast well this day."

The Surfer shook his head. "Not doomed, not yet. Not while the spark of sentience dwells within its remnants, not while *I* remain to plead its case."

"Ever the optimist, Norrin Radd. You've forgotten a few things. You assume that Galactus will be of a mood to hear your case. And you assume that I will allow you to live long enough to plead it."

Ax grasped in both hands, Morg began his charge, feet barely touching polished stone. He had been twenty meters distant when his run started; in seconds, the distance had been covered, and the ax raised, ready to slice the Surfer in half.

But the Surfer had anticipated the attack, knew he and his foe to be so matched in power that stalemate could be the only outcome. He allowed his adversary to close, allowed the deadly blade to fall, straight and true, for his face. Then, he focused his will, compelled his board to carry him out of death's way. The blade missed by scant millimeters, burying itself deep into the polished stone floor.

As Morg struggled to free the weapon, the Surfer wheeled, extended a hand ceilingward, aimed a strand of coherent energy towards an outcropping of stone hung precisely over Morg's head. As the Herald succeeded in liberating his ax, the rock had already started its fall; only by luck did Morg happen to glance up, catch sight of the missile hurtling towards him, and speed himself out from under the point of impact.

Stone shattered upon stone, ruptures spread from the collision. The three spectators—priests and assassin—clasped at

319

walls to maintain their balance. Morg, meanwhile, used the momentum acquired during his escape to gain a wall, speed himself along its surface, and come to ground behind the Surfer. Norrin Radd turned, saw the Herald bearing down on him, blade wielded, teeth bared in a snarl of triumph. Hastily, the Surfer summoned a beam of energy to deflect the ax, but was not able to stave off a collision with his charging foe. In a fraction of a second, the universe seemed to implode, the cave becoming a swirling nightmare of undifferentiated rock. The Surfer regained control of his board, stabilized his flight, used the impetus acquired from Morg's attack to steer himself back towards the Herald.

Morg had already circled around for the next volley, weapon at the ready. Radd doubled his speed, closed in on his prey, skewed course at the last moment to avoid the razor-sharp blade aimed for his midsection. A cry of frustration escaped from Morg's lips; as his weapon continued its flight, he spun, managed to angle the still-speeding handle upwards. One moment, the Surfer was flying past the enraged Herald; the next, he had been caught by a blow that carried the force of an exploding star.

The Surfer tumbled backwards, out of control. He attempted to regain command of his board, aware that at any second Morg would descend, ax closing in to finish its job. The Surfer was still struggling when a blur of mottled flesh obstructed his vision. The blur was followed by a flash of gleaming metal. He possessed enough presence of mind to ward off the blade with a burst of power, but lacked the control to modulate the beam. Even as the ax was repelled, so was the Surfer rocketed across the cavern floor, his body pinwheeling wildly as the board flew out from under his feet. He collided with explosive force where wall met floor, rock dislodging and tumbling around him. The Surfer, maintaining the slightest grip on consciousness, pressed his face against polished stone, shielding himself from the deadly hail.

He could feel it, vibrating up from that floor: explosions, it seemed; explosions that had nothing to do with the conflict occurring within the cave's walls. The three who in terror had witnessed the battle sensed the disturbance as well; grasping walls or dropping to knees, they sought support from the very ground that endeavored to destabilize them.

Morg—who, as Herald, knew the precise import of the tremors—laughed in triumph. "See," he cried to the cavern's ceiling, "the Worldship arrives!" Then, casting his gaze down to the Surfer: "Thank you, Norrin Radd. Your efforts at resistance were pleasant diversions, but in the end a waste. For all your struggles, you have succeeded only in helping me deliver this world to the hunger of Galactus!"

"Cirremon!" cried Evangel Moss. "The ground! What does it mean?"

"It means the end, good priestess," Morg cried. "It means your death, and the death of all you've treasured."

"Why? Haven't we fought in Your name? Haven't we purified this world to further Your glory? Help us now, so that we may continue Your work!"

"Help you?" Morg said, as, teeth gritted, he approached the cleric. "*Help* you? I have struggled all this time to *damn* you. Why should I help you now?"

"You are Cirremon! You are our Lord!"

With a cry, Morg seized the priestess, flung her effortlessly across the chamber. The cleric's body fell to the ground, slid across the polished rock, collided with the foot of the throne. At the chamber's mouth, the two remaining witnesses trembled as they watched Moss splay her hands against the floor, try to rise, but succeed only in collapsing onto her back.

Morg strode to her, sneered as he addressed her. "I am no one's lord. I am Morg, Herald of Galactus, and serve only his needs. You, in turn, have done naught but aid me in my

mission. In your blind devotion to my rule, in your unques-
tioned willingness to wage war without end and serve death
without reason, you have helped me to ready your planet for
his hunger. I am in your debt, dear priestess; such obedience
should not go unrewarded. Now, for all your labors, receive
the thanks of Morg, and of his master, Galactus!''

The Surfer watched as the Herald raised his ax, the treacherous blade hovering precisely over Moss's head. Norrin
Radd tried to rise, found his legs unwilling to heed his summons. With no option left, he gathered will, sought with his
mind the board that served as an extension of his own being,
and urged it into flight. Morg's ax had begun its descent,
had drawn within centimeters of its prey, when the path of
the silver missile intersected with that of its target. The Herald cried out as the weapon flew from his hands, as the blow
threw him off-balance.

The Surfer saw his chance. Marshaling all his power, he
projected a force-beam at the Herald's chest. The blast propelled Morg across the chamber, his flight halted only by the
solidity of the cave's wall. Instantly, the Surfer aimed over the
Herald's head, sliced clean a massive rock formation. Before
Morg had regained his senses, he was buried in a shower of
stone.

The tremors in the ground had doubled. The Surfer heard
Tavah moan, heard him cry, ''We are doomed.''

''Not yet,'' the Surfer replied, managing to rise to hands
and knees, to will his board to his side. ''Galactus knows
Morg is here. He will not claim this world until he has retrieved his Herald.''

''But He is dead! Surely the Galactus will seek vengeance
for the murder of his servant!''

With effort, the Surfer managed to crawl onto the board.
''No weight of rock can kill Morg,'' he said. ''He is unconscious only, and not for long. We must act quickly.'' Still on

hands and knees, he glided towards the center of the room, towards the throne and the prone Moss.

Tavah watched as the Surfer hovered over the priestess' body. "The Head Evangel . . . ?"

". . . lives," the Surfer replied. "Beaten, and a little bloody, but sound nonetheless." He looked down at the priestess. "Can you rise?"

"I think so," she said, and managed with effort to gain her feet.

"Go, join your priest." Then, gesturing to the pair who stood by the entrance, "Assassin."

Jen hesitated for a second, then, slowly, approached.

When he had come within reach, the Surfer seized Jen by his hand. "Sit," he said, drawing the assassin towards the throne.

Jen shook his head, tried to back away. "In Cirremon's place? No, no, I cannot. I'm not . . . I mean, I couldn't . . ."

"Galactus approaches, assassin. If your world is to see the next sunrise, you must sit, now!"

"But upon the God's seat? I would be condemned for my pride! I would . . ."

"*Sit!*"

The command reverberated across the chamber, was caught by walls and carried into the ceiling. Stunned, Jen threw himself into the seat, prepared himself for the divine bolt that he was sure would strike at any moment.

Turning towards Moss and Tavah, the Surfer gestured to a position just before the throne. "Come. Kneel."

The clerics, having seen enough of this being's power, were not inclined to argue.

The Surfer willed his board to carry him by the priests' side, and assumed a similar position of pious respect before the dazed assassin.

"Is this your final joke, demon," whispered Moss, "to have

us damn ourselves with the worship of this low-caste?''

''You have done more than your share in sowing the seeds
of your damnation,'' the Surfer replied. ''Keep your silence,
and there may yet be hope.''

The reverberations had doubled in force and frequency,
to the point where the priests struggled to maintain their
positions of supplication. Without warning, a beam of pure
energy pierced the wall of the cave, mere meters above their
heads. It traveled parallel to the floor, terminating at the
opposite wall. As it swept the chamber's expanse, all above it
vaporized. By the time it had finished its sweep, the former
worshippers of Cirremon knelt in an open arena.

Over their heads, filling the whole of the sky, hovered the
open-work exoskeleton of Galactus's Worldship.

''Morg,'' a voice said, a voice that seemed to come from
everywhere and nowhere at once, the voice of Galactus.
''Good servant, you have labored hard and well, and have
delivered to me a superb world with which to slake my hunger. Come, now. Come rejoin your master, and the feast shall
commence.''

The air above them distorted and coalesced. When it had
resolved, it was the face of Galactus that stared down with
satisfaction upon the assemblage below. Under his breath, to
the priests and the assassin, the Surfer whispered, ''Do not
move, do not speak. Your future depends on what happens
next.''

Galactus's smile vanished, melting as he surveyed the tableau arrayed below him: his Herald, buried under a blanket
of rock, only now stirring; the clerics, arranged in positions
of supplication before a young, filthy primitive; and there,
amongst them, his former Herald. ''The Silver Surfer,'' the
devourer of planets growled.

''Silence,'' the Surfer replied, quietly.

''You again meddle in my efforts, Norrin Radd. How many

times must the lesson be taught you? How many times must Galactus demonstrate that your strength is nothing against his?"

At once, the Surfer stood, cried to the skies, "*Silence!*"

Low menace crept into Galactus's voice: "You dare command Galactus? For the violence you have done my Herald, be thankful I have not incinerated you where you stand."

"Morg receives only the reward he deserves. He has served his worshippers badly, delivering them to your hands."

"Yes, he told me of his plans for this world. But you were not a part of them. Why are you here, Norrin Radd? Why does this boy sit upon Morg's throne?"

"Morg has fallen. Behold Nahl 3's new god."

Silence, punctuated only by the sound of explosions. Then, in poisonous tones, the voice of Galactus: "What do you say? Am I to believe this creature of filth has ascended to the might of one of my Heralds?"

"No. He has *exceeded* the might of your Heralds."

Even as they spoke, the rubble at the cavern's edge stirred. Now, Morg, regaining his consciousness, roused, rose, managed to gain his feet. Staring back at his former resting place, he chuckled softly, as if his vanquishment had been no more than an amusing joke played at his expense.

"Morg," said Galactus, as the Herald dusted rubble from his flesh, "have you heard the words of our foe?"

Morg glanced skywards, smiled. "I have, Master."

"Do you know this creature who has assumed your place?"

Slowly, he approached the throne, studied its new occupant. "I have heard him referred to as an assassin, Master."

Low, almost imperceptible laughter rose from Galactus's throat. "An assassin. And more powerful than Morg."

"Not in the Power Cosmic, Galactus," the Surfer replied. "That's a gift bestowed by your hand, only. His power is mortal, and for it, all the more potent."

"And that would be . . . ?"

The Surfer did not hesitate: "The power to redeem this world."

It was as if his statement had been an incantation, capable of stealing sound from the very air. For seconds, no one dared reply. Then, softly, Morg grunted. "Radd," he said, "too often you have assumed the battle for those powerless to defend themselves. I fear you have invested yourself so in your struggles that you have come to believe powerlessness a power in itself."

The Surfer regarded the Herald. "I believe the desire to heal is stronger than the urge to destroy."

"Morg," said Galactus. "Did you not tell me that you have set these creatures on a path of irreparable destruction?"

"I did, Master."

"Galactus has observed your results, determined your words to be true. Abandon these people, Surfer. They are doomed."

The Surfer cast his glance to the skies, his teeth gritted in anger. "Not while our Lord sits upon the throne!" With a flourish, the Surfer again turned, knelt, averted his eyes floorward. "In His hands, all forces of life converge."

"A life-affirming assassin!" sneered Morg. "How novel. Insanity has indeed claimed you, Radd. Behold, my master, regard our once-powerful enemy. See what a lifetime of devotion to lost causes leads to?"

The world-devourer, however, looked thoughtful. "Imagine the pleasure in stripping him of this last fantasy, in seeing him confront the truth behind his hallucination."

"It can be done, Master. The wars continue, and these creatures' end is not so distant."

Silence followed. The Surfer maintained his position of supine respect before the newly enthroned Jen, imagined he could feel Galactus relishing the malevolent scenario playing out in his mind. Then, from the Worldship, a voice: "You are fortunate this day, Norrin Radd. The hunger does not burn deep, and Air-Walker tells me a smaller, uninhabited world waits nearby. I will spare the creatures of Nahl 3, to play out their fates in whatever manner the assassin god can orchestrate."

The Surfer glanced up to the sky. "Morg shall not interfere?"

"Nor shall *you*," replied Galactus. "But, keep in mind, Galactus *will* return. If, upon my arrival, these people have steered themselves from the path my Herald has set them upon, I will seek another world to relieve my hunger. If, however, the new lord of Nahl 3 fails in his mission"— and at once both Herald and Galactus shared the same, malignant smile— "you shall bear witness to a feast the Worldship has too long been denied. Morg, have you now the strength to rejoin your master?"

"I do."

"Come then, my Herald. Other worlds await."

Morg scanned the floor, caught sight of his ax, stretched out a hand to receive the weapon as it flew into his grasp. "Enjoy your delusion, Radd," he said, grinning at the Surfer, "but be done with it soon. There's unfinished business between us, business we should have terminated a long time ago." With a final grunt of laughter, the Herald willed himself skyward, soaring up to join the Worldship.

There was an all-encompassing thrum of engines; for a moment, Nahl 3 shuddered under the departure of the Worldship. Only after the craft had disappeared into the heavens did the Surfer relax his expression of rapt piety.

To his side, the voice of Moss: "To what end have you delivered us, demon?"

"I have saved your world."

"You have *doomed* us!"

The Surfer turned to behold the priestess's face, twisted into a mask of rage. "You place our fates in the hands of a low-caste? An *assassin*, no less?"

"Understand," the Surfer replied, "I have dealt with Galactus before. The only chance of steering him from his will is to provide him the hope of something greater. That hope is the opportunity to at last see my ruin. I have staked my own soul on the survival of this world. It is a gamble I take no less seriously than you."

"And what now? Shall we be at the beck and call of the primitive who sits upon that throne? Has he *ever* had a thought that extended beyond the dictates of the knife?"

Jen, who since the advent of the Worldship had not raised his eyes from the floor, now said, softly, "Priest . . ."

"High Evangel," Tavah interjected. "I have traveled with the low-caste, witnessed them in battle. It is true they are unlearned. But they are not without courage, or intelligence."

"And the ability to rule?" Moss cried. "Are they perhaps born with that talent instilled in their souls? Do you wish me to cede control to the wisdom of one whose life has been guided by the blade?"

"*Priest!*" Jen cried, rising from his throne.

Startled, Moss and Tavah turned towards the assassin. The High Evangel sought to continue her tirade but, catching the fury playing across Jen's face, decided it best to hold her counsel.

Jen glared down at the priests. "Was it I who almost succeeded in delivering us into the hands of the world-devourer?"

Moss returned Jen's gaze, glare for glare, seemed to struggle for words that would undercut the truth implicit in the question. In time, she realized she had no such words at her command.

After a passage of seconds, Jen continued, more quietly, "I share your guilt, priest. I knelt at the feet of the traitor-god Cirremon, fought his war. The acts I committed . . . the acts . . ."

The Surfer watched as the assassin collapsed back into the throne, grasped armrests with both hands, drew in breath. Did it suddenly seem that a child had been stricken with a weight of years, had been given a glimpse of a knowledge too vast for his unseasoned mind to assimilate? The expression on Jen's face suggested as much. "There was a time," he said. "There was a time when I dreamed of the hunt, of seeing my people prosper through what I would provide by my own blade. Dreams only; my knife has never tasted the blood of honest prey. Only the blood of my own, spilled without purpose, stains its surface." He turned to the Surfer. "You were right to make me throw that knife away, messenger. It is a fouled weapon, capable only of bringing pain to both victim and wielder. The Galactus will accept no other but me as leader. Is that a condition under which he has spared us?"

"Yes," the Surfer replied.

"For the horrors I have committed, it is not punishment enough."

"It is not punishment at all. For the task ahead, it is best you not think of it as such."

Jen turned the words over in his head, nodded. "I have betrayed this world many times over. If I now bring peace, it will not be for my sake, or for the sake of any who had a hand in this evil, but to regain the balance we have too willingly relinquished. The tremors we felt, messenger, how deep did they travel?"

"It is likely the whole of your world felt them."

Jen turned to Moss. "The Field Evangels will then send

messengers to the tabernacle to seek an explanation for this turn of Cirremon's will."

The priestess nodded. "In the next score of days, many will pass through our portals."

"Good. You will return to your temple, High Evangel. You will perform your duties as before. But the message you will convey is a simple one."

"And that is?"

"The war is over. All battles must cease."

Startlement only briefly creased the High Evangel's face, and was instantly replaced by a gloss of cynicism. "My lord, peace is not so easily attained."

"I know. But let's see who responds. Then we can concentrate on those who refuse." Still regarding Moss, he gestured towards Tavah. "Do you have other evangels as skilled in the use of words as this one?"

"A few. Not enough, never enough."

"Prepare a list of them, consider where they might best be used. Their words brought us into war, their words may get us out."

"As you wish, my lord," said Moss, bowing.

Jen regarded Tavah. "You, priest. You ordered the slaying of my people."

"By Cirremon's will, my lord."

"Have you no will of your own, that you could not have denied his evil? If our world were not at stake, I would remove from you the hearts I sought not long ago. But I need you. There's something great in you, priest. I see that you are not constrained by caste, that your judgment comes from the proof of your observations, not the restrictions of your prejudices. I need such understanding, not blind obedience. Can you speak your own will as easily as you once spoke Cirremon's? Will you help me with the task ahead?"

"To save our world, I shall be at your service," replied Tavah, bowing.

"Good." Jen turned to the Surfer. "And you, messenger. I wish to speak to you, alone."

The Surfer watched as Moss and Tavah withdrew from the cave. When he turned back to Nahl 3's newly ascended ruler, it was in time to see the resolve melt from the hunter's eyes, to see his hands grasp in desperation at the throne's armrests. "I wish to stand from this chair," Jen said.

"You don't have to ask my permission," the Surfer replied. "You're free to do as you will."

"Except leave this cave. Except erase all the events that brought me here." He abruptly stood, strode several paces across the floor, turned to face the Silver Surfer. "I can't do this, messenger."

The Surfer glided towards Jen. "And yet, for the sake of your world, you will."

Jen closed his eyes, laughed softly. "What do you see in me? Not an assassin, for you would have been justified in striking me down the moment my knife touched that guard's throat. Not a hunter, for you have denied me that birthright by forcing this task upon me. Is this a joke? Have you steered my ascent only because you knew of its absurdity?"

"The truth, hunter, is that your caste helped convince Galactus to spare your world. It's up to you to prove yourself greater than what he assumes." The Surfer drew close, rested a reassuring hand on Jen's shoulder. "I don't think my judgment has failed me in that regard."

Jen studied the Surfer's eyes, searched for some sign of fault in the visitor's words. Seeing none, he allowed himself a modest smile. "You cannot aid us in our recovery?"

"That, too, was a condition of the wager. But rest assured that Galactus will honor his side of the bargain. He will accord you the time to set things right, but only just. If, upon his return, the madness you have been a part of continues, this world *will* be forfeit."

"Maybe we will then deserve our fate. By the gods of the hunt, I will do all I can to see it doesn't happen." He walked to the throne, rested a hand on its surface. "I would ask one service of you."

"And that is?"

He turned and regarded the Surfer. "If we succeed, I would wish you to return here, to me. I would ask you then to destroy this throne room. One Cirremon has been enough; I will not follow in his footsteps."

"You would surrender your rule?"

"I would seek a village willing to welcome one who wishes to learn at last the ways of the hunt. I would live there, then, serving those who accept me, until my last days."

To Jen's startlement, the Surfer drew himself to full height, then bowed. There was no mock piety in the act this time; only genuine respect, born of a recognition that, on this day, a hunter had achieved a wisdom greater than Nahl 3's prior god.

"As you command, my Lord."

AUTHOR BIOGRAPHIES

PIERCE ASKEGREN lives in Northern Virginia, where he works as a staff writer and in-house editor for a defense support contractor. Lizard-like and fearful of the sun, he emerges from his lair periodically to try his hand at lighter fare. Long ago, after the Earth cooled but before the dinosaurs ruled, he wrote comic book scripts for Warren's *Creepy* and *Vampirella* magazines. He's also contributed to *Asimov's Science Fiction* and will have a collaborative story in the upcoming *Ultimate Superhero* anthology.

JAMES DAWSON is a Los Angeles writer whose work has appeared in publications ranging from *The Washington Post* to *Radio & Records* to the forthcoming *The Ultimate Super-Villain*. He is hopeful that his horror short-story series "Chop House" will be anthologized sometime before the millennium, and that his original comic-book heroines Mammazon and Velveteen will achieve the international acclaim they so richly deserve. A would-be Academy Award winner for best screenplay, Dawson is the proud owner of a 1969 Marvel Comics "No-Prize."

When he was young and impressionable, KEITH R.A. DE-CANDIDO's parents gave him J.R.R. Tolkien, Ursula K. Le Guin, Robert A. Heinlein, and P.G. Wodehouse to read. He was doomed. He has been a writer and editor in the science fiction, fantasy, and comics fields since 1989. His short fiction has appeared in *The Ultimate Spider-Man*, the *Magic: the Gathering* anthology *Distant Planes*, and *Two-Fisted Writer Tales*, and his nonfiction has been published in *Creem, Publishers Weekly, Library Journal, The Comics Journal*, and *Wilson Library Bulletin*. He has served as co-editor of the anthologies *The Ultimate Alien, The Ultimate Dragon* (both with Byron Preiss and John Betancourt), and *OtherWere* (with Laura Anne Gilman). He lives on the Upper West Side of New York City with his lovely and much more talented wife, Marina Frants.

TOM DEFALCO entered the comic book industry in the summer of 1972 as an editorial assistant for Archie Comics. Learning his trade from the ground up, he pasted down character logos, proofread stories, and even served time as an occasional colorist. Within a few months, Tom sold the first of what would eventually become an avalanche of stories. Over the years, Tom has written for such diverse comic book titles as *Jughead's Jokes, The Flintstones, Scooby Doo*, and *Superman Family*. He joined the editorial staff of Marvel Comics during the early 1980s and eventually became the company's Editor-in-Chief. Tom has recently returned to full-time writing. He currently chronicles the monthly adventures of *Fantastic Four* and *The Spectacular Spider-Man*, and will soon turn his attention to two new titles, *The Green Goblin* and *Vandal.*

SHARMAN DIVONO is a freelance writer who lives in Burbank, California with her husband, a horse, and two cats. Her TV animation writing credits include the CBS Storybreak Specials *Hank the Cowdog* and *C.L.U.T.Z.*, and has worked on such series as *Garfield and Friends, Bill and Ted's Excellent Adventure, Droids, Richie Rich, Ducktales, G.I. Joe, Transformers*, and *Captain Power and the Soldiers of the Future*. She's received two Emmy nominations and one Humanitas Prize nomination for her work. She has written for the *Star Trek* and *Bruce Lee* newspaper strips, as well as various graphic novels and children's books and comics. She's a member of the Writers Guild of America, the Animation Writers Caucus, the Screen Actors Guild, the Science Fiction & Fantasy Writers of America, Mystery Writers of America, and the Society of Children's Book Writers and Illustrators.

CRAIG SHAW GARDNER is the author of over twenty books, including *Dragon Sleeping, A Bad Day for Ali Baba, Revenge of the Fluffy Bunnies,* and the *New York Times* best-selling novelizations of the movies *Batman* and *Batman Returns.* He feels that comic books warped him from an early age, and can still remember picking up *Fantastic Four* #1 at the local drug store.

CHRISTOPHER GOLDEN is the author of the vampire novels *Of Saints and Shadows* and *Angel Souls and Devil Hearts,* the YA thrillers *Bikini* and *Beach Blanket Psycho,* and the *Daredevil* novel *Predator's Smile.* Golden has just entered the comic book field with Marvel Comics' *Wolverine '95,* and has created the series *Facelift* for Harris Comics. His short story appearances include *Forbidden Acts, Stalkers 3, The Ultimate Spider-Man,* and the forthcoming anthology *Gahan Wilson's The Ultimate Haunted House.* As an entertainment journalist he specializes in film and comic books, with articles appearing in a variety of genre publications. He edited the Bram Stoker Award–winning book of criticism, *CUT!: Horror Writers on Horror Film.* Golden was born and raised in Massachusetts where he still lives with his wife, Connie, and son, Nicholas.

DAVID M. HONIGSBERG lives, works, and writes in New York City. His short stories have appeared in the anthologies *Elric: Tales of the White Wolf, Tapestries,* and the upcoming *Sorcery: Magics Old and New.* In addition, he has written the *Chaosworld*

Campaign Book with Michael A. Stackpole for Hero Games. A student of Jewish Mysticism, he has taught courses in Kabbalah for many years. A game designer by day, his scholarly pursuits include Arthurian studies and Judaica.

KATHERINE LAWRENCE is a true multimedia writer, having written for television, computer games, and short fiction anthologies. Her most recent projects include *This Means War* from MicroProse, out on CD-ROM, and episodes of *G.I. Joe Extreme* and *Princess Guinevere and Her Jewel Adventures.* When not writing, she can sometimes be found polishing her growing collection of silver Hopi jewelry.

STAN LEE, the chair of Marvel Comics and Marvel Films and creative head of Marvel Entertainment, is known to millions as the man whose super heroes propelled Marvel to its prominent position in the comic book industry. Hundreds of legendary characters, such as Spider-Man, the Incredible Hulk, the Fantastic Four, the Silver Surfer, Iron Man, Daredevil, and Dr. Strange, all grew out of his fertile imagination. Stan has written more than a dozen best-selling books for Simon & Schuster, Harper & Row, and other major publishers. Presently, he resides in Los Angeles, where he chairs Marvel Films and serves as co-executive producer for Marvel's many burgeoning motion picture, television, and animation projects, including the animated series *Spider-Man, X-Men,* and the *Marvel Action Hour.* He is the Editor-in-Chief of Marvel's new Excelsior imprint.

JOSÉ R. NIETO was born in San Juan, Puerto Rico, but now makes his home in Boston. He is a graduate of New York University's creative writing program. His work has appeared in *Terminal Fright* and David G. Hartwell's *Christmas Magic.* José is married to Lisa Delissio, a brilliant and lovely ecologist, with whom he has enjoyed many an adventure.

JOHN J. ORDOVER, *bon vivant* and man-about-town, has been a comic book fan since long before he discovered his mutant powers of writing and editing. Now, dressed in a skintight necktie and Bermuda shorts, he fights the fight for good stories as the Mass Market Editor of Pocket Books' *Star Trek* novel line. He has many short story sales to his credit, most even shorter than the one in this book. He recently sold three story treatments to the *Star Trek: Voyager* and *Star Trek: Deep Space Nine* TV series with David Mack.

But who is **DAN PERSONS**? To some, he is a "familiar name" (*Science Fiction Age*). To others, he is one of "Generation X's most revered voices" (*The Gen X Reader*). In truth, he is a regular contributor to *Cinefantastique* and *Visions* magazines, whose articles have ranged from an appreciation of the cinematic rise of Hannibal Lecter to a lament over the video devolution of *Ren and Stimpy*. His short fiction has appeared in such publications as *Prisoners of the Night*, *Aboriginal Science Fiction*, and Miller, Freeman's *Infinite Loop* anthology; he is currently at work on *Razor Boy*, a *noir*-tinged science fiction novel. When he isn't foaming at the mouth to friends about some especially choice bit of Japanese *animé*, he resides in his luxurious Manhattan apartment with his wife Barbara, and his two alpha-personality cats, Boris and Natasha.

DAVE SMEDS is the author of the fantasy novel *The Sorcery Within* and its sequel, *The Schemes of Dragons*. He has sold short fiction to anthologies such as *Full Spectrum 4*, *David Copperfield's Tales of the Impossible*, *Peter Beagle's Immortal Unicorn*, *Dragons of Light*, several of the *Sword & Sorceress* anthologies, *Flesh Fantastic*, *Nanodreams*, *Isaac Asimov's Earth*, *The Ultimate Superhero*, *Deals with the Devil*, and over half a dozen more; to such magazines as

Asimov's Science Fiction, F&SF, Pulphouse, Ghosttide, Inside Karate, and *Tales of the Unanticipated;* and to Faeron Education's series of booklets for remedial reading classes. He was also the English-language rewriter of *Justy,* a Japanese manga SF mini-series released in the U.S. by VIZ Comics. With wife Connie and children Lerina and Elliott, Dave lives in Santa Rosa, California. Before turning to writing, he made his living as a graphic artist and typesetter. He also holds a third degree black belt in Goju-ryu karate, and teaches classes in that art.

STEVE RASNIC TEM has sold over 200 short stories to date. He's been nominated for the Bram Stoker Award, the British Fantasy award, and the World Fantasy Award for his short fiction, winning the British Fantasy Award for Short Fiction in 1988 for "Leaks" (*Whispers VI*). His novel *Excavation* was published by Avon in 1987 and a collection of his short stories, *Ombres sur la Route,* appeared last year from the French publisher Denoel. He recently edited *High Fantastic,* a collection of fantasy, science fiction, and horror stories by Colorado authors for Ocean View Press. He collects comics, clowns, masks, and antique pull toys.

In more than a quarter of a century as a comics writer, **LEN WEIN** has scripted nearly every major title in the business for DC and Marvel, as well as Gold Key, Blackthorne, and more. He co-created the award-winning *Swamp Thing* at DC, the 1975 revitalization of the top-selling *X-Men* at Marvel, as well as countless other heroes and villains. He wrote the full-length *Spider-Man* novel *Mayhem in Manhattan* with Marv Wolfman, and has collaborated with other writers on two *ElfQuest* novelettes. Len has written episodes of the Emmy-winning *Batman: The Animated Series, X-Men, Spider-Man, ExoSquad, Phantom 2040,* and numerous other animated series. Len has been Editor-in-Chief of Marvel Comics, Senior Editor of DC Comics, and Editor-in-Chief of Disney Comics, perhaps the only person in the history of the business to have accomplished such a hat trick. He currently resides in Southern California with his wife, prominent photographer and attorney Christine Valada, son Michael, no cats, but two dogs: Snowy, the world's happiest Samoyed, and Muffin the Monster Puppy. He is waiting for the San Andreas Fault to rearrange his property values.

ANN TONSOR ZEDDIES was introduced to the Silver Surfer as a student at the University of Michigan, where she frequently neglected her Greek homework to study a friend's extensive comics collection. She is extremely pleased that her studies have paid off at last. She later married the man who owned the comics, had four children with him, and lives with him in Kansas. She has published two science fiction novels, *Deathgift* and *Sky Road,* and recently completed a third, tentatively titled *Typhon's Children.* She is a first-degree black belt in Tae Kwon Do.